I0695182

Also by Phillip Martin

The Cassandra Rho Series

A Witch is Born

The Quest for Zolmex

The Barbarian King

BOOK TWO

THE QUEST FOR ZOLMEX

The Adventures of Cassandra Rho

PHILLIP MARTIN

THE QUEST FOR ZOLMEX
THE ADVENTURES OF CASSANDRA RHO
BOOK TWO

Map art prepared by Shaun Carroll.
Cover design by Teddi Black Design.
Formatting by Author Cultivation.

This is a work of fiction. All of the characters, names, incidents, organizations, and dialogue in this novel are either the products of the author's imagination or are used fictitiously.

ISBN: 979-8-9873344-3-0

I dedicate this book to my sons, Adam and Gabriel. The greatest moments of my life include witnessing your births. I'm proud of the young men you have become.

I also dedicate this book to my stepson, Greg. Another great moment of my life was meeting you and I am equally proud of the man you have grown into.

Lastly, I dedicate this book to Kristin, the mother of my three incredible children. She was with me when I first had the idea to write these books all those years ago.

Contents

Prologue...1

Chapter 1   Deception...9
Chapter 2   Charmed..44
Chapter 3   Acolyte...68
Chapter 4   Disciple of Kane.....................................104
Chapter 5   Secrets Revealed...................................118
Chapter 6   An Evil Unleashed.................................156
Chapter 7   The Quest for Zolmex..........................196
Chapter 8   Ambushed!...217
Chapter 9   Cassandra and Cass.............................250
Chapter 10   Kane's Playground...............................289
Chapter 11   Leo's Tomb?...353
Chapter 12   Homecoming..403

Epilogue..423

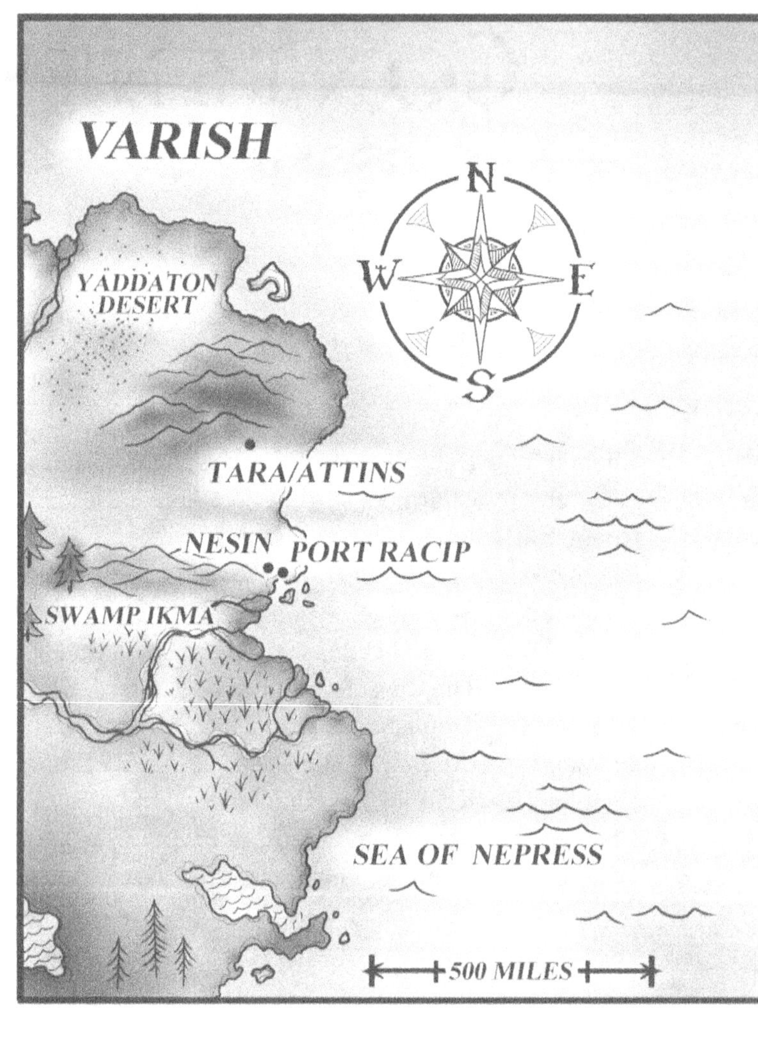

VARISH
N
W
E
S
YADDATON
DESERT
TARA/ATTINS
NESIN
PORT RACIP
SWAMP IKMA
SEA OF NEPRESS
500 MILES

SEA OF NEPRESS
LAKE ELFKIND
GODHOMME
PELESEA
NOVAFONTERA
DARO'S WOODS
TORLIA
OLDORBURG
FARMER'S STOP
MECCA-LORAINE

PROLOGUE

In the woods outside Oldorburg, Kessi watched a familiar and distant memory unfold.

A few feet away, two girls, roughly five years of age, were on an important expedition, their first time outside of the town gates. One had blond locks and blue eyes, and the other brown hair and dark eyes. Though they were happy and innocent in pretty dresses with ribbons to match, the lump in Kessi's throat reminded her that everything was about to change.

The girls leaned in to examine the remains of a bird's nest that their adoptive mother, Unis, had found. They studied the intricacies of the construction, the twine, twigs, and string that helped to make it a home for the birds, and the girls discussed what could have happened to the owners of such a wonderful creation.

Kessi smiled, remembering the joy she felt that day with her mother and sister. She barely remembered Unis, but the woman was crystal clear in this memory, and it filled Kessi's heart with happiness to look upon her once more.

As she watched the scene unfold, her smile slowly turned into a frown, and she wrinkled up her brow. Yes, this was a relived memory, but whose memory was it? Suddenly, she could not recall. Her eyes grew wide, realizing she did not remember which child she was.

A wolf howled, and she jumped at the sound of it. She knew that it would be no ordinary wolf that would soon come into view. She remembered all too well the size of the thing and the intelligence in its eyes and knew there to be at least two of the vile creatures. She remembered everything about that moment, except which little girl she was. How was that possible? Before she could ponder that question, the angelic voice of her long-ago mother broke her from her contemplations.

"Come along, girls, we must be getting back," Unis said.

"We will not make it, Momma," one of the girls answered calmly.

Kessi's heart missed a beat, and she gasped as a giant wolf came into view, nearly as large as Unis. Kessi had to save the little girls and her mother, so she ran toward them, ignoring the fear that threatened to paralyze her. She had to get there fast, for she remembered the wolves being especially quick for their size. Unfortunately, her movement seemed sluggish; the more she struggled to get there, the further away the scene seemed.

Slowly, the sweet memory turned into a nightmare. One girl began to cry and hide behind the other. She remembered that, but was she the little girl crying or the brave one that would stand up to the giant wolf? She tried to remember as she continued her struggle to reach the girls. She saw the wolf quickly spring past her mother. It was upon the children now, the confrontation beginning anew. Her mother would die all over again, and Kessi would not reach them in time.

"No," she whispered in defiance, then pointed her finger at the wolf.

"Bad wolf!" she yelled, drawing its attention.

As it turned to regard her, she could faintly make out a smile, which she knew could not be real; how can a wolf smile, after all? It approached, and she knew she had to protect those two little girls. She felt the ravens in the area and could sense them as if they were a part of her. She summoned them to kill the creature to protect her family.

"Bad wolf!" she cried again, confident that the ravens would answer her call.

They did not. The wolf sprang at her, and time seemed to slow as the wolf hung in mid-air, with Kessi vulnerable and unprotected. She noticed the girls were huddled close, one wagging her finger at the airborne beast, unafraid. She looked past the wolf to see her mother being dragged into the woods by a second wolf.

"Momma!" she cried.

She looked back to the flying wolf just in time to see its fangs up close and felt the strong maw clamp onto her neck. The wolf knocked her to the ground and began feeding on her. Strangely, it did not tear her throat out as she would expect. Instead, she felt it sucking on her like some strange leech. No doubt it would kill her, but not in the fashion she assumed. How could she die? After all, she had killed this wolf before; and could surely do it again. Finally, the creature bit her neck harder, and she screamed out.

The flash of pain brought Kessi from her dreamlike trance. Her vision of the wolf dragging her mother into the woods was gone; the two innocent little girls, her sister and she, vanished. The horrible dream slowly faded away, but the sharp pain in her neck remained. She blinked away the remnants of the terrible vision and tried to reorient herself to her current surroundings. She soon discovered there was no wolf at all but a man biting her neck. She shook the sleep away, trying hard to focus. This man, no, not man; this creature was feeding on her. She could feel it sucking the blood from her neck, slowly killing her.

It took her a few moments to remember the deserted elven village where she was. This creature was Heinsvick, the vampire lord. He had coaxed the dream from the deep recesses of her mind. She wondered then if he had done so for the sole purpose of feeding upon her. She had to stop him, or she would succumb to the curse of undeath. He had bitten her once before already, and she knew from that encounter that Heinsvick could not stop himself. She'd had to stop him then, just like she would have to stop him now. She reached up and placed a finger on each side of his temple, then recalled the words to a powerful spell, expecting to burn him with a bolt of energy. But nothing happened, her magic somehow failing her. She remembered the spell and the symbols that comprised it, but they did not heed her call. Instead, she could feel the creature continuing to suck the life out of her. Her time was growing short.

She closed her eyes and refocused, thinking of a spell to snap Heinsvick from his bloodlust. Something unexpected came to her then, a calmness and clarity offered to her by some deity she should know but could not recall. She was a wizard, a magic user, not a priestess—or at least she thought that was the case. She could not remember but did not question her good fortune at the power she conjured from memory. She cast the holy spell, centering the effects on her hands that now clutched the vampire's head. Divine energy filled her fingers, and they tingled with power. She funneled that energy into the vampire and could feel his sudden discomfort and pain.

In a blur, he released his bite and jumped back with a hiss, seeming more animal than man. He looked at Kessi with an evil smile, blood pouring from his mouth and dripping from his chin. Her blood, she realized, as she brought a hand to feel the puncture wound on her neck.

"Bad wolf," she said flatly, examining the blood that soaked her hand.

"You are mine, girl," the vampire teased, advancing on her confidently.

Kessi tried to call the ravens she knew were in the surrounding woods. She could feel them all around her, and with a confident smile, she said, "Enough of this, Heinsvick. No more games from you. Tell me where my sister is."

The vampire stopped and looked at her inquisitively. "Your sister?"

"Yes, Kessi, my sister. Where is she?"

The vampire's smile grew all the larger. "And do tell, who is it that demands her return?"

"You know me, Heinsvick. Do not make me destroy you," she threatened.

"Your name, girl," he demanded once more.

"I am Cassandra Rho. I have come for my sister and will destroy you if I must."

The vampire lord relaxed then and mumbled, "Excellent," before waving his hand at her.

She felt the weight of sleep take her then. She did not want to sleep; she did not want another vision to unfold in her chaotic mind. She wanted her family back, and this vampire knew where they were. She collapsed then as Heinsvick's spell washed over her. She would have crumpled to the ground if it wasn't for the blinding speed of the vampire lord, who moved quickly enough to catch her gently in his arms. He carried her unconscious form to the elven cellar.

Heinsvick bound Kessi's hands behind her back as she remained unconscious, sleeping soundly. He gently rolled her over onto her back and looked at her pretty face. The wound on her neck still trickled blood, and his eyes grew wide at the sight of it. He wanted nothing more than to feed upon her, to turn her into a creature of undeath, and ultimately be his bride. He wanted nothing more, but he managed to pull his gaze away from her before he bit her again. Doing so would undoubtedly mean turning her. He had bitten her twice already, and a third time would have her become a creature of darkness. Thoughts of Emiline kept him from exploring that path. He needed Kessi unharmed if he intended to retrieve his true love from the vile Matilda.

He had spent the last few weeks with Kessi, brainwashing her into believing she was her sister Cassandra. Then, finally, he had bitten her to reinforce his spells of suggestion that the surprisingly strong-willed young woman seemed to resist. He had bitten her a second time, not to assist the brainwashing process; no, he had bitten her because he liked how she tasted. He was slowly falling for her and needed to make the exchange with Matilda sooner rather than later. If he waited much longer, he would bite Kessi again and lose his chance of freeing Emiline, his true love. Matilda, the evil priestess of the demon-god Marnelphion, had stolen Emiline from him and had demanded he find Cassandra Rho in exchange for his beloved bride. Since he could not find Cassandra, he would exchange Kessi in her place. Kessi was expendable, at least for now.

He examined the back of his left hand, studying the brand that the diminutive priestess had placed there. Matilda had burned him with her power, and now he was her servant. She could telepathically reach out to him through the brand and, more importantly, hurt him. He hated Matilda and would kill her for doing this to him. But first, he needed to remove Emiline from her clutches and hide her away in a safe place where the priestess could not find her. Then, he would exact his revenge on Matilda and perhaps even rescue Kessi if she remained alive. But unfortunately, for now, Kessi was a necessary tool to achieve his goal. Once he had Emiline back, he would recover Kessi and introduce her to a life of undeath. He imagined spending eternity with Emiline and Kessi, sharing his coffin, and the thought pleased him.

He looked back at the peacefully sleeping woman. Heinsvick understood she was doomed if he couldn't rescue her. Matilda would eventually kill her, either sacrificing her to her demon god or torturing her to death after realizing she was not the true Cassandra. He had grown fond of the woman and didn't want her to die. The time had come; the exchange would take place soon. Afterward, he would hide Emiline and track down Matilda to exact his revenge on her. If that meant he would gain the opportunity to rescue Kessi, he would see it through. Either way, he had to have his Emiline back. He would not rest until he did.

A few hours later, the vampire walked the perimeter of the deserted elven village, traces of the werewolf massacre still evident from weeks earlier. He imagined the wails of the dying elves as the werewolves invaded their home. He had discovered that Logan, the werewolf lord, and his pack had decimated the village and now toyed with the unlucky survivors. Ironically, he had further learned of Cassandra Rho through Logan's minions. His trail to Cassandra had led him to Kessi; strangely, she had led him back to this village.

He cared not for the elves at all. However, Emiline had been an elf in her former life and a member of this village. The thought weighed on him as he walked the perimeter, gaining the courage to confront Matilda. Heinsvick was a little nervous about the upcoming exchange, a feeling he had not experienced in many centuries. He was not sure the farce would succeed; if it didn't, he wasn't sure he could defend himself against the powerful priestess.

With a sigh, he moved to the cellar where Kessi rested. The night was young, but the rendezvous with Matilda grew close; it was time to make the exchange. He checked on Kessi, who was still sleeping soundly from the effects of his spell, so he closed his eyes and concentrated on the brand. First, he felt his left hand grow warm where Matilda had burned him, and then he felt her in his head.

"Heinsvick, my faithful servant, I have arrived at Port Racip," Matilda's voice rang through his mind.

"Do you have Emiline?" Heinsvick answered back through the telepathic connection.

"Do you doubt me, vampire lord? I will reward you well if you indeed have Kane's filthy offspring. Your reward will include the return of your precious bride, of course," she answered.

Heinsvick paused, understanding that the volatile priestess could destroy him with but a thought if the ruse failed. He looked down at the slave brand and understood that he had better believe the lie as much as Kessi did, or Matilda might figure out his betrayal.

"Well, do you have the virgin Cassandra Rho?"

"Yes, of course," he lied.

"And she is indeed the offspring of Kane?"

"She has to be," he lied again, unsure if even the actual Cassandra Rho was the one Matilda sought. But, in truth, he couldn't care less.

"Excellent! Meet me at the docks at Port Racip at midnight. We will make our exchange, and I will deem your service to me fulfilled."

"The docks at midnight. I will be there," Heinsvick promised, then broke the mental connection.

He observed Kessi who lay sleeping with her hands bound. She now thought she was Cassandra, and her personality had changed with that delusion. She had become unpredictable. He was glad he had not found the real Cassandra Rho, understanding now the truth of the woman's hideous personality. Regardless, he had finally cracked the mental barrier Kessi's mind had thrown up against him, and the delicious bite had done its work. The transformation process had been lengthy yet complete. It only needed to work for a short time anyway, just long enough for him to once again hold his beloved Emiline and take her far away from the vicious priestess.

Still, he felt great sadness at handing Kessi over to Matilda and ultimately to her death. He desired her as a bride, especially after twice feeding upon her. His eyes fixated on the bite wound on her neck, dry blood caking her soft skin. It took all his willpower not to bite her again, and he reached for her, licking his lips. Finally, he managed to stop himself, and with a shudder, he closed his eyes and thought of Emiline. He soon drifted off to light sleep. He dreamt of a reunion with Emiline, and a smile crept upon his face. Then, he dreamt of ripping Matilda's throat out, and the smile grew even more.

CHAPTER 1

DECEPTION

A vampire?" Penelope asked Daro.

"Yes, Heinsvick by name," the ranger answered.

The beautiful queen of Pelesea and the honorable ranger, Daro, sat in a comfortable study within the castle of Pelesea, a fire burning in the hearth. Daro had decided to come to the city after encountering the vampires from Novafontera. His obligation to the New Order being the deciding factor in informing Penelope of what he had found. Kringus would not return for a while longer, and since Pelesea was the closest neighbor to Novafontera, he had a duty to tell the queen.

"I have heard the name long ago. Heinsvick was a warlock of some renown before the curse of undeath took him. So strange that he is living there, under our noses," Penelope said.

"We cannot hope to know just how long he has been there, but what is most troubling is that the creatures have ventured beyond the walls, making them extremely dangerous," Daro reasoned.

"You told me recently that something was stirring within the dead city. I guess we now know what is stirring, but we don't know why," Penelope said with a worried smile.

They had known each other for many years, and their actions spoke volumes about how they felt about the new information. Daro took a long sip of his tea, which had been made with extra honey, just the way he liked it. Ironically, he enjoyed his visits to the castle, yet felt entirely out of his element, far away from his beloved woods. The tea, the servants, the warm hearth; these were all things he could get used to, but he would never admit as much to Penelope or especially her husband, Kringus.

"What troubles you, my lady?" he finally asked.

Penelope looked at him, her bright eyes staring blankly, as if deep in thought. "Many things trouble me right now. Remember Alleah telling us about the worshippers of Gorl who are gathering in the West, across the sea?"

"Yes, of course. What of them?" Daro asked.

"If that is true, and Novafontera is now home to an undead vampire lord and his brides, we are at a pivotal point in time," she said, the blank look returning once more to her face as she fell inward with her troubling thoughts.

"We do not know how long the vampire has called Novafontera home. The two events are most likely just coincidental," Daro reasoned.

"Yes, that is true, but we should not take any chances. Let us call the New Order to gather and investigate the situation."

The New Order was a group of heroic people who pledged to defend their city of Pelesea and any neighboring lands against the forces of evil. They held no real power and were simply a band of influential friends who pledged to protect the innocent from harm, just as the original New Order had centuries before, battling the demon lord Marnelphion. Penelope and Daro were two of eight members, along with Kringus, the king of Pelesea; Arrin Malik, captain of the king's army; Victoria, the powerful wizard; Von and Lenore, the elven brothers and expert archers; and Alleah Mansuell, the priestess of the goddess, Sinnis.

"A good number of our members are currently in Oldorburg, my lady," Daro reminded her.

Penelope sighed and took a sip of her tea. "Yes, and that is just another thing that concerns me. I am second-guessing our wisdom in going to that town. I need Kringus here; he should know of these new findings you have discovered."

The two sat silently for a few minutes as the logs in the fire popped. The silence was uncomfortable, and Daro was about to suggest that he head back out to his woods. After all, he needed to be there if more of the undead creatures came forth from the city. But instead, he absently rubbed his shoulder where the vampire had struck him almost two weeks earlier, the dull pain still causing discomfort.

"Stay," Penelope said to him, her bright eyes wide and hopeful.

"Where?" he asked, surprised.

"At the cottage on the castle grounds or here within the castle itself," she said, extending her hand wide.

"You think it necessary?" he asked.

"I would say so if the New Order truly is to meet again," she answered with a smile.

He sat back in the comfortable chair and glanced from her to the fire several times before coming up with an answer. "I will stay if you request me to, but I am worried about the woods and desire to be there to protect it and its inhabitants."

"I understand, and I will not force you to stay. I am only asking as a friend."

"Any word from Kringus? When can we expect him back with this early snow?" Daro asked.

"I guess it will be a few more weeks, or a month, depending on how the visit goes," she answered.

"You are worried about the trip?"

"I am beginning to think it is for naught," she said honestly.

"Why? What do you know, my lady?" Daro asked, leaning close.

"Victoria has expelled Cassandra Rho from the school," the queen answered in disappointment.

"What? Why?"

"For fighting another student," Penelope answered with a sigh.

"So, you feel that the lives of her family are not worth the effort? With all due respect, my queen, I think that the two lives he is trying to save are worth saving and have no correlation with the girl's actions," Daro pointed out.

"You are correct, Ranger, and I agree with you. However, I feel that Kringus will not. When he returns and finds that she has not behaved,

I feel his wrath will be swift and severe, especially if he finds trouble in Oldorburg," Penelope reasoned.

Daro sat back and let the information sink in. But, of course, she was correct. He hadn't considered how Kringus would react if anyone became injured or worse. That situation would be bad for the Rho girl.

"Well, let us drink to a safe and productive trip, then," he said, raising his glass in a toast.

Penelope put on her best smile and toasted the drink with the ranger. Then, they again fell into that uneasy silence, both understanding that the king's return could have dire consequences.

Later that evening, Daro found himself in the cottage, happy to stay at Penelope's request. The tiny home had been built per Kringus's orders and afforded him much of the privacy Daro enjoyed. Although he was within a hundred yards of the castle, he felt comfortably alone, with the cottage centered within a small apple orchard. Unfortunately, he found sleep hard to come by that night; thoughts of vampires running wildly through his woods haunted him.

Cassandra awakened with a start, sitting upright in the bed. She immediately regretted her decision as searing waves of pain stabbed through her abdomen. Her hand reflexively went to her midsection and the bandages underneath her gown. The gown was not her own but was similar to the one she had worn when she first came to Pelesea and had awakened in the temple of Sinnis. This room was slightly different, with the window to her right instead of the left, and there was no balcony this time. However, she knew right away that she was in the temple.

Her eyes scanned the room as she tried to recall the events that led her to a second stay at the temple. Images of Binta, her dearest friend, came rushing back to her. She recalled Binta's attack at the hands of Jabell, just feet from where Cassandra had been tied to a tree. Cassandra had not been able to stop the attack and Binta had been seriously hurt.

"Oh, no, what have I done?" she whispered as the fresh memories flooded her.

She remembered the wizard's privilege and challenging Cass and how she had lost that challenge in a matter of moments. Her eyes darted back and forth, panicking at the thought of her failure and subsequent humiliation. Her eyes finally settled on a tapestry on the far wall. The image of a magical wand, leaving a trail of stars behind the tip, met her gaze. It was the symbol of some god but one she did not recognize. It made her feel somewhat at ease, though, primarily since this god centered its power on magic, she surmised. She stared at it for many moments before snapping out of her trance.

She had to get answers about Binta's condition. Was she hurt, or worse, even dead? She would not handle the news well if she learned of her death, primarily if it occurred due to the confrontation Cassandra had initiated. She stood on wobbly legs, and the pain in her abdomen almost made her fall. Cassandra leaned heavily on the nightstand and became aware of a great throbbing in her back. She vaguely remembered the whipping Cass had administered, humiliating Cassandra before most of the students at Victoria's School of Magic. She shook away the pain and made her way stubbornly to the door.

She opened it to find a young man sitting on a bench next to it. He was startled to see her, and he stood quickly. He wore a priest's gown with a star medallion hanging from his neck, and his left arm was in a sling. The shock of seeing her left him at a loss for words, but once she grimaced in pain and leaned on the doorjamb, he jumped to action.

"Miss Rho, you shouldn't be up in your condition," he said, grabbing her gently and coaxing her back into the room, shutting the door behind him.

He helped her to the bed, and she felt much better when lying down again. She watched as he poured her a small glass of water from the nightstand pitcher. She did not expect a priest so young—he was close to her age—or for that priest to be attractive. He helped her sit for a moment, and she took a drink of water, not realizing how thirsty she was. Once the water quenched her thirst, he eased her back down. Once she was lying flat again, she asked him about her friend.

"Where is Binta?" she whispered.

He smiled reassuringly. "Your friend is fine; just a few cracked ribs, is all."

"You are a priest, then?" she asked.

"I am, and I have nursed your friend back to health. Now let me take a look at your wounds. I may need to perform some healing if you are in this much pain."

Cassandra nodded and relaxed. "Thank you," she said.

"Please raise your gown so I might have a better look."

She was hesitant to comply, not knowing what she had on underneath. She figured this priest had probably seen his fair share of female bodies, given his profession. Still, she was shy about showing her naked form to him, especially with him being a similar age, but she tried to put that out of her mind. Finally, she nodded and slowly raised her gown, luckily revealing a thin pair of underwear that at least covered her. The young priest didn't notice and focused on the bandages covering her abdomen. He carefully took them off with his one good hand and examined her injury.

He traced around the edges of the wound, softly chanting. This hurt at first, but then the energy from his fingers began to seep into Cassandra's skin, and she understood the power of his healing touch. The pain melted away, and she relaxed considerably. She stared at the tapestry the whole time, the symbol of the wand giving her strength and hope. Once he completed his healing, his hand lingered as he tested the newly healed skin with a gentle touch.

"Does this hurt?" he asked.

She looked into his eyes and shook her head. That made him smile. "Then you are well on your way to being whole again."

She focused again on the tapestry and the wand as he continued his work. His touch was soft and gentle, and it felt good to her. His thumb brushed lightly against her lower abdomen as he did his job, sending shock waves deep inside her. At first, his touch startled her, and she gasped softly. She tried to make eye contact with him, but he was busy with his work. Surely, he didn't mean to be sensual; he was a priest and only performing a simple healing spell on her. However, when it happened a second time, she grew suspicious enough to stop him. However, before she could say anything, he made eye contact with her, giving her pause.

He smiled and asked, "Do you feel any pain?"

She shook her head, not wanting him to know the effect his touch had on her.

Her thoughts were interrupted when he said, "Good, let's turn you over so I can take a look at your back."

She didn't know what to say, but if his healing made her back feel as good as her abdomen, she would gladly allow him to continue. Also, she liked his touch, whether it was intentional or not. She knew she could stop him if needed, so she allowed him to help her move over to her stomach. Surprisingly, the movement caused her very little pain in her abdomen, which slightly diminished her suspicions of his inappropriate touching. Next, he gently hiked up her gown, bunching it around her neck. She felt very naked at that point and realized that the young priest was probably getting a nice view of her backside, since her underwear left little to the imagination.

He administered his healing to her back, making the dull pain subside. However, the inappropriate touching was still there. He grazed the side of her breast, and twice his fingers gently brushed the top of her buttocks. She would have objected if those touches hadn't sent pulses of energy directly to her loin. She had never experienced this before and was quite ashamed of letting this young man have so much power over her. But a knock on the door interrupted her before she could speak out.

The door quickly opened before either of them could answer. Cassandra covered herself up as much as possible and turned slowly to her side to see who had entered the room. A female priest wearing a symbol around her neck that matched the tapestry entered, followed by Binta. Cassandra's heart filled with joy at seeing her friend, who seemed to be in good health and even wore a smile on her pretty face.

"What are you doing, Greyson?" the priestess asked.

"Greyson?" Cassandra asked, sitting up in the bed at the mention of his name.

She recalled that name as the young man Binta had met at the school, the same one that Binta had ventured into the city to see soon after her kiss with Cassandra. Greyson had been the one who had interrupted the fledgling relationship, or whatever it was she and Binta had begun. Cassandra hadn't liked him when she first discovered Binta's interest in him, the fires of jealousy igniting within her stomach. Now, she felt defiled, letting him touch her as he had.

"Just healing our patient," he said with a shrug, smiling at Cassandra.

"You are not in charge of my healing?" Cassandra asked, now understanding that he had taken advantage of her.

"No. I am," said the female priest, who moved in front of Greyson and motioned him to step back.

She turned toward Cassandra and said, "I am Maina, and I am in charge of making sure you recover fully from your wounds."

Cassandra, still stunned, looked between Maina and Greyson before saying, "He healed me already."

Maina nodded and said, "Yes, we are grateful for his efforts, even if they were inappropriate in the temple of Gella."

"Gella?" Cassandra asked.

"Yes, Gella, the powerful goddess of this temple and to whom I worship," Maina answered, holding up her holy symbol of the magical wand.

Binta rushed up to her friend, enveloping her in a tight hug, and whispered in her ear, "I am glad you are on the mend; I was worried about you."

Cassandra closed her eyes and relished that hug, taking in the smell of Binta's hair and the warmth of her touch. Besides her sister and mother, it was the only time she could remember she hugged someone with that much emotion. It meant the world to have her friend at her side once more. She looked over Binta's shoulder as they embraced, and she could see Maina quietly scolding Greyson for his actions. Cassandra decided not to mention Greyson's touching to

Binta. Instead, that would be a conversation she would share with Greyson at another time.

Her hand dropped to Binta's ribs, and said, "I saw Jabell kicking you, yet you show no signs of the attack."

Binta smiled and glanced back at Greyson. "He healed me. He has a special touch and is blessed with great healing powers."

Cassandra looked to Greyson, who was then approaching the bed, having escaped Maina's silent berating. He looked arrogant, and she wanted to lash out at him for inappropriately touching her. The pompous young man would hear about it the first chance she got when Binta wasn't around. He stopped and put an arm around Binta's waist. She lit up, and a smile engulfed her pretty face when he touched her. Cassandra felt an uneasiness in her stomach when she witnessed that reaction. She felt the familiar pang of jealousy and decided to pry her friend away from Greyson's firm grasp as quickly as possible.

"If you two will excuse me, I must speak with my patient now," Maina interrupted.

The thought of Binta leaving disappointed Cassandra. She suddenly felt very insecure and wanted her to stay. Before she could catch herself, she blurted out, "Can they stay?"

Why had she said "they" instead of "her"? Greyson stopped and turned toward her, a smirk on his face. She felt her cheeks grow flush, and she felt warm all over. She could feel his eyes boring through her gown, knowing what little she had on underneath. She grew angry after the initial wave of embarrassment, though. He had made her feel uncomfortable, and she was tired of people making her feel that way.

"No, I am sorry, but they must leave for now. I will let your friends come in after my examination," Maina said.

"I will be right outside the door, I promise," Binta said reassuringly.

Cassandra watched them leave, hand in hand, and her jealousy of Greyson grew. She did not like him and would let him know the first chance she got. She wanted the sneaky and inappropriate priest out of her way so she could continue her budding relationship with Binta.

Far across the sea at the port city of Racip, Cassandra's sister, Kessi, stood bound and gagged near the docks. Heinsvick stood confidently but nervously behind her, a firm grasp on her arm. He had used his uncanny power of teleportation to send them far from the elven village in a matter of moments. Before his state of undeath, he had been a powerful warlock, and he retained those powers as a vampire, making him quite formidable. Few things frightened him, but Matilda was one of them. He surveyed the docks from his hiding spot behind an outcropping of rocks, trying to find her. Heinsvick found no sign of her, so he waited until the ports were calm and no dockhands lingered. Then, he pulled Kessi along to find a nice dark place on the docks to stay.

Light snow gently fell, and the temperature was much colder than the deserted elven village where the two had spent their last few weeks. Heinsvick could feel Kessi shivering from the cold, though his body felt no discomfort. He had grown fond of the strong-willed young woman and again second-guessed his wisdom of going through the exchange for Emiline. And yet, again, his feelings for Emiline overrode those urges. Kessi would die, and he had to accept that as part of the deal. He would come back for her if the opportunity arose.

A group of lanterns appeared then, separating from the town's lights and drawing closer to the docks. With the fog from the water swirling around the port and limiting visibility, the vampire could only make out the shadowy figures of a small group of people, which he assumed was Matilda and her entourage. Soon, he could hear them speaking, and the one female voice he heard was unmistakably Matilda's. He would never forget that voice for the rest of his existence. Again, he could not make out the words, but knew this was the party for which he was waiting. The new arrivals stopped and waited, lanterns raised as if searching for something or someone, and he knew that the someone was him. He squeezed Kessi's arm until she moaned in pain, then walked toward the group. Now was the moment of truth.

As he got closer, he saw that it was indeed Matilda, along with the large man she called Cerus, and six other men. However, he did not see Emiline or her coffin, which he found very suspicious. He stopped walking just as they caught sight of him. His first instinct was to teleport away, but he knew that even if she didn't live up to her end of this deal, Matilda could still destroy him from halfway across the world. So, there was no need to run now. Instead, he had to try the exchange just in case there was a chance to get Emiline back.

"Heinsvick, you have done well," Matilda purred as she moved swiftly toward them, followed by the group of men.

"Halt!" Heinsvick ordered, grabbing Kessi roughly around the throat, making them all stop.

"I will break her neck if you come any closer," he threatened.

Matilda smiled and gave a small curtsey. "Of course, my dear vampire friend, but why would you do that?"

"I do not consider us friends, priestess. You have used me to get what you want, and now I want my payment."

"And what is that, vampire lord?"

"Emiline, of course! Where is she?" he yelled, sounding more desperate than he intended.

Matilda feigned shock and looked over to Cerus, who only stared hard at the vampire, his massive spear in hand.

"My dear, Heinsvick, she is safely hidden, of course," she answered.

His grip tightened on Kessi's throat, and he could hear her struggling to breathe.

Matilda's demeanor changed, replacing the feigned look of shock with hate so threatening that it made him more than a little nervous.

"You harm her, and you will never see your precious Emiline again, do you understand?" Matilda hissed.

Heinsvick did not answer and let the girl struggle a bit longer. Matilda and Cerus only stood perfectly still, like two petrified beings, their stares boring holes through him. He finally released his grip from around her neck, and Kessi gave him a dirty look and struggled to get away. He shook her violently, which settled her down, but her glare remained.

"I say again, Heinsvick, do not harm her, or you will experience more than just the grief of losing your beloved wife. Now hand her over," Matilda demanded, stretching out her hand and giving him a warning glare.

Heinsvick held firm his grip, not wanting to be intimidated. He thought of his options and considered teleporting away with Kessi in tow. He could then secretly follow the group, and they would inadvertently lead him to Emiline. He knew that wouldn't work, looking at the brand on the back of his hand. Matilda would destroy him if he tried anything that foolish.

"I will have Emiline. I have served you and will gladly serve you again if you keep your word. But if you do not return her—"

He let the threat hang there, understanding he was playing a dangerous game, but one he intended on winning. The desperation in his voice must have been more evident than he realized because Matilda kept her stance, with one hand beckoning Kessi to her. The only change in her demeanor was a broad smile that crept across her face. Reluctantly, he loosened his grip, and Kessi pulled away, giving him a dirty look, and backing a few steps toward Matilda.

"Come to me, child," Matilda coaxed her, speaking softly and with a comforting smile.

Kessi turned her body to face the water, where she could watch both Heinsvick and Matilda peripherally. She looked from side to side, appearing confused about which group to approach. Heinsvick stood perfectly still, showing no emotion, the gently falling snow making him an imposing figure to the frightened young woman. He could see her struggling to recall who she was, why she was there, or even where she was. Nevertheless, he knew he had to make the exchange quickly because Kessi's mind was even now fighting the fake reality he had made for her.

She glanced to her left at the advancing Matilda, Cerus following behind. Kessi struggled with her binds, and Heinsvick did not doubt that she would jump into the icy water if she were free. But instead, the young woman closed her eyes and took a deep breath. It appeared as if she were calming herself or perhaps recalling the pieces of a spell. Heinsvick even wondered if she would go so far as to attempt to summon the ravens as Cassandra had done once before.

Matilda closed in, quickening her pace when she saw Kessi close her eyes, probably suspecting something similar. Heinsvick considered his options then and thought it best to let Matilda take her prize. If they played this game much longer, perhaps Matilda or Cerus would discover Kessi's true identity before they even had her in their clutches.

Kessi's eyes flew open, and she jumped when Matilda gently touched her arm. Heinsvick could see the confused look on the girl's face as her scrambled brain tried to register the events. He hoped she would hold out a little longer, just enough for him to talk to Matilda about Emiline.

"Cassandra, come with me. Let us take you away from this horror who has mistreated you," Matilda coaxed, waving a hand toward Heinsvick.

Kessi studied the woman's face, and Heinsvick knew she was trying to determine her next course of action. But in the end, what could she possibly do? She was bound and caught. As Heinsvick expected, she nodded slowly, and Matilda gently led her to the other end of the pier.

"You are precious to me, and I promise you will have a great life with us. You will live like a queen until the day you die," Matilda whispered while smiling evilly at Heinsvick.

Kessi mumbled something into her gag, and Matilda reached up and removed it from her mouth. Kessi worked out the stiffness in her mouth, flexing her lower jaw for a moment. Then she looked into Matilda's eyes and did something that no one expected: she spat in her face. Cerus stepped toward her, clutching his massive spear, but Matilda waved him off. She left the saliva on her face and only continued to smile.

"Why, child, you have no reason to hate me; after all, I offer you the life of a queen," she said, wiping the spit from her cheek with a finger, then putting it into her mouth. She sucked it dry and smiled once more. "You see, I worship you and will never lay a hand on you. What more could you ask?"

"You are gross," the fake Cassandra stated. Then she added quickly, "I want my family. He knows where they are," she said, nodding toward the vampire.

Matilda flashed Heinsvick a wicked smile, then said, "We will find your family, I promise. But first, I must save you from this creature. Come with Cerus and me where it is safe, then we will discuss your family."

"He knows where they are," she said again, nearing tears.

"Yes, and he will tell me everything, do not doubt, young one. I have complete control over him, which is why he so easily handed you over. Now come, let us be on our way," Matilda said, motioning for Cerus to take her from the docks.

It appeared to Heinsvick as if Kessi neared rage as tears streamed down her face. She looked back and forth from Heinsvick to Matilda for a few moments, seeming unsure of her next action. Eventually, she gave in to Matilda's desires and walked with Cerus and the other men to the end of the pier. With a final glance back to Heinsvick, they escorted her to a waiting carriage.

"Matilda!" Heinsvick called, his anger and impatience growing with the diminutive woman. "I will take Emiline now, as we agreed."

Matilda turned to face the vampire, the evil smile on her face telling him everything he had feared but expected. "I am keeping her, Heinsvick; she is far too precious to return to you."

"We had a deal," Heinsvick stated flatly, the unspoken threat plastered across his face.

Matilda stood confidently on the pier, alone against the vampire lord but showing no fear at all. She crossed her arms over her tiny frame. "Yes, and you have performed admirably, vampire lord. But do not make me destroy you, for I have big plans for you once my god arrives.

"Give me my Emiline, and you will never see me again. I don't want anything to do with you or your demon-god," Heinsvick quickly said.

"Come, now, Heinsvick, be reasonable. You can be the general of my army once we take power," Matilda said, dramatically waving her hands.

"I do not want to be your general; I simply want my Emiline," Heinsvick demanded, taking a step toward the small woman.

Matilda sighed and dropped her arms to her sides, shaking her head. "Very well. You leave me no choice."

Heinsvick was about to teleport to her when he felt her in his mind, quickly gaining control of his actions. He concentrated on the teleportation that would take him close enough to strike the killing blow. If he were quick enough, she would be unable to stop him. He would then interrogate the crew and find out exactly where Emiline was. He had played this scenario out in his head a million times, assuming Matilda intended to betray him all along. However, one thing the vampire lord had forgotten was the power she exuded over him. Once the priestess was in his mind, he felt sluggish, and his thoughts were jumbled, the same as that fateful night they had met in Novafontera. How could he have forgotten the power she held over him?

She controlled his actions before he could even move, so he just stood there helplessly. Then she approached him confidently and arrogantly, and all he could do was watch until she was standing before him. He knew his mistake then; his love for Emiline overruled his senses, and now he had failed them both. Hot waves of agony rolled through him as the flesh of his forearm ripped open to the bone. He screamed and fell to his knees, grabbing at the searing wound.

"You have chosen incorrectly, foolish vampire. Now you will perish once and for all," Matilda whispered, disappointed.

She raised her arms to the sky, and the flesh ripped across his back. He screamed once more in pure agony and fell over on his side. He had planned to teleport away if something like this happened, but she was in his head, keeping him from executing his plan. Another wound appeared on his abdomen, and it felt like his insides would spill out onto the pier.

Kessi felt what was happening to Heinsvick, though she could not see it. The bite had connected her to him more than she understood.

She screamed, "No, I need him!" standing up and trying to exit the carriage.

Cerus sat next to her, and two other men sat across from her in the vehicle. Cerus quickly grabbed her and clamped a hand tightly around her mouth, pulling her into a sitting position.

He breathed into her ear through gritted teeth, "You might be a queen to her, but you are nothing to me. If you cause me trouble, I swear I will beat you within an inch of your life. Do you understand?"

She turned her head to look him in the eyes as best she could. She found no hint of a lie there, and she calmed immediately. The other two guards smirked at her as she nodded her agreement. Cerus kept his hand tightly around her mouth and turned once more to watch for Matilda to exit the docks.

Heinsvick was rolling around on the pier, screaming in pain. Matilda stood near him, her arms raised to the sky, her eyes closed, summoning the power of Marnelphion, her demon-god. Deep gashes ripped open all over his body, and he knew this was the end. She was destroying him slowly, savoring the event, and toying with him as if he were a small child, not a powerful vampire lord. His hate for her grew somehow beyond what it already was. He scolded himself for falling into the trap. She had tricked him easily, and he felt like a fool as his last bit of life force began to wane.

Kessi had to do something if she had any chance of finding her family again, so she did the only thing she could think to do and bit Cerus's hand. Blood squirted into her mouth, and she briefly considered that she enjoyed the taste for some reason. So, she bit harder, tearing the skin.

Cerus screamed out in shock and pain and let go of her. The guard across from her leaned in to grab her, and she kicked out as hard as she could, connecting solidly with his crotch. The man fell to the carriage floor, and she opened the door, jumped out, and ran toward the docks.

Cerus and the third warrior jumped out, and as that third warrior began to take up the chase, Cerus put a firm hand on his shoulder, stopping him. The man looked back at his leader and saw the stern visage there.

Cerus shook his head and said, "She is mine."

With that, he took off after her with surprising speed for a man of his stature. The lesser warrior could only watch Cerus with great appreciation as he bound away.

"Leave him alone!" Kessi shouted as she made her way back to the docks as best she could, her hands still secured behind her.

Her screams caught the attention of several passersby, who stopped to watch the spectacle but did not dare interfere. Unfortunately, a scene such as that was not uncommon in Racip, and interfering meant the risk of death. So those that did notice quickly turned and hurried away. Racip was chaotic, and law and peace were non-existent.

Matilda opened her eyes and turned toward Kessi, who was nearing the docks, Cerus close behind her. She regarded the vampire briefly, who lay in a bloody mess on the pier, not putting up much of a fight and faintly moaning in pain.

At the edge of the docks, Cerus tackled Kessi and knocked the wind out of her as his full weight fell on her. He pinned her easily and quickly backhanded her hard across the face.

"Cerus, no!" Matilda screamed, now ignoring Heinsvick's broken form altogether.

The vampire vaguely felt her leaving his mind.

Kessi had never felt such a mighty blow before. The vampire had struck her, she recalled, and although those hits had hurt her, Cerus could injure her badly, she understood. Her jumbled thoughts recalled when Lord Ronnis had hit her in the orphanage yard after he had taken her drawings. She could not remember exactly how that had felt, but she knew this was worse. She saw stars right away and swooned with a dizziness that threatened to take her into a deep sleep. She had hit her head reasonably hard, but she only felt the throbbing in her left cheek from the tremendous slap.

Cerus, half-listening to Matilda, did not strike her again. Instead, he picked her up by the throat and stuffed the gag back in her mouth. His hold on her throat was like a vise, and she could not breathe. Pain assaulted her as her cheek and head screamed with each move. Her lungs burned from a lack of air. The crazed man was killing her, his face inches from hers, as he spoke to her. She did not focus on his words as her eyes rolled into the back of her head, and she neared unconsciousness, but she knew the gist of what he was saying. Kessi could faintly hear Matilda screaming as if she were a hundred miles away.

"Cerus! Release her!" Matilda called, running toward him.

Heinsvick lay on the pier, next to unconsciousness, as Matilda ultimately left his mind and confronted Cerus. Six deep wounds showed in various places on his body. Blood pooled around him, but he knew he had to block out the pain and move while Matilda was distracted. Although he was vaguely aware of her conversing with someone else, he knew the reprieve was only temporary. Heinsvick had only one chance at this, so he shook the cobwebs from his mind the best he could and quickly recalled his teleportation spell. The world blurred from existence temporarily, and he felt hurled across the continents. When he refocused, he found himself in his lair, near his coffin in Novafontera.

He would fully heal in that coffin with a bit of rest. But first, he had to stop the threat. He staggered on shaky legs to an old desk in the room. He opened the drawer to find the one item he had taken from Kessi's pack when he snatched her from Oldorburg.

Kessi lay on the ground, moaning, where Cerus had dropped her. With his reckless anger, he had come close to killing her. Matilda was furious.

"Fool! Do not dare touch her again. You nearly cost us everything with your blind rage," she scolded, leaning over the girl.

Cerus smirked. "Cost *you*… not me. I care nothing for her."

"I need you with me, my husband, in this great mission. If you work against me, then all is lost. Do you not see the greatness that is within our grasp?" Matilda lectured, confirming Kessi was not seriously injured, then rose confidently before him.

"I see the greatness for you, and I am pleased, but I do not worship Marnelphion as you do, and so no reward awaits me with his summoning," he answered stubbornly, grabbing his spear, and slamming the butt hard on the ground.

Matilda understood his frustration; after all, he was the son of Gorl, the god of war, and war was all he craved. He had been willing to follow Matilda, hoping he could lead many battles with his bloodthirsty men. But, as of date, her war-mongering husband had only had the one easy invasion of Attins, then twice had lost his dignity to Greyson Kavince, the young priest she had taken as a lover. First, Greyson had cuckolded him; then, he had broken Cerus's nose when her proud husband had caught the arrogant priest with the intent of paying him back for that humiliation.

Since then, Matilda had pressured him to play with Emiline more and more, which she knew he resisted. Perhaps she would need to soften her stance and let him take more of a leadership role between them. She knew she could manipulate her proud husband by doing so, so she bit her tongue and knelt to help Kessi into a sitting position. He towered over them as Matilda took an inventory of the girl's injuries. Her cheek swelled, and her neck would surely bruise, but she was not permanently hurt. Matilda gently stroked her uninjured cheek and smiled, but Kessi pulled away.

Matilda rose and looked up at Cerus, who stood there defiantly. "I love you and need you. Please help me protect her. I cannot do it myself, and we must keep her safe for the next few years. I promise I will reward you in more ways than you can imagine if you can help me see this through," she teased, running a finger over his breastplate, and looking at him lustfully with her big brown eyes. She took his torn hand and kissed it gently. "Surely you can endure some discomfort for the greater good?"

"He is gone," Cerus said, ignoring her and looking over her shoulder at the pier.

Matilda turned and found Heinsvick missing.

Cerus chuckled and said, "Seems that the vampire lord has escaped your grasp."

"Hardly," Matilda answered. She focused on the brand that bound her to the vampire.

She could feel his essence and forced her attack on that very life force once more. He was weak, his power waning, and she would not stop until she destroyed him. She felt his flesh rip from his shoulder to his hamstring, and his life force weakened even more. In a few moments longer, Matilda would utterly destroy the vampire lord.

Heinsvick lay his left hand down on the desk, the evil brand on that hand killing him. He raised the small hatchet he had stolen from the pack but hesitated momentarily, losing the courage to complete the deed. Severing his hand was not something he could do now that the time had come. The delay cost him dearly as a tear in his back cut him down. His screams echoed throughout the castle, and he fell to one knee as dizziness began to take hold. He had to stay conscious; he had to sever contact with Matilda. He stubbornly rose, sweat now pouring into his eyes from the pain of many garish wounds.

He could hear the rustling of his brides as they began to stir, and he knew they would come to him, overjoyed at his presence, but not like this. He had to end this before the evil priestess destroyed him. He could not take one more wound from the brand without the possibility of blacking out. So, he quickly lifted the hatchet just as he felt the next tear in his skin forming on his chest. That gave him the motivation to follow through, and with one great swing, the hatchet came down.

"The task is complete," Matilda said triumphantly, opening her eyes and turning back to Cerus with a broad smile. "I no longer feel the essence of the vampire; I have destroyed him," she continued.

Kessi screamed into her gag; the only link to her sister and mother was gone. She began to sob, the emotions overcoming her finally. Matilda bent down and put an arm around her.

"There, there, child. I destroyed the creature that captured you and your family. I avenged you; now, we are your family, and you need to forget your previous life. None of that matters," Matilda said, lifting Kessi's chin to look her in the eye.

Kessi only sobbed harder, so Matilda helped her to her feet and led her back to the carriage that would take them home. Kessi re-took her seat; Matilda sat beside her, and Cerus was across from them this time.

"Take us home, my powerful husband," Matilda said, looking at him pleadingly and giving him back some control.

He sat motionless for some time, and his men waited for his order, standing just outside the carriage. Then, finally, he nodded and said, "Lead us home, men."

They went into action as two mounted the carriage to drive it home, and the other four men found their horses and formed an escort. They were soon out of Racip, and all the commotion they had caused while there vanished into the history of the evil port, not one witness daring to help Kessi.

Heinsvick awoke shortly after severing his hand to find blood gushing from the wound. His brides huddled around him, most of them crying. Allustria was there, cradling his head in her lap as she sat on the floor, sobbing gently. He managed a weak smile and summoned the energy to produce a small flame in his hand. Allustria froze, not understanding his intent.

Heinsvick took the flame and, with a grimace, burned the stump of his wrist to stop the bleeding. He held the fire there as long as he could, screaming in pain but successfully sealing off the blood flow. He kept his bearings, knowing that he was near death. He could feel the many places on his torn body where Matilda had attacked him. His entire body throbbed with pain, and he was as close to destruction as he ever had been. Heinsvick needed his coffin, and he needed much rest to recover. He would need to do so quickly if he wished to survive.

"Help me to my coffin," he whispered to Allustria.

She nodded and gently helped him to a standing position. He leaned heavily on her, and she walked him to the coffin, opening it and helping him inside. She felt so powerful to him at that moment, and he realized how weak he indeed was. She stood at the coffin, the lid still up, and his other brides joined her, each poking their head around the top tentatively. Most were terrified and crying, and they gently touched him, stroking his legs or hand. He smiled, trying to be strong. He knew that if Matilda entered the castle now, this would be the last time he would see any of them. Hopefully, she thought he was now dead and would leave him be.

"Guard me while I heal. I will be whole in but a few days. Guard me and kill anyone who comes near. We will start life anew once I am at full strength," he instructed.

Allustria nodded and slowly closed the lid. The smell of the earth in his coffin was strong, and the temperature was cool. His left wrist ached and throbbed, and his entire body was seared with pain from the gashes caused by Matilda. The healing powers of his coffin began to take hold immediately, and he closed his eyes. He drifted off, and his last thoughts before sleep took him were how he would enjoy destroying Matilda and bringing Emiline home. Nothing else in the world meant anything to him now. He would have his revenge.

Having examined Cassandra's wounds, Maina stood straight and said with a shrug, "You are almost as good as new. Greyson's healing is impeccable."

Her diagnosis offended Cassandra more than it reassured her, and she quickly pointed out the flaws in that statement. "Greyson touched me without permission and in the temple of Gella, where he does not belong."

Maina looked at her patient with a perplexed expression and said, "I agree, but the fact is, he healed you willingly and broke protocol only because he is a friend and cares for you."

"He is not a friend; I hardly know him. He also doesn't care for me; he seems only interested in molesting me," Cassandra pointed out with a huff.

Her words brought a smile to Maina's face. "He is a bit promiscuous," she replied, shaking her head.

Cassandra rolled her eyes and gingerly stood on shaky legs.

"Where are my things?" she asked.

"What are you doing?" Maina asked.

"Getting dressed and going back to my room at the school. I feel better and can easily fend for myself now."

"You can't do that, Cassandra."

"Why not? You said I was as good as new."

"I am afraid the queen has ordered you to stay in the temple until further notice."

The realization she could not leave knocked the wind out of Cassandra, and she sat back down on the bed, a stunned expression on her face.

"You mean I am a prisoner here?" she asked.

Maina shook her head and said, "No, I do not think that is the queen's intent, but until she resolves things, she wants you here."

"What do you mean by 'resolve'?" Cassandra asked defensively.

"Well, I am not sure, but a representative from the school will be here soon to go over things with you."

Cassandra just sat there, dumbfounded, trying to absorb the latest news. Was she kicked out of the school a few weeks into her first semester? Would she have to stay at the temple now if she could not return to school? Why was she treated like a prisoner if Pelesea was such a righteous place? These thoughts swirled in her mind as she stewed over her new situation.

Her thoughts were interrupted by Maina, who had made it across the room and was about to exit, but turned and offered some advice, "Pray to Gella, dear; she will provide the answers."

Cassandra's eyes moved to the tapestry, and she felt the warmth of Gella's symbol once more.

"Shall I send in your friends?" Maina asked.

Tears welled in Cassandra's eyes. She needed Binta very much but could not tolerate being around Greyson. She just shook her head and lay down on the bed.

"No, I am tired. Please tell Binta I will speak with her later."

"As you wish," Maina said with a smile.

She left, closing the door gently behind her, and Cassandra strained to hear the conversation that followed. She briefly listened to some mumbled discussion, but it soon stopped, and Cassandra assumed Binta and Greyson had left. Again, Cassandra felt very alone, and thoughts of her sister and mother filled her head. Then, not for the first time since arriving at Pelesea, she cried softly to sleep.

She awakened sometime later when she felt someone holding her hand. She opened her eyes to find Binta sitting on the edge of the bed. Her smile was warm, and the sadness immediately melted from Cassandra's thoughts. She sat up and hugged her friend. It was a long, much-needed hug, and Cassandra rested her head on her friend's shoulder. She needed the support right then.

"You have slept the day away," Binta said, breaking the hug and brushing Cassandra's hair out of her face.

"I guess I was more tired than I realized," Cassandra said sleepily.

She noticed the setting sun through the window and realized that the day was truly gone. She looked back at Binta and saw the concerned look on her pretty face.

"What is it?" Cassandra asked.

"You could have died, you know?"

Cassandra looked down at her hands and nodded. "She tricked me, Binta."

"What do you mean?"

"Before you arrived and before that fool, Jabell, attacked you, she countered my magic," Cassandra explained.

Binta shook her head, confused. "How?"

"She had some device, a medallion, which absorbed my magic."

"She knew," Binta reasoned.

Again, Cassandra looked down and nodded in embarrassment. "She baited me to attack her. She prepared for it, and I was the fool who—"

"Acted irrationally," Binta finished for her.

They laughed at that, and Cassandra looked lovingly at her friend. She needed Binta in her life. They understood each other and complimented each other. However, the smile soon faded from Cassandra's face, and Binta looked at her, puzzled.

"What bothers you? If it is Cass, do not—" Binta began.

Cassandra waved a hand at her, as if dismissing the notion, and shook her head. "I am not concerned about Cass. I will repay her for what she did to me."

"Then what troubles you? Tell me," Binta pleaded.

"You are not going to like what I have to say."

Binta sat back a bit and smiled once more. "It is about Greyson, then?"

Cassandra's eyes widened, and she slowly nodded her head. "Yes, but how could you know?"

"He told me what he did to you."

"What? He did?" Cassandra asked, now very curious.

"Yes, when he healed you earlier this morning."

"What exactly did he say?" Cassandra asked.

Before she could answer, a knock on the door startled both of them.

"Come in," Cassandra said.

The door opened, and Greyson was there. The sight of him made Cassandra's blood boil, especially when she saw how Binta lit up upon his arrival. He made his way across the room confidently, too confidently for someone his age, Cassandra realized. Whatever ordeals he had been through in his short life had built his confidence and reputation within the temple. Binta had become obsessed with him, and the simple fact was that Cassandra was jealous. She wanted her friend to be happy, but she needed Binta right now. She felt selfish and wanted Binta to herself.

He kissed Binta on the cheek, then sat in the chair in the corner of the room. Cassandra could not deny that he was handsome, but he was too smug for her, too confident. She didn't like it and didn't like that he might hurt her friend.

"Hello, Cassandra, how are you feeling?" he asked.

"Better," was all she could say, and she couldn't bring herself to look him in the eye.

"Good. I could call on the powers of Plath to heal you some more if you wish."

Cassandra did look at him then, snapping her head quickly to meet his gaze. He sat there with a smile, as if he had done nothing wrong. Cassandra turned her gaze to Binta and could tell her friend was oblivious to the potential heartbreak the priest offered. She wanted to scream out the accusations of what Greyson had done earlier that day, how he had touched her, but it sounded like Binta knew. Was she tolerant of that kind of behavior?

"I am fine, Greyson, and I'd prefer it if you left your hands to yourself," she finally spoke, unable to hide the venom in her voice.

"Cassandra, I healed you because you were in pain. Healing such as this is no small thing and usually earns my temple a few gold pieces for performing such a feat," Greyson said smoothly.

"I have no money, Greyson, and didn't ask for your healing," she snapped back a little more hatefully than she intended.

"And I expect none. I do hope that you tolerate my company better if we are all going to be friends," he answered, holding his one good arm wide to emphasize the three of them.

"Friends? I hardly know you, and I have a feeling you and Binta don't truly know each other yet," she spat back, knowing that Greyson would decipher the hidden message in that retort.

"Oh, but you are wrong, dear Cassandra," he said dramatically, rising from his chair and making his way to the edge of the bed.

Cassandra did not know what to expect from him, but Binta seemed enthralled, her big, dark eyes wide, taking in his dramatics. It made Cassandra sick to know she was under such a spell with the smooth-talking young man. Of course, she held her tongue, but having Greyson this close to her made her uncomfortable as much as it made Binta happy.

"Cassandra, I expect the three of us to be best friends. Binta and I have discussed this in detail, and I think the three of us will be happy together."

Cassandra's mouth fell open, and she stared at him in disbelief. Did he think she was so dense that she would forget his actions from this morning? Binta seemed not even to have a clue as to his indiscretions. Cassandra wondered how many women he had touched inappropriately or worse.

"I can explain my theory with three kisses," he explained.

"What are you talking about?" Cassandra asked.

"Behold, kiss number one," he answered, cutting her off and turning toward Binta.

He grabbed a handful of Binta's hair and pulled her head back. Binta gasped, and her lips parted slightly in anticipation. Her eyes darted back and forth, studying his face, awaiting his next move. Finally, he turned and smiled at Cassandra, then bent low to engage Binta in a deep kiss. She eagerly returned it, and they kissed passionately as Cassandra watched.

Cassandra struggled to register the scene as her friend kissed the idiot priest right in front of her, and pangs of jealousy shot through her heart. She recalled the kiss she had shared with Binta just a few nights ago. It had meant so much to her and somehow meant even more now. As she watched the kiss become even more passionate and Binta moaned slightly into his mouth, Cassandra felt the need to use her magic to hurt Greyson for taking that special kiss and making a mockery of it. She wished it was her kissing Binta, and the thought startled her a bit.

She had never considered herself bisexual, but that kiss meant her world. It dawned on her then that the kiss they had shared may have triggered her attack on Cass, and it was all Greyson's fault. The kiss had meant everything to Cassandra, and Greyson had taken Binta away from her before they could take the next step, whatever that might have been. She was sure this was why she had lashed out recklessly at Cass.

They broke the kiss then, and Greyson turned back to Cassandra. "And now, kiss number two," he said, interrupting her thoughts.

He still had a handful of Binta's hair, and she had such a lustful look in her eye that it made Cassandra's heart pound in her chest with anticipation. Greyson lifted Binta by her hair gently to go from sitting on Cassandra's bed to kneeling on it.

"What are you doing, Greyson? Let her go," Cassandra demanded, but without much conviction, her words coming out in a whisper.

Greyson only smiled and walked toward the head of the bed, leading Binta by the hair. She straddled Cassandra's body and crawled toward her, a playful smile on her face. Cassandra did not know what to do; Binta looked more beautiful to her than she ever had.

"Binta?" she whispered and sat back as far as she could against the headboard.

Her friend did not respond, and Greyson moved her closer so that Binta's pretty face was only inches from hers. Cassandra could feel the heat of Binta's breath and could only close her eyes as Greyson pushed Binta's face closer.

Their lips touched, and Binta's tongue darted into her mouth. That was all it took to dissolve Cassandra's resistance; soon after, they kissed passionately. It was a deeper and more sensual kiss than the first time and more sexually charged. Cassandra loved the way kissing Binta made her feel. She was on a cloud, and at that moment, there were only two of them, and she didn't realize Greyson even existed then. He said something, but it was far away, and instead of listening to his words, Cassandra concentrated on Binta and how she tasted and smelled. The kiss was blissfully amazing, but then it was suddenly over.

Cassandra opened her eyes to see Greyson leading Binta back down the bed, still holding her by the hair. She crawled backward, just the way she had come, and obediently sat down on the end of the bed. Greyson finally released her hair and smiled down at her. She smiled back and bit her lower lip. Cassandra found Binta so desirable at that moment and felt a tingling sensation in her loins as she watched her friend submissively follow his lead.

He then turned and walked back to Cassandra, who once again sat as far back as she could against the headboard, her attention finally focusing on the aggressive priest.

"Greyson, what—" she whispered.

"Shhh," he whispered back and knelt so that his face was close to hers.

He was handsome, and she knew he meant to kiss her. She wasn't sure at that point if she wanted him to stop. She felt that if the kiss happened, she would betray Binta, but her friend was not objecting to this and appeared to want it to happen. She could no longer see Binta, but she knew she was still sitting on the bed. She felt her hand gently lay on her leg, as if giving her permission to kiss the young man. Cassandra closed her eyes and opened her mouth.

"And finally, kiss number three," he whispered and moved in.

Just before their lips touched, there was a knock on the door. Cassandra's eyes flew open, and she pushed Greyson back.

"Come… come in!" she yelled, almost hysterically.

Greyson and Binta both stood as if caught in some illegal activity. Then, the door opened, and Instructor Baxter from the school of magic entered.

"Baxter!" Cassandra exclaimed.

"Cassandra Rho, you do not look hurt at all," he said happily, walking briskly into the room and moving quickly to the bed. "You seem to have made a miraculous recovery, similar to your friend, here," he added, extending his arm to Binta.

He nodded at Binta and Greyson, "Miss Mulay, Greyson."

"Good evening, Instructor Baxter," Binta replied nervously, her face flush from the kissing.

"Good to see you again, sir," Greyson quickly added.

"Greyson has been using his gift of healing to help us recover from our injuries," Binta added, giving Greyson a loving look as she did so.

Cassandra noticed a strange expression on Baxter's face then. Was it jealousy, she wondered, and if so, who could the instructor be jealous of? He noticed her look and quickly composed himself, the strange expression melting away with a fake smile.

"I appreciate your good work, Greyson. I assure you; Lady Victoria is delighted that the temple was able to heal both students. I'm sure a generous donation is forthcoming from the school to the priests responsible for their quick recovery," Baxter answered.

"A donation would be much appreciated, sir. I have just begun allocating a section of the temple to Plath. I'll need funds to build it into something worthy to attract followers," Greyson said with a slight bow.

"Yeah, but I am under the care of Maina, priestess of Gella," Cassandra butted in, nodding toward the tapestry on the wall depicting the beautiful wand.

Baxter looked over at the tapestry, then back to Greyson, who blushed a bit. "She is correct; Maina has healed most of her wounds; I am following up with any extra healing she may need," Greyson answered.

Cassandra rolled her eyes at the ridiculous comment, and she thought Baxter noted her reaction, but said nothing.

"Well, we must be going; I'm sure you need to discuss some things privately," Binta said, then moved over to hug Cassandra.

Cassandra hugged her friend tight and whispered in her ear, "Thank you."

Binta pulled away, smiled, and said, "Get better, and hopefully, we will see you back in school soon."

"Well, then, nice seeing you again, sir," Greyson said to Baxter, then looked at Cassandra and added, "I will come back soon to finish the healing we started today."

Cassandra froze, not knowing how to respond to that as a hundred different feelings bombarded her, including annoyance, anticipation, and lust. She watched Baxter as he nodded goodbye to Binta and Greyson, and the look on his face indicated he suspected something amiss. His knowing eyes bore holes through her, and she felt her cheeks flush. They held a silent gaze until the door shut, leaving them alone.

Once they were, Baxter sat on the edge of her bed and shook his head, saying, "How could you have attacked a fellow student?"

Cassandra's cheeks reddened at the comment. The embarrassment of her failure, compounded with Baxter blaming the event on her, made her temperature boil.

Finally, Baxter seemed to relent a bit at her embarrassment. "I'm sorry, I should not critique your actions so," he said with a smile.

"I understand your disappointment; I am equally frustrated," Cassandra said, looking down at her hands.

"Victoria will discuss your actions in great detail soon enough. But, for now, I am here to tell you the punishment that Lady Victoria has decided to exact on you."

"On me? Cass nearly killed me, Baxter!" Cassandra said, leaning toward him as she spoke, her face red with anger.

"Calm down, Cassandra," Baxter said, patting his hand in the air. "All three of you will face punishment: Cass, Jabell, and you."

Cassandra sat back against the headboard and crossed her arms over her chest. She said nothing for a long while and looked into his eyes, determining what other bits of information she could extract from him. She finally gave up and diverted her gaze, becoming more frustrated as the moments passed.

"I should have won," she finally said, more to herself than Baxter.

"Perhaps, but the real question is—should you have challenged her in the first place?" he answered.

She gave him a look that hinted there would be a better place and time for this conversation. He seemed to pick up on that and said, "Look, Cassandra, all I want you to remember is that I care for you very much and have very high hopes for you. So does Lady Victoria. I don't want you to throw your future away on petty altercations with a fellow student."

"She provoked me."

"Then rise above it," Baxter answered, standing from the bed, and crossing his arms. "You are better than this, and I expect more from you."

Cassandra looked down at her hands again and sniffed away a tear. Baxter sighed and sat back down, patting her leg. "Look at me, Cassandra."

She looked up, eyes filled with tears, her face still flush. Baxter's demeanor changed to that familiar, stupid look she had caught him giving her several times before. It was the look a schoolboy with a crush might give, except Baxter was old enough to be her father. Finally, he seemed to catch himself and smile, dismissing the look. She did not return the smile but wiped away her tears and pulled herself together a bit.

"I care for you, Cassandra, and I will fight for you. You know this, right?"

She nodded and smiled ever so slightly but kept her emotions in check. Instead, she just glared at the wizard, waiting for the news he had to deliver.

"So, what is my punishment?" she finally asked, with a catch in her throat.

"Victoria has expelled you for the rest of the semester," he answered quickly, seemingly wanting to get the news out fast.

"What? The whole semester? What about my classes? Where will I stay?" she asked in rapid succession.

Baxter patted his hands in the air once more. "Calm down, Cassandra, and I will explain everything if you will just listen and not interrupt."

Cassandra sat back against the headboard once more, her arms over her chest again, and her bright blue eyes bore holes through the instructor.

"First, you will withdraw from your classes and will need to retake them in the spring. You will live here at the temple for the rest of the semester. Victoria has arranged it with the high priests."

"Here? What will I do all day?" she asked in a huff.

"I'm glad you asked, because we have arranged for you to work here to pay off your debt for the healing and lodging. At night, I would suggest studying," he answered and awaited her response. None came, so he added softly, "I could even come in the evenings to tutor you."

She did smile at that, realizing then that she enjoyed Baxter's company and wouldn't mind some one-on-one tutoring. He smiled back and patted her leg again. She watched his hand touching her leg, and he seemed lost in thought for a moment. He soon realized what he was doing and retracted his hand.

"So, what about Cass and Jabell? Their crimes were much worse than mine, so what are their punishments?"

"They are for Victoria and the instructors to decide," Baxter said.

Cassandra pouted a bit, keeping her arms crossed and rolling her eyes again. Baxter waited patiently until she finally gave in and looked him in the eye. A smile crept on his face, and she returned it with one of her own.

"Fine, then. What did Victoria decide for them?" she asked, throwing her hands up in resignation, unable to maintain her anger with Baxter.

"Well, Cass will receive the same punishment as you; expulsion until next semester."

"What? She nearly killed me—"

"Yes, that is true, Cassandra, but the rules of wizard's privilege allow her to if she had chosen. She could have killed you if she wanted to," he interrupted again with enough force to show her how serious the situation had indeed been.

Cassandra sat back once more and reflected on his words. She could not believe why her punishment was as severe as Cass's. Cassandra had been injured and humiliated in front of the student body. She managed to bite her tongue, though, and let Baxter continue.

"Jabell has been expelled permanently from the school. His severe punishment is because his actions were deemed more violent, and he did not have the protection from the rules as wizard's privilege provided the two of you," he finished.

She took some satisfaction from that but would still have to tolerate Cass once the spring semester rolled around. Perhaps she would not be nearly as nasty without her lackey, Jabell, hanging around.

"So, that's it, huh?" she asked.

"For now," Baxter agreed, and stood once more. "I will have Miss Mulay bring your belongings to you tomorrow; I didn't feel right rummaging through them. I will be in touch as soon as possible with more information. Lady Victoria will want to meet with you and Cass to resolve this issue before the next semester, and I will make that happen soon. It is still up to Lady Victoria whether she will let either of you back in school when the spring comes."

"I may not be allowed back? I am the best student in my class!"

"And Cass is second in your class. That is what makes this whole thing a tragedy," Baxter sighed. "Don't worry about it; work hard while you are here and prove to her you are serious about school. I will say a good word for you as much as possible."

Cassandra nodded and smiled, and Baxter stood there, seemingly lost in thought.

She finally broke the awkward silence. "Is there anything else?"

"Oh, yes... as a matter of fact... there is," Baxter stammered, searching his pockets for something.

"Ah-ha!" he finally exclaimed and brought forth a massive tome from one of his pockets. The book was far too large to fit in such a small space. Cassandra surmised that the pocket was probably an extra-dimensional space to keep many useful things.

He laid the tome on her lap and asked, "Do you remember this?"

"My book," she said excitedly. "Well, Instructor Franklin's book on the New Order," she corrected.

"Yes, I asked Franklin if you could use it the rest of the semester, and he gladly agreed," Baxter said with a wide smile.

Cassandra quickly moved out of bed, pulling the covers off and ignoring the dull pain in her abdomen. She rushed right up to Baxter and gave him a big hug. He didn't seem to know what to do initially and was in a bit of shock at her reaction. Slowly, he returned the hug.

"Thank you," she whispered in his ear.

"Of course," he said, moving back at arm's length. He smiled and kissed her forehead.

They shared a knowing look then and said their goodbyes. As Baxter left, he promised to return soon to check on her and discuss her readings. Cassandra slept soundly that night, temporarily at peace with the world and the hefty tome tucked into the bed beside her.

CHAPTER 2

CHARMED

About eight miles south of Oldorburg, Boz, who frequented the small farming community known simply as Farmers' Stop, requested Kringus's company stop there. Kringus readily agreed, due to the injuries his small party had sustained. Boz arranged for the three most significantly wounded men to convalesce in the home of an elderly couple, Quentin and Ella, and employed the local herbalist to care for them.

Although his healing practices were crude and had little effect, the herbalist did his best to keep Arrin's fever under control and Marcus's pain to a minimum. Kringus had berated himself for not bringing Alleah, a proficient healer, along on this excursion; he just hadn't planned for the difficulties they ended up facing at Oldorburg.

Kringus and his remaining sojourners assembled in a large barn, their horses nearby, along with various other livestock that belonged to their gracious hosts. The cold wind howled outside and beat against the old but sturdy barn. He looked around at the men huddled together near the few lanterns they had lit, the light dancing across their faces, as he addressed them. Some of his most trusted men, including the elven brothers Von and Lenore, and the cavaliers Franklin and Jimmon, gathered to hear their king's words. Their mood was dour, as it should have been, as their friends, Arrin, Erik, and Marcus, were so severely injured. Arrin especially so because he remained unconscious and in the throes of a devastating fever.

Their new ally, the carofex, Boz, also joined the group at the request of Kringus himself. Carofex were similar in appearance to humans but possessed strange powers over fire. Boz wore a shaved head, which he rarely displayed, for he preferred to keep the hood of his robe pulled tight, hiding most of his features. He was a curiosity to Kringus and his men, having known him for only a few days, but they all trusted him, for he had helped them defeat the attack in Oldorburg that had decimated their group.

Kringus stood as the rest sat around him, his large arms crossed over his massive chest. He looked each one in the eye, except for Boz, who stared blankly ahead. The carofex wore his hood pulled down so that only his mouth and chin were visible. The group waited patiently for Kringus to speak while making that critical eye contact. He read no judgment on their faces, no accusations, even though he had erred by being too reckless at Oldorburg. That had cost him the lives of four friends, which weighed heavily on his shoulders.

At long last, he spoke, "We leave at the break of dawn."

There were no objections, as most of them had already guessed that would be his decision after the group had stayed put for the last two days.

"Our time out of the kingdom grows long. The queen expects us back soon, and so we will go. We have six bodies to bury: our four friends, the sheriff of Oldorburg, and Cassandra Rho's mother. We also have news to deliver concerning the troublesome town of Oldorburg. I feel our friends are safe here, and sadly, we will leave them behind. We will send for them once we reach home, but until then, they are in good hands with these folks," Kringus continued.

Kringus's bandaged forearm began to bleed through the wrappings for the second time that day. The king casually changed his dressing as he addressed the gathered men. He applied more healing salve the herbalist had given him. It was a grim reminder that they had used all their healing potions on their three injured friends who needed a true healer. Kringus had stubbornly refused to take any of the curing liquid when it was rationed among the injured. He wore the bandages as a reminder of his mistake of not bringing a healer or at least more curing potions. A mistake he would not make again.

"We will leave at the first light of day. Get some rest, for we will ride hard and long to reach Mecca-Loraine as quickly as we can," Kringus declared, and the gathered men nodded in agreement.

"Then it is settled. We ride for Mecca-Loraine at dawn and find passage home from there," he proclaimed with as much enthusiasm as he could muster, and under the circumstances, it wasn't much. "But first, we will discover the true identity of our new, mysterious friend here," he said, extending a hand toward Boz.

The carofex made no move at first, and as usual, the only thing visible on the man's face was his chin, which seemed made of rock in the lamplight. All the other men looked toward the carofex, and after many moments, he slowly raised his head to look the king in the eyes, but still, only half his face was visible. Finally, Kringus approached the carofex to stand right next to him.

"Do not get me wrong, Boz; we are all indebted to you and appreciate your help thus far. But as a king, I must remain vigilant with any new acquaintances. Therefore, I wish to know more about you and how you were so conveniently able to assist us," Kringus said.

Boz pulled the hood of his robe back to reveal his shaved head and crystal blue eyes. He rose slowly and powerfully to stand before the king. Kringus was an imposing man who stood six and a half feet tall with massive shoulders and a chiseled chest. Boz stood just as tall but was not nearly as imposing, especially with his robe, which hid his finely toned muscles. He bowed to the king, which was more of a slight nod.

"You assisted us in battle and just happened to have the antidote that may save my good friend's life. Why did you help, and how did you happen to have an antidote? It seems too convenient to me," Kringus asked, crossing his arms over his chest.

Boz slowly removed his robe, leaving him in only a pair of light pants and sandals. It was the first time they realized the man was wearing little clothing in the bitter cold. A large tattoo of a burning fist covered his back. He slowly turned, facing the men, and letting Kringus see his tattoo.

"I am Boz from the Brotherhood of Fire Monastery of Mecca-Loraine. I am a carofex, proficient in martial arts and most other fighting styles. However, as with my brothers and sisters of the monastery, I carry no weapons and desire no conflict. We are fighters but fight only for peace," the young carofex answered, lifting his arms out straight by his sides and turning once more to face Kringus.

"My brotherhood took an interest in the Rho girls when word first reached us concerning the tale of the wolf and the ravens. I assume you have heard of this?" he continued.

Kringus glanced at Von and Lenore, who remained seated and shared a knowing look.

"Yes, some of us within my kingdom know of this story, including myself," Kringus answered, recalling the meeting with Victoria all those years ago when she had told him of the rumors of the strange encounter.

Boz nodded slightly, then continued, slowly bringing his arms back to his sides. "The brotherhood sent me to Oldorburg then to observe the girls, and I did so for nearly a year before returning home."

"To what end?" asked Kringus, uncrossing his arms and cocking his head slightly.

"To study them; to understand them. My brotherhood thirsts for knowledge of the human race, and the extraordinary ones are most worthy of our time."

"So, why did you return to Oldorburg?" Kringus pressed.

"Word reached us that the Rho girls were in trouble. My masters agreed that I should return to Oldorburg to investigate and assist them, if truly in peril. Alas, I found them gone once I reached the town and, after some research, discovered that Cassandra had presumably fled to Pelesea and Kessi had gone missing. Once I heard you were from Pelesea, that solidified my allegiance to you. When they attacked you, I went into action," Boz answered.

"And the antidote?" Kringus asked, staring hard at the man, locking his accusing gaze with the carofex, looking for the slightest hint of a lie.

"I never go anywhere without being prepared for a place's worst-case scenario. I know the poison of the priests of Oldorburg, and I travel prepared," Boz answered, unblinking.

"And what would you prepare for if you came to Pelesea?"

Boz thought for a moment and finally said, "I would prepare for a good night's rest, knowing that the city is just and that I am with friends," he finally answered.

Kringus stared hard at him for many moments, and Boz quickly matched the intensity of the gaze with his own, showing no emotion. Eventually, a smile crept across Kringus's face, and he clasped Boz on the shoulder, noting how his firm grip did little to move the strong carofex.

"Then you are most welcome to travel with us and visit Cassandra Rho. You are now considered an ally of Pelesea, Boz from Mecca-Loraine," the king declared and clasped hands with the carofex.

The others cheered and came together around Boz, welcoming him as an official member of their band. It was many hours before they all settled down to sleep. And when they did at last nod off, Boz rested comfortably, the next step in his goal quickly reached. Winning the king's trust was key to getting close to Cassandra Rho.

"Cassandra? Time to rise."

The voice was distant and unfamiliar. Cassandra wasn't sure if it was a dream, and she was so tired she could not open her eyes.

"Kessi?" she asked.

"It is I, Maina."

"Maina?" Cassandra repeated, shaking away the fog of sleep and opening her eyes.

There stood Maina by her bedside, a small candle in her hand. She wore a magnificent gown, and a headdress made of metal, perhaps even gold, that covered her head and ears and ran down the sides of her face. Cassandra sat up, remembering where she was. She glanced out the window and saw that the sky was still dark. She rubbed her eyes and yawned.

"It is still dark outside; why do you wake me at this time?" Cassandra asked.

"Today is your first day of service to the temple of Gella. I have chores for you, but first, I want you to put this on," Maina answered and laid a gown on the bed at Cassandra's feet.

Cassandra sat up and pulled the white gown to her, feeling the soft material. Gold trim ran around the edges of the sleeves and the bottom of the dress.

"What is this?" she asked, puzzled.

"It is an acolyte's gown. You must wear this if you are to join me in the temple for the morning worship."

"Worship? I'm not a priest or an acolyte or even a follower. So why do I—?" Cassandra began.

"You are under my command, young lady, and I suggest you obey my orders if you ever want to attend Victoria's school again. I want you to be familiar with our customs if you are to assist the temple's priests. Understand?"

Cassandra nodded, and she could feel her face turning red. It was bad enough having lost to Cass in the first place but having priests who understood nothing of true magic order her around only added salt to her wounds.

Maina set the candle on the bedside table and said, "I will be outside the door. Get dressed quickly and bring the candle. We mustn't be late."

Cassandra rose and dressed as quickly as she could. She noticed very little pain in her wounds and was happy to have recovered from the vicious attack. She understood that Greyson's magic had helped her recover quickly. Cassandra tucked her book of the New Order under her pillow and put on her sandals. With a sigh, she joined Maina, and together they made their way down the long hallways of the temple. Small lanterns hanging from various spots on the wall provided additional light as they passed, Cassandra's candle offering little assistance. They passed many decorative doors along the way, and she noticed the countless beautiful tapestries that hung on the walls, depicting various gods and heroes.

"This building is home to more than two dozen gods, all of them of the goodly persuasion," Maina explained as they walked.

"Great," Cassandra said, unimpressed.

"Gella has one of the largest followings here and, therefore, has a grand section of the building dedicated to her. We are going to the temple of Gella now to pray," Maina continued.

"Is that why you are wearing that weird hat?" Cassandra asked, determined to mock her instead of taking an interest in her god.

"This is called a head crown, and high-ranking priests of Gella wear it during our holy days," Maina said, slightly annoyed.

Cassandra hid her smirk, satisfied that she had gotten under the woman's skin. If Victoria forced her to serve in some temple as punishment, she would make the temple priests suffer as much as she. She was not a religious person and didn't belong there.

They reached the temple a short time later, and two guards opened the decorative doors. Inside was a vast chamber containing gold-colored furniture, candelabras, and braziers. Many tapestries and banners bearing the familiar holy symbol of the goddess, similar to the tapestry in Cassandra's room, hung on every wall. Several more high priests walked around the altar at the far end of the giant room, preparing their communion as the golden pews began to fill with the priests and acolytes, who streamed in from several other entrances to the large chamber. The first rays of daylight began to shine through the windows on the eastern side of the room, making the golden furnishings glow with power.

"What do you think of our grand temple?" Maina asked.

Cassandra did not answer, but could only stand there, agape, taking in the most beautiful sight. As sour as her mood was, and as much as she wanted to say something witty, she was at a loss for words. Maina smiled and seemed to be pleased with Cassandra's reaction.

A few hours after Cassandra's first glimpse of the grand temple of Gella, Cass found herself in her father's study. Very rarely had she been allowed in that room, and only occasionally had her father invited her. Today she found herself sitting in an oversized plush chair near a window overlooking the city proper. The harbor was only a rock's throw away, and her father's men loaded the ships there for the day's trading. The sun shone through the window and warmed her, making the visit a little more tolerable. She closed her eyes and soaked in the warmth. She had tuned out the conversation between her father and Lady Victoria. She knew she was in trouble for her actions, so the conversation didn't interest her.

She opened her eyes and trained her gaze past the harbor to the giant structure that housed the priests of Pelesea. With the stained-glass windows and steeples, it was not hard for even a stranger to recognize the building as a place of worship. She did not know how many gods the temple housed, but she knew that Pelesea openly accepted all goodly gods. She also knew that Cassandra was in there somewhere. The one part of the conversation she had paid attention to was when her father asked how the "Rho girl was doing," and Victoria informed him that she was on the mend. Cass smiled at the thought of the embarrassing beating she had given her rival. Then, unable to control her glee, she let out a small giggle. Cass covered her mouth instinctively and looked over at her father and Victoria to see them both staring at her.

"Is there something funny, young lady?" her father asked, absently rubbing his massive mustache as he always did when pondering something of great importance.

His glare immediately changed her mood, and the giggles were no more. "No, father, please forgive me."

She looked over to Victoria, who only smiled at her, but the gesture seemed fake to Cass, and she realized then that perhaps she had better pay more attention to the conversation.

"As you were saying, Lady Victoria?" Franklin Ruben motioned with his hand to their guest.

"I discussed the punishment with my instructors and determined that expulsion for Cass and Cassandra is appropriate for the remainder of the semester," Victoria explained.

"What?" Cass screamed and stood from her chair.

"Sit down, Cass!" her father yelled back.

Ignoring him, she turned her attention to Victoria and pleaded her case. "I was defending myself. I had every right to do what I did."

"That is enough, Cass. Sit down now, or your punishment will be much worse than it already is," her father vowed in no uncertain terms.

Cass knew her father well and played on his emotions to get her way most of the time, but she could tell he was reaching his breaking point, and she was pushing too hard. She wanted to say much more about the situation and explain how she had every right to kill the snotty little Rho girl. She used her better judgment, closed her mouth, nodded, and sat down as her father had instructed.

"You must understand, Cass, you had the right, but you should never strike a fellow student. You would not be in trouble if you had refrained," Victoria explained calmly.

Cass nodded, then looked down at her hands in her lap. She bit her tongue, knowing not to push her father on this.

"You see, Lady Victoria, my daughter seems to forget that attending your school is a privilege and not a right," Franklin continued, giving Cass a stern look. "I will side with whatever punishment you have deemed appropriate and ask forgiveness from you and the instructors for my daughter's act of violence," he continued.

"Thank you, Mr. Ruben. I think highly of Cass and would like to see her again in the spring to start her education anew," Victoria answered.

"Excellent, my lady. I will do my part to support your decision by making my daughter work on the docks for the rest of this semester," Franklin added.

Cass stood again and was ready to unleash a mouthful of curses, but her father cut her short with his stern gaze.

"You will scrub the docks every day until the next semester starts to repay the gold wasted on the tuition for the fall semester. After that, you will think about what you have done and if you want to attend the school in the spring or if you would prefer to stay on as a dockhand permanently," Franklin ordered.

The tears began to well in Cass's eyes as she pondered the idea of working at the stinky docks. "But—" she began but was quickly cut off.

"No buts," Franklin said, then added, "Go straight to your room until dinner and hope that I forgive you enough to allow you to eat."

Cass left quickly, with her head down, while sniffing back the tears the best she could.

"And you are at this moment forbidden to ever associate with that boy, Jabell, again," he demanded, just as she shut the door.

There were a few moments of silence as Franklin watched the door, waiting to ensure his daughter wasn't coming back in. Franklin struggled to remain stern and all in the house, including Victoria, knew his bark was worse than his bite where Cass was concerned.

He finally turned to Victoria and said, "I do not condone her actions, and I will punish her accordingly, I promise."

"Very well, Mr. Ruben. We hope to see Cass again in the spring, then," Victoria said with a smile as she stood to leave.

Franklin escorted her to the door and asked again, "How is the Rho girl?"

"All accounts say she has recovered from her wounds. Her ego may still be a little bruised, but I believe she will be fine after some time passes."

"That is comforting to hear. And what of Jabell?" Franklin prodded a little more.

"We usually don't discuss student punishments with anyone other than close family, but since his fate directly affects Cass, I can assure you that one will never attend the school again."

Franklin nodded and opened the door for her. "Good day, my lady."

"Good day, Mr. Ruben; thank you for understanding," Victoria said and left the study and walked into the hall, where a butler showed her to the door.

Franklin watched her go, and once she was out the front door, he closed the study door and smiled. It was common knowledge that the

Rho girl had started the confrontation and Cass quickly dispatched her. The large man shook his head and chuckled, his anger with Cass melting away.

Greyson held the metal ball in his left hand with his left arm extending parallel to the ground. Just keeping that pose for any amount of time was excruciating, and he had held it there for a long while before Alleah let him put his arm down. Finally, he dropped the ball to the floor and rubbed his recovering shoulder. Once the throbbing subsided, he wiped the beads of sweat from his forehead and looked up at Alleah.

She picked up the five-pound metal ball and held it before him. Then she said, "Again, when you are ready."

He slumped back in his chair and answered immediately, "That will not be any time soon."

With a frustrated look, she lowered the ball and fetched him some water from a nearby pitcher. He drank it greedily, watching her over the edge of the glass as he did so. Her beauty exceeded anyone he had ever met, even Binta, with whom he was very obsessed. He had learned his lesson the hard way that the worshippers of Sinnis were chaste and were not easy to seduce. Still, he could not help but have wicked thoughts about Alleah whenever he was around her.

She pulled up a chair, sat beside him, examined his arm, and took it through several range-of-motion exercises. Greyson winced and pulled his arm from her, tucking it back in the sling.

"Greyson, you must do these exercises, or your arm will never heal properly," she scolded him.

"I am in no hurry, my dear Alleah. I have my church to establish before I am ready for the road. It will not be until spring, and I am sure to be better by then," he answered with a genuine smile.

"A temple to Plath?" she asked inquisitively.

"Yes, Eldrick and the other high priests have granted Plath a temple in your grand building," he exclaimed, standing and holding out his good arm.

"Greyson, that is great, and I wish you the best of luck with the temple. I am certain that your story will draw many new worshippers for you."

"Yes, and so will Plath, once word spreads as to his magnificence and prowess," he exclaimed. "Now, if we have finished here, I must be going; I have much work to do," he answered excitedly, gathering his gown and holy symbol.

He smiled and bowed to the beautiful woman, and she returned the smile yet seemed distant, as if lost in thought. The smile melted from his face, and he lay his belongings back on the bed. Something was troubling her, and he couldn't leave without asking her what it was. After all, they had grown close in the short time they had known each other, and he considered her a friend. If something was wrong, he needed to ensure he hadn't caused it.

"What is it, Alleah? I know something troubles you," he asked.

She didn't answer at first, only looked him in the eyes and held her gaze until the silence became uncomfortable. Then, finally, she said, "Please sit down, Greyson; there is something I must discuss with you."

Greyson did as she asked, now concerned about what was on her mind.

"Tell me, Alleah."

"I need you healed sooner than the spring if you are to journey with us to Tara," she said bluntly.

Greyson sat back in his seat, dumbfounded. The mention of his home had his thoughts reeling back to the day he lost everything he had ever known. The image of the burning buildings and the bodies swinging from the trees filled his thoughts. He saw Darian, his good friend, again at that moment, and Berro, the only father he had ever known. He recalled the destruction of his home and all of his loved ones. He must have daydreamed about it for some time because he heard Alleah calling him, and it sounded like it was not the first time she had done so.

"Greyson, are you all right?" she asked.

"What?" he answered, snapping out of his trance.

"Are you all right? You seemed lost in thought. Were you thinking of Tara?" she asked.

He looked her in the eyes and nodded. "Yes, Tara, and the awful memories of my final moments there."

"I understand. If you do not wish to go, we will not hold that against you, but I was hoping you would join us."

"Join who?" he asked curiously.

"There is a small troop consisting of sisters of Sinnis only, including myself, who the queen has granted permission to go to Tara on a reconnaissance trip."

"The queen has granted this?" he asked.

"Yes, and she said you should go if you feel up to it."

He thought again about that day he left there and how he had narrowly escaped death and was lucky to live. He knew that to be the will of Plath, and he would do his part, even if that meant showing Alleah and her friends the graveyard he formerly called home. He would see it through.

"Greyson, do you want to think about it and let me know later?" Alleah prodded, interrupting his thoughts again.

"No, I do not need to think about it," he answered with a shake of his head. "If you and the queen need me, I am there for you. I owe you that much after your hospitality. The two of you saved my life, and I am forever in your debt."

Alleah smiled and grabbed his hand. The strength in that grasp made Greyson aware of two things: she was indeed very grateful to him, and the young woman was strong, much stronger than her slight frame made her look.

"So, when do we leave?" he asked.

"When the king returns. Perhaps within a week or two."

He nodded and looked at the sling on his arm, then back at Alleah, who seemed content now, having delivered the big news. He sighed and shook his head and slid the sling off. He extended his hand, and Alleah smiled, took the lead ball, and handed it to him to perform his exercises. He vowed to be ready for her and the queen; he would not let them down. But, more importantly, if he had a chance to help avenge the death of his family and friends, he would gladly die doing it.

That night, Greyson shared with Binta the plans to travel back home with the priestesses of Sinnis. They were alone in the partially constructed temple of Plath. A giant star of the god hung above the altar, and Greyson had hung several tapestries he had found in storage that depicted worldly things attributable to Plath. One showed an older man walking down a dirt path toward the rising sun, while another displayed a man painting. The temple was well on its way but needed a lot more work.

"In just a few weeks, I will travel back home to the other side of the world. I will have to leave the temple unfinished until I return," Greyson explained to her.

"Why such short notice? You have so much to do here with the temple, and you and I are at the beginning of whatever wonderful thing this is between us. So, I feel it is bad for you to go," Binta argued.

"No, my dear," Greyson began, reaching for her hand and looking her in the eyes. "This is my destiny, and I will gladly go and even sacrifice my life if that is what it takes to avenge my family and friends."

"What of us? I mean, what will happen to us?" she asked, and he knew she was trying to remain calm.

"We will see what Plath decides. If he deems we should be together, then we will meet again. After all, our objective is not to fight these murderers, but to find more information about them. I shall return within the year, and in the meantime, you will be busy with your studies. You will hardly know I am gone," he reassured her and kissed her gently on the forehead.

"No, I will think about you all the time and long to be by your side once more," she disagreed.

"Yes, and that will make it all the more satisfying when I return," he answered.

He stroked her face with the back of his hand and gave her a reassuring smile. She tried to smile back, but he could tell she was worried.

"I am falling in love with you, Greyson Kavince," she said softly.

"And I am falling just as much for you, my love. However, we must put those feelings aside for the greater good. I must travel with Alleah."

"Yes, I understand that. I hope that—" Binta began, but looked down at her hands, losing the energy to finish the sentence.

Greyson had learned from their long nights staying awake and telling their life stories that Binta had always been a loner until she met Cassandra. The two quickly became friends, and they seemed to have a special bond that stretched beyond that. Even though Binta would not fully admit it, he knew they had shared some sexual experiences. Greyson meant to exploit that, especially after witnessing Cassandra's near-naked and perfect body. But he also knew that Binta had fallen hard for him and enjoyed their sexual affairs as much as he did. He had stoked the fires in her loins and would take advantage of that to lure Cassandra to their bed.

Greyson gently pushed her to the floor next to the altar.

"What are you doing?" she whispered.

"I will make love to you here, in the holiest of places. And after that, we will discuss how we can expedite our seduction of Cassandra. Time is now of the essence, and I want us to have at least one encounter with her before I leave."

"I care for her, Greyson. I do not want to hurt her."

"Neither do I, my love. We will not make her do anything she doesn't want to. I feel the three of us will have a nice future together, don't you think?"

Binta seemed to tremble at the thought of being with Cassandra, and Greyson knew it could soon become a reality. He knew she felt guilty about trying to seduce Cassandra, but she would quickly see its advantages. She had hinted to him several times that she had genuine feelings for her friend, and Greyson had come up with the plan to seduce Cassandra shortly after. The possibility of the three of them involved in some strange sexual relationship enticed him. Binta finally nodded to Greyson and closed her eyes, fully aroused and open to his advances. He fell over her, and they made love for many hours that night in the temple of Plath.

The following day, Greyson found himself near the docks, watching the sun come up as light engulfed the forest beyond the city's eastern gate. Rays of sunlight began to filter through the trees and fall on the hard snow that had frozen during the night. It was beautiful, and he felt closer to Plath at the dawn of each day than at any other time. It was similar to how he had felt in the holy cave. He had sensed Plath with him during the trials, just as he did now. He remembered the otherworldly being that he only assumed was an angel in the cave with him. He could almost sense her with him during the first moments of each dawn, when he was deep in prayer.

He recalled at that moment the wonderful sanctuary the elders had constructed back in Tara. The eastern side of the room was made of glass and was filled with the sun's warmth each morning. The thought made him smile, recalling many wonderful mornings in worship of Plath. However, his smile quickly melted into a frown as he remembered the slaughter of his people. He was the only survivor of that community. Why had Plath spared him? What was his purpose now? Those questions were the center of his prayers that morning.

The temple stood directly in front of him, and the angle from standing on the docks let him watch the sun rays bathe the incredible building. He felt Plath's presence, closed his eyes, and reached out to his god. He removed the sling and stretched out both arms, feeling no pain in the wounded shoulder. And even though the wind was blowing hard that morning, he felt no cold as he had enacted a simple spell of weather resistance before heading to the docks. He felt perfectly comfortable in his thin gown.

He prayed, "Dear Plath, I need your guidance. I feel tasked with avenging your people of Tara, which I gladly embrace. I will use your strength to help battle the evil that has taken our family away. I will die carrying out this goal if I must, but I ask that you give me the strength to see it through. I also feel torn between that objective and a beautiful woman for whom I am falling. It is not a good idea for your priests to take brides, but this one is different. She is not jealous and openly accepts the possibility of me enlightening other women. She is one of a kind. My heart tells me to leave her behind, though I may risk losing her if I do. Please guide me on this decision. Also, there is the matter of Cassandra, who I desire greatly. Please provide insight into the best way to carry out her seduction."

He felt Plath's presence grow even more as the heat from the rising sun warmed his face. A thought came to him then, and one that he gave Plath full credit for: he would introduce Binta to the order! She would become an acolyte of Plath and would carry on with establishing the temple in his absence. It was a fantastic idea and one that he was sure came from the will of Plath. He raised his arms to the sky with a smile, thanking his god for such a revelation.

His thoughts were interrupted by a woman's voice. "What are you doing?"

He slowly opened his eyes to find that he was no longer alone. Several dock hands were tossing salt on the docks to melt the snow and ice, and an olive-skinned woman stood in front of him with a sack of salt lying at her feet. She was young, perhaps not yet twenty years old, and very exotic-looking. Her dark eyes matched her dark complexion, and she had a natural beauty.

He slowly put his hands down and responded, "Pardon me, dear lady. I was deep in prayer."

"The temple is that way," she said, poking her thumb over her shoulder.

She then pulled her hood tight and picked up the bag of salt while Greyson eased his arm back into his sling. She gave him a weak smile, then moved around him. He stepped out of the way to give her room and took in her most intoxicating perfume as she passed.

"I can help you with that," he said as she made her way to the end of the dock.

"No thanks. I have to do it, or I don't get credit for the day's work," she said, dropping the heavy bag and turning toward him again.

He approached her, drinking in her beauty. "What do you mean?"

She looked over his shoulder and nodded. He turned to see a large, portly man in a small building at the edge of the docks, which Greyson assumed must be the dock boss. He stood with a book, scribing notes as he observed the various dockhands.

"Besides, you are injured and would probably not be much help. Now, if you'll excuse me," the beautiful girl said, blowing air into her hands to warm them.

Before she could turn, he grabbed her hand and held it tight in his, which was nice and warm, despite the bitter cold. Her eyes widened with surprise at his warm touch. Her reaction only made her seem more beautiful.

"You are a priest, then?" she asked.

"Yes, I am Greyson Kavince, priest of Plath," he acknowledged.

"Greyson?" she repeated.

He could see a hint of recognition at the mention of his name. Perhaps stories of his escapades had made their way through the kingdom, after all. If a beautiful girl like this knew of him, could others know his tale?

"I can help you with the cold if you wish," he offered.

"With a protection spell?"

"Yes, you know of priestly spells?" he asked curiously.

"No, but I know some lore on magic, both arcane and priestly," she answered.

He took out a small vial of holy water and put a drop on the palm of her hand; he closed it tight, said a few words of praise to Plath, and waved his hand over hers. Soon she became warm and comfortable.

"That is amazing!" she said with a laugh.

The dock boss cleared his throat, and the two looked over at him. He was standing with his hands on his hips, looking her way, and did not seem pleased.

"I have to go," she said, quickly picking up her bag.

"Your name?" he asked of her as she walked away.

She turned with a smile and said, "Cashmere Ruben."

He nodded and waved. "Perhaps I will see you down here again, Cashmere."

She smiled but did not answer. Greyson turned and left the docks, nodding to the dock boss, who looked none too happy about him being there, but did not say anything as he passed. As he returned to the temple, he decided that Cashmere had also been a sign from Plath. What it meant was beyond him, but he was determined to find out quickly.

After his encounter with Cashmere that morning, Greyson spent the rest of the day in his temple, praying to Plath, searching for his answers. Eventually, he felt a peace come over him, similar to the one he felt in the caves back in Tara during his test, a calm that allowed him to open his mind and receive the clues from Plath that he desired. A vision of Binta filled his thoughts, one with her dressed in the priestly robes of Plath, the star-shaped holy symbol hanging from her neck. She looked as lovely as ever in that vision, and he knew then that she would stay and maintain the temple as he went on his journey. She would fulfill his duties in his absence, and the word of Plath would grow strong in Pelesea.

Late that night, after continuous prayer and an entire day of meditation, he had his answer concerning Cassandra. He opened his eyes and found himself in his temple, the candles long since burned out, and the room filled in total darkness. Although he had no window in this part of the massive holy building, he knew it was late at night. He had not eaten the entire day, and his stomach growled in protest. But he had his answers. Binta would become an acolyte of Plath without question because of her submissive nature. She might be a little disappointed to quit the school of magic, but she would see it his way in the end, he knew. Plath would be with him on his journey to Tara so that he could avenge his family for the evil that had befallen his home. He also had the perfect answer from his god on how to seduce Cassandra Rho. A smile crept across his face. Life was good for Greyson, and it was about to get better!

With a heavy heart, Kringus and his men left their injured friends behind with the good people of Farmer's Stop. It was especially hard for the king, who felt the loss of his men, especially his good friend, Arrin, who wasn't guaranteed to survive his wounds. Leaving him there only compounded Kringus's guilt. However, after saying their goodbyes and being reassured by Quentin and Ella that their friends were in good hands, the troupe rode hard for Mecca-Loraine. They stopped only twice and made the gates of the small town in less than three days.

They were permitted entrance quickly enough when the guards recognized Boz, a known member of the legendary monastery. Once inside, Boz led them to the stables, where their exhausted steeds could find shelter and much-needed rest. He left them there to settle in while he took the six bodies to the temple for safekeeping, after convincing Kringus he would handle that task responsibly. Afterward, he took them to a famous inn named The Friendly Genie, which offered the best accommodations in the town. Once they unpacked and washed away the filth of travel with much-needed baths, Kringus looked out the window, surveying the town proper. The elven brothers were with him, which reminded them of the not-so-distant past in Oldorburg, where they had shared the same view and felt the same pending dread.

The view was more splendid than the one in Oldorburg, with winding cobblestone roads wrapping around the many stone buildings of the town. They had entered the northern gate, the only gate available to access the small port community. The gate gave way to the heart of the various government and proprietary buildings. Snow blanketed the roads, and the wind was deadly cold, but the beauty of the architecture was still breathtaking.

A large bay extended into the heart of the town, cutting it into two sections. On the north side of it rested the city proper, including The Friendly Genie Inn, where they now stood, and on the south side, the residential buildings. The bay separated the two sections, except for a small strip of land between the docks and the wall. The bay was void of activity due to the cold front that had settled over the land. However, a dozen ships lined the harbor, with a few more anchored where the bay spilled into the ocean.

"There are plenty of ships here for us to gain transportation home," Kringus said, turning to Von and Lenore.

"Yes, we shall find passage easily enough," Von agreed.

"What of the bodies?" Lenore asked.

"We will preserve well your fallen comrades for the trip home," came a voice behind the three.

All turned to see Boz at the doorway, his hood again covering most of his face, adding that all-too-familiar aura of mystery to their new ally.

"The priests here have ways to preserve the body after death. They will make the trip home with little decay," he continued.

The bluntness of his statement made all three of them cringe, and although no one said it, the fact that the carofex could approach them unnoticed made them more than a little uneasy.

"Boz, we again are indebted to you. Do you think you or your brotherhood can find quick transportation for us?" Kringus asked hopefully. "We can pay any price," he added.

"I will do what I can. However, sailors may not be too eager to leave port with this early snow."

"I understand, but please emphasize that we are desperate to travel and will pay well for passage," Kringus reminded him.

Boz nodded slowly, then, without a word, quickly shut the door and was gone once again. Kringus turned to regard the elves, who shared a concerned look with him.

"That one is a mystery to me," Kringus said with a frown.

"Yes, but he has only shown loyalty since joining us," Lenore pointed out.

"True enough, and he has given me no reason to doubt him. However, he has been overly helpful, and the reason he gave us sounds—"

"Made up," Von finished for him.

Kringus nodded and said, "Yes, and we should be vigilant and, more importantly, find out more about this monastery from which he hails when time permits."

The three shared another look of concern. Again, none of them spoke, but Kringus knew what his elven friends were thinking and thought the same thing. Boz seemed a perfect ally, helpful, and with all the answers at all the correct times. Unfortunately, he seemed too good to be true, which bothered the king more than he was willing to admit.

Cassandra stood in the temple of Gella, an empty bowl in her hand that usually held holy water for the priests. She had just cleaned it as Maina had instructed her, one of many menial chores she had performed over the last few days. Cassandra focused on the tapestry depicting Gella and not the bowl. The symbol had always been comforting since she first saw it in her room. Standing there and looking at it made her forget her problems with the school of magic and, more importantly, the pain of not having her family with her. She had lost track of time and became mesmerized by the image of Gella. When a hand landed gently on her shoulder, she was so surprised that she dropped the bowl and let out a small gasp. She turned to find Maina standing behind her with a smile on her face.

"Sorry, I was just—" she stammered to the priestess.

"Don't apologize, Cassandra; she is calling to you, is all," Maina answered with a smile, bending and picking up the dropped bowl.

"Who is calling to me?"

"Gella, of course."

Cassandra took the bowl back and was at a loss for words. Eventually, she found her gaze entirely on the tapestry again. The beautiful wand had her under a spell once more. There was something comforting about it, and she didn't resist it. The young woman felt Maina take the bowl from her hands, but Cassandra did not divert her gaze from the holiest tapestry. She also felt Maina move behind her at some point and felt her breath on her ear. She tried to turn around, but Maina held her by the shoulders to face the holy symbol.

"Do not turn around. Keep your eyes on the symbol, Cassandra," Maina whispered in her ear.

Cassandra felt she could not turn away and felt Maina's words very comforting. She focused on the tapestry and felt a warmth wash over her.

"Do not deny her call, Cassandra; you are one of the lucky ones. I've seen you become entranced by her symbol since you first arrived. You are her chosen."

"I am not a priest," Cassandra answered, her eyes filling with tears but still locked on the tapestry.

"Oh, but you are, deep down. Can you not feel it?" Maina reasoned.

"I feel—"

"You feel your calling is at the school of magic, correct?" Maina interrupted.

Cassandra nodded slowly and whispered, "Yes."

"We all were wizards at one time, Cassandra, all of the priests of Gella. Some of us are even graduates from Victoria's school."

Maina's hand then reached in front of Cassandra, a small flame upon her open palm. Cassandra once saw Baxter perform the same cantrip back at Oldorburg. She watched the flame dance across her palm, and tears streamed down her face. She slowly held out her palm beside Maina's and called to the flame, quickly seeing the simple magic for what it was. The flame eventually jumped to her palm, where it began to dance. Maina moved to stand in front of her, and Cassandra's eyes slowly moved from the flame to the priestess, more tears joining the fresh tracks of the first ones.

"Pray with me, Cassandra," she said, slowly closing Cassandra's palm and dissipating the cantrip.

Cassandra wiped her face as Maina led her to the altar at the base of the tapestry. There they knelt and prayed. The pent-up emotions Cassandra had held in for so long came out as Maina began her prayer. Soon she was sobbing, letting go of her pain, and Maina draped an arm around her, holding her tight as they prayed together. Cassandra let her guard down, letting in the warmth and the good feelings that seemed to be seeping into her soul. Little did she know, some of those good feelings were from a source other than Gella.

Greyson watched the spectacle unfold as he hid in the shadows at the back of the temple. He felt a little guilty about witnessing Cassandra's tender moment, for he understood the feeling one experienced when becoming dedicated to a deity. However, Plath had granted him a great gift, and he intended to use it. At that moment, Cassandra was vulnerable, participating in her first prayer to Gella. Greyson took the opportunity to cast the powerful charm spell Plath had granted him. He concealed himself from sight so he could flee if Cassandra felt the intrusion. The magic was powerful; the young priest could feel it as it left him, as if Plath magnified its effect. When Cassandra started sobbing, he knew she had not detected or resisted his magic. Her mind and heart were open to receiving her deity and absorbing the spell Greyson had sent her way. If it worked, she would trust his judgment, and he would have her in his bed soon after that.

He waited a few moments to see if she would react negatively to the charm spell, and when she did not, he slowly slid out of the sanctuary, convinced the magic had taken effect. He could not wait until he and Binta visited Cassandra the next day. If the gift from Plath was successful, he would have his answer then.

CHAPTER 3

ACOLYTE

The small caravan had traveled nearly a day out of Port Racip and now had Nesin in its sights. Matilda and her escort would reach the cave fortress within the hour, and she was anxious to get Cassandra deep within the caves where she would be safe until the great sacrifice. Cerus, on the other hand, was looking forward to the subsequent invasion. They had discussed at great length the events that had occurred in Racip. Cerus was none too happy about appeasing his wife to protect the newly acquired sacrifice. He wanted war, and none of the details involving Cassandra Rho interested him. As if reading his thoughts, Matilda turned to him and gently touched his injured nose. He pulled away from her touch, which only made her smile.

"Don't be like that; your nose is healing nicely. Soon, there will be no trace of the injury that has caused you so much humiliation, my love."

"There is no humiliation; I have killed the lesser man who caused this minor injury," he snapped back. "Go to Tara and dig up his ashes and ask him yourself," he added with a growl.

Matilda maintained her smile but looked through the carriage window and saw their home fast approaching. "That may be the case, but I know he wounded your pride, my love."

He turned to her, his face red with anger. "You cuckolded me, and I will not tolerate it again."

"Dear Cerus, you shouldn't become so defensive; you know we have an open relationship," she said, tracing a finger over his chest.

"I will not tolerate your unfaithfulness in front of my men," he said sternly.

"Agreed. And in return, you agree not to touch my most precious sacrifice," she said, motioning with her chin to Cassandra's still form as she slept on the seat.

"Is she that precious?" he asked.

The smile melted from Matilda's face, and she leaned back. "What do you mean by that?"

"Perhaps the vampire lord was not as ignorant as you assume."

"He is dead, is he not?" she retorted.

"Perhaps, but you betrayed him. Do you think he did not expect that?"

"Even if he did, that information did not help him defeat the betrayal," she said, a smile creeping back upon her pretty face.

"True enough. But perhaps you have not given the vampire credit for deceiving you similarly."

"What do you know?"

"Nothing; it only stands to reason that he gave you a decoy because he knew you would not hand over his bride."

Her smile quickly vanished and was replaced by a look of panic, which made Cerus smile. But, of course, she had not thought of that possibility, and he had taken her completely off guard with the reasonably obvious comment.

"You do not think we have the offspring of Kane?" she asked meekly.

"Perhaps, perhaps not," he said with a shrug.

Matilda stared out the carriage window, then looked at her hulking husband and said, "I have a way to find out for sure."

"How?" he asked curiously.

"Vasheba, the demon lord," she answered grimly.

Neither said another word until they reached home; the thought of contacting the powerful demon did not sit well with either of them. Matilda, especially, with the near-death experience she encountered at the gates of the underworld still very fresh in her mind.

The caravan arrived home soon after and without incident. Matilda had Cerus and his men escort Cassandra to her quarters, and there, she had several female servants bathe her and clean her up. Matilda watched as they dressed her in a silky gown, showing the girl's fantastic figure. She noticed her husband watching with a vulgar expression, and Matilda elbowed him and shook her head, indicating that he was not allowed to touch her prize under any circumstances. He frowned at her, then continued to watch. She knew he would not deflower the girl, no matter how attractive he found her. Too much was on the line for them both.

Their new prisoner was frightened, and she fidgeted, her eyes darting around the room as if she expected her execution. Matilda was impressed with the young girl's deductive skills, but now she had doubts that this was even the prized sacrifice. If she weren't, Matilda would need to know immediately so the search for the real Cassandra Rho could continue. Time was of the essence, and Cerus's words echoed in her head. The more she thought about it, the more confident she was that the nasty vampire lord might have betrayed her.

A bed had been set up next to theirs for their prize captive to sleep. Matilda had the servants walk the girl over to the bed and sit her down. Matilda came and sat down next to her. She had installed a chain in the wall about six feet long, with a collar attached to one end. The collar lay on one of the cushiony pillows, and Matilda picked it up.

"What is that for?" the frightened girl asked.

"It is for you to wear, Cassandra."

"Why?"

"So you will not have silly thoughts about leaving us."

"I thought you said you would treat me like a queen here."

The girl's cheek had swollen slightly from the hit she had taken from Cerus the night before, but it did not detract from her beauty, Matilda could not deny. She was so young, perhaps only seventeen or eighteen, but carried herself well above that. Matilda could only smile as she put the collar on the girl. To the girl's credit, she did not struggle and probably knew that to do so was futile. Matilda locked the metal collar with a key and gave it to Cerus.

"I've never seen a queen wear a collar before," she persisted.

"You'll get used to it, for it is only a minor inconvenience compared to the luxurious life you will lead here."

"In a stupid cave?"

Matilda had to refrain from smacking the girl for her arrogant and unappreciative tone, but she smiled and stood. Then she grabbed her roughly by the chin and bent so they were eye to eye. "Sleep; you will need your energy for tomorrow."

"Tomorrow? What happens then?"

Matilda only smiled, electing not to give her an answer. Whether she was indeed Cassandra Rho or not, she was brilliant, and Matilda surmised that their captive had already figured out she would never see the light of day again. Matilda joined Cerus and watched from the other side of the large room as the girl's eyes darted about, coming to terms with her new home. She hoped this was indeed Cassandra, but there would only be one proper way to verify that; a way that would include summoning a demon more powerful than Matilda could control alone.

When Kessi awoke the next day, Matilda was gone, and the nasty creature, Cerus, was her only company. He only stared hatefully at her as she ate her breakfast. Neither spoke, and being in the room alone with him made her uncomfortable. When she finished her food, which was surprisingly good, Cerus unlocked her leash from the wall and led her deeper into the caves.

"Where are you taking me?" she asked, but the large man only pulled harder on her leash each time she spoke.

Finally, they reached a large room, which appeared to be some strange sanctuary, with the walls decorated with pentagrams and skulls. Worshippers of Marnelphion, dressed in their black priestly robes, sat in stone chairs carved from stalagmites and other rock formations near a large pentagram drawn on the floor in the center of the room. The place reeked of evil, and Kessi's nervousness grew as Cerus led her by her leash to a large, circular steel contraption in the center of the large pentagram. It was about ten feet in diameter, with two chains hanging from the top, ending in shackles. There were also more chains with bonds lying on the ground. Both chains ran through the giant circular construction center and were attached to four cranks. She could only imagine what kind of tortures the enormous machine could exact.

Spectators filled the room, standing behind the seated priests, seemingly eager to witness what show Matilda had planned for them. Kessi knew that whatever it was, she was the main attraction. The men looked purely evil and flashed her wicked smiles as she passed them.

Matilda stood next to the contraption, waiting for her with a determined expression. Once they reached Matilda, Cerus handed the leash off and then made his way to the back of the room, where his men eagerly awaited the show.

Matilda removed the leash and then signaled for two of her fellow priests to come up and strip her captive of her silky, transparent gown. Kessi struggled but realized she had no choice but to let them and eventually gave no resistance. The priests had her naked quickly, and each took a firm grip on her arms, presenting her to Matilda. Kessi kept a hateful look focused on Matilda as she stood there in her nakedness. Nevertheless, Matilda seemed quite impressed with what she saw, taking in Kessi's form, as did everyone in the large room.

Matilda smiled as Kessi covered her virginal body the best she could, uncomfortable with so many eyes on her. Kessi could tell Matilda approved as if she had passed the first test. Matilda led her to the center of the circular contraption as the two priests attached the shackles to her wrists and ankles, prying her hands away to reveal her nakedness in full. Kessi covered herself again after they secured the chains, the slack allowing her to move freely momentarily. She stood there staring into the crowd of gathered men, who all wore expressions of anticipation. Matilda stood next to her, seeming to enjoy Kessi's struggle to keep herself covered.

"Do not be shy, my dear; show them your beautiful body. I assure you, none of the men will touch you," Matilda said.

Kessi only gave her a dirty look in response, which made Matilda smile all the more. The two priests moved to the cranks to which the chains were attached, and as they turned the handles, the chains tightened. Her arms were slowly forced above her head, exposing her fully to everyone in the room. She kept her stare on Matilda, who only looked her up and down as much as the men did, making Kessi extremely uncomfortable.

A third priest brought a small vial, handed it to Matilda, and took his seat quickly. She unstopped the vial and brought it up to Kessi's lips. "Drink this, Cassandra Rho, child of Kane," Matilda instructed.

"No. I am going to die now, so why would I?"

Matilda smiled and said, "You will not die, my dear. But you will feel great pain if you do not follow my instructions."

"Again, this does not seem to be the way to treat a queen," Kessi said.

"Drink it," Matilda instructed her once more, her smile turning into a frown.

"Never," she answered, closing her lips defiantly.

Matilda motioned for the priests to stop the cranks. The contraption had Kessi's hands stretched far above her head, and she painfully stood on her toes. Matilda held her hand toward one of the priests, who went into the shadows to retrieve something. Kessi tried to maintain her resolve, but she could only wonder what implement of torture the priest was fetching.

"And now, you will be punished for not following my orders. You are our queen, but if you act like a spoiled child, I will treat you as such," Matilda explained as the priest brought her a coiled whip and traded it for the open vial.

Kessi's eyes widened at the sight of the vicious weapon, and her defiant look quickly changed to fear as Matilda uncoiled it. There was a murmuring from the crowd, and Kessi knew the men approved of what they saw so far. But, unfortunately, the stirrings of the group only seemed to fuel Matilda's anger.

"I am ready to drink from the vial," Kessi pleaded desperately.

Matilda walked up to her and said, "Then open that spoiled little mouth of yours."

She did as instructed. Matilda slid the whip up and down her leg, teasing her. Finally, Matilda signaled for the priest to return the vial, and Kessi drank it without a fight.

"Good girl," Matilda whispered.

"What did I just drink?"

"Something that will help you tell the truth when I ask you questions. If we get the correct responses from you, and I am certain you are who you say, then we stop there. On the other hand, if you give me any doubt concerning your identity, you will meet Vasheba face to face, and that is something far worse than this," Matilda said, holding up the uncoiled whip.

Kessi was relieved that the tasteless liquid was not some poison that would lead to a slow and agonizing death.

"And now for your punishment," Matilda said, walking to stand behind her.

"What? I complied!" she pleaded.

"Your delay will cost you, my dear. You are our queen, but I am still in charge. You would do well to remember that."

Matilda delayed the first strike for some time, building up the tension, and Kessi closed her eyes tight, waiting for the strike to fall. She could imagine the wicked men in attendance, leaned in for a better view, and eagerly anticipated her cries of pain. When Matilda finally struck, a perfect red-hot wave of pain creased her back as Kessi felt the weapon tear into her skin. She screamed and stood taller on her toes as the whip cut deeply into her tender back. Then, with a similar effect, Matilda let fly a second strike, which had Kessi weeping.

Matilda walked to stand before her once more and motioned for the priests to continue cranking. Soon, poor Kessi was hanging a foot off the floor, the shackles digging into her wrists. The crank workers then switched to the legs and began tightening those chains. As they did, her legs began to spread. They did not stop until Matilda gave the signal, and by that point, she hung in the air, spread-eagle. She managed to stop crying, but silent tears continued streaming down her face. Likewise, blood ran down her back and legs from the two nasty gashes from the whip.

"Behold, our most sacred prize!" Matilda addressed the gathered men. "We will discover now if she is truly the child of Kane."

There was a cheer from all those gathered as the priests praised their demon god for such a gift. As Matilda spoke, Kessi could tell the truth serum was affecting her, and she shook her head, trying to clear her thoughts. Matilda moved to stand before her once more, her head even with Kessi's breasts. Kessi looked down at her with as much hate as she could muster. The liquid prevented her from resisting, and she was spread for all to see. Kessi was also in more pain than she had ever felt in her young life. After all, she knew what the sting of a whip felt like now, and Matilda's two strikes had been perfectly placed.

Matilda still had the coiled whip in her hand to add motivation, but Kessi's stubbornness faded at that point as the serum did its work. Matilda cast a simple spell then, and Kessi felt it wash over her, digging at memories and opening her mind. Once complete, Matilda began questioning, "What is your true name, child?"

"Cassandra Rho," she answered.

"Are you still a virgin?"

Kessi did not answer, trying to fight the intrusion into her mind, so Matilda uncoiled her whip.

Her eyes widened, and she said, "Yes," and immediately felt her face turn red from announcing such private information.

Matilda focused on Kessi's responses and pried each answer from her as if she were inside her brain, determining which parts were true and which were lies. After a few moments, a wicked smile spread across Matilda's face.

She turned and announced to the gathering, "She is Cassandra Rho and is still a virgin!"

The men cheered again as Matilda closed her eyes and held her arms wide, basking in the possibilities.

"I hate you!" Kessi spat, frustrated and embarrassed.

"Shut up, Cassandra, and only answer the questions I have for you. Do you understand?" Matilda asked, rubbing the whip on her inner thigh once more.

She nodded, not wanting anything else to do with that vicious whip but still keeping a hateful stare on Matilda.

Matilda smiled that evil smile and said, "Good, then tell me, Cassandra Rho, can you summon and control ravens?"

Without hesitation, she quickly answered, "Easily."

"Tell us all, child, who is your father?" Matilda asked, raising her voice for effect.

"I am an orphan," was her simple response.

Matilda studied her, the smile slowly melting from her face. "What did you say?" Matilda asked in disbelief.

"I don't know who my father is," was Kessi's short response.

Matilda brought the whip back to strike, and Kessi tensed her body and closed her eyes tight, preparing for the nasty bite of the whip. The strike never came. Finally, after many moments, she dared to open her eyes and stared anxiously at the uncoiled whip in Matilda's hand.

"Tell me who your father is, child," Matilda asked a third time, her patience growing thin.

"I do not know," Kessi answered truthfully.

Matilda stood there for many moments, just looking her over, her eyes darting back and forth, trying to digest the answer.

Finally, she whispered, "Bring her down," to the priests and handed the whip to them.

She turned to the gathered priests as Kessi was lowered and said, "By all accounts, this is Cassandra Rho, the key to our great summoning. She speaks truthfully about being an orphan, so an element of doubt shrouds our prisoner. Therefore, we will meet tomorrow night as the moon is high to prepare the sanctuary for demonic contact. All of us will need to attend the summoning, for the demon I seek is quite powerful. We will find our answers through her. Until then, we will treat this potential impostor as if she is truly Cassandra. The mighty Vasheba will reveal her identity."

Matilda stepped close to Kessi as the other priests unwound the cranks that pulled the chains taut, giving Kessi's poor limbs a reprieve from the pain. Matilda grabbed her roughly by the chin, then said, "And I hope you are Cassandra Rho because there are worse things than being sacrificed on an altar."

Kessi swallowed hard in response, and Matilda released her firm grip and walked briskly from the room, leaving a murmuring crowd in her wake. After she exited, the chatter grew louder, and Kessi heard the panic in their voices, most of them fearing the summoning. She knew if these evil men who worshipped such creatures of hell were afraid, she should be concerned. Nevertheless, Cerus ignored them and made his way to her. They lowered her to the floor, where she collapsed and curled into a fetal position as the priests undid her chains. She was experiencing so much pain that she couldn't walk, so Cerus picked her up roughly and carried her back to his room, where he again leashed her to the wall. Kessi then crawled onto the bed and lay on her stomach, quickly finding sleep, naked and still bleeding.

Cassandra awakened the day after her spiritual enlightening with a smile, perhaps for the first time in many years. She rose to sunlight spilling into her room and sat up and stretched, noticing immediately that an acolyte's robe lay draped over her chair. She looked back and forth between the robe and the giant tome that Baxter had given her. She placed a hand on the old book, tracing the leather cover with her fingers. Cassandra had perused that massive work many times, trying to find the solution to who she was and from where she came. Perhaps she could discover her answers elsewhere. Instead of reading the tome that morning, she put on her robe and prayed to Gella.

Cassandra made no delusions about her status as an acolyte. She surely wasn't an acolyte and didn't necessarily want to be one. But she could not deny her connection with the goddess Gella. Something about the goddess called to her very being. Maina was right; although Cassandra didn't want to admit it, she could feel the goddess pulling her in. She had never considered religion much other than what Kessi had taught her about Adlesk. And Cassandra had never felt interested or moved by the notion of worshipping an invisible being. She was much more comfortable manipulating the strange symbols that seemed to follow her. That way, she felt more in control of her surroundings and more in touch with her magic. Priestly spells didn't seem logical to her, as they were gifts from deities, not something the worshipper could control. But she could not deny their potency.

The previous night, when she prayed with Maina at the altar, she had felt something more powerful than she could have ever expected. Not only could she detect the presence of the goddess in the temple with her, but she felt a strange sensation, almost pure bliss, which she had never felt before. So perhaps she would give the goddess a chance during her stay. She would keep an open mind and an open heart.

When she entered the temple that morning, the holy symbol above the altar drew her eyes. She smiled and instinctively walked toward it, her heart filling with joy and her thoughts of her troubles at Victoria's school were suddenly not so important. She prayed hard and even wept as she took her next step toward becoming a faithful acolyte of the wonderful goddess.

She spent most of the day there and happily wore the acolyte robe of Gella. The priests and other acolytes there treated her nicely, another characteristic of the temple she found endearing. Never had she ever been so welcomed, and it made her realize just how wrong all the other places had felt to her. By the end of the day, she was tired but satisfied. She had performed some menial chores and attended lectures on the goddess Gella. She made her way to her room that evening, feeling very contented.

Greyson met Cashmere at the docks as the exotic woman completed her evening tasks. Finally, he had all the answers he needed from his prayers the previous day. He knew what Plath had intended for him, and no mysteries remained. The only exception was the appearance of Cashmere. How did she fit into his god's plans? He was anxious to find out. Perhaps if the charm failed with Cassandra, he and Binta could seduce Cashmere instead. All possibilities seemed pleasant to him.

"You again?" she asked as she made her way from the docks and noticed Greyson standing there.

"You sound disappointed," Greyson responded with a smile.

She stopped in front of him, and although her hair was messy and her face dirt-streaked, he still found her beauty overwhelming.

"I am just tired and don't feel like being preached to," she answered and started past him.

"I am not here to preach, just to talk," he said, turning and walking with her.

"I don't feel like talking," she said without even looking at him.

"Dear woman, why are you forsaking me? Have I offended you?"

She stopped and turned toward him, pulling her coat tightly around her as the chill wind bit her. From their meeting the day before, he knew she was aware of his powers to protect himself from the elements. Even so, she did not seem impressed by his comfortable stance and rolled her eyes.

"No, but you can help your chances by protecting me from this cold," she said.

"I am sorry, but my spell powers are exhausted for this day because of the heavy workload of healing I have performed," he lied. "My warmth spell will protect you if only you come closer."

She looked at him skeptically and still did not approach. Then, finally, he let out a small chuckle and approached her. When he did, the temperature around her became very comfortable, and she closed her eyes and sighed.

"Oh, my, that feels good," she said, opening her eyes with renewed vigor.

"You see, I'm not so bad to have around, right?"

"You have your purposes, priest, I have to admit," she said with a slight smile.

"Good. Let me walk you home and keep you warm on your trek," Greyson suggested.

She thought about that for a bit, and he knew she was trying to judge his character. Finally, he spoke up when it looked like she might decline his offer.

"Come on, I am a priest of the order of Plath and am a bit of a celebrity within the temple if I may brag a little," he said, nodding to his left arm that was still in the sling.

"The temple, huh? Well, then, you may walk me home on one condition."

"Very well. What is the condition?"

"I just need a little information from you."

"Well, I guess that all depends on what information you require," he said, suddenly intrigued.

"I need information about a patient staying at the temple," she said bluntly.

"Sorry, I cannot give any information like that. It is against my priestly code."

"Then I guess you will not be walking me home," she said, tightening her coat around her and stepping out of the protective sphere.

She walked several steps without turning around and Greyson almost let her go. But he felt she was an answer to his prayer, and it felt wrong to let the opportunity pass, and so he caved.

"Very well. What information do you require?" he asked, catching up to her and enveloping her in his protective sphere once more.

She looked at him excitedly and said, "I need information concerning Cassandra Rho. Do you know of her?"

That rocked Greyson back on his heels, and he stopped walking. She did not notice at first and continued to walk until she exited the circle of warmth. Then, once the cold breeze bit her, she turned and walked back toward him.

"What is wrong?" she asked.

"You know Cassandra?"

"Yes, and you must, as well!" she answered excitedly.

"Well, I have treated her, yes."

Her eyes widened, and she grabbed him by the arm, pulling him along. "Come with me. You will eat dinner with us tonight," she said, a renewed vigor in her step.

"I cannot; I have to—"

"Don't be silly; we have a lot to discuss, Greyson Kavince," she insisted and pulled him along even faster.

Soon after, he found himself at her home, one of the nicest in the city. He shared a delicious meal with Cashmere and her father and lost track of time, spending most of the night talking. He shared all he knew about Cassandra's status at the temple, except for his plan of seduction.

When Cassandra finally returned to her room from her first day in the service of Gella, she was tired but content. Something in her heart told her that she could indeed one day become an acolyte of the fantastic goddess, that she could live a life dedicated to Gella. She felt fulfilled, working hard at the temple, and keeping her mind off her troubles. And as a gift, which seemed to be straight from the goddess herself, a pleasant surprise awaited her outside her door.

Binta stood there casually, smiling broadly. Cassandra rushed up to her friend and hugged her tight, which Binta returned.

Cassandra pulled away suddenly and said, "Sorry, I am filthy. I have been cleaning the supply room all day and need a bath!"

Binta laughed and replied, "You do not stink, but I am surprised at your choice of clothing."

Cassandra did a half twirl, letting her acolyte robe flow around her. Then, finally, she smiled and asked, "Do you like it?"

"I'm not sure what it is," Binta replied honestly.

"These are acolyte robes, of course."

"But why are you wearing them?" Binta asked, now more intrigued.

"Well, I am working for the followers of Gella, and it is appropriate that I wear the garments that they have issued me."

"Issued you? Cassandra, have you joined the faith?" Binta asked, now concerned.

"Of course not; I am just trying to do my job properly so that Victoria might reinstate me at the school," Cassandra answered, but left out the part where she considered the possibility.

"Good, because I miss you," Binta said, coming close and taking Cassandra's hands.

Cassandra's heart missed a beat, and her knees weakened at Binta's touch. Binta came closer, and Cassandra pulled away.

"Wait, I *must* take a bath. I have much to talk to you about, but I am filthy. Please wait in my room, and I will return shortly," Cassandra offered, unlocking her door and rushing Binta inside. "I will be back soon, I promise."

"I will be here, waiting," Binta said with a flirty smile.

Cassandra shut the door and immediately put her back against it, trying to catch her breath. Her heart pounded in her chest. What was going to happen when she returned? Would Greyson be there? The possibilities made her tingle all over. She quietly thanked Gella without realizing she did it and then quickly went to the bathhouse.

Cassandra took extra care to ensure she was clean and ready for whatever may happen with Binta. She hoped that Greyson would be there and continue what they had started earlier. After her bath, she returned to Binta, chewing her lip in nervous contemplation. With a slightly shaking hand, Cassandra grasped the doorknob and paused just a moment to catch her breath. Her heart raced, and she tried to steady her nerves. Finally, she took a deep breath and opened the door.

"Sorry it took so long—" she began before she realized all was quiet and Binta was asleep in her bed.

Her lamp had been lit and flickered on her nightstand, making shadows dance across Binta's still form. It made Binta look more beautiful than ever. She slowly shut the door and locked it. A feeling of disappointment washed over her briefly as she realized Greyson was not there. It was short-lived, though, as she was overwhelmed by her deep desire for Binta. She crept to the bed, intending to wake her gently. But she stopped when she saw the pile of clothing on the floor, including Binta's underwear. Was Binta naked in her bed? She froze, and her heart somehow beat faster.

Cassandra did not know what to do next; the anxiety was paralyzing her muscles, and her heart was pumping in her ears. She glanced at the clothes pile and summoned the strength to move to it. She bent and picked up Binta's shirt, rolling the soft fabric with her fingers. She could smell her friend's perfume, brought the material to her nose, and breathed in her scent. She took a deep breath, which made her tingle all over again.

"Smell something you like?" Binta asked from behind her, making Cassandra drop the shirt immediately and turn to face her friend, her cheeks flush.

Binta was lying in bed; her hair splayed across Cassandra's pillow. She wore a warm smile on her face, which made her look beautiful to Cassandra.

"I—" Cassandra began.

"You don't have to explain," Binta said, sitting up in the bed while holding the covers to her chest. "Where is Greyson?" she continued with a smile.

"I haven't seen him. I hoped he would be here when I returned from my bath."

"That's strange; he was supposed to meet us here tonight," Binta said, disappointed.

Cassandra sat on the bed, wanting to discuss an important topic while Greyson wasn't there. It took her a few moments to choose her words. After all, she did not want to hurt Binta's feelings, especially if she was as infatuated with the young man as Cassandra suspected. She wanted to get it out in the open before Binta and she did anything else romantic or even sexual.

Finally, she looked into Binta's beautiful brown eyes and said, "You acted so different last night. Why?"

"What do you mean?"

"I mean with Greyson. You were just very submissive to him," Cassandra explained.

"You don't like him, do you?"

Cassandra wanted to tell her that she did not like Greyson and that Binta should not trust him. She wanted alone time with Binta to see what was next for them. Were they good friends who had shared a random kiss, or was there more? Cassandra desperately hoped there was more in store for them. She wanted to tell Binta to avoid the perverted priest. For some reason, though, she could not bring herself to say those words. Instead, something washed over her that made her feel at peace with Binta's choices concerning Greyson. She felt a pang of jealousy, but she barely recognized that strange feeling and dismissed it immediately.

Finally, she smiled and said, "You know what, I do like him. He seems like he is good for you."

"You mean that?" Binta asked.

"Yes, I do," Cassandra answered with a genuine smile.

"I had the feeling you did not... I mean, you seemed a little standoffish toward Greyson last night."

Cassandra thought about it for a moment, then said, "I found him untrustworthy at first and did not like how you were submissive to him. But now, after thinking about it, I understand he could have that power over women. After all, he is good-looking and charming and—"

"You do like him!" Binta interrupted.

Cassandra stopped herself and thought about her words. Why was she building Greyson up. She wanted nothing more than for Binta to leave him. But the promise of the three kisses floated in her head, and something in her loins wanted that little experiment to continue.

Her naughty thoughts were interrupted as Binta continued, "Besides, me being submissive has nothing to do with him, my dear friend," Binta explained. "I am a very sexual person, and I am a submissive. When I first met Greyson, I knew he would fit perfectly with my fetishes, and he quickly embraced the role. I have not changed for his sake; he has changed for mine."

There was a long pause as Cassandra pondered her words. "And what of us?" she dared to ask.

"Well, I have kissed you twice, and it was amazing to me both times. What I feel for you is closer to love than lust. But, with Greyson, it is all about lust. Does that make sense?" Binta asked.

Cassandra swallowed hard and suddenly could not speak. Binta lowered the sheets, exposing her nakedness. She whipped the sheets aside quickly to reveal her entire body. Cassandra caught a strong whiff of her perfume and found it intoxicating. At that moment, Cassandra remembered the night they first kissed, and that feeling of love and togetherness came flooding back. As she took in her friend's naked body, she felt a tingling all over again, but this time, the feeling was even more powerful.

"Come to bed with me," Binta said lustfully, sliding over to make room for her.

Cassandra nodded without realizing she was doing it and began to get into bed, but Binta stopped her. "No, take your clothes off first."

Cassandra flushed and looked at her friend apologetically. "I have never been with a woman before... or a man, for that matter, remember?"

"Yes, I remember. I remember you once told me you are not gay, but does any of that matter right now?"

Cassandra looked at her for a few moments, trying to process what was happening. She had powerful feelings for Binta; there was no doubting it. At that moment, Cassandra knew two things: her virginity would be lost to Greyson, possibly that very night, and she was falling in love with Binta. Cassandra had never been a sexual creature, nor had she ever considered romance until recently. She looked lovingly at Binta and slowly undressed with the sexiest smile she could muster. When finished, Cassandra felt comfortable in her nakedness. Binta admired her body, chewing on her lower lip as she looked her friend up and down.

"You have a beautiful body, Cassandra," she whispered and softly patted the bed.

Cassandra slid in, and they kissed lightly. As Cassandra lay down,

Binta wrapped her in her arms and put her head on her shoulder. Cassandra closed her eyes and breathed in her perfume. She felt more at peace at that moment than she had ever in her life. Binta turned her head and began kissing her neck, which sent shockwaves through her body. At the same time, Binta's hands began to explore, touching places that no one else had ever felt. A flash of memory came to her, just an instant of something she remembered while drugged at the temple in Oldorburg. It was an image of Ronnis undressing her as she was bound to the bed. He touched her in places then as well. She panicked.

"Wait," she pleaded, gently taking Binta's hand, and bringing it back from under the covers, intertwining their fingers.

"What is it?" Binta asked, raising her head from Cassandra's neck.

"I am nervous, that is all."

"I will not do anything you do not desire," Binta reassured her, squeezing her hand tight.

"I know that, and believe me, I want to be with you more than anything. I never expected this when I came to Pelesea. When I started Victoria's school, it was the same as the orphanage; I felt like an outsider. Then I found you and—"

"I know; I feel just as glad to have met you," Binta said, breaking Cassandra's tight grip and gently stroking her hair.

"Then, as I prayed last night in the temple, a feeling of peace came over me, one that I have not had ever in my life. It was like Gella was showing me what I was missing. That moment changed my life and opened my feelings toward you and even Greyson. It felt as if Gella was permitting me to like Greyson, to embrace the idea of our potentially strange relationship with him."

"I am glad, but are you saying you are becoming a follower of Gella?"

"I don't know. All I know is that moment at the temple made me forget my troubles; it made me not dwell on Kessi and Sera. It made me realize that I should put more faith in others, such as Kringus and you."

Binta smiled and kissed her gently on the cheek. "Whatever

happens, whether you come back to the school or become a priestess here at the temple, we must promise each other that we will stay together, if not as lovers, then as best friends."

"Yes, I want nothing more. I also trust your judgment in Greyson and will freely give myself to him if that is what you want."

"I want nothing more than the three of us to be intimate and happy together."

Cassandra smiled, and Binta reached up and kissed her gently; then, she wrapped her arms around her again, and they held each other tight.

"What do you want?" Binta asked, laying her head on her shoulder once more. "Right now, I mean. I can show you pleasures you have yet to experience, or we can wait for Greyson to make your first experience more memorable. Just tell me what you want."

There was a moment of silence before Cassandra finally said, "I just want you to hold me."

Binta squeezed her tight and snuggled her face into her neck. The two friends held that position for a long while, enjoying the moment. Then, finally, they fell asleep while waiting for Greyson.

The following day, they awoke, and although their sleep was peaceful and refreshing, both thought of Greyson immediately.

"What happened to him?" Cassandra asked, sitting up in the bed, covering herself as Binta rose and dressed.

Her friend looked just as distressed at Greyson's absence but had no answers. "I know not where he is, nor why he did not show."

"Do you think he forgot?"

"No," Binta shook her head. "He is probably with another woman."

"What? Why?" Cassandra asked, suddenly alarmed.

"It is his way, and I have given him permission to be with other women, even if we are together."

"So, that is why you are fine in sharing him with me? You know he will be with other women anyway, so it is better if it is with me, right?" Cassandra said, suddenly understanding more about her friend's strange relationship with the young priest.

Binta smiled uneasily and said, "I have class and will be late if I don't go now."

"I have many chores to do anyway," Cassandra replied.

Cassandra watched her dress, admiring her perfect body. "I wish we had more time this morning; I wish we hadn't waited for him last night."

Binta smiled and came over to the bed, only half-dressed, which made her all the more mysterious and desirable to Cassandra. Binta leaned over and kissed her gently.

"Just wait until Greyson joins us," she breathed huskily. "Perhaps this very night. The wait will be worth it, I assure you. He is an amazing and thorough lover."

"I look forward to it," Cassandra answered, suddenly tingling at the thought.

The two then shared a deep kiss before Binta left. Cassandra stayed in her room for a bit longer. She thought of the complexity of Binta's relationship with Greyson and how Cassandra was slowly becoming entwined in that most unusual situation. The thoughts only brought a smile to her as, deep down, Cassandra felt Gella was pushing her to be with Greyson; why else did she so readily accept the man? She could almost sense the goddess's approval the night she took Gella into her heart. Cassandra knew nothing would change that now. She would be with Binta and Greyson, and she desired that as much as they did.

Later that day, Cassandra worked in the sanctuary, polishing candlesticks for the upcoming holy day of Gella, her thoughts entirely focused on Greyson Kavince. She was lost in thought, polishing a particular candlestick for many minutes, staring at the tapestry of Gella, when she was interrupted by one of the other acolytes named Maleiah.

"Maina wants us to go to the cellar and bring up a case of candles for the coming festivities," she said, startling Cassandra and making her nearly drop the candlestick.

Maleiah was a little older than Cassandra, and the rumors suggested that she had dropped out of Victoria's school during her second year there. She was quiet, and Cassandra didn't know her well, so neither said much as they made their way to the temple's lower levels. Soon, the two were standing at the doorway leading to the cellar with stone stairs winding down into the darkness. The two girls looked at each other, a little hesitant to proceed. A lantern hung on the wall, which Maleiah lit, then, with a nod of her head, they started down the steps, side by side.

The lantern cast dancing shadows on the stone wall, and the temperature became much colder and the air mustier as they descended. They walked silently, and the stairs seemed like they would never end. But, finally, they did, spilling into an old, stone hallway that proceeded into the darkness. They found another lantern hanging on the wall that they quickly lit, and Cassandra took, giving them double the light to combat the shadows. They moved down the hall, Cassandra noticing the irregularity of the unpolished floor at that temple level. Both wanted to be done with their business and out of the cellar as quickly as possible. Something felt unnatural down there, and it spooked both girls.

As they walked, they began to pass doors on the left and right at regular intervals, each containing an engraved symbol of the goodly gods that had sanctuaries within the temple. Phena and Sinnis were among the first two doors, those symbols they knew. But they came across many that they did not. Eventually, they did come to a door with the familiar magical wand and stars symbol of Gella, and Maleiah quickly fished out the key and fumbled nervously with the lock. The sudden sound of a door slamming from the depths of the dark elicited a sharp scream from each of them, and Maleiah dropped the key, which clanged loudly on the stone floor.

Both of them froze with fright, and after several moments, Cassandra managed to ask meekly into the darkness, "Hello?"

Her voice echoed through the hallway several times before dissipating, but there was no answer. They stood there as still as statues, listening for another sound, but none came.

"What was that?" Maleiah eventually asked quietly.

"You mean, who?" Cassandra corrected.

The acolyte nodded dumbly in agreement. "Yes, who was that?"

Cassandra shrugged and picked up the key, handing it to Maleiah. "Not sure, maybe another acolyte gathering supplies. Let's get our job done and get out of here; this place gives me the creeps."

Maleiah took the key and nodded her agreement, trying to open the door quickly. Eventually, the tumbler clicked, and the door opened. Both girls entered the storeroom rather swiftly and shut the door behind them. Once inside, they felt a little safer, especially when Cassandra relocked the door. The room was more significant than they expected, with many crates and boxes stacked neatly around it. Also, shelves containing rolls of cloth, acolyte robes, priest vestments, vials of liquid, which Maleiah reasoned were probably holy water or healing potions, scrolls, and various tomes filled the room.

"So, where are the candles?" Cassandra asked.

"Maina said there would be a box of them, and we should bring the whole box," Maleiah said with a shrug.

They started searching the room, reading the inscriptions on the sides of the various boxes, until Cassandra finally found several of them labeled as candles.

"Help me pry this lid off," Cassandra said, pulling one of the boxes out.

"Why?"

"Because if these aren't candles, do you want to return to this place?" Cassandra reasoned.

"Good point," Maleiah agreed and grabbed one edge of the wooden box lid.

After some struggle, they pried off the lid and saw it was full of unused candles. They put the top on the best they could, which wasn't very tight, and headed for the door, each carrying one end of the fifty-pound box, their lanterns now attached to their belts. They sat the crate down, and Cassandra unlocked the door.

Cassandra turned to her companion and asked, "Are you ready?"

Maleiah nodded and swallowed hard. They just wanted to be upstairs again, and neither wanted to spend much time in the hallway.

"When we clear the door, set the box down, lock the door, then pick it up again quickly. Understand?" Cassandra instructed.

Again, the young acolyte nodded and took a moment to compose herself. Then Cassandra opened the door, and they quickly made their way into the hall. Cassandra immediately saw a hunched-over figure within the light of her bouncing lantern. It lifted its arm to cover its eyes and fled into the darkness. Cassandra screamed in surprise and dropped her end of the box. It fell over on its side, and the lid came undone, spilling candles all over the stone floor. Some even rolled into the darkness behind the fleeing creature.

"Are you mad?" screamed Maleiah.

Cassandra pointed to the dark and stammered, "A figure! That way!"

Maleiah looked and saw nothing but did not doubt Cassandra's claim. "Was it human?"

"Not sure," Cassandra answered, her heart pounding in her chest.

"Enough of this!" Maleiah screamed.

The young acolyte grabbed her holy symbol from around her neck and whispered a few words. Then, with a wave of her hand, the entire hallway was bright as the midday sun. But unfortunately, the entirety of the hallway only stretched about fifty feet past the storage room of Gella and ended in a dead end with another door slamming shut when the light spell resolved.

Cassandra turned to the acolyte, eyes wide, and said, "Why did you not do that before?"

Maleiah shrugged and said, "I am not a priestess, just an acolyte. Sometimes my powers fail me."

"But not this time; Gella is with us," Cassandra replied with a smile.

That statement made her stop for a moment. Was she that caught up in the belief in some deity? She had lived at the temple for a week but had grown very close to Gella during her stay. So much so that now, when she needed help, she believed the goddess was with her.

She would have previously resolved the issue by using her skills with arcane magic. Had she changed that much in the short time she had been there? Again, the thoughts of becoming an acolyte of Gella overcame her, and her pondering caused a delay in her actions. Maleiah called her several times before she even responded.

"What?" she asked.

"Let's hurry and pick these up and get out of here!"

Cassandra realized then that the girl was busy picking up the spilled candles and pointed to a few that had rolled down the hall and up against the door that had just slammed shut. She did not move at first and looked at Maleiah doubtfully. The acolyte furrowed her brow and nodded with her head toward the door. Cassandra took a gulp and proceeded down the hallway. She focused on the door in front of her as she walked, fully expecting it to burst open and the hunched-over figure to come running out and attack her.

She finally reached it, and she froze in place. Like all the other doors in this hallway, it had a symbol engraved on it, and to her surprise, the symbol was very familiar to her. She had seen it before in her dreams. It depicted the scepter on the table in her dream, the one with the topaz tip that always vanished when she reached for it. She absently ran her fingers over the engraving.

"Cassandra!" Maleiah whispered forcefully.

Cassandra didn't hear her, but focused on the engraving, her eyes filling with wonder. "What is this place?" she whispered to herself.

Maleiah dropped a handful of candles into the crate and put her hands on her hips in frustration. "I want to leave this place, Cassandra, if you don't mind. Let's pick up—"

She was interrupted by the door quickly opening a few inches. Both girls screamed as a hand shot out from behind the door and grabbed Cassandra by the arm. Maleiah screamed and turned to flee, only to run into the box of candles, tipping it over once more and falling in the process. Cassandra did not see her but focused on the darkness within the door. She tried to pull her arm away, but the grip was tight and forceful. Finally, she realized she was caught and began to panic.

"I'll get help!" Maleiah said, regaining her footing.

"Hurry!" Cassandra responded, finally turning to acknowledge her.

With that, Maleiah grabbed her lantern and ran up the stairs and out of the cellar. Cassandra was breathing hard; fear overtook her as she tried to pry the fingers off her arm with her other hand. She kept glancing at the pale fingers that had her in a death grip. They appeared human, not monster-like, but she tried to stay focused on the darkness beyond the door and catch a glimpse of what had a hold of her. The young woman was afraid of what creature it could be as her mind wandered with possibilities, despite the human hand holding her. Was she going to die down there alone? Thoughts of her family, Binta, and even Greyson filled her head, and she started to panic as the fear of death overcame her. The hand was human, but what kind of creature would haunt the cellar? Did anyone know it was even there? She had to free herself.

Then suddenly, a calming, male voice filled her head, *"Cassandra Rho, do not be afraid. I will not harm you."*

The voice sounded human and quite intelligent. It was a telepathic intrusion, so whatever this creature was, it was clever and maybe more powerful than it first appeared.

She stopped struggling and managed to ask, "Who are you?"

"I am a friend of your father's. I am here to help answer the many questions you have."

She relaxed at that statement, and the hand released her as she did. The door then cracked open a little more, and the light from Maleiah's spell revealed a human face, one of an older man with unkempt hair and a shaggy beard. Though his expression was friendly, he eased her mind even more with a gentle smile.

"You know who my father is?" Cassandra asked, her fear now replaced with curiosity and excitement.

The man spoke out loud this time. "Yes, I know him, and I know all about you. I have waited many years for your arrival."

Cassandra stared at him, unable to move or speak, the shock of his words gripping her tighter than his bony hand had just moments earlier.

"I apologize for scaring you. Unfortunately, it was a necessity to remove your pesky friend. My words are for you only," the man explained.

"What?" Cassandra asked, still in a daze.

"Your friend. She is returning with help in tow, which means our time is ending. Come back tonight as the moon is high in the sky, and I will tell you everything you wish to know."

Cassandra could hear people coming down the steps and Maina's voice yelling from that direction, "Cassandra, are you hurt?"

She glanced that way, but only for a moment, still unable to find her voice. She turned back to the man, who once again was hunched over with a crazed look. He held a candle in one hand, one of the candles of Gella that she had come to retrieve.

His voice was suddenly in her head again. *"Remember, come back this very night. We have much to discuss!"*

Cassandra nodded, still in shock and still not able to say anything. A million thoughts filled her head just then. Was this a gift from Gella? She looked at the candle he was holding and considered that possibility. The older man slowly raised the candle to his lips and took a large bite, pulling the wax from the wick and chewing wildly. He began making weird guttural noises as he chewed, making her step back.

Then he was in her mind once more, *"Act afraid!"*

"Cassandra!" Maina yelled from the bottom of the steps.

Cassandra feigned a frightened look on her face as the eccentric man continued to chew and gave her a quick wink. Then she ran toward Maina, who was taking in the strange scene.

"Are you all right?" Maina asked, grabbing her by the shoulders and looking her over for injuries.

Cassandra nodded, trying to play the part the strange man had instructed. But, in truth, her mind was a jumbled mess, trying to process what had just transpired. All of her life, she had wondered who she was and exactly who her parents were. Could this strange man have all the answers for her? Of course, she would not believe in that theory under normal circumstances, yet the peculiar man knew her name, and his door contained the same symbol as the rod in her dreams. How could that be? Instead of answering Maina's question, she stared blankly at her, nodding slowly.

Confident that Cassandra was not injured, Maina smiled and said, "It is fine, girls; this is Cedric. He is eccentric, but completely harmless. I am sorry he frightened you."

Maina walked down the short hallway and soon stood before Cedric, who greeted her with a big smile, which allowed chewed pieces of the candle to drop to the floor.

"Uh-oh!" he said in a childlike voice, utterly different from the one he had used to communicate with Cassandra.

He then scooped up the dropped wax and stuffed it back into his mouth, chewing it with renewed vigor.

"Cedric!" Maina scolded, her tone showing she was none too pleased with him.

He stopped chewing, and Maina held her hand under his mouth. He slowly spat the gob of wax into it, then looked at her with shame and guilt.

"Not food?" he asked.

"No, Cedric, not food," she answered, quickly disposing of the wax in one of her pockets. "Dinner will be served later. Also, you may not scare the acolytes that come to the stores; you know better."

Cedric looked down at his feet and nodded. Maina turned to the two girls and said, "He is harmless, and I should have told you about him before you came down here."

"Who is he?" Maleiah asked.

"He once was a priest of an old and forgotten god. He has lived down here well before my time in the temple. But, again, he is harmless, so please clean up this mess and take the candles to the temple. I will be there shortly."

With that, she gently took the half-eaten candle from Cedric and stuffed it into another of her pockets. "Come, Cedric, let me get you settled back into your room. I will serve your dinner soon, but you must be patient."

She took the older man by the hand and led him back into his room, gently shutting the door behind her. But, before it closed all the way, Cedric made eye contact with Cassandra, and the childish look he wore in front of Maina disappeared for just a brief moment, replaced with a look that told Cassandra that he did indeed know something about her.

The young acolytes quickly picked up the spilled candles and left the cellar without speaking another word. Cassandra was deep in thought and didn't even remember picking them up. The rest of the day was a blur as life bombarded her with tidal waves of emotions.

Binta was going through her own turmoil as she attended her classes that day. Greyson had not shown up at Cassandra's room as he had agreed. She wondered what had happened and hoped that he was all right. Deep down, she felt that he was probably with another woman. He had warned her that the demands of his god called for him to be with many women. She could live with that because she was falling in love with him. She was also falling for Cassandra just as much. Her perfect world would be the three of them involved in a romantic fling. She didn't mind sharing Greyson, but it made her feel uneasy when he disappeared like he had the night before. So it was with great relief that she found Greyson waiting for her outside her dorm room after classes.

She ran to him, wrapped her arms around his neck, and kissed him deeply. She did not care about the other students in the hallway who watched the spectacle. Let them look; she was in love and did not care what they thought.

She finally broke the kiss and asked, "So, where were you last night?"

Greyson only smiled, and she could tell by the smug look on his face that her feelings had betrayed her. She was falling for him, and now he knew it would give him more control in their strange relationship. But she didn't care; she needed him and would do whatever it took to formulate a romantic relationship that included

Greyson and Cassandra. He would allow that and desired it, so she needed him.

"It was another woman, wasn't it?" she asked.

"Yes, and no," he answered cryptically.

She gave him a puzzled expression and pleaded, "Tell me what is going on."

"Of course, my love. First, you must tell me how things went with Cassandra last night," he answered, motioning to her door.

She quickly found her key, and they entered her room. Once there, Greyson fell over her, embracing her passionately. Then, he removed her clothing and said, "On second thought, I must have you now."

Greyson listened to Binta as she told him about her night with Cassandra as he made love to her. She told him how they had waited for him yet slept together in the nude, and the words seemed to energize his lovemaking, sending her to orgasm quickly. Also, she mentioned how Cassandra had positively referred to Greyson during their time together, which piqued his interest. So much so that he had her repeat the information, especially about how Cassandra reacted to his mention. Afterward, Greyson offered a wry smile. He would not elaborate, but she knew he was pleased with Cassandra's behavior.

Later, as the couple lay in bed, embraced in each other's arms, basking in their lovemaking, Binta finally asked him again, "So tell me of this other woman."

Greyson smiled and kissed her forehead, stroking her hair with his wounded arm. She noticed how the movement still caused him discomfort, but the arm seemed to be healing. His range of motion also increased, so Alleah's exercises had indeed helped.

"Well, there is not much to tell," he lied.

During their time together, Cashmere had told him why she was so interested in Cassandra. He eventually discovered that Cashmere was Cass, who had beaten Cassandra at her challenge.

"Tell me," Binta prodded softly.

"You are not going to like it, my love. I will tell you, but you must know upfront that I did not sleep with her yet. That may come in time, and you must be tolerant of that."

Binta sat up on one elbow and looked at him curiously. "Go on, tell me," she pressed, anxious to find out the meaning behind his cryptic words.

"Very well. Last evening and through most of the night, I found myself at the residence of Cass Ruben."

She sat up straight in the bed at that point and yelled out, "What?"

"It is true; I was visiting Cass because she came to me as a sign from Plath, an answer to a prayer."

"You know who she is. She nearly killed Cassandra, and her creepy friend kicked me hard enough to break my ribs, remember? How could you spend time with her?"

Greyson raised a hand, indicating she should stop, and she obediently ceased talking. She sat against the headboard and pulled the sheets tightly around her. Greyson sat up next to her and turned her face toward him.

"To be honest, I did not know she was Cassandra's nemesis until I was already eating a meal with her and her father. I know this is hard for you to accept, but I feel she has changed. She asked how Cassandra was doing, not out of hate but concern. I feel she regrets what happened, even though she did not start the conflict," he explained.

"But she did, Greyson. Can't you see?"

"Was she not the one attacked?"

"Yes, but she provoked the attack. Cass set Cassandra up to do just that. And Jabell is—"

"No longer in the picture," Greyson interrupted. "She no longer associates with that fool."

Binta bit her lip for a few moments, struggling with this new information. "Do you believe her?" she finally asked him.

"Yes, I believe her because she is a sign from Plath."

"In what way could she possibly be a sign from your god?"

"I don't know yet, but I intend to find out. I want you beside me when I discover the reason."

He kissed her gently and said, "You mean everything to me, Binta, and I want you to be beside me in my life. The idea of me sleeping with Cass is a big test for you, and I need you to pass it, understand?"

She nodded and put on the best smile she could muster. "Yes, of course. Cassandra will not like it, though."

"She does not have to know right away. We can tell her sometime after tonight, if at all."

"I do not want to betray or keep secrets from her."

Greyson cut her off once again, "We will not betray her. Cass's involvement in all of this is still unclear. She came to me for a reason, and it is more than a coincidence that the three of you have a history. Tonight, the three of us entwined in Cassandra's bed will be perfectly magical, and I want you to enjoy it as much as I do. Are you not looking forward to it?"

"Yes, of course. Tonight will be wonderful, I'm sure."

"Good. Now I must be getting back to the temple. I have much to do. I will meet you at Cassandra's room at the designated time," he said as he rose from the bed and dressed.

"Greyson?"

"Yes, my love?"

"I will not betray her or keep secrets from her. But if you want to continue this thing with Cass, you need to tell her," Binta said.

She was not afraid of Greyson, but she knew he liked to take advantage of her submissive nature. So, she would let him control her to a certain degree, mainly to satisfy her sexual needs. But she was determined not let him hurt her friend. Greyson smiled, nodded, and was on his way after a quick kiss. Binta sat there for a long while, pondering Greyson's words. She did not like Cass and knew Cassandra liked her even less. She did not want Greyson to ruin their night by mentioning Cass, but Binta would not go along with any betrayal that would hurt Cassandra. With a sigh, she eventually gathered herself and took a long bath. She had to prepare for the coming night, which promised a plethora of delights.

Cassandra was late returning to her room that evening, and Greyson and Binta were already outside her door when she finally arrived.

Cassandra looked dirty and exhausted, but there was a sparkle in her eyes, and Greyson reasoned that it was in anticipation of what was about to occur between them.

"Binta, Greyson, I am so glad to see you! I have fantastic news!" she said, giving each a hug.

Greyson noticed the sincerity of that embrace, which was a far cry from how she had treated him just a few days before. He knew then, without a doubt, that the charm spell had been effective. She quickly shuffled them into her room and locked the door behind her, ready to share her big news.

"What is it, Cassandra?" Binta asked excitedly.

"First, I apologize for being late; there was an incident in the temple cellar."

"An incident?" Binta asked.

"Yes, it is a long story, but through that mishap, I may have found an answer to something I've been searching for all my life," Cassandra said.

"What do you mean?" Greyson asked, now intrigued.

Cassandra explained the encounter with Cedric and how she planned to visit him that night. Greyson was immediately disappointed in the news, realizing their night of intimacy might have to wait once more. He sat in a chair and watched the two friends sit on the bed and talk. By the tone of Cassandra's voice, he knew it would be difficult to convince her to do anything but visit the old hermit that night. Even the powerful charm would not have the desired effect. Still, he had to try it; but he wouldn't push his luck if she resisted. He thought for quite a while about the best way to keep her from going, but after some time, his thoughts returned to focus on the two girls.

"How do you know this Cedric person is not tricking you?" Binta asked.

Cassandra shook her head. "I don't know, but I must take the chance." She walked to her dresser drawer, retrieved the tome, and said, "I have read most of this and do not have the answers I want.

This Cedric person can tell me exactly who I am and who my parents are. It is the ultimate gift for an orphan."

"Shall we go with you?" Greyson interrupted.

Cassandra paused and thought about it for quite some time before shaking her head. "No, I must do this alone."

"What if something happens? Can you defend yourself?" Binta asked nervously.

"I have a few spells still memorized, and I have my spellbook. I will pray to Gella, and she will protect me as well," Cassandra assured her.

"This seems too convenient, Cassandra. Are you sure this meeting isn't some trap?" Greyson asked, trying to plant a little doubt in her mind.

"I don't think it is. I mean, who would be trying to trap me?"

"How about Ronnis D'Breeth?" he answered.

He could tell that mentioning Ronnis took her aback. Binta had told him about Cassandra's history and how Ronnis was after her. It was a long shot, but he needed to plant that doubt if he had any chance of being with her this night. A meeting of this kind could also destroy her delicate mental state and lessen the charm's effects. Cassandra should focus on him, not on some crazy man in the temple's basement.

"We should all go," he suggested, standing up and approaching the bed. "But first, we should finish what we started the other night."

"No, Greyson. As much as I would like to—" Cassandra began.

She stopped mid-sentence when Binta grabbed her hand and squeezed it. Greyson watched as they made eye contact and Cassandra's resistance seemed to melt. He smiled on the inside; his hope renewed at achieving his conquest of Cassandra. The look they shared was a mix of love, friendship, and lust. Binta smiled, and Cassandra blushed. Then it was time to take it to the next level, so Greyson approached, and they both looked up at him, their expressions were quickly lust-filled.

"So, we shall start over from the other night with the three kisses. After that, I will show both of you the true meaning of Plath's will and the enlightenment that follows," Greyson began, gently grabbing a fistful of Binta's hair and bending down to kiss her.

He stopped just short of their lips touching and looked over at Cassandra with a smile. He tightened his grip, pulling Binta's head back slightly. A small gasp escaped Binta's lips as he did so. He lowered his mouth slowly to devour hers, embracing her in a passionate kiss that lasted several minutes. He never broke eye contact with Cassandra, as she seemed mesmerized by the unfolding events. Unlike the first time he tried this, he saw lust in her eyes, not jealousy. The charm was working perfectly; Cassandra was his. According to Binta, Cassandra had never been with a man. Greyson would resolve that issue this very night. Cassandra's face grew flush as he finally broke the kiss. She swallowed hard with anticipation.

"Now for the second kiss," he whispered.

This time, instead of taking Binta by the hair and making her crawl to Cassandra, he roughly took a handful of Cassandra's hair. He eased her head back so that she was looking him in the eye. She did not stop him, and the look of lust plastered across her face made his groin ache. He wanted her more than anything at that moment.

"This time, you go to your friend and kiss her like never before. Show her how much you care for her, how much you desire her," he demanded, releasing her hair so she could do as he instructed.

"I—" she began, but he cut her off quickly, hoping that his planted suggestion would be too overwhelming for her struggling mind.

"Will do as I say because that is what you want anyway, and there is no need to resist something you desire," he finished for her.

Cassandra leaned in, following his instructions, believing in his words. Binta looked as lovely as ever, and Greyson took a step back to enjoy the show. Binta chewed her bottom lip in anticipation and closed her eyes, more than ready for the moment. Cassandra also closed her eyes and parted her lips, eager for the kiss. Something happened when she closed her eyes; her expression changed to one of concern, the lust melting away as she slowly opened her eyes.

"Kessi?" she whispered, pulling back.

"What?" Binta asked, opening her eyes.

Cassandra sat back on the bed and shook her head. "I saw an image of Ronnis just now. It reminded me of Kessi and my mother. I have thought only of you the last few days. And you as well, Greyson," she added, turning to him.

"What is it, Cassandra?" Binta asked, taking her hand.

Cassandra looked at her friend pleadingly and said, "I do not want to kill the mood between us, but I can find the answers this night that can give me and Kessi information about our origins, about who we are."

She looked at Greyson as well with a disappointed look. He made no move and did not speak, hoping her guilt over her family would be short-lived. But he could not help but feel frustrated, and perhaps his visage gave that away, for Cassandra simply turned to Binta and said, "Not tonight," while squeezing her hand.

"But—" Binta began to respond.

"It is not that I don't desire it; it is just not a good night. I must find my answers; I must go to Cedric. Kessi needs me."

Greyson sighed and returned to the chair to take a seat. He watched the two friends talk as Cassandra assured Binta that she wanted nothing more than to be with her. He watched as they hugged and made peace with the decision. Binta asked again if she wanted them to go with her, but she declined once more. As he watched, his mind spun. He was so close to his goal, but in the end, he could not risk jeopardizing the budding relationship the two women shared for his selfish desires. Instead, he would focus on Cass until Cassandra finished her silly business in the cellar. He and Binta said their goodbyes a short time later and left Cassandra's room, both more than a little disappointed. Binta took his hand in hers, and although unhappy, she appeared content, even giving him a reassuring smile. He loved her and would eventually have Cassandra, and he knew Binta would help him realize that goal.

Chapter 4

Disciple of Kane

After they left, Cassandra prepared for her journey to the cellar. She packed the few components she still had, along with her spellbook, and took the giant tome that Baxter had delivered. Cassandra was ill-prepared for this meeting, but this man might have answers to her questions, answers she had searched for her whole life, and so she intended to go. She was disappointed that she had to send her friends away, but she would make it up to them soon. The thought of giving up her virginity to Greyson and sharing that experience with Binta sounded like bliss. With a deep breath, she refocused her thoughts, putting her potential lovers out of her mind. She quickly put on her pack, grabbed a lantern, and set off for the cellar.

A short time later, she found herself in front of Cedric's door, again studying the scepter's carving. She hadn't dreamed of it for some time now, but it was the same as the one in her dreams, she did not doubt. The tingling sensation of fear she felt earlier was gone, replaced by feelings of excitement and hope. She was not afraid of Cedric, for she believed him. There had been something comforting in his words, and with confidence that she was making the correct choice by being there, she knocked softly on the door. There was no answer, but the door opened slightly with a creak. She saw only darkness beyond the door, and her confidence began to wane.

"Hello?" she asked into the tenebrous room.

There was a brief pause before Cedric whispered to her from within, "Miss Rho, I am glad you came."

The room suddenly lit up inside, brighter than her lantern, spilling light into the hallway. She could see the old hermit then, his messy hair and bushy eyebrows more pronounced in the lantern's light. Cedric had decorated the room with a small table and single chair, a hearth in the corner, a cot in the opposite corner, and various utensils and bowls littering the place. Also, many scrolls lay strewn about, some so old that they had begun to decay. The smell was a mix of old food and rot, and Cassandra made a face despite herself.

Cedric noticed it right away and only smiled. "In with you, then, young lady. Shut that door," he ordered, then turned and walked toward the cot on the far side of the room.

Cassandra entered and shut the door as told. Cedric turned and waved his hand, and the door behind her creaked slightly and swelled against the doorjamb. Cassandra began to doubt her wisdom in coming and suddenly wished that she had allowed her friends to come along. She understood that the only way out of the room appeared sealed off.

Cedric noticed her discomfort and said, "Do not worry, dear; it is not to keep you in but to keep out the riffraff. I truly mean you no harm."

Cassandra looked around and doubted seriously that this seemingly crazed priest had any of the answers she so desperately desired. Again, she questioned her wisdom in coming. "You live in this?" she finally blurted out.

"Of course not," he answered with a wounded expression. "I am a crazy, harmless hermit, at least to all the mighty and wise priests."

Cassandra nodded with a smile.

"Good, then you understand why I must maintain such a façade?"

"Yes, I suppose. But, if this is not your real home, where do you live?" she asked, still puzzled by his strange abode.

"Here, of course," he answered cryptically, holding his hands out to his sides to acknowledge his messy surroundings.

She looked around at the messy and straightforward room, and her heart sank just a bit. She had held onto so much hope during their encounter earlier that day, but now it seemed possible that he was crazy, and she would find no answers.

"Damn it, Cassandra Rho, wake up and become who you should be!" Cedric yelled at her.

The anger in his voice had her backing toward the door. "Perhaps I should go," she mumbled.

"Nonsense. Look around you, girl."

"I am looking. What am I to see other than a small and filthy room, along with its crazed occupant?"

Cedric approached her calmly and reached out to her, and she recoiled another step. He smiled warmly and held his hand in the air.

"Again, I am not going to hurt you, child," he reassured her, then gently put his hand on her shoulder.

His touch was gentle, and he slowly turned her to face the back wall. "Again, tell me what you see."

Cassandra sighed and wanted to say that she saw nothing, but a dirty cot secured to a wall with garbage strewn all around it, but he interrupted her before she could get the words out, "Don't say that you see my room with debris all over the floor. Instead, see the energy; see through the magic."

She looked confused, and he smiled and nodded to the wall. "Un-focus your eyes. See what it is that stands before you," he whispered.

She looked back at the wall and concentrated. She tried to un-focus as the strange man suggested, but nothing changed. She felt he was trying to get her to recognize some magic in the room, so she called on her ability to see magical energy. The familiar arcane shapes came into focus and danced in her head, just as they had when she was younger. Then she realized she did not need to *lose* focus; she needed to *sharpen* her focus. Slowly, the wall swirled and became transparent, and she could see through it. Beyond the wall was another much larger room, richly decorated and filled with furnishings, complete with a library.

Cedric released her as her eyes widened, and a small gasp left her mouth. He smiled as the young woman walked through his powerful spell, the illusion that had defeated many high-level priests over the years. Cedric followed her through and into his actual chambers. There was much to discuss, and it would take more hours than the night offered for him to tell her all he had to say.

He offered her a seat in a plush chair that stood very low to the ground. It was the most comfortable chair in which she had ever sat. Mesmerized, Cassandra looked around the great room, which consisted of many shelves of books and tomes, neatly stacked and in good order. A tidy bookcase stood behind a large desk and contained various bottles, beakers, and jars, most holding what she assumed were spell components. The carpeting in the room was just as plush as the chair, and the smells were intoxicating. It seemed like a mix of cinnamon, sugar, and other aromas she could not identify.

Cedric took a seat behind his desk, and she could sense the magical energy emanating from him. He was far more powerful than she gave him credit for, and as she studied his smiling face, it melted away, similar to the illusionary wall. Cedric dismissed the illusion and revealed his true self to her then. He was much younger than the older man he portrayed and rather nice-looking. Grey hair peppered his goatee and hair, and he reminded her very much of Instructor Baxter. His actual looks made her feel more at ease, and she sank into the chair further than she thought possible.

"This is a most exciting night for both of us, dear Cassandra," Cedric began while rummaging through some drawers of his desk.

"What are you looking for?" she asked, craning her neck to see.

He did not answer but kept at his searching. Finally, he exclaimed, "This!" holding up a chunk of a dark clay-type substance.

He quickly stood, grabbed two mugs from a shelf, and set them on his desk. He then took the clay and broke it, spilling crumbs on the desk, which she then realized didn't look much like clay. Was it some magic component? She watched intently as he found a beaker that held water and poured some into each mug. He took one cup in each hand and smiled. He then closed his eyes and whispered a quiet spell, making his hands glow warm. Next, both cups began to steam, and the clay-like material sank into each mug. Finally, he set them on the edge of his desk with a proud smile.

"And?" she asked, unamused.

"Why, it is hot chocolate, my dear!"

"Hot what?" she asked, again sounding a bit pessimistic.

"Smell it, Cassandra," he bade her.

She reluctantly leaned over the mug and felt the warmth coming from it. She made eye contact with him and, at the same time, inhaled deeply. The scent was rich and inviting, and a smile crept over her face. She looked down at the rich liquid and was mesmerized by the look and smell of the drink. She looked back at him, and he still wore a big smile, as if he had created something unique.

"So, what now?" she asked.

"So, now we wait. It must cool before we drink it."

"Drink it?" she asked, sitting back in her chair as if the mug contained deadly poison.

"Yes, it is quite delicious, and few in the world have it."

"It is a magical potion?"

"No, just a treat. Trust me; it will be worth the wait. In the meantime, I will answer your questions to the best of my ability."

Cassandra stared at him, not knowing where to even begin. There were so many questions, so many mysteries. Her thoughts were interrupted by the strange priest.

"May I?" he asked, pointing to the hefty tome she had borrowed from the school.

"Yes, of course," she said, handing the book to him.

He opened it and studied it for many moments, licking his fingers and flipping the pages eagerly, becoming entranced with the work. Cassandra could hear him mumble things under his breath in amusement, and he would occasionally chuckle.

"Cedric?" she said, trying to get his attention.

"Yes, yes, I remember that!" he exclaimed.

"Cedric!" she repeated more loudly.

Again, he seemed not to hear, too caught up in the writing. Frustrated, Cassandra finally stood and grabbed the book from his hands. His expression was sad and disappointed as he watched her close it and set it on the chair. Cedric looked at her again, finally understanding that he had become too entwined in the book, as he was apt to do, with exciting things. His gaze settled on the book again; his eagerness to read more drew his attention to the fantastic tome.

"A member of the original New Order or someone close to them probably penned that tome," he said.

He sat there staring at the work for a bit and began to speak again, but Cassandra cut him off. "Cedric, who are my parents?"

"Ah, yes, the first of many questions we must discuss this night," he exclaimed, pointing a finger excitedly toward the ceiling as he said it.

"To answer it, we must understand the bigger picture," he explained, taking a mug of chocolate, and testing it with a sip. Then, finally, he nodded his approval and motioned for Cassandra to take the other mug.

"I do not want a treat, Cedric. I want answers."

Cedric took several large gulps of the chocolate, then set his mug down. He turned his attention back to Cassandra, and she immediately noticed that the melted treat drenched his goatee and mustache. She was in no mood to tell him about the mess, so she ignored it.

"With all due respect, you hold the answers that I have searched all my life for, and I am anxious to hear them," she said more calmly.

His expression was one of resignation. "I understand that, girl, but you must practice patience if you are going to save the world."

"What are you talking about?"

"According to the prophecy of Kane, you are to usher in the darkness and then abolish it again," Cedric explained, kneeling in front of her and taking her hands gently in his.

Cassandra shook her head and tried hard to ignore the chocolate mess around his mouth. "Usher in what? And who is Kane?"

Cedric looked her in the eye and held her gaze, slightly squeezing her hands as he spoke. "He is your father, the lich-god."

"Wait, my father is a lich?" she exclaimed, drawing her hands back from his hold.

"Yes, and a god. He is my god."

The weight of the words settled on her shoulders like a ton of rocks. She had always wanted to know who her father was and always thought she would feel whole once she discovered his identity. The news didn't make her feel complete; it only made her want to ask more questions. She sat there, dumbfounded, as he continued.

"Kane was a powerful warlock long, long ago. He could use arcane magic without the use of a spellbook or components. Just like his daughter."

She looked at him even more confused and slowly shook her head. "Not me, I—"

"Haven't lived up to your potential, girl. That is why I am here; I will show the door you are meant to walk through," he interrupted.

She studied him, more confused now than she could have imagined. The revelation of her father's identity did not make her feel at ease with things. Instead, it made her feel quite afraid.

"Your father searched his whole life for the answer to immortality. He was powerful and, at the time, the world's only known warlock. Unfortunately, being the most powerful man in the world didn't help him cheat death. Well, not at first. As he grew old and his body began to shut down, he desperately turned to lichdom to prolong his life. He temporarily found a way to prolong his existence in undeath as he searched for immortality."

He took another large gulp of his chocolate and finished the rest with a satisfying smack of his mouth. He licked his lips and wiped his mouth with his sleeve, then pointed to Cassandra's mug.

"You going to drink that?" he asked.

Cassandra shook her head, so he picked it up and chugged the contents.

"So, how can my father, the lich, have children?" she asked while he drank. "I mean, a lich is nothing more than the skeletal remains of a human and incapable of reproduction."

"Ahhh," Cedric exclaimed as he finished the chocolate and let out a silent burp. "Pardon me, dear, but I do love chocolate!"

He wiped his mouth once more and stared excitedly at her. He only found a frustrated look mixed with a heavy dose of curiosity and doubt. With a sigh, he answered, "It took him more than five centuries, but your father finally found the answer to immortality."

After a few moments of the two staring at each other uncomfortably, she finally blurted out, "Yeah, and what is that?"

"Possession, of course, child," he answered, as if that explained everything.

"So, to become immortal, you possess people?"

"Yes, and no," he answered cryptically.

"Cedric, this is making no sense. Please start making sense, so I know that you are not completely crazy and that I shouldn't be in my room sleeping at this very moment."

"He possesses a new body every fifty years, transferring his very soul into the host while leaving the quivering soul of his victim in the husk of the old, dying body."

Cassandra sat silently, trying to soak in all the information. Cedric gave her the time she needed, knowing there was a lot to absorb that night.

Finally, she spoke, "So, the last time he came down to our world, he not only took a new body but also procreated, so that Kessi and I would be born into this world?"

"You are partially correct, girl."

"Kessi is not my sister, is she?" she asked after a few moments of silence.

Cedric shook his head and replied, "No, she is not."

"Who is she?"

"A decoy."

"What?"

"She is a decoy to protect you if you are hunted," he answered bluntly.

It took her a few minutes to let all of that sink in. She stood and paced the room, running her fingers through her hair. After several trips back and forth across the room, she approached the crazed priest once more. "Cedric, who is my mother?"

"I do not know."

The look of disappointment on her face seemed to bother the old priest. How could he know who her father was but not her mother?

He took her hands again and eased her back into the plush chair. "Listen, Cassandra, I do not know her identity, but I can assure you that Kane would only select the perfect mate. She would have to be of high regard and have good blood. Moreover, he would want the mother of his children to be special."

Cassandra nodded and bowed her head, her gaze falling to the floor. He brushed her hair behind her ear and continued, "Besides, you have had a mother who loves you. Your biological mother does not matter now. Your true mother is the one who raised you as her own."

Thoughts of Unis and the wolves, of Sera, and mainly of Kessi flooded her thoughts. She wanted Sera and Kessi with her to hear all this news. She missed them very much, and she was nearing tears. So, she asked her next question anxiously, "Are Sera and Kessi alive?"

"I do not know that, either, dear."

"I must know; I cannot keep waiting for news of their safety," she sighed.

"Of course you can't, child. Therefore, you must become who your father wants you to be."

"I am to usher in the darkness so that I may banish it, according to Kane's prophecy?"

"Yes, that's right. You are the most powerful living person. You don't understand or believe that yet. Once you do, you will become legendary, my dear."

"How do I become legendary? I cannot even protect my family, Cedric," she said in frustration, her voice growing louder than she intended.

"By finding Zolmex," he stated.

"Who?"

"Not who, but what."

Cassandra looked at him, puzzled, but after a few moments, her eyes widened, and she stood. "The rod in my dreams!" she exclaimed.

"The very one," Cedric whispered with a smile.

"And the dark man, the one in my dreams, the one in the mural in

Victoria's tower? That is my father?" she said, the pieces coming together.

"Dark man? That is not a good way to describe Kane, my dear. Why do you refer to him like that?"

She thought for a few moments and said, "I do not have a good reason, except that his face is a little blurry in my dreams, and mostly all I can see is his dark hair."

"Well, I assure you, your father is anything but dark. On the contrary, he is amazing: the only known self-made god in the history of the human race."

"I would love to hear more about him, and the story you hint at. Perhaps he is amazing, but the visions I have of him do not convey that. And I am not convinced he is good or just. I must know his tale, Cedric. Tell me everything you know."

Cedric rubbed his chin, studying her with a smile. Finally, he began the story, "Your father is the only known mortal who defied death, Cassandra. He was a powerful warlock in his mortal years, and his research led him to the study of undeath. More specifically, he understood that lichdom would grant him eternal life, and he achieved it through his control over arcane magic. Once he had achieved his goal of immortality, he quickly understood the life of a lich was not the final version of himself he desired. From there, he studied possession and found he could live forever, procuring a new body every few decades."

"And his ability to walk among the heavens, and live among the gods?" Cassandra asked.

"Only he knows that part of the tale. Perhaps one day you will get to ask him yourself."

Cassandra let his words sink in and shook her head, slowly, trying to process the story. "Yes, perhaps you are correct," she finally said.

"I know I am, dear. Your dream, the vision in the tower, was your father's way of communicating with you," he said with a smile.

"So, what does it do?"

"Zolmex? Why, it will make you more powerful than you already are."

"I do not feel powerful," she said doubtfully, her face frowning. "If I were, my family would be with me now."

"Yes, yes, I know. You doubt yourself. That is because you have not properly tapped into your abilities as a witch. You do not need Lady Victoria's school. Nor do you need a spellbook or components of any kind. You are more powerful than any wizard alive!"

"No, I am not, Cedric!" she yelled. "I lost my home and family and was recently humiliated in front of the whole school. I am not powerful."

"Oh, but you are, you have to believe, and with Zolmex, your powers will be god-like. The prophecy states that the offspring of Kane will wield the rod to destroy Marnelphion once more. That is you."

"Marnelphion? The demon lord?" she asked, her neck hair suddenly standing on end.

"Yes, the same. You will battle the creature, and the prophecy predicts that you will beat the demon with Zolmex in hand," he explained.

There were a few sobering moments when the two sat in silence. Cassandra finally stood and paced the room, contemplating his words. Finally, she stopped and walked to him quickly.

"What does the prophecy say about me bringing darkness into the world? Does this mean I am responsible for Marnelphion coming back? If so, how do I stop it from happening in the first place?"

"Yes, you will be the one responsible for his return, but rest easy; you will be the one to banish him once more."

"Rest easy? Are you crazy, Cedric? I do not want to be responsible for summoning a demon lord. How can we stop it from happening?"

"We cannot, I'm afraid. Nevertheless, the prophecy will come to pass."

"Whose stupid prophecy is this, anyway?" she asked, with an edge to her voice.

"Why, your father's, of course," he answered excitedly.

"Wait, why would my father use me to bring Marnelphion here, only to have me destroy him?"

"Now, you ask questions only your father knows the answers to, my dear. Why do gods play their games? We, as mortals, do not know."

Cassandra resumed pacing, having heard enough of the story to be frightened. At that moment, she wished that Cedric was crazy and that he was speaking gibberish that she could not understand. She could accept that better than what he had just told her.

She turned to him and asked, "How do we know the prophecy is real? And how do I know that what you say is the truth and not some elaborate story?"

He chuckled and patted his hands in the air. "Dear child, I have waited here for more than twenty-five years. Your father told me the year you would come and the day you would be at my door. I have played the part of the idiot priest all of this time to have this most important discussion with you now. It is up to you to believe it."

"I'm not sure I do," she answered somberly.

"What does your heart tell you? The dreams, the visions, the fact you are here now. No one can see through the illusion that hides my home except perhaps a powerful warlock or an equally powerful witch. Are all of these facts just a coincidence, or are you truly the child of Kane?"

She shook her head and sighed. "I do not know. Deep down, I believe you, but I will not let some stupid prophecy dictate my life. I will find this rod, and I will become powerful. Then I will use that power to protect my family, not summon a demon lord."

"As you wish," he said, but she could tell by his expression that he believed in her; he believed she would fulfill the prophecy, whether she wanted to or not.

He believed her to be the daughter of Kane, and somewhere deep in the recesses of her mind, she also knew it to be true. But she didn't want to believe it.

"The New Order used the rod to defeat Marnelphion all those years ago. Did you read about that in your book there?" he asked, pointing to the old tome.

She looked at it and shook her head. "Not yet. Tell me more about Zolmex."

"Kane was a lich when Marnelphion first came to our world, and he had not established himself as a god yet. The one thing he knew was that he did not want to be controlled by that filthy demon, the lord of all undead. So, Kane created one of his many artifacts, his most powerful creation ever: Zolmex. He allowed it to fall into the hands of Leo, the great wizard and member of the original New Order. Have you heard of him?"

She nodded in response, and he smiled. "Good, because he is an important piece to this puzzle. With Zolmex, Leo could instantly cast his most powerful spells without components. The rod served as a conduit for his magical energy."

She looked at him quizzically and said, "He could then do things you tell me I am already capable of doing. How will Zolmex help make me more powerful?"

"Only your father knows that, my child, and there is only one way to find out."

"Possess the item."

"Naturally."

"So, where is it?"

"Zolmex?"

"Yes, the rod; where can I find it?"

"I wish I knew, Cassandra," he said, standing and strolling toward a chest in the corner of the room.

"Great, you don't know where it is? So then, what am I to do? You tell me that I am the catalyst to summoning a great demon into the world, but my father likes to play games and wants me to defeat him, no doubt with a rod that no one seems to know how to find!" She threw up her hands in frustration.

"I did not say that I did not know how to find it, dear; I simply said that I do not know where it is," he corrected, pulling a tiny metal chest from a larger chest.

"What is that?" she asked, sensing a most unusual power coming from the small chest.

"A gift. From your father. The first step in finding Zolmex."

She reached for it, but he pulled it back from her grasp. "Not yet, dear. First, we have much to discuss, and I think we should start by perusing that most wonderful tome you brought. So please sit, and I will make us some more chocolate."

"I told you, I do not want any."

"Nonsense, you must try it. It is exquisite! Also, it will help you stay awake; we have a long night ahead of us."

She didn't respond but let the man prepare the mugs as a prelude to their long night of discussions. Instead, her attention remained on the tiny chest on the desk beside him as he prepared their drinks. The energy emanating from it gave her the same feeling she had in her dreams just before she grasped the rod. Powerful waves of magic rolled from the chest, almost as a warning that what she was about to embark on would change the world. She thought of her broken family, the prophecy, and the idea of being powerful, and she liked it.

She was ready. As Cedric said, it was time to become legendary.

CHAPTER 5

SECRETS REVEALED

Captain Biggles looked on as his men loaded the six bodies onto his ship, *The Siren's Scourge*. Kringus stood beside him, watching them take the precious cargo below deck. Kringus could feel the captain watching him peripherally, understanding how important this trip was to him. The captain had just negotiated a deal with Boz to take Kringus, his men, horses, and their dead to Pelesea for a large sack of gold. Biggles was happy to accept the money but told Kringus that his men had just docked at Mecca-Loraine two days prior and were looking for a few weeks of rest. Instead, they would spend that time traveling the rough, stormy sea. The captain and his men were probably unhappy with the prospect, but money was money, and a sack of gold was a lot to the crew of *The Siren's Scourge*.

"How long will it take to reach the docks of Pelesea?" Kringus asked.

"Not more than two weeks, assuming the weather continues to hold off," Biggles answered, studying the overcast evening sky.

The weather had become freezing over the last week, turning the thick snow from the previous week into a hardened sheet of ice. And the ocean's cold waters promised a choppy voyage to Pelesea, regardless of potential snow.

"Will the bodies remain preserved that long?" Kringus asked, slightly disappointed at the prospect of a two-week trip.

"Yes, of course, we have large blocks of ice below, as you witnessed, and the embalming of this town carries the reputation as the best. Therefore, your most precious cargo will not spoil, Your Highness."

Kringus nodded and watched as the last body, fully wrapped in cloth, was taken below. Before the bodies were loaded, Kringus had watched them pack six large slabs of ice into one storage room of the hull. The six bodies, four of his squires, the sheriff of Oldorburg, and Cassandra Rho's surrogate mother would fit easily in that room and remain cold during the voyage. He had lost his squires in a deadly battle at Oldorburg and had cut down the sheriff and Cassandra's mother from the gallows, where they had found them upon their arrival at the wicked town. He wanted to see Penelope again and end this costly, ill-advised mission.

"We will be here at dawn, ready for a quick departure, Captain," Kringus said and started away.

"We will be ready, Your Highness. Sleep well," Biggles called behind him as he walked down the plank and made his way off the docks.

Agatha, Biggles's first mate, walked up and stood beside the captain and watched the large king make his way toward the town proper.

"Wow, a real king on our ship," she said in amazement.

"Yes, a real king," Biggles repeated absently.

"What is wrong, Captain?" Agatha asked, suddenly concerned.

Biggles turned to her slowly, still with a distracted look in his eyes. "One of the carofex will be joining us."

Agatha's chin nearly hit the floor at the mention of the powerful and unpredictable carofex. But instead, she lowered her gaze to the ship's deck and said, "It will be a long two weeks."

"That it will, Agatha, that it will," Biggles answered, turning once more to watch the big man make his way toward the inn.

Once Kringus had arrived at the inn and could no longer see the captain, he paused at the door, and his gaze drifted to the eastern side of the small town where the giant monastery stood. He thought of their strange new friend who had arranged this voyage. The city seemed to fear the carofex as a whole, and even the captain seemed anxious about the prospect of Boz joining them. Kringus wished he knew more about Boz's race and his monastery home. He made a mental note to learn more about their friend during the voyage home.

Ronnis D'Breeth watched Kringus intently from the top floor of one of the small town's most prominent homes south of the bay. The ship in question, *The Siren's Scourge,* was anchored in the bay the city surrounded, giving him an easy view of the king of Pelesea. He watched the mighty warrior leave the vessel and return to the inn where the rest of his men waited. He knew the pesky elves were not there; they were out, keeping an eye on their king. He did not see them, but the Black Adder knew. He absently rubbed the snakehead handle of the mighty sword, which had permeated his soul over the last few months. He and the sword now had a powerful connection, even communicating through thoughts alone. Ronnis smiled and gulped the remainder of his brandy.

"Why so troubled, my friend? The carofex is with the king of Pelesea and will bring you the treasure you so desperately desire," Barktuck said from behind him, putting a hand on his shoulder and stepping beside him to take in the view.

Ronnis did not answer but instead just stared out the window. He watched the reflection of his old friend standing next to him for a moment, but his vision slowly refocused on himself, specifically the hole in his cheek. The wound represented the hole in his heart caused by Cassandra Rho. He slowly took the mask from the nearby table and placed it on his face, covering the ugly scar.

"Come, my friend, I worry about you! We have all we need here; once my congregation grows, we will be even more powerful than we were in Oldorburg. We are home, and life is good," Barktuck continued, gently turning Ronnis to take in the crowd of people partaking in Barktuck's latest celebration.

Ronnis did not feel much like celebrating, and in truth, he felt angry. Cassandra had taken everything from him. Barktuck had lost a lot, but he had started over quite quickly in Mecca-Loraine; Ronnis had not. There was no orphanage in the town for him to run, and there certainly wasn't a new face for him. He blamed it all on

Cassandra, never considering how much of the damage had been avoidable. Barktuck's parties, the comfortable lifestyle, the new town, and the new beginning meant nothing. Still, Barktuck was one of the few people he liked and could trust with his life. In truth, the old priest was now his only friend.

He turned to the window again, ignoring the cold air seeping through it and making goosebumps on his arms. He did not doubt the ability of the carofex, especially Boz, who seemed to be the best at finding people who wished to remain lost. The carofex had sent word of his plans to sail to Pelesea with Kringus at daybreak. Ronnis's prize was still weeks away, and he would have to find some semblance of peace during those long days of waiting. A powerful surge of energy came from the sword at that moment, and the Adder promised him in no uncertain terms that if the carofex did fail, the blade would help him obtain his objective. A genuine smile crept across his face, a confident smile that he kept hidden by the mask.

"There are some ladies here who will help you relax. I will send them over. So, take advantage, and enjoy your time as you await the carofex's return," Barktuck encouraged him, patting him on the back and walking back to the gathered throng of guests.

True to his word, two lovely ladies of the night came to him shortly after. He turned to regard them, one a gorgeous redhead and one a pretty blond that reminded him of Sera. The sight of her conjured a vivid memory of his lovemaking with Sera. He missed those nights, taking advantage of her good nature to protect Cassandra. Ronnis would hurt and often bruise her, and she would say nothing of it. All for the sake of the spoiled Cassandra Rho. He missed those days dearly. Suddenly, he felt very interested in the women standing before him.

"I like your mask," the redhead breathed huskily, running a finger over his injured cheek.

The cool porcelain of the mask hid the hole, and all she felt was the smoothness of the cover. Ronnis chuckled at the irony of it and offered both of his elbows to the women. "Shall we?"

They giggled and locked their arms with his. Then, they made their way to the stairs that would take them to the next floor, to his private room, where he would show them the true power of his lovemaking. It would be a night neither would forget; the bruises would eventually fade, but they would never forget their night with Lord Ronnis. Barktuck nodded at him as he passed and raised a glass of wine in a toast. Ronnis nodded in return. Perhaps the wait for Cassandra would not be so long after all.

Cassandra and Cedric talked through the night and into the early morning hours. At first, neither felt the effects from lack of sleep as their discussion was intense and one that each needed to have desperately. Cassandra had lived without answers, while Cedric had waited years to give them. Unfortunately, most of Cedric's explanations had left Cassandra with more questions, leading to a very long night. They had each partaken of Cedric's delicious chocolate, which helped maintain their stamina. Now, as the sun rose outside, a fact to which they were utterly oblivious, both began to feel the effects of exhaustion.

"It has to be morning by now," Cassandra said, laying back in her comfortable chair with a deep sigh.

"Yes, I would say it is. We have progressed but are far from finished with our discussion."

"I agree; I could stay here and talk with you for days; there is still much I want to discuss."

"And so we shall, but not here."

"What do you mean?" she asked, sitting up again.

Cedric had been full of surprises that night, telling her about her father, whom she wasn't sure was a hero or a villain in the battle against Marnelphion. He had also enlightened her that she was the centerpiece of some strange prophecy concerning the return of the very demon lord her father had helped to defeat. Unfortunately, he had no answers about her mother or any information concerning her strange incidents with the ravens at various points in her life. Most of their discussion had been about arcane magic and how to control it without using spell components of any sort. She had hesitantly shared her spellbook with him, and by the end of the night, she was mastering the technique of spell crafting without it. He had opened her eyes to the fact she had already used spells in the past without components, such as when she attacked Ronnis and when she had taken the dancing flame from Baxter's palm all those months ago. More recently, she had defeated Cedric's illusion when she entered his home. It had been a productive night, but he assured her that she had only begun to tap into her powers.

"I mean that our time at this temple is over. I have taught you all I know about who you are, and the priests will not tolerate you being down here with a crazy hermit as we work together to find the rest of your answers," he explained.

"Where are we to go, then?"

"I don't have the answer to that, but your father does."

"What do you mean?" she asked with renewed curiosity.

Cedric turned to the chest that still sat on the desk behind him. Cassandra's eyes were drawn to it at once, having forgotten about it during their long night of discussion. She turned her senses inward, using her newfound skills to detect the magic that emanated from the small chest. She closed her eyes and focused. She quickly felt the energy in the room and manipulated it into a magic detection spell, one of the first spells she had ever learned. When she was ready to cast it, she released the energy and opened her eyes wide in anticipation. To her great disappointment, she discovered no magic within the chest. She sat dumbfounded for a few moments before noticing Cedric's smile.

"What?" she asked.

"There is no magic within the chest contents; you have discovered this fact just now?"

"Yes," she nodded absently, her gaze going to the chest again.

"There is no magic, but the contents are no less important. Your father delivered this to me on your date of birth, using a vivid dream. He told me the contents are for your eyes only and that it was my life's goal to see that you receive them. When I had awakened that morning, the chest was at the foot of my bed."

Cedric got up and retrieved the chest, handing it over to her. She gently took it, sensing its other worldliness, feeling the powerful energy centered around it. The chest might not contain magic, but there was no denying that it was not of this world. She sat it on her lap, with the catch facing her. Cedric took his seat and looked on anxiously. She undid the latch and placed her hands on either end of the lid. Cassandra glanced up at him one last time for reassurance. He gave her a slight nod, and she lifted the lid.

Cedric sat quietly, letting her take in the sight. He could not see what was inside and knew it was for her eyes only. If she wanted to share the contents with him, it was her decision. Delivering whatever precious items were in that chest had been the one thing he had waited his whole life to do. He had done his part; the rest was up to Cassandra.

Inside the unusual little chest were two items: a simple chain necklace with a key attached to it, depicting a lion's head on the key grip, and a tiny, rolled-up parchment, no longer than six inches in length. Cassandra slowly lifted the chain with the key and let it dangle in mid-air. The lion's head was exquisitely carved, with the mouth spitting out the key neck and teeth, forming what looked like a skeleton key. She watched it spin slowly at the end of the chain before shifting her gaze to Cedric.

"So, what is it?" she asked him.

"A key."

"Yes, I know, but to what?" she asked with annoyance.

"Only your father knows, but it must be an important piece to uncovering Zolmex," he explained excitedly. "Go ahead and put it on, dear."

Cassandra did just that, putting the ordinary-looking necklace around her neck. Then she retrieved the small scroll, unraveled it, and held it up to the light, tilting her head back and forth, trying to make out the various symbols and words on the old, fragile paper. Cedric moved over next to Cassandra so he, too, could review the ancient scroll.

The two studied what appeared to be a map, but neither could make out the coordinates. Then Cedric gently took the scroll from her and turned it over. Cassandra let him as he appeared to become lost in the map, studying it intently.

"Yes, yes," he muttered.

"What do you know, Cedric?" Cassandra asked.

"I know of this place, and it is where your journey begins for Zolmex."

Cassandra took the map back and studied it, but it made little sense to her. She looked from the map to him doubtfully.

"Trust me; I know this place. It is a gravesite."

"This only looks to be a partial map. How can you be sure?" she asked doubtfully.

"Because I have been there before when I was a young man. It is not far from here, and the rumors suggest it to be the burial site for Leo, the wizard."

"Leo, of the New Order?"

"The one and only, my child."

She gently rolled up the scroll and retied it, placing it back in the box. She then shut the lid and fastened it. "So, what do we do now?" she asked.

"We go to Leo's grave. That is our starting point, I am certain."

"We will find Zolmex there?"

"Perhaps!" Cedric answered excitedly.

"When do we leave?" she asked, her eyes growing heavy as weariness began to overtake her.

Cedric smiled and said, "Tonight. Go back to your room and rest. Say your goodbyes to your friends because you will probably never return to this city."

That was something that she had not thought of and something that rocked her back on her heels. She could not leave Binta, and it troubled her greatly to consider it. Her mind was a jumble as she made her way back to her room. She was so deep in thought, replaying the conversation with Cedric, that she never even noticed Greyson following her.

Greyson had spent that night in prayer after secretly following Cassandra to Cedric's room in the bowels of the temple. He had stayed and listened at the door after she had entered but detected no sound. He had even tried to enter, but the door had been locked tight, or more accurately, jammed. He returned to his temple, as he had the previous few nights, and asked his god for guidance with many things that were transpiring in his life. At the very least, his prayers included an answer for Cassandra and his failed attempts at seducing her. Finally, after meditating most of the night, he received his answer in the form of Cassandra walking down the temple's main hall. He followed her for a bit and noticed she carried a small chest. He knew she believed wholeheartedly that this Cedric person held some critical answers for her, and he assumed the chest came from him.

"Cassandra," he yelled from down the hall, then waved as she turned with a jump.

She smiled at him and stopped walking, turning to wait for him. She looked exhausted, and he thought briefly that this might be an excellent time to seduce her, as her resistance would be low. Instead, he shook that thought away and focused on the real issue. He needed to know what she had discovered and what that meant for Binta and him.

"You look like you've been up all night," he said, catching up to her.

"Yes, I have, actually," she confirmed with a yawn, then started walking again.

"And?"

She stopped, the question stirring emotions within her. At that moment, it looked to Greyson like he could knock her over with a feather, and he noticed tears forming in her eyes.

"I am leaving, Greyson, and will likely never return."

"What? When?"

"This very night. You must bring Binta to me. I must say goodbye before I leave, and I don't think I should try to enter the school."

He felt a great sense of sadness at the fact she was leaving. He had not expected such an answer from her. "Why must you leave? Because of what Cedric told you?"

"Of course. My destiny is before me, Greyson. After speaking with him last night, I understand that I do not belong in Victoria's school, and I am certainly not a priest of Gella. I have work to do, and it is not in Pelesea."

They walked the rest of the way in silence. Once they reached her room, Cassandra gave him the chest to hold as she unlocked the door. He ran his fingers over the smooth metal surface and realized it was unlike anything he had ever seen.

"What is this?" he asked, handing her the chest back.

"A gift. From my father."

"Cedric is your father?" he asked in shock.

"No, of course not. It is a long story," Cassandra said with a sigh. "Now, if you will forgive me, I must rest."

"Of course," Greyson said, stepping away from the door so she could shut it.

She leaned her head against it and smiled weakly. "Greyson, promise me one thing."

"What is that?"

"Please bring Binta here before sundown, perhaps after her classes."

"You have my word," he said with a nod.

She closed the door, and he stood there momentarily, letting the interaction sink in. He would bring Binta to see her friend, but he decided it would not be to say goodbye.

Matilda stroked Kessi's hair as they sat upon Kessi's large, comfortable bed. Kessi, whom Matilda still dared to believe to be

Cassandra, suffered from the injuries she had sustained at the hands of Matilda's apparatus. Deep cuts lined her back, with her wrists and ankles bruised and swollen. Kessi pulled away from her touch, and Matilda smiled.

"You are so full of anger, young one. Don't you see how special you are to us? That is, as long as you are who you claim to be."

"You speak with a forked tongue," Kessi whispered.

Matilda stood then and laughed. "We will see who has the forked tongue, child," she said, leaning over the girl, who naturally recoiled and continued, "And you had better hope it is not you."

"I hate you!" Kessi blurted out.

"I love you, my child, as long as you pass my final test. As long as you truly are the child of Kane."

"What test? Are you going to strip me down and humiliate me again, then strike me with your whip?"

"That sounds like a wonderful idea, and I might do that if you have lied to me. At that point, your virginity will mean nothing to me, and I'll have my priests teach you exactly what it means to deceive me."

Kessi did not deny her words and had no rebuttal. Instead, Matilda grabbed her by the chin, made her look her in the eye, and said, "Pray to whatever pathetic god you worship that when we perform the ritual in two more nights, we will discover no lies."

With that, Matilda left Kessi to her thoughts and the painful gashes in her back from the whipping. She knew the girl would not intentionally deceive her again, as Matilda had left her wounds unhealed as reminders of what consequences awaited her for such deceptions.

As Kessi rested uncomfortably that night, the pain in her back keeping her from finding proper sleep, Matilda and Cerus lay in their bed just a few feet away, discussing her.

"She passed the lie detection serum; she has to be Cassandra Rho," Matilda whispered.

"That is good. So, you are certain the girl is the sacrifice?"

There was a long pause before she answered, "No, but I am as sure as I can be. She is not lying to us willfully."

"Then what troubles you?"

Again, there was a long pause before she answered, "I only have one concern."

"That is?"

"Heinsvick."

"What of him?"

"Your words about his cunning have sunk deeper into my thoughts than I would care to admit."

"When I planted the seed of doubt in your mind about the legitimacy of the sacrifice?"

"Yes, Heinsvick was powerful, and he could easily have brainwashed any fool into thinking they are someone they are not. He could make things seem not as they are."

A smile crept across Cerus's face. She did not notice, especially in the dark.

"So, I only have one option left," Matilda said.

"Vasheba?"

"Yes."

"When you met the beast at hell's door, she nearly killed you."

"She won't this time. I am a high priestess of Marnelphion and the chosen one to gate him back into our world. Besides, I am more powerful now. I can control her," she said confidently.

"Is this truly necessary?"

Matilda sat up on one elbow, and he could faintly see her silhouette in the dark. "Cerus, I cannot take a chance at the summoning failing. If she is not truly the offspring of Kane, then the gate will fail, and our goal of world domination with it. I must know for certain."

"When will you do this?"

She lay her head back down and stared into the darkness for many moments before answering, "In two nights, during the full moon. It will take me all day tomorrow and the next to prepare the sanctuary and Cassandra."

Cerus nodded, although she could not see the movement. She draped an arm around him and was soon asleep. Unfortunately,

Vasheba was far too powerful to contain, and he would have to be there to protect his wife. As Matilda's breathing became steady and shallow as she fell asleep, he heard weeping coming from Cassandra's bed. The girl was in tremendous pain, and Matilda had denied her any healing so she would not soon forget the consequences of her defiance. That brought a smile to his face as he drifted off to sleep.

As soon as Greyson left Cassandra's room, he headed straight for the cellar and soon found himself in front of Cedric's door. He studied the symbol engraved there, a rod of some sort, and understood that it must be the man's holy symbol, though he did not recognize the god. His own sacred symbol, the star of Plath, shined brightly, enchanted by his light spell and giving him plenty of visibility to study the door.

Finally, he knocked and waited a few moments. Again, there was no answer, so he pounded on the door a little louder. He listened intently for some sign that someone was on the other side. But, again, he heard nothing and was about to strike a third time when the door slowly cracked open. The room was dark beyond, and the stench of filth wafted from the opening. The light from his holy symbol spilled into the room, and he caught a glimpse of a wild face before it recoiled from the light. Greyson took that opportunity to push into the room. The man was slumped over with his arms up, covering his eyes. His greying hair was wild and unkempt, just like the room.

"Is it breakfast for Cedric?" the crazy man asked in a childlike voice.

"I am Greyson Kavince, a friend of Cassandra Rho. We need to speak."

The man slowly lowered his arm and squinted at Greyson, slowly blinking out the invading light. Once his eyes adjusted, the old priest looked around with wide eyes, a crazy look settling on his face. "Not breakfast?" he asked with a disappointed sigh.

Greyson was not about to play that game with him and restated, "I am Cassandra's friend; I know all about you. Stop acting like a fool and speak with me. As you know, we haven't much time."

Cedric just nodded furiously, his wild hair bouncing on his balding head. "Time, yes, time to eat," he said eagerly.

"Fine, if you will not speak, I will be forced to summon the elders to investigate this impostor that lives under their temple before you take Cassandra on some crazy adventure."

Cedric looked at the floor and rubbed his chin for a few moments. He then stood straight, and when he raised his head to look into Greyson's eyes again, the crazed look was gone. "I could kill you, you know?"

Greyson smiled, calling the bluff, and said, "I do not wish to stop you; I wish to help you. I want to know where you are taking her."

"It is not for me to say," the old priest said, pulling Greyson in fully and shutting the door. "It is her decision, not mine. I will only guide and protect her on her quest."

"She has friends that want to do the same. The more who go would increase her chances for success, I think."

Studying Greyson's face, the old priest thought about it for a long while. He seemed torn about what to say or do, and Greyson sensed he did not want Cassandra's friends involved. That made Greyson wish to tag along all the more, not fully trusting this person who conveniently held all of the answers to Cassandra's questions.

"So be it," the old man finally nodded and opened the door again so that Greyson could leave.

Greyson returned the nod and turned to leave but stopped when Cedric grabbed his arm, saying, "Be advised, the road will be full of danger, and Cassandra is my priority. If we run into trouble, you and your friends may be putting yourselves at great risk," Cedric warned.

Greyson looked at him a moment longer, then answered, "Understood."

He gently pulled his arm from Cedric's grip and walked back down the hall, the light following him. Cedric shook his head and whispered, "Stubborn kid, come along then, but you better order a coffin for you and each of your friends before you go."

Greyson soon found himself at the temple of Sinnis. He wanted to tell Alleah about the new adventure that awaited him, but she was in the middle of her morning prayer. He waited a few moments, but when it looked like it would not end soon, he left. He wanted to assure her that he would join her on her quest to Tara and return from Cassandra's adventure in time to go. Prayer sounded like a good idea then, and he headed straight for the docks like he had done each morning over the last few days.

He was later than usual arriving, and the dockhands were already busy with their morning chores. The sun was almost mid-morning, indicating that he was several hours later than expected. He scanned the docks until he found Cass, using a small blade to scrape the ice off the side of a docked ship. He knew it was probably busy work for her, handed out by the dockmaster as direct orders from her father. He watched her work a bit longer, enjoying the way her body moved.

He eventually turned from her and faced the rising sun. He closed his eyes and said a prayer to Plath:

"Dear Father, bless me with the wisdom to make the correct decision concerning Cassandra Rho. I wish to return to Tara with the good priests of Sinnis and avenge the murder of your people. I also think I should be by Cassandra's side as she undertakes her urgent adventure. I feel the gesture will help break her will and allow my sexual victory over her. More importantly, it will make Binta more enamored with me and hopefully more submissive to my will. Please, Plath, show me a sign. Should I stay or go with Cassandra?"

As soon as he finished the prayer, he heard Cass yell, "More praying, Kavince? Don't you have anything else better to do?"

He opened his eyes with a smile to find her carrying some crate to the dockmaster's small quarters. She was smiling at him as well, but the dockmaster was not. Greyson waved to her, then did the same to the dockmaster, who mumbled something under his breath and followed Cass into his small office, shaking his head. Greyson closed his eyes in meditation again, confident that she would return soon.

Moments later, he heard her say, "I'm on break now," as she exited the small building.

She walked straight up to Greyson and said, "Warm me." She

entered his personal space, and his enchantment of cold resistance enveloped her.

"Yes," she sighed and lay her head on his shoulder, snuggling close and tucking her cold hands between their bodies. "It is too cold to be doing this, and I think I am officially sick of it."

"But your father demands it," Greyson reminded her, silently enjoying her closeness as he gently hugged her.

She picked her head up and looked him in the eyes. "You are starting to sound like the dockmaster."

Greyson laughed at that, and she smiled, putting her head back on his shoulder. Greyson rubbed his hands over her back briskly, trying to keep her warm, though he knew his spell would soon have her nice, toasty, and not so close to him. He realized that this was the second time he had asked for a sign from Plath, and on both occasions, his god had delivered Cass.

"So, what is the latest information on our little patient?" she asked, lifting her head, and looking him in the eyes.

He knew she was referring to Cassandra and didn't know how to feel about her obsession with her. Finally, he decided it wouldn't hurt to tell her the truth about Cassandra's pending adventure, so he said, "She is leaving the temple."

"What? Where is she going? She cannot return to the school; Lady Victoria would never allow it."

"That is not her intention. She is leaving the temple and the city altogether."

"What?" Cass asked, suddenly very interested in Cassandra's adventure. "Come, let us go to the temple, and you can tell me all about it."

Before he could object, she took his hand and started leading him to the temple. But, before she got very far, the dockmaster opened the window to his office and yelled at her, "Miss Ruben, you may not leave. Your shift is not over."

"Yes, it is. Go tell my father if you wish."

The man stumbled over his words for a moment, not expecting the young woman to be so bold. All he could do was watch her walk away with his mouth hanging open. He shrugged and shut the window; he had far too much work to do than concern himself with some spoiled child. He knew her father would handle that appropriately.

Greyson and Cass found themselves in Greyson's room near the temple of Plath soon after.

"Tell me about Cassandra," Cass said while stripping off her warm coat and taking a seat next to Greyson on his bed.

Greyson's blood boiled. Having her this close in his private chambers aroused him. She was a beautiful girl, and though she had just been working at the smelly docks, she looked and smelled pleasant to him.

"Greyson?" she asked, breaking his daydream.

He stood so that he could concentrate better. "Yes, Cassandra. She has decided to leave the city to pursue a personal quest."

"Quest? What kind of quest?"

"I am not sure, but I believe it is to find her origins, to find out who she is."

Cass's eyes darted back and forth, and he knew she was processing the information. Whether that was a good thing or not, he could not tell, for he did not know whether he could trust her. Was she plotting some kind of scheme? After all, she and Cassandra were enemies as far as he knew, so he doubted any interest she had in this so-called adventure would be in Cassandra's best interest.

"Who is going with her?" she finally asked.

"Well, there is a priest in the temple who is going as her guide. Also, Binta and I would like to go. We could be assets on a trip such as this to help protect her in case of trouble."

"Yes, that is a good idea, Greyson. She may need your healing, and you have some experience as a traveler, but Binta?" Cass asked, standing up with a questioning look on her pretty face.

"Binta is her dearest friend, and I will leave it up to first Cassandra, then Binta to decide whether they should undertake this journey together. Besides, Binta does know some spells and can be helpful if danger presents itself."

"Please, Greyson, Binta is an average student of magic at best and does not excel in her craft. She would be a hindrance more than an asset to you," Cass said, crossing her arms over her chest and tapping her lip with one finger.

She looked into his eyes, and he knew what she would say before she even asked, "Take me with you instead."

"I don't know, Cass," he replied, throwing up his hands and walking away from her.

She grabbed him by the arm and gently turned him back so that he faced her again. "Think about it; I am the best student at the school and more powerful than Cassandra. I think I have proven my worth."

"Yes, but Cassandra will never go for it," he argued.

"She will if I have the chance to apologize."

"What?"

"I am truly sorry for what happened, Greyson. I was mean to her, and I egged her on so that there would be an eventual conflict," she said, hanging her head and fidgeting with her fingers. "Besides, most of that was Jabell's idea. I no longer associate with that fool, so my thoughts are clearer now, and I am truly sorry for what happened."

Greyson looked into her beautiful dark eyes and could not tell if she was sincere or just playing childish games. But her words made sense to him, and he could not deny that she would be more of an asset than Binta. Perhaps this way, Binta could stay in the city where she would be safe. Still, if this was a ruse, and Cass traveled with them, it could jeopardize the whole party and the quest.

"Besides," she said, moving up close to him, "It will give us a chance to grow our friendship as we travel. Nothing makes people closer than when they travel together, and I will need your magic to keep me warm on the road."

Greyson thought about that for a moment, and her not-so-ambiguous words promised a more profound connection, implying more than just a simple travel companion. The thought of sharing his bedroll with Cass made his temperature rise. In his opinion, she had been a sign sent by Plath, and therefore, should join them. Sleeping with her would only be an added benefit, one which he would truly enjoy.

"Very well," he finally said, as a big smile spread across her face. "We will let Cassandra decide. Meet me here this evening at sundown with your traveling gear, and I will allow you to apologize to her and state your case to come with us."

Cass hugged him, then pushed him out to arm's length. "You will not regret this. I will be here at sundown."

"What will you tell your father?"

"Leave that to me; manipulating him is a skill I have developed over the years. He cannot say no to his little girl."

Greyson, enthralled by the idea of sleeping with the beautiful woman, missed the connection between her being a skilled manipulator and how she persuaded him to let her go.

She pulled him back in and kissed him lightly, smiled extra big, showing her perfect teeth, and left. As the door closed behind her, Greyson took a seat once more on the bed. The events were getting a bit out of control. First, he would have to tell Alleah of his plans, which he already knew she would not like, then he would have to tell Cassandra about Cass's plea to join them. If the charm spell was not still in effect, that could be disastrous. He ran his fingers through his hair and gave a deep sigh. He looked over to the door that connected his room to the temple of Plath and decided a little more praying couldn't hurt.

Maina came to Cassandra's room later that morning, using her key to enter. Cassandra was fast asleep, and Maina went to her and gently shook her. "Cassandra, are you well?" she whispered.

It took several shakes to get her to stir, and once she did, Cassandra sat up with a start, her eyes wide. "What time is it?"

"It is mid-morning. You did not report to the sanctuary for chores, so I came looking for you," Maina answered.

Cassandra looked around the room wide-eyed, trying to remember where she was.

"Are you all right, dear?" Maina asked. "I knocked, but there was no answer, so I used my key."

Cassandra nodded. "Yes, I am fine," she said, getting out of bed and opening the drawer to her nightstand. She fished around for a moment before bringing out her holy symbol of Gella, letting it dangle from the necklace, admiring its beauty. She offered it to Maina.

"What is this?" Maina asked, not making a move to take the most precious symbol.

"I am leaving."

"The temple?"

"The city."

"Cassandra, you are not allowed. I have strict orders to inform Lady Victoria immediately if you leave the temple."

Cassandra nodded. "I am aware of your orders, and I do not care. I have made up my mind, and I am leaving."

Maina did not say anything and only shook her head in disbelief. The proclamation confused the priestess as Cassandra had made quick strides to becoming an acolyte of Gella. Maina had seen it happen to more than one of Victoria's students, and Cassandra's connection with the goddess was more substantial than most. After a moment, Cassandra extended her arm once more, offering the holy symbol to her.

Maina took Cassandra's hand and placed the holy symbol in it. "You keep this. The Lady will always be with you if you need her. Pray to her for anything at any time, and she will hear your call."

Cassandra put the chain around her neck. The lion-shaped key had hung there a few hours before but was now safely hidden under her bed. The symbol of Gella felt good around her neck, and she smiled warmly at Maina.

Maina smiled back and hugged her. "I wish you the best, Cassandra Rho. When are you to leave?"

"Tonight. I need rest or I would leave now while it is light outside."

"Do me a favor. Pray to Gella and ask her for guidance on this most important decision. I will check with you this evening. If you are gone,

I will tell Victoria of your departure. That will give you a day to think about it."

Cassandra smiled and said, "I will. Thank you, Maina."

With a hug, Maina left her alone with her thoughts. Cassandra climbed back into bed, exhaustion getting the best of her. She held the symbol tight to her chest and did as Maina suggested, praying to Gella as she drifted asleep. Cassandra did not know what the night held for her, but she could use all the help she could get. Cedric had put events into motion for her; there were things she truly wanted to discover, and he could help. He had thrown her life into disarray, not that she felt settled in Pelesea.

She would leave in a few hours to a future she did not expect. The coming days were clouded with doubt, and she did not know what they held for her. The worst part was she did not have time to ponder those questions. Things were moving much too fast for her now. Hopefully, she would find her answers at the end of the journey. That was something special, and she knew in her heart that this was her destiny. If Zolmex was real, it would answer her problems, and her family would be safe and happy. For the first time in her life, she would be content. She drifted off to sleep quickly and had pleasant dreams for the rest of the day.

Later that day, Greyson left the temple of Sinnis after having told Alleah about his plans. As expected, she was not too happy about the decision. In no uncertain terms, she told him they were leaving for Tara in precisely three weeks, with or without him. He could tell by how she spoke that she expected him to be on that ship.

So, he left the temple with many thoughts swirling through his head, wanting to please Alleah but not daring to miss the adventure with Cassandra. He walked briskly toward the school of magic to tell Binta of his plans. At least he did not have to worry about her being upset with him. Sure, she would be disappointed that he was leaving and would not be too happy about Cass going, but her passive nature would allow him to make that difficult decision without much resistance.

As he walked across the school grounds, he removed the sling on his arm. He grimaced, the lingering injury still causing a dull ache if he moved it the wrong way. He reflected on that day of his injury and how close to death he had come. He had no desire to face that evil again, but he would not allow the old wound to hamper him. Unfortunately, he was deep in his thoughts concerning Tara, and before he realized it, he found himself outside Binta's room. She had locked the door, so he waited patiently in the hall, knowing she would be there soon.

Sure enough, she showed up shortly after and ran to him once she saw him. The two embraced in a hug and shared a long kiss. "What brings you to the dorms?" she asked with a wry smile as she unlocked her door.

"I have something important to tell you," he answered, rushing her into the room and locking the door behind him.

"Is it concerning Cassandra?"

"Yes, actually, it is. How did you know?"

"Because you have been obsessed with her lately. I still will not do anything that will hurt her, so I hope this does not concern some trick to get her to sleep with us," she said, taking a seat on her bed and patting it with her hand to indicate Greyson should join her.

"No, nothing like that," he assured her, sitting next to her.

Her eyes widened as she remembered Cassandra's meeting with the crazed priest the night before. "Cedric?" she asked.

"Yes, Cedric has something to do with it," he confirmed.

"What did he tell her?"

"Well, he told her who she is and what he expects of her now."

"What do you mean?"

"I mean, she is leaving the city."

"What?" Binta exclaimed, suddenly standing up. "She cannot! The queen demands she stay at the temple. Where is she going?"

"She is going on a quest with Cedric. I do not know all of the details yet."

"She is leaving just like that? Victoria will never allow her back in the school if she does this. I must talk to her before she makes this decision," Binta exclaimed, heading for her door.

Greyson grabbed her gently by the arm and turned her toward him. "She wants you to come to her room to say goodbye. That is why I have come."

"Very well, let's go; perhaps I can still talk her out of doing this," Binta said, turning toward the door.

Greyson would not release his grip and turned her back to him again. "Wait, there is more. Please sit back down; I have something to say."

He might as well have slapped her across the face as he watched her expression change from anxiety to stunned silence. Instead, he slowly guided her back to the bed and sat her down, and she did not utter a word as he did so. He remained standing before her to maintain his domination over the submissive woman. He needed this conversation to be easy, but he had not counted on her being so emotional about the news of Cassandra leaving. He should have known better, but he was confident she would do as he asked. He stood there for a moment, his hands across his chest, watching her squirm uncomfortably.

Finally, she spoke. "Tell me, Greyson, what is it?"

"I am going with her."

Binta wrinkled up her brow in confusion. "Why?"

"I want to be there to protect her."

"But you are leaving soon to go overseas. Why would you leave now with Cassandra?"

"I haven't asked her yet. She may not want me to, but I will offer my services as a friend. I do not know this Cedric fellow, but she believes in him, and I want to be there with her in case this is some trick by that Ronnis fellow."

Binta nodded her agreement. "I will go as well."

"No," he stated.

She looked up at him, her eyes wide, and he saw a look of shock and perhaps anger. That was one emotion he had never elicited from his lover, which made him nervous.

"I do not want you to be in harm's way; also, you must not miss your classes," he reasoned.

She looked down at her hands that lay still in her lap. It was the perfect reaction that the young priest desired. Her submissive acceptance of his decision spoke volumes about their relationship and how much authority he held over her.

"Also, Cass has offered to go," he added, wanting to get that news out in the open while Binta was in a submissive mood.

"What?" Binta asked, raising her head.

He knew this would be the biggest challenge of the conversation because of their history. Still, he felt confident in his power over Binta. She would accept this as well, even if she wasn't pleased about it.

"She wants to make amends, and she thinks this trip to be an opportunity that could put her and Cassandra on friendly terms."

"Greyson, she hates Cassandra, and the feeling is mutual, I assure you!"

"No, I feel that she is sincere and wants to apologize to Cassandra, despite the history the two have," he reassured her, patting the air with his hands.

Instead of resuming her submissive posture, she stood and walked around him. He turned to watch, and she went straight to her chest of drawers and started rummaging through her clothes, laying outfits on the bed.

Now it was his turn to crease his brow in confusion. "What are you doing?" he asked.

"Packing."

"I said that I wish you to stay here. So, I will go, and you will stay here where it is safe."

She turned to look him in the eye, and he saw anger and power there for the first time since he had met her a month ago. She walked to stand close to him, so close that he had to take a step back. She grit her teeth, lifted a finger, and waved it in his face.

"Now, you listen to me, Greyson Kavince. I am submissive to you because I like it and am only that way in our sex life. I allow you to have that power over me for my satisfaction, not yours. But in the real world, I make my own decisions, and you have no authority over what I will and will not do."

Her voice gained volume as she spoke, so her last few words were nearly a shout. Greyson tried to calm her down, but her hand still waved in his face, and she continued to take steps toward him until he had backed into the bed and involuntarily sat down. Now she stood over him and continued to scold him.

"Cassandra is my friend. If she is going on some quest that means so much to her that she has to leave the city, I will find out why it is so important. If I agree with her that it is or cannot convince her to stay in the city, I will offer to go with her. There is nothing you can do to stop that. I will protect my friend, and if you want to bring that witch Cass along, I will keep one eye on the dangers of the road and one eye on her. Do I make myself clear, Greyson Kavince?"

"Yes, of course," he whispered.

"Good!" she said, then resumed her packing.

Greyson sat on the bed without saying a word and ran his hands through his hair. He felt things were spiraling out of control, and the day wasn't even over.

As the sun began to set, Greyson found himself in his room, packing his things, with Binta waiting impatiently by the door for him to finish. As he folded his clothes, it dawned on him that he had never traveled anywhere. He stopped and thought of Darian. They would have already been on the road to adventure by now. He wondered how many experiences they would have shared already. His heart sank at the thought, and he stopped packing and just stared into space. His god demanded that he travel the world, and he had done nothing of the sort thus far. This adventure would be the first in the name of Plath. He would go with Cassandra and, upon his return, travel with Alleah and avenge his friend's death. He would avenge all of those who died that day. He missed them all terribly.

Binta's hand on his shoulder made him jump. "What troubles you?" she whispered.

He put his hand on hers and smiled. "Just chasing ghosts."

He finished his packing quickly, and within a few moments, he and Binta were ready. Cass was to meet them at Greyson's room, so they waited. He knew Binta disapproved of Cass going, and he also doubted the wisdom of that choice. But he believed Plath had a plan for Cass, so he welcomed her offer. The wait was uncomfortable for both of them. Greyson knew that Binta did not want Cassandra to leave without speaking to her first, and he didn't think there was a chance Cassandra would do that. The relationship that Cassandra and Binta had forged was genuine, and he did not doubt Binta's sincerity in joining Cassandra on her quest. He knew Binta would try to convince her to stay; if that were not possible, she would offer to go. He watched her pace and knew she grew anxious, waiting. Greyson's anxiety was slightly different as he focused on how Cassandra would react to Cass being there.

They both jumped when at last, there was a knock on the door. Binta looked at Greyson, her eyes wide, and he detected a hint of fear mixed with anger. Nevertheless, he smiled and kissed her cheek.

"It will be fine," he assured her.

He opened the door, and there stood Cass, decked out in expensive traveling gear, complete with a backpack and a staff. She wore thick makeup, which made her seem more like a princess than a traveler. She smiled at Greyson when he opened the door and hugged him. Greyson then stepped aside so Cass could see Binta. It was evident that Binta did not welcome her company, and Cass seemed to understand that and appeared to expect it. Cass walked right up to her and stood very close. The two sized each other up for a few moments and Greyson didn't know what to expect next. Finally, he decided he would let them work it out.

"How do you feel?" Cass finally asked.

That unexpected comment stunned Binta, and when she didn't reply, Cass continued, "I am sorry for what Jabell did to you; that was not my intention. He acted of his own accord."

Binta shook her head. "It is not my forgiveness that matters. Cassandra's anger with you is great, and she will not be as easy to win over."

Cass smiled. "So, you forgive me?"

Binta thought about it for a moment. She had not expected that attitude from the spoiled girl, and given that Greyson was all right with her going, she felt compelled to at least try to keep the peace.

"No, never. I will not forgive what you did to Cassandra, but I will learn to let that become a thing of the past," she finally said.

"Fair enough," Cass conceded.

"As long as Cassandra finds it in her heart to forgive you, that is," Binta added.

Cass only smiled, accepting her sharp words with understanding, then turned to Greyson and said, "Well, then, shall we go?"

"It will not be that easy, Cass," Greyson said.

"I understand that, and I'm sure her anger with me is great."

"More than you can imagine," Binta agreed.

"So, what do the two of you suggest? Is there a way I can make peace with her?" Cass asked doubtfully.

Greyson rubbed his chin, pondering the question. Finally, after a few moments, he said, "A gift would help."

"A gift?"

"Sure. Cassandra was born an orphan; if you gave her something of value, I bet she would treasure it. At the very least, it may soften her hatred."

Cass thought about it for a moment and eyed both of them suspiciously. Binta said nothing but agreed with Greyson. Finally, with a sigh, Cass pulled a necklace over her head and grasped the attached medallion. As the chain tried to spill from her hand, she held it up to Greyson first, then Binta, and said, "This is worth a lot of gold."

"Perfect," Greyson said.

"Very well, a gift for Cassandra," Cass agreed.

Greyson made eye contact with Binta, letting her know with a smile that he believed Cass to be sincere, and Binta returned a weak smile.

Greyson motioned toward the door with his good arm and said, "After you, ladies."

Soon, they walked down the temple's main hall toward Cassandra's room. All three were nervous in their own right, fearing something a little different from Cassandra. The walk was quiet, with each of them contemplating how she would react. At that moment, all three truly felt like brave adventurers, regardless of whether they would travel with her or not.

Cassandra had packed for the road and now looked out her window at the setting sun. Her heart sank at the thought of leaving, and she panicked at the thought of leaving without saying goodbye to Binta. Cassandra would be going soon, and there was no way she could walk out of the city without seeing Binta one last time. Greyson promised he would bring her by before Cassandra left. She wasn't sure what she would say to Binta, but Cassandra decided then that she wouldn't go without seeing her; she simply couldn't. She checked her pack and dresser drawers to ensure she had left nothing in the room. She did not plan on coming back. Pelesea had not been kind to her, and it was not home. She would find Zolmex, then find her family and eventually find a home. She would miss Binta tremendously.

She let out a sigh as she contemplated those things, and that is when the tapestry of Gella caught her eye, and she instinctively felt for the holy symbol around her neck. She still felt a kinship for the goddess and decided a quick prayer wouldn't hurt anything. She dropped to her knees and silently thanked her for giving her the peace she longed for.

Soon after, the knock upon her door made her jump. She stood quickly to open it, but before she reached it, Greyson and Binta entered. She was so pleased to see her friend that she ran up to Binta and hugged her tight, burying her face in Binta's long hair. Tears came to her eyes as she breathed in her scent. She knew this might be the last time she would see her friend. They would never advance their most precious friendship or develop romance if that was indeed in their future. That hurt the most, losing Binta. Greyson also, for Cassandra considered him a friend and potential lover, and she would miss him too.

She broke the hug and went to Greyson and embraced him as well. Again, she felt a strange sense of closeness to him, almost enough to make leaving him equally unbearable. That is when she noticed the pack that he wore. Her eyes widened, and she turned to regard Binta, who wore a similar backpack.

"What is this?" she asked suspiciously.

"Well, it is not goodbye, I hope," Binta responded.

"What? You cannot be serious?"

"We are," Greyson confirmed with a warm smile.

"We want to come with you if you are truly leaving. I want you to stay, of course, but if it is something you must do, I ask that you allow us to accompany you," Binta said.

"I don't know. What about your classes?" Cassandra stammered.

Binta approached her and stroked her friend's hair. "Our friendship is more important. Besides, I think Greyson has plans to convert me to a follower of Plath."

Both women looked at Greyson, who shrugged and smiled.

"I don't know what to say. I mean, I did not expect this," Cassandra said, nearing tears.

"I need to know if you feel that this adventure is vital. I mean, the consequences to you could be devastating if you leave the temple," Binta said.

"And worse if you leave the city," Greyson added.

"Your arm," Cassandra said, walking back to Greyson. "Where is your sling?"

"I no longer need it. I will not be a burden on your journey but will be there to protect you from any dangers you face," Greyson said, moving his arm in a circular motion to emphasize his lack of pain.

"I have not had much time to think about this, but I assure you, I feel it is the right thing to do. Something about Cedric feels right, almost like he is filling in the gaps in my life. I have a birthright out there. For the sake of Kessi and Sera, I intend to find it!" Cassandra promised.

She walked back to Binta and hugged her tight. "It would mean the world to me if you came. You, too, Greyson," she said, turning back to him as she maintained her hug with Binta.

"That is excellent news. However, there is another who wishes to journey with you," Greyson said as he shared a nervous glance with Binta.

Cassandra broke her hug with Binta again, but this time with a puzzled look on her face. "Another?" she asked.

"Yes, someone who wishes to partake in your great journey, but for a different reason than us," Greyson said, moving a finger back and forth between himself and Binta.

Cassandra thought about it for a moment; already caught off guard by the request of Binta and Greyson, she could not come up with another person in the city who would wish to go. Then she thought of how she had first arrived at Pelesea, and it came to her just who the other person might be.

"Baxter?" she asked.

Greyson and Binta looked at each other, but neither spoke. Finally, Greyson moved to Cassandra and grabbed her by the shoulders. "Listen, this may be hard for you to understand, but there is a surprise offer of help from an unlikely source. You will never guess who it might be, so I shall bring her in."

"Her?" Cassandra asked, even more confused.

Greyson nodded to Binta, who returned the nod, then went to the door to let Cass in. Once she stood aside for Cass to enter, Cassandra took a step back in shock. Her face became flush, and her eyes widened.

"You!" she said through gritted teeth.

Cass walked straight up to her, not backing down and showing no fear of how Cassandra might act. Cassandra only grit her teeth harder and balled up her fists, holding them at her sides.

"Cassandra, please, I ask your forgiveness," Cass said.

"You humiliated me in front of the whole school," Cassandra growled.

"Yes, and I realize that was wrong," Cass tried to explain.

"You are a bad person, and I don't want you anywhere near me. Leave my quarters before I lose my temper," Cassandra spat back.

"Please, Cassandra, I only want to—" Cass began, but before she could finish, Greyson stepped between the two girls and took Cassandra's head gently in his hands, moving her head to look him in the eyes.

She was furious at him; how could he have brought Cass into this? Was she supposed to share her most important journey with the hateful woman? She was about to unload a verbal assault upon them both, but then she locked eyes with Greyson and became lost. Something in the way he looked at her calmed her. Her anger melted away as he smiled warmly. Little did she know that the powerful charm that Greyson had cast upon her was very much still in effect, and his words held great power over her.

"Your anger with Cass is great, and rightfully so. I truly feel that she is sorry, and I would never have brought her here if I didn't feel Cass was sincere. Do you trust my judgment, Cassandra?" he asked, smiling warmly.

She reached up, removed his hands from her head, looked over his shoulder at Cass, who smiled weakly, then looked down at her feet, unable to hold Cassandra's hateful glare.

"I do, but it is hard to trust her. Even if you believe in her, I do not."

"Perfectly understandable," Greyson agreed.

He turned himself so he was no longer between the two women and addressed Cass, "So, Cassandra doubts your sincerity, Cass, and with good reason. What do you have to offer to prove that you are truly sorry for your actions?"

Cass gave him a scour but approached Cassandra and held her closed hand toward her, the necklace chain still visible. "I offer this to you as proof of my sincerity."

Cassandra just stared hatefully and did not move. As they shared their awkward exchange, Greyson slowly positioned himself behind Cassandra to speak in her ear. His breath was warm, and his voice was soothing.

"She is offering something of value for your friendship. Do you accept?" Greyson whispered.

Cassandra made no move to take the jewelry, so Cass slowly opened her fist to reveal a topaz necklace. Cassandra recognized it immediately as the item that had absorbed her spell during their confrontation. The stone had turned a beautiful green as it had absorbed Cassandra's magical dart, but the actual color was blue, very similar to that of Zolmex. Her eyes widened, and she scrutinized Cass's smiling face, trying to determine whether she was somehow playing a trick on her.

Cass only smiled and said, "Yes, it is the item I wore to defeat your magic. It is worth a lot of gold, and I want you to have it. Consider it a token of my friendship; hopefully, this will clean the slate."

"Do you accept this most generous offer?" Greyson whispered in Cassandra's ear.

Cassandra nodded slightly and took the jewelry from Cass's hand. She examined the valuable topaz, holding it up and letting it reflect the light. Cassandra had never owned something as powerful or as expensive as the necklace. She was impressed with the gift and had to admit Cass's intentions seemed genuine. Still, the beating she had endured at the hands of the nasty woman was fresh. Greyson slightly squeezed her shoulders, and his warm breath felt terrific on her neck. Her resistance melted a bit with his touch.

"I accept your gift. I will forgive your actions at the school, but I will never forget them," Cassandra said, donning the necklace but maintaining her stern demeanor.

After a few awkward moments, Cass nodded and asked, "So, am I in?"

Cassandra did not answer at first, and Cass seemed to fidget, shifting her weight from foot to foot. Cassandra imagined that Cass expected the gift to make things right; in truth, it did for the most part. Cassandra still didn't like her and surely didn't trust her.

Then Greyson whispered soothingly in her ear, "You have accepted her gift therefore, you cannot hold the past against her ever again. If there is any hope of trusting her, the past must remain in the past."

His words had a powerful effect on her, and she relaxed, almost leaning against him for support. She noticed Binta chew her bottom lip as she looked on. Cassandra loved that look and found Binta very desirable at that moment. But then, her thoughts shifted to the promised threesome they had arranged for this night, and she nearly forgot about Cass standing in front of her. Instead, lust filled her thoughts, and she sensed Greyson's sensual touch on her shoulders, a gentle rubbing that promised so much more.

"The decision rests with you, Cassandra. Will you allow Cass to travel with us? If so, it must be made clear that you are in charge, and there can be no challenge to your authority. Cass must understand that you are the leader of this group," Greyson continued whispering, moving his hands gently up and down her shoulders and upper arms.

Cassandra responded to his touch by leaning back against him, becoming more relaxed and further subject to the charm he had cast. Her reactions to his words and touch felt natural. She felt good in his arms and could feel every inch of his body pressing against her. Greyson slowly massaged her shoulders, relaxing her even more. She was vaguely aware of how his massage was manipulating the front of her shirt, making the gap between the buttons larger if he moved his fingers a certain way. She was also very aware of how her nipples reacted as the material rubbed them.

"Cass must prove her loyalty now," he continued.

Cass's eyes narrowed as Greyson spoke those words, but he only returned the glare with a shrug and a smile. Cassandra did not notice the exchange as she fell more and more under Greyson's spell, finally closing her eyes and laying her head back on Greyson's shoulder.

"You must prove your loyalty to me, Cass, if you wish to accompany us on the journey," Cassandra breathed huskily.

Cass looked hatefully at Greyson, who only offered a wink as he continued his sensual massage.

Cass looked perturbed by the fiasco but remained calm. She put her hands on her hips and stared at the priceless magical necklace between Cassandra's breasts, the one she had just offered as a gift.

Finally, she asked Cassandra, "In what way are you referring? I pledge my allegiance to you, do not doubt, and I will prove myself in time. You will not be sorry for letting me travel beside you; I promise you this."

She directed her words at Greyson, not Cassandra, although Cassandra failed to pick up on that fact as she was approaching a sleep-like state.

Greyson whispered more soothing words in Cassandra's ear, and Cassandra smiled, her eyes still shut, and said, "Bow before me, Cass. Show me you are willing to follow my commands," Cassandra ordered, pointing to the floor at her feet.

"What?" Cass asked, looking at Greyson in confusion.

He only nodded slightly and smiled as if to say everything would be all right. Cass looked back to Cassandra, who stood there calmly, her finger pointing toward the floor. Cassandra did not see Cass's cheeks flush red or notice her eyes narrowing again at Greyson. It looked as if Cass would attack Cassandra for such a demeaning request, and Binta even stepped a little closer in the event she did. But Cass eventually knelt, never taking her eyes off Greyson. She sighed and placed her hands on her thighs and waited.

When Cassandra made no move, she stated, "There, I am on my knees, and I will follow your commands."

Greyson whispered something quickly, and a smile crept across Cassandra's face. She relaxed even further, which seemed impossible without crumpling to the floor. Greyson slowly reached down and undid several buttons of Cassandra's shirt. Cassandra was unaware of the action and awaited his following command. Greyson winked at Cass, then smiled at Binta as he continued his work on the buttons. If Cassandra had been more conscious of her surroundings, she would have noted the sexy look Binta now wore. She would also have noticed Cass roll her eyes at the strange display.

Then Cassandra took things to another level. "Lick my boot," she ordered, her eyes still closed and her head resting on Greyson's shoulder.

"What?" Cass asked with surprised disgust.

When Cassandra did not respond and Greyson only gave a quick nod, she issued a low growl and began the humiliating task. Cassandra was not even aware of the action, but there was no denying Cass's anger.

Greyson could not comprehend his good fortune. Cassandra was putty in his hands, and Cass was somehow following her orders, which he was implanting subconsciously into Cassandra's thoughts. With Binta standing aside and letting it happen, he could only foresee many pleasures on this trip. First, he wanted to help Cassandra in her quest, but more importantly, he desired sex with all three of these women, and he would see it to fruition.

He slid his hand down Cassandra's shirt and cupped her breast in his right hand, eliciting a gasp from the semi-conscious woman. Her breasts were perfect, and her nipples were erect. He caressed her for a few moments as Cass looked on and licked Cassandra's boot. He slowly kissed Cassandra's neck and made eye contact with Binta as he did. Binta only chewed her lip and her face flushed as she took a few steps closer, seemingly ready to pounce on them. He knew she was becoming very aroused at the scene. Cassandra leaned heavily on him, and he nearly lost his balance, breaking the trance with Binta in the process.

Cass paused long enough to pick dirt off her tongue when she heard Cassandra say, "Now the bottom."

That was enough for Cass, and she dropped Cassandra's foot, making Cassandra snap out of her trance. Cass stood and was about to say something to Cassandra that Greyson knew would break the charm and renew the fight between the two enemies. Before she could speak, there was a voice from the doorway, and all four jumped at the sound.

"Now, I must say, I do not approve of this," Cedric said.

Cassandra pulled from Greyson's embrace, and he had to work to extract his hand from her shirt, which she rebuttoned as she made her way to the door, giving Greyson a quick, confused glance.

"Cedric, I am glad you are here," she said, trying to regain her wits.

As Cassandra greeted the old hermit, Cass approached Greyson with a sour expression and whispered, "Was all of that necessary?"

He only smiled and said, "Of course, if you truly wanted her forgiveness and if I plan on bedding her during this trip."

Cass only shook her head and walked away, moving to introduce herself to Cedric. Greyson watched her backside lustfully as she did. Cedric was a heavy, wet blanket with impeccable timing and Greyson cursed his continued bad luck when trying to seduce Cassandra. Then he picked up on the conversation as Cedric finished saying, "It is up to you, Miss Rho, but are all of them going?"

Cassandra looked over at Cass and nodded. "Yes, all of them."

So, there it was, confirmation that Cass was in the group. Cass turned to Greyson, and he nodded, eliciting a smile from the woman.

"Very well, but remember, I am here to protect you only. If we run into trouble, which I am sure we will, I will use my resources to protect you, no others," Cedric explained.

Cassandra nodded her understanding and glanced Binta's way. None of them had ever been on a quest before, and not one of them could imagine what lay ahead of them. Cedric tossed a pair of boots to Cassandra, which were high leather and lined with wool.

"Another gift from my father?" Cassandra asked.

"No, a gift from me, child. They are magical and will keep you warm, even in the harshest weather."

Cassandra nodded and moved to her bed to change her footwear. While she did so, Cedric addressed the group. "I am Cedric, Cassandra's guide on her most magnificent journey. I must tell you that this is not a simple quest that will make you rich and fill your life with adventure. No, this is a quest that will change the world as we know it. There will be danger and if you have the least bit of doubt about going, step aside now. For once we leave, there is no turning back. I have waited many years for this, and I aim to see it through."

Everyone looked at each other, but no one said anything until Greyson finally said, "We are here to help Cassandra."

"Yes, I could see how you were helping yourself, son, when I walked in."

Greyson smiled and shrugged, and Cassandra's cheeks reddened even more, but she pretended not to hear.

"There will be none of that on the trip," Cedric scolded him.

Greyson's smile slowly disappeared, and it was Cass's turn to smile at his disappointment.

"I'm telling you, none of you have the experience required for this journey, and I will want you focused on what we are doing," Cedric lectured. "So, no more of this activity until we have completed our quest."

"I have some experience, sir," Greyson blurted out, not appreciating the lecture.

He had not thought of the older man intervening with his seduction of Cassandra, and it frustrated him to be this close only to have him stand in his way. But he would work around it and accomplish his goal, whether Cedric approved of it or not.

The old priest walked up to him, looked him straight in the eye, and said, "You have no idea what you are getting into, lad. Whatever experience you have is irrelevant, and you might want to consider the possibility of just what you will find on this quest; what dangers you and your friends are about to face. Are you and these young women going to be of assistance to Cassandra, especially if all you think about is bedding them?"

The threat of danger to his friends reminded Greyson of his minimal adventuring experience, and he began to doubt the wisdom of the quest. His arm and shoulder throbbed at the idea of Cerus and his wicked spear, and thoughts of his dead family and friends flashed in his mind. The images of them hanging from the trees were still very fresh, and it made him even more motivated to defeat the evil of the world, but it also made him worry about his friends' safety, especially Binta's. Then, for an awful moment, he saw her hanging from a tree; her entrails spilled upon the ground. He shook the thought away, and when he snapped out of it, Cedric had moved on and was now discussing something privately with Cassandra.

He took that opportunity to speak with Binta and Cass alone. "Perhaps the old man is right. Maybe the two of you should stay; this sounds dangerous," he reasoned.

A cloud crossed Binta's face, and he knew by her glare that he would not convince her to stay. "I told you, Greyson, this is not your call. I'm going to help my friend," she explained in no uncertain terms.

He nodded his understanding and turned to Cass, who only shrugged and said, "And I am going to help my new friend."

Within the hour, the five of them were heading out of the city's eastern gate. Cassandra thought little of the consequences of leaving the temple or even the city. Instead, her thoughts were on her family. If anyone were to protect them adequately, it would have to be her, as she had always believed. The quest for Zolmex had begun.

Chapter 6

An Evil Unleashed

"I am hungry," Kessi said, not for the first time.

She stood in the center of a pentagram drawn on the floor with a red, chalky substance. Chains attached to a metal pole jutting from the rocky floor held her hands above her. A priest, wearing a dark robe and sporting a shaved head, drew symbols on her face while another held her head still. His strong hands squeezed her throat whenever she struggled too much. She learned quickly to cooperate so they could paint her; to prepare her for what was coming.

She could not turn her head, but peripherally, she could see Matilda sitting on the floor, outside the pentagram, cross-legged and with her eyes closed, deep in meditation. She ignored her as well, making Kessi even angrier. She had been brought to the lightless caves days ago and had not eaten recently. She could only assume that they would kill her, which she would gladly accept if it meant she would be free of their clutches. Her lonely nights, thinking of her mother and sister, had been much worse than she could have imagined. The lack of food only fed those despairing thoughts, and the cuts in her back remained untreated and caused her discomfort in every position. And now, this, whatever this was, would probably kill her.

"I said, I am hungry!" she yelled and tried to spit in the priest's face.

Unfortunately, she was so dehydrated all that came out of her mouth was a thin string of saliva, which landed on her chin, making both priests stop their work and look at her in disgust. Then they shared a laugh at her expense.

"Shut your mouth, spoiled one; hunger is a necessity. That way, Vasheba can more easily devour your thoughts."

"And your robe is stupid-looking," Kessi managed to retort weakly, still believing she was Cassandra and playing the part perfectly.

One of them grabbed her hard by the cheeks, squeezed her face, and leaned in with a smirk. The look in the priest's eyes told her he was serious, and she believed what he said.

"No god can help you if Matilda finds that you have lied to her. She does not take betrayal lightly," he hissed.

He slowly released his grip on her cheeks, and the two priests shared another laugh and finished their work. Once done, Kessi sported a pentagram in the center of her forehead. She did not complain again; regardless of her hunger, her will to fight began to wane. She knew something terrible was coming, something that would make her forget about her pain and suffering.

She felt the fear creeping inside her as the two priests left her and began inspecting the pentagram outline's red powder. She knew the priests were about to start a horrible ritual with her at the center. Suddenly, the whipping from Matilda didn't seem like such a bad thing for poor Kessi. She closed her eyes and tried to think of better times when Sera, her sister, and she shared a decent life at Oldorburg. But unfortunately, that time seemed like a distant memory at that terrible moment. She slipped in and out of consciousness as the priests scurried around her like ants, efficiently completing their tasks for whatever came next. She lost track of time.

Nearly a day later, Kessi slowly came to and felt her arms aching and her belly rumbling from hunger. The cuffs from the chains dug deeply into her wrists, and her legs no longer supported her. She had been chained to the metal pole, weakening her resolve, and sapping her strength. The priests of Marnelphion sat outside the pentagram, hands joined, eyes closed, and all were chanting silently in a tongue she did not understand. She did not know how many there were because the ring of priests circled the pentagram, and she was too weak to look over her shoulder to find them all. But she could see Matilda at the head of the gathering, facing her.

Many candles lit the cavernous room, making shadows dance across the walls and ceiling. This room was much bigger than the one they used to whip and humiliate her. Because of that, Kessi could sense something awful was happening; why else would they need a bigger room? In her weakened state, she could not tell if the shadows were simply from the candles, or if creatures of unnatural origins were dancing around the cave. It was as if the moving shapes warned of things to come.

She shook her head and tried to think back to the events that had led her to this moment. She remembered Heinsvick telling her that she would die, but it would save her family and possibly humanity. But she couldn't remember how. She took a deep breath and prepared for whatever would happen next. She came here for death, and she would see it through. The cadence of the chant increased, as did the tempo. She knew the time was near. She would not have to wait much longer for whatever she was about to face.

Her suspicions were confirmed when an awful odor assaulted her. Unlike anything she had ever smelled, it was a sickly mixture of sulphur and blood. To her, it just smelled like evil and death. She would have vomited if there had been anything in her stomach. Instead, she dry-heaved for many moments, only making the cuffs dig deeper into her bruised wrists. Then her pain was replaced by fear, so great that her heart nearly beat out of her chest. Something was coming for her, and it would kill her quickly. The candles outside the pentagram flickered and changed hues, from white to dark red to light blue, then back to white. The hairs on her neck stood straight, and she began to shake. Something was in the circle with her, something evil and otherworldly. Kessi lost control of her bladder but hardly noticed the wetness on her legs, for the creature suddenly took shape before her, a dark cloud that slowly took the form of a terrible beast.

It was hideous, standing at least twice her height with black, leathery skin and substantial bat-like wings. The red eyes promised death to anyone who met its gaze. The creature had a misshapen head and a mouth filled with razor-sharp teeth that comprised most of its facial features. Drool continuously dripped to the stone floor with a sickening splat, desecrating the very stone it touched. Its elongated arms ended in fingers like talons. The thing had no clothing but wore a thick, black, barbed chain around its waist like a belt, with the ends long enough to reach the floor on either side of it. Those ends were primarily red, stained with the blood of its victims, with fleshy bits impaled in many places along its length. If she had the strength, she would have screamed. It approached her, and she knew she was doomed.

Five hours after leaving the city, as the night reached its coldest peak, the party of five companions from Pelesea turned off the northern road and headed into the wilderness. The trees were thick with pines in this part of the world and covered with snow. As a result, the cold seeped into every pore of Greyson, Binta, and Cass, who had no way to keep warm other than their thick winter clothes. Greyson's spells of warmth had been adequate for the three as long as they stayed close; although, he had exhausted those spells hours ago and could not keep his friends protected for any length of time. So, as the night reached its halfway point and the moon was high in the sky, the party slowed considerably due to the conditions.

"We must stop and build a fire, Cedric," Cassandra pleaded.

Cedric stopped and turned to regard her three friends, who huddled together, shivering. He and Cassandra were perfectly comfortable thanks to their magical boots, but the other three came ill-prepared for the journey and with no experience traveling the wilderness. He shook his head at the apparent burden the extra travelers had become.

"They should not have come," he stated.

"That is beside the point," Cassandra said, her hands on her hips and staring hard at the old priest.

He sighed and said, "Very well, we will find warmth, but not from a fire. We do not want to draw attention to ourselves."

"So, how do we warm them without a fire?" she asked curiously.

"I'll show you, my child," he responded with a grin and started digging around in a sack he kept tied to his belt.

Greyson, Binta, and Cass came over to speak to Cassandra as he searched. All were shivering badly and were grossly losing their battle with the frigid temperatures. She could tell that they would not last much longer in the harsh environment.

"I am sorry, Cassandra, I did not expect this situation in which we find ourselves. I thought my powers would protect us long enough," Greyson apologized with chattering teeth.

Binta and Cass each snuggled up beside him, trying to keep warm. Cassandra made eye contact with each of them, and her heart went out to them, especially Binta.

"Do not apologize, Greyson; you have come to assist me, and I love you all for doing so. I will not let you die to the cold; Cedric is working on it," she reassured them.

She bent to undo the protective boots. "In the meantime, we will take turns wearing these, so no one freezes to death out here."

"No, Cassandra, do not take them off," Binta pleaded through clenched teeth.

Cassandra smiled at her but shook her head and continued to undo her boots. "I will not stand by and watch the three of you freeze to death. We will share in this burden."

"There is no need," Cedric said from behind her.

All looked toward him to see that he held a tiny cottage in his hand, made of polished stone. It was pure black, and the craftsmanship was highly detailed, right down to the shutters on the windows.

"What is that?" Cassandra asked.

"Another gift from your father, this one given to me."

"Well, whatever it is, can you please make it work? We are freezing here," Greyson pleaded.

"Of course, young man, you and your friends are just moments away from warmth," Cedric answered happily.

"I think he is crazy," Cass whispered to Greyson and Binta as

Cedric took Cassandra over to a clearing. They both nodded in response.

"What is this thing?" Cassandra asked as he placed it on the ground at their feet.

"An extra-dimensional space created by your father."

"What?"

"No time to explain; let us get your friends comfortable first," Cedric said, looking back to her three shivering friends huddled together. Cassandra nodded and looked on in anticipation.

"Your father was good at making such pockets in space. He also chose his activation phrases carefully, usually using a normal saying, but backward," Cedric said.

Cassandra just looked on in confusion as he tried to explain the workings of the magical device. "So, to activate the cottage, you must touch it and say, Red Rowen."

"What does that mean?" she asked, scrunching her nose.

"It is backward, as I have told you."

"So, it is Newor Der pronounced backward?" she asked, shaking her head in confusion.

"No, dear, it is New Order pronounced backward. Now try it, quickly, before your friends freeze to death."

That was all the motivation she needed, as she quickly knelt and touched the trinket while saying the command phrase. Immediately, the item multiplied in size, and she and Cedric had to take several steps back to give it room to grow. Finally, it rose to the height of a small cabin, about twenty feet square. Then, once it completed its transformation, it immediately vanished from sight.

"What happened?" Cassandra asked.

"Your device is broken," Cass shouted over the howling wind and chattering teeth.

Cedric took Cassandra's hand and moved her to where they last saw the magical cottage. The tiny door remained open and hung in mid-air, about a foot from the ground. Inside, she could see a cozy little room with a lit fireplace.

"Amazing!" she said, her eyes wide.

Cedric only smiled and crossed his arms over his chest. "Your father is quite talented."

Cassandra turned to her friends and waved her arm. "Get over here quickly!" she said excitedly.

They made their way beside her, then stared in disbelief. "Where is the rest of it?" Greyson asked.

"I assure you, it is there, and once we are inside and close the door, no one from outside the cabin can see us," Cedric explained. "Now inside, all of you, before the cold turns you to icicles."

He did not have to tell them twice, and within a few moments, all five were sitting near a warm fire that crackled in the fireplace. Binta, Cass, and Greyson sat very close to it and started to peel off their coats, letting the warmth infiltrate their frozen extremities. Cedric took one final look out the door to make sure no one was watching, and once satisfied that no one had seen them, he shut it.

No one could see the cottage outside of it; since it was an extra-dimensional space, one could pass through it and never know it. The small sculpture became part of that extra dimension, so it was no longer visible. The friends were safe and soon were stretched out on the floor in front of the fire, sleep overtaking each of them. Only Cassandra and Cedric were awake as they sat together on one of the cabin's two comfortable couches.

"This place is amazing, Cedric," she whispered excitedly, looking around the nicely decorated room and sipping some more of his hot chocolate.

"Yes, I agree, and it is only one of many extra-dimensional spaces that your father constructed with his powerful magic, or so the rumors say."

Cassandra stared off into the fire as if in deep thought.

"What troubles you, child?" Cedric asked, noticing that the mention of her father made her distant and uncertain.

"It's just the idea that I know who my father is, and it makes me nervous. It is nice to know but also scary, especially given this prophecy I seem to be centered around. Also, even though we suspected it, it is difficult to learn that Kessi is not my true sister."

"She is as true a sister as you could ever have."

"Yes, I agree," she said with a smile. "I miss her, Cedric. I must find this artifact so that I can save her."

"Save her?" Cedric asked.

"Yes, I feel that she is in trouble. My mother as well. I must find Zolmex to be powerful enough to save them."

Cedric nodded his understanding, and it was his turn to stare blankly into the fire.

"You are afraid," she reasoned.

He looked at her, puzzled. "Oh?"

"Yes, afraid. I can see it in your eyes."

He smiled weakly and nodded. "Perhaps a little," he agreed.

"Because of the prophecy?"

"Yes, the prophecy."

"A prophecy orchestrated by my father?"

Cedric only shrugged and nodded, smiling weakly at her.

"I am going to summon the demon lord using Zolmex, you think? Is that how the prophecy goes?"

"Not exactly, child."

"Then how?" she asked, suddenly concerned.

"It is not my place to say."

"I have a right to know, Cedric. You told me I would become powerful after I find Zolmex, and I believe it. But you have not elaborated on the other part concerning Marnelphion. So how do I play a part in his return?"

Cedric turned and looked her right in the eye. His expression was severe enough to make her very nervous, and a chill coursed down her spine when he finally spoke. "The prophecy declares that you will be sacrificed to the demon lord, your blood bringing him back to destroy the world. There is nothing you can do to stop it, my child. Your father conceived you for this very purpose, and it will come to pass. He told me that you would stop at nothing to gain the artifact. Even knowing it will mean your death, you have decided to proceed, just as he predicted. Embrace the prophecy and understand your father has great plans for you. Your legacy will not stop upon your death."

She sat back on the couch and considered his words. She was still sorting out everything he had told her the night before, especially items concerning the prophecy. What did he mean by her legacy? Was her father planning on making her a lich, or even immortal? She suddenly felt tiny and very powerless. She looked at her friends lying on the floor, and her heart went to them. She could not let the prophecy come to fruition for her friends' and family's sake. First, she would beat it; then, she would use the artifact to defeat anyone trying to bring back the demon lord. She would not willingly become a sacrifice for such an atrocity. It took her a long while to fall asleep that night, her mind processing the new information. Cedric stayed awake a bit longer and watched over her. When she finally did fall asleep, her dreams were not of the pleasant variety.

Cassandra awakened with a start in the middle of the night. Her heart was racing, with her hair matted to her face. Tiny beads of sweat dotted her brow, and her breath came in gasps. It took her a few minutes to realize where she was, the dancing shadows from the fire playing tricks on her tired eyes. She took a deep breath and told herself it was only a dream. She tried to remember the details, but nothing came to her. All she knew was that she felt terrified, and as she reoriented herself to her surroundings, she realized that perhaps she was making a mistake going after the artifact. She put her friends in danger and could not live with herself if something happened to them, especially Binta. She wondered if her father was trying to communicate with her through her dreams again. She had not dreamed of him for a while, but those dreams had always been very vivid, and most importantly, she always remembered every detail of them.

She remembered Cedric's words before she drifted off and craned her neck to look behind her at the other couch he occupied. She only saw a mound of blankets and assumed that the old priest was under them, sound asleep. She looked to the floor and then at her three friends—well, two friends—and Cass. She stared at the sleeping girl, her former enemy, wondering why exactly she had come. Her actions seemed sincere, but it didn't make sense why she was there. Greyson had convinced her to let Cass go with them, and Cass did seem sorry for what she had done. Still, Cassandra knew she would have to keep an eye on her. Something was out of sorts. She felt for the necklace Cass had gifted her, and the touch of it made her relax a little. It was still there and evidently a true gift. That made Cassandra feel a little at ease.

Her attention turned to Greyson and Binta, who slept soundly by the fire, cuddled in each other's arms. A pang of jealousy coursed through her then, and she wished she could join them. She longed for the day the three of them would finally consummate their strange relationship.

She sighed and thought of her family. She grew weary of worrying about them, and she missed Kessi dearly. She wished she could have that simple life back that she once shared with her sister. Why had all of these troubles found her? Was that part of the prophecy also?

She lay back on the plush couch and tried to shake the curious thoughts from her mind, but they wandered, and soon she focused on the events of the night before. Greyson had molested her right before everyone, and she gladly let him. The thought made her tingle, and she bit her bottom lip. His touch had been electric, shooting bolts of energy through her body, and it had taken all of her willpower not to embrace him then and there, to allow him to take from her what was so precious. Her virginity had never been something she considered until she met him. She had never been interested in men, especially after growing close to Binta, but something about him made her want to experience her first sexual encounter. Cassandra knew that she and Greyson would be intimate soon enough, and her loins tingled with anticipation of that day. Finally, she closed her eyes and drifted back to sleep, this time with pleasant thoughts. For the rest of the night, her dreams centered on Greyson and his magical touch, which was most sensual.

Cass had awakened moments before Cassandra did, but when she saw her sit up on the couch and look around deliriously, she pretended to remain asleep. Cassandra had looked quite panicked, and it had taken her a long time to gain her bearings. Eventually, her gaze had fallen on Cass herself, and she had closed her eyes fully then and played the part of a sleeping companion. Then, when she heard no movement from the couch, she slowly cracked her eyes open and found Cassandra resting once more and drifting fast to sleep.

A smile formed on Cass's lips, and she thought about how easy it had been to gain Cassandra's trust. Fortunately, it had been almost too easy, and from the events that had occurred in Cassandra's room between her and Greyson, Cass knew that Greyson was the only reason she was there at that very moment. He held some power over the two idiots, Cassandra and Binta, strengthening her position within the group. She would have beaten Cassandra into submission for making her lick her boots if she hadn't realized that Greyson was behind that sick game. The memory of her beating Cassandra in the schoolyard made her chuckle, and she had to cover her mouth to muffle the sound.

She turned over and began to drift back to sleep. She could not believe her good fortune at being invited along on this adventure, and she couldn't wait to wield the powerful artifact if there was one waiting at the end of their journey. She especially couldn't wait to dominate Cassandra with it. Her dreams were delightful that night as she dreamed of the tortures she could exact on Cassandra. Her dreams were also pleasant when they morphed into how she could reward Greyson for manipulating Cassandra into letting her come.

The beast looked into her soul, and Kessi knew despair. The thing was powerful and pure evil. Whatever Matilda had summoned, it would be the death of her and probably all of them. The creature grabbed one side of its chain and began to twirl it lazily. The action caused bits of the flesh, hair, and other remains of previous victims to dislodge from it and fall at the creature's feet.

"Death is upon you, child. Now is the time to weep," the demoness whispered to her through a telepathic intrusion that shot through her brain.

"Vasheba, lord of torture and eater of souls, I welcome you to our world!" Matilda's powerful voice echoed off every inch of the large chamber. Her voice seemed amplified and powerful, and Kessi guessed it was due to the combined powers of the joining priests.

The demon stopped and turned her head toward the small woman seated directly behind the creature, just outside the giant pentagram. Matilda sat cross-legged and stared straight at the powerful demoness. She grasped hands with the priests next to her, and they, in turn, joined hands with the ones next to them, forming a chain around the perimeter of the pentagram. Matilda was the only one with her eyes open, and the power of the joined priests seemed to collect in her very being. She sat strong against the demon's gaze, knowing she could show no weakness.

The creature of darkness turned to face her summoner, and with a quick flick of her arm, she had the chain snapping right toward Matilda's face. To her credit, Matilda did not flinch, confident in her hold over the creature. The chain struck an invisible barrier at the edge of the pentagram, just a few feet from Matilda's face, and fell harmlessly away. The invisible wall held, but Matilda and the two priests beside her tightened their grasp. The other priests also felt the tremor, just not as amplified. All of them had expected the attack, so none were surprised. They did well to maintain their concentration, holding the demoness at bay.

"Foolish mortal! You dare summon me and believe you are powerful enough to hold me as a prisoner? I recall meeting you recently at the gates of hell, weakling, your soul slipping through my fingers. Do you so eagerly wish to see me again, fool?" Vasheba spat, drool falling to the stone floor as she spoke.

"No, most powerful ally, I do not hold you as a prisoner, but know that I do not fear you here," Matilda answered, recalling that near-death experience in Novafontera.

The demoness paced the perimeter of the pentagram then, studying the runes on the stone floor, looking for weaknesses in the markings and the priests themselves. The priests understood what the beast was doing and were confident they had adequately prepared for the summoning. So, when Vasheba suddenly lashed out at one of them, they knew the beast had found a weakness. The barrier held, but the attack disturbed a particular priest, and his concentration waned. A smile crept across Vasheba's lips.

"Vasheba, I command your attention!" Matilda yelled, her voice rising in strength as she pulled more energy from the combined power of the priests.

Vasheba marched back to where the woman sat and bent low so that her face was level with Matilda's. "You command?" the demoness asked.

"I command," Matilda replied calmly, matching the demon's unblinking stare.

"You are a fool, mortal. Be careful what you command of me."

"I command a deal from you, nothing more."

"You offer nothing that I could not obtain on my own, foolish woman," Vasheba spat and slowly began teasingly raking the invisible barrier with her claw, digging deep into the power that held her at bay.

"He is coming. I will be preparing the great summoning very soon. He will need generals for his army. I can make sure you are one of them," Matilda promised.

Vasheba stood straight then and looked curiously at the diminutive human, appearing interested in what she had to say. "What do you want in exchange for such empty promises?"

"The promise is not empty, oh great one. I will make sure you rule by our lord's side."

"You presume much, little one."

"Do we have a deal, or shall I send you back to hell?" Matilda asked, trying to sound confident in the face of such raw power.

Vasheba narrowed her eyes and said, "Proceed with caution, human."

"The woman within the pentagram is the child of Kane, the one chosen for the great sacrifice, so we believe."

The demoness turned to regard Kessi, who seemed quite pathetic at that point. Vasheba smiled as Kessi shivered with fear as a tiny animal might when facing a predator.

"You have doubts, though?" wise Vasheba asked.

"Our sources indicate that she is the offspring of Kane, but yes, I have doubts," Matilda confirmed.

"And if I tell you the truth of this wretched creature, you will uphold your pretentiousness and demand of he that I serve as a general?"

"You have my word," Matilda nodded.

"Your word means nothing. But yet, I am curious. This wretch cannot be the offspring of Kane," Vasheba said, pointing a long and crooked finger at Kessi. "She is far too pathetic for such a grand sacrifice."

Kessi swooned and nearly lost consciousness as the great beast approached her again. Her gaze bore through her soul, and she felt naked before the great demoness. Vasheba bent low so that her face was near hers, and Kessi could smell the stench of death, the smell of evil. She closed her eyes and prepared for the worst.

Vasheba grabbed her roughly by the throat and lifted her from the ground with one hand. Kessi's eyes popped open as she struggled to breathe. She kicked her feet with what little energy remained in her starved body. The creature tightened its grip enough that she would surely die. If she wanted to kill her, she would easily do so, and nothing would stop it. Instead, she reached out with her other hand and extended a finger to touch Kessi's forehead, just where the priests had drawn the pentagram. The touch burned at first, as if she were branding her. She tried to cry out, but the ever-tightening grip choked off her voice.

"Tell me your secrets, child," Vasheba's voice echoed through her head.

Kessi tried to fight the intrusion, but her effort was in vain as the demoness quickly pilfered her thoughts. At first, there was just white-hot pain, and her mind seemed like it would implode. But then, the creature was there, peeling away the memories and destroying any feeble barriers Kessi managed to put up in the hopes of blocking her out. As a result, Vasheba removed all of Heinsvick's brainwashing in just a few moments.

"Who are you? Are you truly the filthy spawn of Kane?" the demoness screeched.

Memories flew through her mind. She recalled Oldorburg, Ronnis, her mother, the wolves, the ravens, and Heinsvick! She was not Cassandra Rho; she was Kessi Rho! She tried to block those damning thoughts and hide them from the beast in her mind. She had to, for Cassandra's sake. Kessi was supposed to be the sacrifice, the one chance she had to save her sister.

"Liar!" the voice screeched.

Kessi knew no more as the mental intrusion became too much for her beleaguered mind to handle, and the lack of oxygen finally overtook her. She felt the creature releasing her just as she slipped into darkness. Before she faded away, she felt the beast devouring her true memories. Vasheba knew her secret; Vasheba knew everything.

The next day's journey was more profitable for Cassandra and her friends as the weather cooperated, warming the frozen snow, and giving the adventurers a reprieve from the arctic wind. On that day, they made good progress, and Cedric and Cassandra shared their magical boots so that the entire party enjoyed the comforts the footgear provided. In addition, sharing the magical boots allowed them to cover much more terrain than the day before.

As they stopped for a meal around midday and Cedric started a small fire to warm them, Greyson and Binta joined Cassandra on a fallen log. Cedric and Cass sat on the other side of the fire and similarly shared a seat. Cedric observed Cassandra interacting with her friends. Cassandra's conversation with Binta seemed genuine and natural. Still, every time she spoke with Greyson, she appeared to go into a dreamlike state, almost as if she were mesmerized by his every word. Her actions raised concerns for the old priest. He stole a glance Cass's way, and she seemed to be content eating her meal. She did not seem to be the least bit interested in her friends' conversation. He found that to be just as curious.

"Your friends seem very close," he said, which startled Cass a little, eliciting a small jump.

"Yes, almost sickeningly close, I would say," she responded with a nod, followed by a small bite of her food.

"And you are not as close to Cassandra?"

Cass stopped chewing and let her gaze fall on the three friends who seemed to share such an incredible bond. She eyed them many moments before responding, "No, I am Greyson's friend, but I know Cassandra from school. I just thought I would help."

"And you were licking her boots when I walked into her room before we began our journey," Cedric added.

Cass blushed at that, and he saw her glare at Cassandra for a moment. "Yes, it was all in fun."

"In fun?"

"Sure, like a pledge to follow her and assist her on her grand journey."

"Did the others do that?" Cedric asked curiously.

She became a little flustered and shook her head slightly, then took another small bite.

"Curious," Cedric said, rubbing his chin. Something was amiss with his travel companions; he was far too old not to see it plainly in their actions. Kane tasked Cedric with protecting Cassandra, and he vowed not to fail.

At about the same time the party of friends was sitting around the fire, an angry Franklin Ruben pounded on the tower of Lady Victoria. He could not find a door, so he marched around the building, trying to find one.

"Not even footprints in the snow to indicate where a door might even be?" he yelled, then stopped and pounded on the tower wall.

"Lady Victoria, let me in! I have business with you!"

He stepped back and shielded his eyes from the bright, midday sun, trying to find a window or any opening the magic structure might have. He found nothing and, with a growl of frustration, started for the school itself. He noticed some students were stopped, staring at him. He realized then that he was making quite the spectacle of himself.

He was about to say something in defense of his actions when he heard Victoria's voice from behind him. "Dear Mr. Ruben, whatever is the matter?"

He turned to find her standing at the tower's base in one of her fanciful robes, blue with red and orange arcane symbols printed on it. Her matching red hair spilled over her shoulders, and her bright blue eyes warned of the power she possessed. She also carried a carved staff that shared similar symbols. He immediately understood from her scowl that his high standing in the city meant little here. He was one of the wealthiest men in Pelesea, but he was simply a visitor on these grounds.

His cheeks flushed immediately, and he tried to apologize, "I—" he began, walking back toward the tower.

"Go to class, students. Everything is fine here," Victoria reassured the students before Franklin could get the words out.

He turned to see the group leave, feeling embarrassed by his actions. He turned back to Victoria, and a door appeared at the tower's base. He looked at it, confused, knowing there had not been a door there moments earlier.

"Well, Mr. Ruben? I haven't a lot of time," Victoria said with an outstretched arm toward the door.

"Yes, of course, my lady," he said and hurried in.

Inside, he found himself at the end of a great flight of stairs, with murals adorning the ceiling and walls. Sculptures of exotic, magical beasts lined the stairway, silently noting him as he passed. The two did not speak until Victoria escorted him to a small, comfortable room at the top of the steps.

Once inside the room, which contained only two chairs and a fireplace with a burning log, he regained his senses. The powerful wizard offered him a seat with an outstretched hand, and she sat in the other one, letting her great staff rest against the wall beside her.

"Now, what is the meaning of your most hysterical visit, Mr. Ruben?"

"Yes, I am sorry about that, but I have a very urgent matter to discuss with you," he said, pulling a rolled parchment from an inner pocket of his coat. "A letter penned by my Cass last night."

He unraveled it and read it, every word as Cass had written it:

Dear Father,

I have decided to go on an adventure of a lifetime! My new friends and I are to travel together and share in the spoils. I assure you that I am safe and do this to honor you. I am traveling with Cassandra Rho, and we will fix this mess we made at the school and prove to Lady Victoria that we are worth reinstating. I trust you understand my reasoning for leaving without saying goodbye, only because I knew you would not want me to go. I will make you proud, Father, and I will see you soon.

Love,
Cashmere

Then, with an edge again to his voice, he leaned over in his chair and said, "My Cass would not have voluntarily traveled with that Rho girl. I also investigated at the docks, and my girl was with the young priest, Greyson Kavince, who has been sniffing around my home more than I care to admit. I do not trust him or Cassandra Rho."

Victoria sat up in her chair, a concerned look on her face. "When did they leave, Mr. Ruben?"

"According to the priests at the temple, it was last night. But unfortunately, I only just found this note."

"They left at night? That is strange."

"Yes, and it makes me trust the situation even less. I fear not all is as it appears," Franklin said, distress in his voice.

Victoria sat back and closed her eyes, losing herself in deep thought. Why would the two girls suddenly work together, given their recent history? What did the young priest, Greyson, have to do with all of this? Who else went with them? Why did they leave at night? So many questions needed answering.

Franklin broke her thoughts by asking, "So, what do you intend to do?"

Victoria opened her eyes and looked at him with a frown. "Do?"

"Yes, magically. Surely you have a way to find their whereabouts. You tell me where they are, and I'll have my men bring them home."

"Mr. Ruben, magic is not that simple."

"What am I to do, let them go into the wilderness to be killed or to freeze to death? We must do something, Lady Victoria. I cannot lose my little girl," he said, nearing tears.

Victoria patted the air in front of her and nodded. "I know someone interested in Cassandra Rho and would gladly go to find her if I asked him."

"I care nothing for her! But, if this person is willing to find Cashmere, I am grateful," Franklin said.

"He will be willing to find both women, Greyson, and whomever else may have gone. Also, Daro the Keeper is currently here in the city. He is one of the best trackers in the area. I'm sure he will volunteer his time if he is not engaged in other matters."

"That is great news. What could be more important than finding my girl?"

"Girls, Mr. Ruben, and whoever else might be with them."

"Yes, yes, of course," Franklin said, standing and stuffing the scroll back into his pocket.

He walked briskly out of the room and toward the staircase before Victoria could even react. "Mr. Ruben, where are you going?" she called after him.

"To the castle to meet with this ranger fellow. Find the person you speak of and meet me at the castle gate as quickly as possible. Time is of the essence!" he called over his shoulder as he ran down the steps.

Victoria sighed and gave the command word to open the hidden door at the base of the stairs. She had a feeling that if she didn't do it in time, the excited man would crash through the wall. So, with another sigh, Victoria grabbed her staff and made her way down the stairs and to the school. Soon after, she found Baxter, the goal of her search, administering an exam to his students, and quickly beckoned him to the hallway.

"What is it, Victoria?" Baxter asked, coming immediately, wearing a concerned look.

"It's Cassandra, of course."

"What of her?" he asked, suddenly alarmed.

"She has left the city."

"What? Why? Where has she gone?" he asked rapidly, almost panicking.

"No one seems to know, but I have come to you because of your... shall we say, interest?" she answered, trying to find a sensitive way to address his feelings for the girl.

"What do you ask of me?"

"I want you to find her."

"Yes, yes, of course. I can leave within the hour, but what of my classes?"

"I will teach in your absence."

"That will work. Thank you," Baxter said and started toward his office.

"Baxter?" she called after him.

"Yes?" he asked, stopping, and turning back.

"I have more information for you."

His face turned red, and he nodded, returning to her, and trying to collect himself. He was out of sorts and seemed as if he were deep in thought, perhaps contemplating Cassandra's actions. Victoria interrupted his thoughts, calling to him, and her tone indicated she would not tolerate anything less than his full attention.

"Yes, I'm listening," he finally said.

"Good, because she could be in danger. I need you focused if you are going to do this, understand?"

"Yes, of course. Please, tell me what you know."

"No one knows where she went, but we know she left last night and was not alone."

"Who is with her?" he asked, with more than a hint of jealousy.

Victoria picked up on the inflection and just stared hard at him. He took a deep breath, and she waited for him to calm down. Finally, after a few moments, he nodded.

"Sorry. Do you know who was with Cassandra?" he asked, trying to remain focused.

"I believe she left with Cashmere Ruben, believe it or not. I also suspect Greyson Kavince."

"And Binta," he added.

"Why do you think that?" Victoria asked.

"Cassandra and Binta are always together, and Greyson is always with them. The women seem to be the best of friends. It makes sense that those three would be together, but Cashmere?"

"It doesn't make sense to me either; we must find them quickly."

"I'm on it," Baxter said and started to hurry off again, unable to contain his anxiety.

"Baxter, Cass's father, has asked you to meet him at the castle gates. He is talking to Daro and asking him to go with you."

"Good, good," Baxter answered with a wave of his hand, not even turning to acknowledge her.

"I left the carpet in your room. It will greatly assist you," Victoria called out just before he turned a corner.

Baxter stopped and turned to her and nodded solemnly. The mention of the carpet brought back memories of Cassandra when he rescued her from the temple of Oldorburg. Baxter had held her close on the flight home, not wanting her to fall in her dazed condition. He had entirely fallen in love with her on that flight. It was appropriate that Baxter might rescue her again with it. He shook the thoughts from his head and realized he had been standing there for quite some time. He glanced up at Victoria to find her arms crossed over her chest and shaking her head. He cursed under his breath and hastily made his way to his room.

Once there, it took him very little time to prepare. He had his spellbook, several wands, and all of his components ready quickly. He strapped the carpet to his back and made his way to the castle gate, where he promptly recognized Cass's father and the legendary Daro the Keeper, ranger of the woods. About half a dozen men had packs ready and bundled for the road.

"Mr. Ruben, Daro, and good men," Baxter greeted them with a nod.

"You are Victoria's emissary?" Franklin asked.

"Yes, I am Baxter Von Glord, an instructor at the school."

"Very good, Wizard; I have assembled some men to travel with you," he said and extended an arm toward the gathered men.

"I was just telling Mr. Ruben that we will not need these men, that they will only hamper our progress," Daro responded immediately.

"Look, that is my daughter out there, and I say the more men you have, the greater the chance of finding her," Franklin responded.

"No, they will only slow us down," Daro said, stubbornly shaking his head.

Franklin turned to Baxter and said, "Please talk some sense into the stubborn ranger!"

Baxter looked at Daro, who had a smirk, and understood that the ranger was correct. "Sorry, Mr. Ruben, but I agree with Daro; we will find her. But, unfortunately, though worthy and with good intentions, these men will only slow our progress."

Baxter held up a hand before the enraged man could respond and quickly removed the flying carpet from his back. He unrolled it and said the command word that had it levitating two feet off the ground. He crawled atop it and sat cross-legged, leaving room for one more person. "Good ranger, if you please, climb aboard, and we will be off," Baxter bade Daro.

Daro just stood staring at the wizard, but finally seemed to understand this was a way to get the pushy and slightly annoying Franklin Ruben off their backs. He climbed atop the carpet shakily and found his seat, looking over the edge uneasily.

Franklin walked up to the carpet and said, "I like the way you think, and my men are ready if you change your mind."

"Very well, Mr. Ruben. And now we are off," Baxter said.

Before they could move, Cass's father grabbed Baxter by his shoulder and said, "Find my daughter. I will reward you well if you bring her back to me."

"We plan on finding all of them and bringing them home," Daro added.

The big man only looked at the ranger sternly, showing no expression on his face, and whispered, "I care not for the others, and if they harm my daughter, I would advise you not to bring them back here, or they will deal with me."

"Very well, we are wasting time, so if you would please release me, we will begin our quest," Baxter interrupted.

"Find my daughter," Franklin said once more as he released his grip and stepped back.

Baxter willed the carpet to the front gate, where they met briefly with the guards who had witnessed the party leaving. They determined that the party was five strong from the guards' testimony, with one much older man leading them. Neither Baxter nor Daro could imagine who that person was, but Daro found the tracks quickly enough, the only set leading north. It took some convincing, but Baxter was able to talk the ranger into riding on the carpet, which he kept hovering about five feet above the ground. Daro could easily see the tracks at that height, allowing them to travel much faster than if they were walking.

Baxter only hoped that they could find the party before something horrible happened. Perhaps everyone was overreacting, and the five travelers were just fine, but the situation just seemed strange and out of character for Cassandra. He was deeply disappointed that she hadn't consulted with him first or at least told him goodbye. He tried to keep his personal feelings out of it and focus on the road ahead. He glanced back one last time to the shrinking gate of Pelesea, and the realization of the dangers out in the wilderness set in. He and Daro would need to find the party quickly; the longer the group was out in this weather, the less chance they had of finding them alive.

Vasheba turned from Kessi's limp form, a wicked smile upon her face, and hissed, "This fool is not of Kane's seed."

"What?" Matilda wanted to scream, but it came out as a whisper, knowing the creature spoke the truth.

"She is a decoy; the vampire has tricked you," Vasheba spat, followed by a deep and sinister laugh. "He has played you for a fool."

Matilda summoned all of her strength to control her rage. She knew Vasheba's tactics and knew that the beast was trying to distract her while looking for a weakness in the link of priests. Unfortunately, Matilda didn't have the power to hold the volatile creature much longer, so she moved on with her questioning just as the demon lashed out with her chain to smack the invisible barrier. It struck precisely at the same spot as before, right at the youngest priest, who waned with the initial strike. Matilda felt his resolve falter again, knowing she had little time left.

"Vasheba, who is the decoy? She passed our lie detection, so she must know much about the real Cassandra Rho."

The demoness growled and attacked the barrier again with several heavy strokes from her giant chain weapon. Matilda saw the young man's arms quiver, his eyes wide with fear.

"Hold the circle, do not break!" Matilda yelled, her voice booming over the crashing chain. "Who is the decoy, Vasheba, the Powerful? You must answer; you cannot deny me!"

Vasheba growled and paused her attack, compelled to follow Matilda's commands. "She is her sister," she spat.

"Sister? But you tell me she is not the child of Kane. How—?"

"Not by blood, but by word only," Vasheba interrupted.

"Then she knows where Cassandra is. Tell me, Great One, where is the real Cassandra Rho?" Matilda commanded, her voice becoming more powerful and commanding as she spoke.

The demon attacked the barrier with abandon, and the power of the circle began to give. Matilda knew that breaking the barrier would spell instant doom for them all. Vasheba was her tormentor and loathed her. She could not control the demon if she broke free of the pentagram.

"Answer me; I command it!" Matilda screamed, her voice reverberating throughout the large cavern.

Vasheba turned to her once more, a look of pure hate splayed across her face. The beast knew the answer, and as Matilda's captive in the pentagram, she had to comply. So, she hissed a reply in a low, gravelly growl, "Pelesea."

As soon as Vasheba answered, Matilda made the mistake of relaxing just a bit. She knew the great city and could reach it quickly. Even though Heinsvick had betrayed her, all was not lost. Her precious sacrifice was still within her grasp. Then, in her moment of delight, the demoness struck, summoning a ball of fire at the weakest link in the chain, the same spot she had attacked before.

The blast engulfed half of the pentagram and nearly caught Kessi in its destruction. She moaned, still unconscious and unaware of her surroundings, and her clothing smoldered. Matilda could not see the young priest, the attack's focal point, as the fireball licked at the barrier in front of him for several seconds. His name was Ralf, and he had been with them for less than five years, always good at his studies and rituals but never really radical enough to belong. She always thought that he would have made a fine worshipper of a more lawful demon or some other creature of darkness that would not require the power Marnelphion demanded of his followers. She knew it was a mistake to add him to the circle, and now she knew real fear as she felt his concentration collapse entirely.

"Vasheba, I dismiss you!" she commanded above the sound of the flames. "Hold the circle, just a bit longer," she pleaded with her fellow priests.

Vasheba roared in rage as her form began to smoke and become insubstantial, the pull of hell drawing the demon back home. Matilda was relieved to be sending the creature back, and as the flames dissipated, Vasheba did as well, pulled back into the darkness from which she had come. The smoldering clothes of the priests near the fireball attack showed Matilda just how close the creature had come to breaking the prison. The barrier had held, but the intensity of the fire had seeped through and blistered Ralf. The fool relaxed for a moment; that was all it took for Vasheba to strike. A whirling sound buzzed through the air, and the young priest jerked wildly, his eyes wide with shock.

He looked down at his chest in disbelief, a line of blood appearing across it from his right lower rib cage to his left armpit. Matilda could see the expression of pain and confusion on his face as he slowly looked at her, barely making eye contact before the top half of his body separated and fell to the ground.

Vasheba and the chain cleaving the young man in half became visible again, appearing at the edge of the pentagram. Matilda understood the farce quickly as Ralf fell in two. Vasheba was beyond her abilities and had faked her banishment back to hell. The demoness swung her wicked chain back in, decapitating the priest to Ralf's right. The priests scattered as a clawed foot stepped outside of the pentagram. Vasheba was free.

Baxter sat on the hovering carpet as Daro walked around the area, inspecting the various footprints they had stumbled across. The light of the day was running low, and the temperature was dropping. The ranger seemed puzzled, which made Baxter nervous.

"Is it them?" Baxter asked.

"Most likely; the prints match those of the party that the guards witnessed leaving the city," Daro answered, but knelt to get a better look at the tracks.

Baxter hopped off the carpet with a smile on his face. "Then let us command the carpet to greater speeds so we can catch them before nightfall.

"It's not that easy, my friend."

"Why not? We have time remaining in the day. You have found the prints. We can follow them quickly, and we will end this search. So where does the problem lie?" Baxter asked.

"First, the light is waning, and I cannot see the tracks clearly from up there," Daro said, pointing to the hovering carpet behind Baxter.

"I can make light, Daro," Baxter argued, and began casting a spell to bathe the area in bright light.

Daro grabbed his arm and pulled it down, disrupting the spell. Baxter looked at him, puzzled, but the ranger shook his head. Daro then moved to an outcropping of trees and began to unpack.

"What are you doing?" Baxter asked.

"Making camp."

"I do not understand Daro; I feel—"

"A new set of tracks has joined the first," Daro interrupted, unrolling his sleeping pack.

"What?" Baxter asked, an uneasy feeling overcoming him.

Daro stood and patted him on the shoulder. "It is all right, Wizard; it's probably nothing, but we have run out of daylight to find that answer. Tomorrow, we will start again."

Baxter scratched his head in confusion, looking around the crushed snow at the various prints. Unfortunately, he could make neither heads nor tails of any tracks or see any newly added ones. He had no choice but to trust the ranger.

"How many do you see?" Baxter asked.

"Two more," Daro answered, again attending the camp as the sun disappeared behind the trees, making it nearly impossible to see.

"Not human?" Baxter asked.

Daro turned to his traveling companion and shook his head. "Too small, and the footgear is primitive. Most likely goblins or goblinoid creatures, and if so, most likely hostile."

"How old are the tracks? Can you tell?"

"Yes, not more than a few hours."

Baxter's heart raced, and panic nearly overtook his thoughts. He needed to be calm for Cassandra's sake but hearing that she could be in danger made him nervous.

"Well, let us be on our way, then," he said, moving to the carpet once more.

He turned to see Daro unpacking some food from his backpack and shaking his head.

"No, we must camp," the ranger said.

"What? You just said that the new tracks are probably from hostile creatures," Baxter sputtered, not believing what he was hearing.

"It is too dangerous in the dark, especially with goblins about," Daro reasoned.

"Which is why we must find them!"

"No, my friend, we must camp here and start our search again in the morning."

"But I have light, I have my spells. We can find them, I know it!" Baxter pleaded.

"Trust me, this is my area of expertise. We cannot fly around on this thing at night, and we certainly can't have a light going, especially if goblins are in the area," Daro explained, then sat upon a rock and began eating some jerky.

Baxter knew he should trust the ranger, especially a member of the New Order, but he was worried about Cassandra. He could not let her die out there, not to goblins. A thought suddenly came to him. "How about I fly a little higher and just scout the area? I might be able to see them."

Daro stopped chewing his food and said, "Listen, my friend, if you fly off without light, you will never find me again in this darkness. Then we will have failed your friends due to your lack of patience."

"You are not building a fire, are you?" Baxter asked.

"Of course not; it would draw too much attention."

Baxter finally admitted defeat with a great sigh and commanded the carpet to land. He helped set up the camp the best he could, and luckily, he fit in the small tent with Daro because the temperature dropped considerably over the next few hours. Baxter was nervous and slept very little that long night. He recounted the various spells in his mind as he lay there. He had a bad feeling he would need them the next day.

Vasheba's primary objective would be her, Matilda knew. Then, with another swing of the heavy chain, Vasheba cut the arms off Leskin, a minor priest who was in the middle of casting a spell. The demoness then teleported away before his brain even registered what had happened.

The beast blinked out of existence and reappeared beside Matilda, dwarfing her. Visions of hell's door flashed in Matilda's brain then. Just months earlier, she had first met Vasheba, the great demoness, as Matilda's crumpled body failed her. The terror she felt then flooded back to her as the beast stood before her. She was foolish to think they could hold the mighty creature, and although she successfully gathered the desired information, the effort could cost her life.

Vasheba lashed out with her chain to capture the priestess, but Matilda saw the attack coming and held up her hand. Vasheba slowed, and the chain lost its velocity, striking the cave floor near her feet. Matilda did not flinch, only concentrated on her attacker, holding her perfectly still. Vasheba froze in place, a gift from Marnelphion, assuring Matilda that he still believed in her. Furiously, the demoness tried once more to teleport away, but Matilda negated the effort with but a thought. Vasheba was powerless against her, and Matilda's confidence grew.

"I still control you, even outside the pentagram, Vasheba. Marnelphion has given me this strength, the ability to control even the most powerful of demons. Now, I have no choice but to destroy you, to send you back to the bowels of hell, where you must stay while we conquer the world. You could have been his general; now you are nothing," Matilda said in a calm, cold voice.

Vasheba was still trying to come to terms with the turn of events when the vicious spear dug deep into her side. She had seen many centuries of war and destruction and had felt the most intense of pains, battling fellow demons to the death, but nothing bit at her like Cerus's spear. Matilda looked on gleefully, knowing the pain the spear inflicted, having witnessed it against Cerus's enemies many times.

His sudden appearance baffled Matilda, but she did not question her good fortune. Her guards had been instructed to summon him and he was asked to be close by, so she surmised the guards had alerted him when she lost control of the beast. Even powerful Vasheba was no match for Cerus the Grey, son of Gorl! Cerus's muscles corded as he plunged it deeper into Vasheba's flesh, making the beast howl in pain.

Cerus smiled as he roughly pulled the spear from her side and plunged it deep into her gut. Matilda could feel the life force of the beast waning as the hateful spear did its work. Nevertheless, Matilda concentrated on holding the powerful demoness while Cerus joyfully gutted her.

Vasheba caught Matilda off guard by entering her mind as quickly as she had Kessi's. The demon flashed images of the tortures that awaited Matilda in hell, while feelings of despair and horror accompanied them. Matilda's hold on Vasheba waned substantially at the sudden intrusion. She was vaguely aware of Cerus pulling his spear from Vasheba's gut and black blood splashing on the floor. A moment later, the great demoness was gone, and Cerus's next thrust hit nothing but air. He looked confused, trying to find the great beast, as Matilda collapsed on the floor. Vasheba managed to leave a parting thought in Matilda's mind, a threat that she knew the beast meant to carry out.

Matilda slowly regained her bearings, trying to shake away those awful images. Cerus stood guard over her, waiting for Vasheba to show herself again, his great spear dripping with the black ichor of the demoness. Matilda knew the creature to be gone but was more concerned with the threat she imparted before her exit.

It took her some time to regain her senses. She was still on her knees when she looked up at her husband, who now stood over her, offering a hand to help her. The other priests and some of Cerus's men also surrounded her. She shook Cerus's hand away and took a deep breath.

"What is it?" Cerus asked, bending down to look her in the eye.

"She plans on killing Cassandra. She has gone to Pelesea with the intent of killing the sacred offering and thus putting a stop to the Great Summoning," Matilda answered, fully panicked and unable to catch her breath.

The five weary travelers settled in front of the cozy fire once more. Greyson and Binta shared a bedroll, and Cass lay off to their side, tucked in her own. Cedric and Cassandra sat on the plush couches, sipping Cedric's home-brewed hot chocolate, just as they had the previous night. Cassandra felt very comfortable and a bit exhausted as she watched Greyson and Binta interact in their snug sleeping quarters. Cassandra could hear Greyson whisper something unintelligible, then Binta would giggle and whisper something back. As the previous night, a pang of jealousy ran through her, but she also had the notion of getting up and joining them. She longed to be between the lovers to enjoy them both. Her feelings of jealousy slowly dissipated, and that old feeling of lust replaced it. She had longed to be with Greyson and Binta for several days, and the world's craziness had prevented it repeatedly. There had been too many obstacles for them to have an opportunity. She recalled sleeping with Binta, both naked and very much aroused, but both had drifted off to sleep while waiting for Greyson to join them. She was growing impatient; she needed the sexual release, and soon.

She set her mug down and contemplated going over to her friends, biting her lower lip with lustful thoughts, when Cedric said, "A copper piece for your thoughts, Cassandra?"

"What?" she asked, turning toward him, and shaking the naughty thoughts from her head.

"You seemed deep in thought and were not listening to anything I was saying."

"Oh, sorry, Cedric, I do have a lot on my mind, I guess," she replied, trying to change the subject before he found the truth of her contemplations.

He looked over at her friends and nodded. "It is an unusual group we have here, wouldn't you say?"

"Yes, most unusual," she agreed.

A few moments passed between them before he blurted out something she did not expect. "You love her, don't you?"

"Excuse me?" she stammered.

"Binta, you cannot hide your feelings for her. Well, not from someone as old and wise as I am," he added with a chuckle.

"Well, yes, I do love her. She is my closest friend," Cassandra admitted.

"And Greyson?"

"What of him?"

"When did you first realize you were in love with him?" Cedric asked intently.

"What? I do not—" she began, but trailed off and did not complete the thought.

Her gaze shifted to the two lovers, who continued whispering and kissing. Greyson's back was to them, but she knew he enjoyed Binta, and she imagined his hands exploring her body as he had done to Cassandra while healing her wounds. She could not see what he was doing, but the way Binta was gasping and moaning spoke volumes. The jealousy crept back into her thoughts then. Did she want

Greyson? Or did she want him to leave her friend alone? She suddenly felt very confused by all of it.

"Cassandra?" Cedric asked.

"I don't know. I want Greyson, or at least I did at some point, but now I'm unsure. I don't love him, though."

"That is strange," Cedric added slyly.

"Why?" Cassandra asked, sensing that he knew something.

"Because, when he speaks to you, you look at him so lovingly, as you do with Binta. You hang on to his every word and trust his judgment. For instance, was it his idea to bring Cass, or was it yours?"

"It was mine—" Cassandra began, but stopped and shook her head. Her eyes widened, and she looked over at Cass's sleeping form. Her most hated enemy was amongst them. Why had she allowed it? It slowly dawned on her that Greyson had orchestrated that. The pledge, the licking of the boots—all of that was Greyson's doing. How could she not have seen that?

"It was Greyson's idea," she managed to squeak out, then slumped back against the couch. "He has played me for a fool," she whispered.

"No, my dear, I think other things are at work here," Cedric corrected.

"What do you mean?"

"I mean that you are showing classic symptoms of someone who has been charmed."

"What?" she asked, but before the words ever left her lips, she understood his reasoning to be correct.

Greyson had charmed her at some point! She thought back to the day in the sanctuary when she had first felt the strength of Gella when she had opened her heart to the goddess. It was after that revelation that she started liking Greyson and desiring him. She thought it was a sign from the goddess, but no, it had been Greyson.

"Oh, no," she whispered, sitting back up. "Do you think Binta is involved in the deception? Could she have known about the charm?" she asked.

"I highly doubt it, Cassandra. And I would not pass judgment on either of them yet. After all, we do not know for certain that you have been charmed," the old priest reasoned.

She slumped back once more, and tears welled in her eyes. Greyson and Binta seemed to be in the middle of making love, which suddenly repulsed her. She had a mind to take Greyson by the ear and throw him out in the cold. She wiped away a tear that ran down her cheek. Then she thought of Cass and how much she hated her for the beating she had suffered. She grabbed her holy symbol of Gella and closed her eyes, praying silently until the evil thoughts disappeared.

"Are you all right, my dear?" Cedric asked, seeing the tears streaming down her cheeks. "I do not think Greyson is your enemy; he only wanted to exploit you for his lustful gain. I also believe that Binta cares for you; I can see it. The next time Greyson touches you inappropriately, you will either melt in his hands or slap him. Then you will know if he has charmed you, and the same will happen with Binta's touch," he tried to explain.

Cassandra stared at the two, making love just a short distance away, their moans telling the story that her eyes could not see.

She was almost in a trance, her eyes unblinking and the tears still spilling, when she said, "Cedric?"

"Yes, dear?"

"Tell me of the prophecy. Tell me how this all ends. Am I going to die?"

Cedric sat up and thought a few moments before speaking. Cassandra knew that he had told her a lot that night in his room because Cedric needed to convince her that he was the prophet of Kane. But she knew he had left out the parts he didn't think she would want to hear.

"Your father's prophecy simply states that you are the key to bringing back the greatest evil this world has ever known," he eventually said.

Cassandra turned her head toward him, the tears still silently running down her face. "Continue."

"The very act of you finding Zolmex has begun the prophecy. You are to find it, and once you do, you will trigger the coming of the great demon lord. But your father will use you and the power of Zolmex to destroy the creature once more."

"Then what?"

"Then you will be the most powerful living person in the world."

"How is that possible if I am dead?"

"Only your father knows that answer, child," Cedric reasoned.

"Will my mother and sister be there with me afterward?" she asked, looking intently into his eyes, awaiting the answer she desperately needed to hear.

"I'm sorry, my dear, I do not know," he answered truthfully.

Cassandra let her gaze fall back on Greyson and Binta, and her heart broke. They were through with their lovemaking and now held each other as they drifted off to sleep. She knew then that there was no one she could trust, and that she would have to do this alone. She would find Zolmex, fulfill the prophecy, and once Marnelphion was banished, she would take the mantle of the most powerful human in the world. But then she would make them pay, all of them! Anyone who had crossed her or threatened her family would suffer the consequences. She closed her eyes, the weariness found her, and she drifted off to sleep.

Cassandra awoke from a terrible dream, sitting up and breathing hard. Her hair was matted to her face, and it took her a moment to orient herself. Everyone was asleep except for Binta, who lay beside her, her body pressed tightly against hers.

"Are you all right?" Binta whispered, opening her eyes.

Cedric's words flooded her, and her heart's pain flared again. She wanted to wrap herself up with her beautiful friend and stay in her arms forever. But if Binta had betrayed her, what was she to do? If Binta knew all along about Greyson's charm spell, could they still be friends? Her thoughts began to run wild, and her anger boiled, but then she remembered that there was no proof Greyson had done anything wrong, and she indeed loved Binta. She needed to give her a chance.

When Cassandra didn't answer, Binta sat up and turned Cassandra's face toward hers. "What is wrong? Do you not want me to lay with you? We haven't had a chance to be alone on this trip, and I just wanted to be with you, even if only for a short time."

Cassandra smiled and whispered, "I want nothing more. I need you to lay with me right now."

"Why? What has happened?" Binta asked, becoming very concerned.

Cassandra then noticed that her friend was nude, and her breasts were in full view. Cassandra looked at them, wanting nothing more than to ravish her friend's perfect body.

Binta smiled and asked, "Do you like what you see?"

Then she leaned in and kissed her lightly on the lips. Cassandra grabbed her head as she broke the kiss and pulled her back almost immediately. The two kissed passionately for several moments before Cassandra broke it off.

"Lay with me," Cassandra said, and they lay back down to face each other.

Cassandra played with Binta's hair as she ran her fingers up and down Cassandra's arm. Cassandra felt whole in that moment of bliss. There was no mistaking it. Her feelings for Binta were real, and the love she felt from her friend seemed genuine. There was no charm spell involved where the two of them were concerned. She only wished that she could have Binta all to herself. She didn't realize it then, but only a few short hours earlier, she had wanted to climb into bed with Greyson and had been more than willing to give him her virginity. Thanks to Cedric, the charm was failing.

Daro and Baxter started back on the road as soon as there was enough light for tracking. Neither had slept well, and both knew they had been very close to the group the previous night. The weather was cold, and the wind blew snow on and off as they began the search anew. It didn't take long before Daro wanted down from the carpet, noticing a change in the tracks. A quick inspection indicated that one of the goblinoid creatures had turned south, away from the group, but one still followed.

"What does it mean?" Baxter asked.

"I guess that the two creatures are scouts, and one went back to the clan to summon an attack group," Daro answered with a frown.

"Then we must hurry. I will command the carpet to a quicker pace if that is acceptable to you," Baxter urged.

Daro nodded and climbed back onto the carpet. They made rapid time, and Baxter occasionally climbed to a higher altitude to see if they could make visual contact with the party or a potential goblin war band. Baxter was intent on looking at the trail ahead of them, knowing they could see the group at any moment. His heart raced at the thought of it. What if Cassandra was dead? He realized at that crucial moment just how far in love he had fallen with the young woman.

"Wait! Go back," Daro suddenly yelled in his ear.

"What is it?" Baxter asked, turning the carpet around and lowering the altitude.

"I've lost the trail. Go back the way we came, and slowly, if you don't mind," Daro answered, his gaze on the ground.

They backtracked nearly a hundred yards before the ranger again picked up on the trail. Baxter willed the carpet to land, and the two stepped off. One didn't have to be a ranger to understand Daro's confusion at that moment as he bent low to examine the ground where all of the tracks, human and goblinoid, seemed to merge into one area, breaking the frozen snow in many places. Daro found the second set of goblin prints running south, just as the other one had done a few miles earlier, but the human footprints seemed to vanish at the same point.

"What does it mean?" Baxter asked nervously.

"I don't know; I have never seen anything like it," the ranger answered honestly.

"Perhaps a teleportation spell?" Baxter reasoned. "Perhaps the old man with them is more powerful than we realize, and he sensed the goblin following them and teleported them to safety?"

Daro just stood there with his arms crossed, looking at the various spots in the snow for many moments. Eventually, he answered Baxter, "Possibly. I think it is safe to say that magic is at work here."

"Now what?" Baxter asked.

"Well, a group of goblin hunters is not far from here. They have a stronghold where we can sit in front of a warm fire for a bit, with plenty of food to fill our bellies," Daro reasoned.

"And leave the trail?"

"Baxter, there is no more trail. Besides, these hunters know more about the terrain and the goblins than anyone. Their knowledge could be beneficial."

With a sigh, Baxter nodded his agreement and climbed aboard the carpet. Daro put a hand on his shoulder and said, "Fly high and to the east. The sun has almost fully crested the horizon now, and we may spot Cassandra and her friends on the way if they are still in the area."

The two made their way toward the stronghold of the goblin hunters. They had no idea, of course, that the party they were looking for was right beside them, tucked away safely in an extra-dimensional pocket.

Heinsvick was awakened from a profound sleep by the feeling of weightlessness. As he quickly came to, he realized he was hurling through the air and simultaneously ejected from his coffin, which crashed into the castle wall and splintered. He managed to brace himself just before the impact, the shock of which awakened all the injuries he had suffered at the hands of Matilda. The tears in his abdomen and left hand throbbed, and he nearly lost consciousness. He held up the stump where his left hand used to be, then looked around at the remains of his coffin; the healing dirt from his grave lay all around him and still poured from the broken casket, which leaned heavily against the wall. He knew he would not heal fully without the soil from his grave.

Before his mind could register what had just happened, a heavy chain hit him and wrapped around him, its barbs digging deep into his skin. He screamed out in pain as he was lifted several feet from the floor at the end of the nasty chain to be brought face to face with a hideous, demonic creature. He knew immediately that its power was beyond anything he had witnessed since Marnelphion had roamed the world nearly seven hundred years before. Perhaps the demon lord had once again arrived? How else could a creature this powerful inhabit the world? He thought of Kessi in that awful moment and what a terrible ending she must have already endured.

"Heinsvick, I presume?" it hissed at him.

He hadn't the strength to answer, so overwhelmed was he by the intense pain, and when he did not respond, the demoness shook him, making the chain dig deeper into his flesh. Finally, the severe pain made him answer in the form of a scream. The beast only smiled and brought him up close to her great maw.

"I am sparing your life only because I know you hate the little wretch known as Matilda. She keeps your pet in a cavern fortress on Varish, known as Nesin. So, I release you to exact your revenge."

"Emiline?" he managed to mumble.

With a growl, she jerked her arm, unraveling the great chain and hurling him to the floor, where he lay face down, the jolt of the impact making his body throb in pain once more. He tried to remain conscious as the beast moved to stand over him, dragging the nasty chain behind her.

"Get out!" she growled. "I am the new master of Novafontera. Do not return on pain of death."

He reached over and grabbed a handful of healing soil from his demolished coffin, then weakly stammered, "And my brides?"

He knew the answer even before the beast started to laugh. He shook his head, knowing they were already destroyed. He could not sense them; he could not call to them. He had failed them in his weakened state, and now his harem was gone, except Emiline. He heard the chain lift from the floor and knew the beast was gearing up for a deadly strike. He concentrated on a place he knew well and vanished before the strike could connect.

He teleported to the elven cellar that he and Kessi had shared not so long ago. It was full daylight outside, and it poured into the earthy cellar through various cracks in the trap door. He crawled to a dark corner and brought the handful of dirt to his face, breathing in its delicious aroma. He soon lost consciousness from the immense pain, and he knew as he faded out that he was defenseless if anyone happened by. The darkness called, and he succumbed to it, not caring if he ever woke again. Only the thought of reuniting with Emiline gave him the will to survive. If anyone found him in that cellar in his weakened state, he was surely doomed.

And that is how Vasheba, the demoness, became the new lord of Novafontera.

Chapter 7

The Quest for Zolmex

Kratoo, the goblin scout, had followed Cassandra and her travel companions for nearly a day before suddenly losing their trail. The goblin was trained well on the actions of humans and understood that many of them were magic-wielding weaklings. He thought that especially true with Cassandra and her friends because they were not heavily armed or armored and certainly didn't look like any warriors he had ever seen. He had served as a head scout of his clan ever since Gramous became their leader. Gramous was a very cranky but fair leader, an ogre of some renown in the area. He had taken over the clan's leadership when their old goblin patriarch, Buzpat, had been killed by the nasty goblin hunters who lived in the area. The filthy brothers that led those humans had beheaded poor Buzpat and continued to plague Kratoo's clan, hunting them and stinging them with their swords. All Kratoo knew was that Gramous would not be pleased to see that he had lost the trail.

He and Suzzy had found the prints a day earlier and made visual contact with the strange humans shortly after. Kratoo had sent Suzzy back to Gramous with word of the human prey who so brashly walked the land of goblins. Kratoo thought about running after Suzzy and killing him before he reached the caves of Gramous. That way, the volatile leader would never know about the humans and, more importantly, never find out that Kratoo had lost them. Even if he ran as fast as he could, there was no way to catch Suzzy now. He could maybe think of a good excuse and blame it on Suzzy, anyway. With the utterance of a few goblin curse words, he left the area, trying to think of a good way to blame his fellow goblin scout for their failings. He walked very close to the hidden cottage, never realizing that his prey was safely tucked inside.

Cassandra was the first to awaken that morning and found herself facing Binta's bare back, her arm wrapped around her friend. She snuggled her face into her hair and breathed deeply. Her scent was intoxicating and was just one of the many things she loved about her. Her moment of bliss was interrupted by Greyson as he rose, completely nude. She had never seen a naked man before and became more than curious. According to Binta, he was well endowed, and even though Cassandra's anger with him was great at that moment, she couldn't help but be curious.

He had his back to her, and from this angle, he looked in excellent shape. As she strained to get a look and, at the same time, act like she was sleeping, she realized he was murmuring to Cass. He was getting out of her bedroll, not his own! Had he slept with her during the night? Before the thought could register in Cassandra's groggy mind, he turned and walked to his bedroll, glancing Binta's way. Cassandra quickly closed her eyes, not wanting him to catch her looking him over, but not before she got a good look at his manhood. She had mixed feelings about Greyson Kavince at that moment, and she couldn't tell if it was from the remnants of the charm or her genuine curiosity. Either way, she couldn't help the lustful thoughts filling her mind again at that moment.

As Greyson nonchalantly slipped back into his bedroll, Cassandra snuggled Binta, burying her face in a tangle of hair. Cassandra drifted on and off again for the next little while, until Cedric finally awoke and made breakfast. Binta awakened at the sound of the old priest milling about. With a smile at Cassandra and a quick peck on her cheek, Binta stealthily made her way back to Greyson's bedroll while Cedric rummaged through his food supplies.

Soon after breakfast, they set out on the road once more. The going was slow because there was no longer a path to follow, and the group of travelers had to stop occasionally for Cedric to get his bearings. The terrain was steep in some parts, and the snow hid many slippery rocks or tangles of brush, making the going even slower than normal. Some parts were so treacherous that the party had to backtrack at several points to find another way around. They grew wearier as the day went on, and they all felt restless at their lack of progress. None of them, including Cedric, had much adventuring experience and the difficult travel conditions began to wear on them.

On one occasion, as Cedric stared into the woods, a finger tapping against pursed lips, trying to gain his bearings, Cassandra approached him. "Do you remember the way?" she asked.

He jumped slightly and laughed, "I am old, my dear, and have not been this way for several decades. It will come to me; Kane will show me the way."

They sat there for a few moments, the wind howling through the trees. Then, finally, Cedric must have sensed her unrest and said, "Do you doubt me, child?"

"No, of course not. I have followed you faithfully because I believe you are here to help me."

"And, right you are, young lady, right, you are," he said with a cackle. "Ah, yes, it is this way!" he added, pointing to the east.

As the group started to move again, Cassandra decided to ask him something that had been on her mind since they started the trip, "How did you know, Cedric?"

"To go east? That is easy. The terrain slopes upward, and that is how we need to go."

"No, not that," she interrupted. "How did you know I was the daughter of Kane? How did you know I was even in the city?"

"Because of this, child," he smiled, fished around in his robe, and finally pulled out an amulet with a large topaz in a setting of silver.

The stone was about two inches in diameter and attached to a necklace of shining silver. It sparkled in the sun and appeared to be valuable. "It is beautiful," she exclaimed. "What is it?"

"It is another gift from your all-knowing father," he answered, handing it to her to study.

"What does it do?" she asked after looking it over for a few moments.

"It tells me where you are, child."

"What?"

"It is a mighty item that he created the night you were born. It connects to your life force, and as long as you are alive, it will give a sense to the wearer of your location," he explained.

"I don't sense anything," she said, handing it back.

He laughed and tucked it away. "Of course you don't, but I had worn it all those years, so I knew when you entered the city a few months ago."

"So, why did you wait? I mean, if you knew I was in Oldorburg, why did you not come and find me? I mean, why act like some strange hermit down in the dungeon of a building for all these years?"

He turned to her with a solemn look in his eyes and said, "Because he told me you would come to me when the time was right."

"The prophecy?" she asked doubtfully.

"Exactly."

The two marched on in silence after that, Cassandra deep in thought. Not too far behind them, Cass, having listened intently to the conversation, took a great interest in remembering into which pocket Cedric tucked the amulet.

As the party continued their expedition, Baxter and Daro found the stronghold home of the goblin hunters a few miles to the southeast. The main building looked like a small castle, with a fortified wall surrounding the other structures. Those structures included one building slightly smaller than the castle, several smaller buildings, and a large stable that housed hundreds of horses. The eastern side of the wall had the only visible gate, and beyond that, the area opened up into wilderness as far as the eye could see. The road stopped at the stronghold and did not continue into the rolling hills, which seemed to be nothing more than untamed land.

"Welcome to Godhomme, the stronghold of the goblin fighters," Daro said. "Do keep a safe distance from the wall; those boys know how to use their bows and probably wouldn't look too kindly to us flying very close to them."

Baxter set the carpet down about fifty yards away from the gate so the guards could quickly identify them. As he collected the magical rug, he looked out into the open hills that seemed to stretch forever to the east. The rising sun made for a fantastic scene as the snow-covered land sparkled with the sun's reflection.

"Magnificent!" he exclaimed, holding his hand over his eyes to block the blinding sun.

"Looks can be deceiving, my friend; that is goblin country, a perilous place," Daro warned.

"The party was only a few miles away from this when they disappeared," Baxter said with more nervousness.

Daro could only nod his agreement, then he put his arm around Baxter's shoulders and turned him toward the wall. "That is why we must find Gabriel and see if Godhomme can provide any information. Time is of the essence."

"Gabriel?"

"Yes, he and his brother, Adam, run this place and know all goings-on in this wild land. If anyone has seen Cassandra or can find them, it is them," Daro explained.

Once they approached the gate, the guards eagerly welcomed them inside, as all of Godhomme knew who Daro the Keeper was. Then, several men escorted them to Gabriel's chambers, where he and Daro shared a hug.

"Daro the Keeper, how long has it been since you have honored us with your presence?" Gabriel asked cheerily.

"Now, Gabe, you know I have duties to the south, with my woods and the New Order," the ranger replied.

"I wish you'd reconsider moving to Godhomme; we could use you here. Unfortunately, the nasty goblins multiply faster than rabbits!"

"Maybe one day, my friend," Daro answered.

Gabriel clapped him on the shoulder and looked over at Baxter. "And who is this? Not a fellow ranger would be my guess?"

"I am Baxter of Pelesea, High Wizard of Victoria's School of Magic," Baxter answered, extending his hand.

Gabriel clasped it in a firm shake and a warm smile. "Glad you are both here. Please join Adam and me as we are about to partake in breakfast. You can tell us why you have come out to goblin country as we all share a meal."

Gabriel was a tall and slender young man with a neatly trimmed beard, which seemed to shine from the tonic he used. He was handsome, and Baxter did not doubt that he could wield a weapon if he knew Daro. His brother, Adam, was equally handsome and just as tall, but clean-shaven and quieter than his brother. Baxter found them both charming, and all four ate their share of the fine food.

During their meal, Baxter learned that the two brothers lost their parents early in life as a goblin raiding party had killed their family. They had rebuilt their home, which still stood as the centerpiece of Godhomme, and as word got out of the raid, more and more people came to help fight the goblins. Some came with weapons; others came with money, enough to build the stronghold. It had grown over the fifteen years since their parents' murders. They were not the rulers of Godhomme, but everyone living there relied upon the brothers to make critical decisions.

After the meal, Gabriel leaned back in his chair and lit a pipe. "Now that you know a little about us, Baxter, tell us, why has Daro dragged you over to our part of the world?"

Baxter looked at Daro for guidance, and the ranger nodded for him to proceed. So, he said, "We are tracking friends."

"Hope they are not goblins; we may have killed them by accident," Adam chided in.

The brothers shared a hearty laugh. When they realized Baxter didn't join in, they sobered up quickly. Gabriel cleared his throat and said, "Please continue."

"We lost their tracks a little way north of here and wanted to know if you have seen them or their tracks," Daro answered.

"How many days since they have passed here?" Gabriel asked.

"Less than a day ago. As I said, their tracks suddenly stopped. They were not traveling southeast to reach Godhomme but were going northeast, so they may not have come anywhere near your grand home," Daro answered.

"That is most peculiar. I can tell you this; we have not seen humans out in the wilderness for many months," Gabriel confirmed.

"When was the last time you went out?" Baxter asked nervously.

Both brothers shared a smile and a knowing look. "We go out every day. We are going out soon if you care to come," Adam answered.

Baxter looked at Daro, who nodded and said, "We do not wish to be a burden, but perhaps we can come with you just to see if we can spot them."

"Great!" Gabriel exclaimed, smacking his hands together.

"When do we leave?" Baxter asked.

"How about now, dear wizard?" Gabriel answered as he stood and patted him on the shoulder. "Meet us at the stables within the hour so we can pick some excellent steeds for you."

Shortly after, around mid-morning, a small group consisting of Daro, Baxter, Gabriel, Adam, and four other men left the safety of Godhomme and headed east into the wilderness. Baxter had refused a steed, electing to use the carpet instead. The others rode magnificent horses, spectacular enough to match the ones used by the cavaliers of Pelesea. Gabriel and Adam wore light leather armor, similar to Daro's. The other four wore polished plate mail. Baxter noted that the brothers from Godhomme also had giant bows strapped to their backs. Baxter flanked them and flew about twenty feet above the ground, keeping a sharp eye out for Cassandra. He knew she was out there somewhere and could be in serious trouble. Time was of the essence.

Kratoo knelt in front of Gramous's giant stone seat, his head down. Gramous stared hatefully at him, and he could feel those eyes burning through the back of his head. Kratoo tried to calm his nerves, but with little success. He knew that his life might be forfeit after bringing the bad news to the volatile leader, but he also knew that Gramous was reasonable for an ogre. He was deep in thought, still trying to conjure a lie about Suzzy, when he saw the giant foot coming at his face. He partially blocked the kick, throwing an arm up at the last moment but the impact still launched him across the cave room and against the far wall.

"You let them escape?" Gramous roared but, to his credit, remained seated.

"No, no, never!" Kratoo began, trying to regain his bearings.

"You just admitted it. So why you speak in riddles?" Gramous roared.

"They used dark magic to hide themselves. It wasn't me fault!" Kratoo pleaded.

Gramous stood from his throne and grabbed his spiked club that rested against it. The ogre was almost ten feet tall, with bright yellow skin and matching yellow eyes. What little hair he still had on his head was a pale greenish color. When he grabbed his mighty weapon, that usually meant at least one goblin was about to die. And as he stood, the gathering of goblins in the room, which consisted of the generals, shamans, and other high-ranking members of the tribe, all took several steps away from Kratoo, knowing what was about to happen.

"You lost the trail of humans and cost us five slaves," Gramous roared, holding up three long, crooked fingers.

"No, no, I... I... " Kratoo groveled, backing as far into the cave corner as he could.

"You have failed me, Kratoo. You have failed us all!" the leader said, waving his arm toward the other goblins, who stupidly nodded their agreement.

Gramous hoisted the spiked club onto his shoulder; its length was at least six feet long and nearly twice the height of Kratoo.

"Have mercy on Kratoo! I beg you!" he pleaded.

The giant ogre grabbed his weapon in both hands and began to stride across the cave, gaining speed as he went.

"No, please, Kratoo, sorry!" he continued to plead.

There was no stopping the ogre, and Kratoo just closed his eyes. Perhaps it wouldn't hurt too bad. He braced for the impact, but then a thought popped into his head, something he had forgotten, which goblins tended to do from time to time.

He yelled the thought out as fast as his mouth would let him, "Kratoo knows where they go!" he cried, then quickly closed his eyes again.

The killing blow never came, and after a few moments, Kratoo dared to open one eye. Instead, he found Gramous standing right in front of him, his club held over his head, ready for a devastating blow. His muscles tensed and he grimaced, wanting nothing more than to finish the swing and kill him. But, somehow, he held that swing.

Kratoo's eyes widened, and he realized he had hope, and blurted out, "Kratoo, take Gramous there. Yes, right away!"

Gramous growled and relaxed his grip. He knelt, so his face was even with Kratoo's and said through clenched teeth, "It hard for Gramous to not crush goblin skull once club is swinged."

Kratoo looked around nervously and pointed to the first goblin he saw. "Kill Stinkus."

Gramous glanced to where Kratoo was pointing and saw poor Stinkus standing there, picking his nose. All the other goblins nodded eagerly and took several steps away from Stinkus, who just stood there with his finger lodged in his nostril and his mouth hanging open stupidly. Goblins were neither overly intelligent nor faithful to their kind, so Kratoo deflected the leader's ire toward Stinkus, who was daydreaming of nothing in particular at that moment, thinking only of what he could dig out of his clogged nostril. The last time it was a worm, which he decided to eat, and it was tasty. Perhaps this time, it would be something just as juicy! He eventually noticed the other goblins slinking away, which is when he first registered something was amiss. Gramous saw red, and soon after, poor Stinkus's brains decorated the cave wall. A goblin war party, fifty strong, exited the caves not long after that, including Gramous and led by Kratoo.

The goblin scout would not fail his leader a second time; he knew the consequences of doing so. He kept repeating the location in his head that he had heard the nasty humans discussing: a cemetery. Kratoo's mastery of the human tongue had a lot to be desired, and he could not recall if a cemetery meant a place where human priests worshipped their weakling gods or if it was a burial ground. He guessed the latter and knew of one burial ground not too far away that humans had used in the past. The rumors hinted that it was haunted, but that mattered little to the goblin scout. He needed to please Gramous, and he meant to do it.

The questing party stopped for a meal late that afternoon, weary from their travels and battered by the wind, making the conditions nearly unbearable.

"Can we not summon the cottage, Cedric?" Cassandra asked.

"No, my child, we mustn't tax the magical device. We may only use it once per night, and even then, we are stretching its limitations."

"But I am so cold out here," Cassandra pleaded, pulling the collar of her coat tight around her neck.

"Take these, Cassandra," Greyson offered, unlacing the boots. "I have some spells that will help me for a bit."

Cassandra did not argue the point, nodding and quickly scoffing down the last bite of her meal so she could untie her boots. She watched as he unlaced and handed her the footgear, replacing them with his own ordinary ones. Cassandra thought of his naked image from that morning, and she couldn't help being intrigued. Then her thoughts dwelled on the idea of him and Cass, and her anger dominated her emotions; she hated him for treating Binta that way. She would never treat her like that. He did not deserve her.

"Yeah, it's my turn as well," Cass pipped in, pointing to Binta's boots and breaking Cassandra's thoughts.

Binta gave her a fake smile and began to unlace her magical boots as Cass came over to sit beside her. Cassandra took the magical footgear and moved to sit beside Cedric, hoping to cool her anger with Greyson by moving away from him. Cass took the opportunity to let Binta know what had transpired the night before.

"I noticed you slept with Cassandra last night," she whispered.

"What?" Binta asked, startled by her forwardness.

"I guess she is your girlfriend, after all. I mean, Jabell used to joke about the two of you being lesbians, but I guess I never thought it was true until I witnessed it for myself," Cass continued.

"What does this have to do with these boots?" Binta asked.

"Nothing, of course," Cass agreed with an innocent smile.

As Binta gave her the boots and started putting her own back on, Cass could tell she had hit a nerve. The girl's face was red, and she refused to make eye contact. Cass honestly couldn't figure out what kind of relationship Binta and Cassandra had, or Greyson and Cassandra, for that matter. All she knew was that Greyson was an expert lover, and as she pulled the boots on and laced them up, she made sure to mention it to Binta.

"All I know is that Greyson must have been cold last night because he came to me for warmth while the two of you were cuddling," Binta said, lacing the boots.

Binta turned to look at her, and Cass could see the anger in her eyes. It was then that she realized just how similar Cassandra and Binta were. Words easily manipulated them, and Cass was an expert at using them. That was very convenient, she decided then.

"It is Greyson's calling to make love to as many women as possible," Binta reasoned through gritted teeth. "We have an understanding that he may sleep with other women because of his faith. I am also allowed to spend time with Cassandra as I please."

"Is that what he told you?" Cass interrupted. "He told you his faith calls for him to be unfaithful? You're more foolish than I thought," Cass said, standing up.

"What do you mean?" Binta asked, standing up as well.

"I have read about the tenants of Plath, and I assure you they say nothing of making love to as many women as possible."

Binta had nothing to say in response to that, and it appeared to Cass as if someone had smacked the poor girl right in the face. Cass smiled, knowing she had just won that verbal battle. But she needed to add one more barb to feel good about it, so she continued as she walked away, "I hope you and your girlfriend snuggle again tonight, so perhaps Greyson can pleasure me once more. He is a most excellent lover."

Binta could not respond and only stood there staring at her as she walked past Greyson, playfully ruffling his hair as she did so. Cass made eye contact with Binta as she did that, then looked at Greyson with a lewd smile, who returned the look. Cass could feel Greyson stare at her as she walked toward Cedric, and she swayed her hips even more than usual to hold his attention as long as possible.

Now very unnerved at the thought of Cass traveling with them, Cassandra just watched the spectacle for a moment and wondered how she could ever have agreed to let Cass tag along. She also wondered how she even considered sleeping with the fool, Greyson. She knew the answer, of course; Cedric had pointed it out for her. Greyson had charmed her, compromising her most important mission. She watched as Greyson quickly fell into Cass's trap, which made her sick to her stomach, especially when she saw the look of hurt on Binta's face. She got up and went to her friend to provide whatever comforting words she could.

When Greyson completed his ogling of Cass's backside and turned to Binta, Cassandra made sure he understood her true feelings. She gave him the most hateful look she could muster, and for Cassandra, that would make most people wilt. Of course, Greyson pretended not to notice and just laced his boots. She knew he had seen her expression, and she knew a conversation would soon follow. It was time for her to take control of this adventure and clean house.

Kessi awakened with her head throbbing. Luckily, there was very little light in the room, and she could squint enough to observe her surroundings. She had difficulty remembering where she was or the events that had gotten her there. Her mind was a whirlwind of confused thoughts, and her surroundings did not look familiar. She was lying in a pile of straw, and her clothes were new to her; a simple dress made of a thin, very transparent white material. She realized then that she was actually in some natural cave-turned-jail cell. A stone wall was a few dozen feet to her left, and a set of iron bars immediately to her right. Beyond the bars was a larger room where several braziers burned brightly enough to shed some light into her cell.

She struggled to prop herself up to her elbows and view the room beyond the bars. It was larger and also seemed to be a cell because the bars from Kessi's cell formed its back. She noticed that her cell had a door leading to the larger enclosure and a similar door on the far side of that one led to a hallway. Only one thing was in that giant cell, a coffin. Kessi tried to shake the cobwebs from her head, and that movement created a sharp pain, and she let out a soft groan, raising a hand to her temple and lying back down.

"Here, drink this," came a soothing female voice from her left.

She jumped as she did not realize someone else was in the cell with her. She turned her head to regard the source and found another young woman about her age dressed in a similar white dress. She offered a small cup to her.

"It is only water. Drink it; it will counteract whatever poison Matilda has given you."

"Who?" Kessi managed to whisper.

"Matilda and Cerus, of course. Do you not remember?" the woman asked curiously.

"No," Kessi whispered and reached meekly for the cup.

The woman helped her by gently cradling her head and holding the cup for her as she drank. At first, Kessi wanted to gulp it down, but she wouldn't let her and pulled the cup back.

"Slowly, or you will get sick," she warned.

After Kessi had drunk her fill, she rested her head on the soft straw and looked around the cell for the first time. She realized behind the young woman stood another five, all female, young and dressed in similar white gowns.

"Who are you?" Kessi whispered.

"I am Sabrina, and these are the other virgins," she answered with a smile and a thumb pointing over her shoulder toward the others.

"Where am I?"

Sabrina laughed gently and said, "I can explain it to you once you have recovered. You should sleep now; that is the best medicine for your condition."

Kessi didn't argue with the wise words and let herself drift off into a deep sleep once more, already comfortable doing so, surrounded by her new cellmates.

Kratoo stood at the tree line, looking out over the rolling hills. It was still morning, and the sun shone brightly on the frozen snow, hurting his eyes. He and his tribe preferred the darkness of night or a deep cave. But he had to quickly find the human party he had lost, so daylight was a necessity for now. Unfortunately, Gramous was not a patient leader. Kratoo was squinting into the painful sunlit hills, watching a human band ride by on horseback, when Gramous walked up behind him.

"Why we stop?" the ogre growled.

"Because of the pointy sticks," Kratoo answered, pointing at the men on horseback.

"I am not afraid of pointy sticks!" The ogre said, taking up his spiked club and beginning to break the tree line.

"Wait!" Kratoo pleaded.

Gramous looked at him, gnashed his teeth, and said, "Why should I?" threateningly.

Kratoo gulped and pointed to the sky, "Because they has a skeeter."

Gramous followed the direction of Kratoo's shaking finger to see another human riding around the sky on a wool blanket. He scratched his head, uncertain of what he was witnessing, so he just played along with the goblin's assessment of the strange creature. "A skeeter, huh?"

"Yup," Kratoo answered with multiple nods of his head. "Also, not the weakling group we seek; they not go that way. They not powerful," he continued.

Gramous finally nodded his approval, and the party of goblins waited until the humans had passed. Once out of sight, they broke the tree line and made haste across the open hills. Kratoo breathed a sigh of relief, knowing that was not the party he was tracking. That party was much more dangerous because of their metal shirts, long pointy metal sticks, and a skeeter. Those humans were better left alone!

Baxter, Daro, and the men from Godhomme passed by Gramous and his goblin party without noticing them, and by midday, they arrived at a giant lake. They had seen no sign of goblin or human tracks on their ride. Daro had spotted a few massive tracks to the north, and Gabriel explained that giants and their kin were not uncommon in the area. Intent on finding the party from Pelesea, the group gave up tracking the giants and instead made their way to Lake Elfkind. There they stood, marveling at the giant lake, which spanned nearly one hundred miles north to south and almost fifty miles east to west at its widest point.

"If they crossed the lake, the elves would know it," Adam told Daro as Gabriel spoke with the elves at the small, fortified docking and ferrying station they controlled.

"The lake is massive; I could not see the start or the end, even at a high altitude," Baxter agreed.

"There is no way they could have crossed here unless they did teleport away," Daro reasoned.

"Aye," Adam agreed, "But that means they could be anywhere in the world."

"But why would they have traveled by foot for several days, then have teleported away? Why not just teleport to where they were going in the first place?" Baxter asked.

Daro shook his head, just as puzzled as the rest. Then, finally, Gabriel returned and said, "The elves have seen no one for months, and no humans have passed nearby, or they would have known about it."

"That leaves two possibilities, assuming there is no teleportation at work here," Adam reasoned. "Either they are to the north in the thickly wooded and stony mountains or the south in the thickly populated goblin woods."

Daro and Baxter shared a concerned look, and Baxter said, "We should go back to where you lost the trail. Maybe there are clues there that you missed before."

"That is as good a plan as any," Daro agreed.

"Very well, let's make haste back toward Godhomme, then we will backtrack to where you lost them. We have many good trackers; perhaps one of them will find a clue if the great ranger from the south does not!" Gabriel said, slapping Daro on the shoulder with a laugh.

Soon the party was heading back the way it had come, all feeling uneasy at the prospect of not finding the lost party. The goblin hunters from Godhomme didn't say it, but they knew this was no country for inexperienced adventures to be wandering.

Late that afternoon, they found the goblin tracks leading from the southern tree line to the mountains to the north. Daro and Gabriel studied the tracks intently as Baxter flew high, trying to visualize the large group. Unfortunately, he had no such luck with the thick canopy that the woods offered on the northern slopes, so he landed the carpet beside Daro as the ranger and Gabriel discussed the tracks.

"There is at least one giant with them. Perhaps not a true giant, but something much bigger than a goblin," Daro was explaining.

"Most likely an ogre; the southern woods are thick with them," Gabriel reasoned.

"How many goblins?" Baxter asked.

"More than twenty, less than one hundred," Daro guessed.

"Sounds like we have a decision to make, gentlemen," Adam

chimed in. "Do we proceed back to where you lost the tracks or follow these prints, which we know are fresh?"

"It is a tough decision, but one we must make quickly," Gabriel replied. "On the one hand, these tracks may have nothing to offer us other than the thrill of slaughtering goblins. On the other hand, we know there were two goblin scouts following your friends. These tracks could easily belong to the assembled party responding to those scouts."

"Yes, but you are giving credit to stupid goblins. They are heading into the mountains as if they know exactly where they are going," Adam added.

"Which means this may be a stray party that has absolutely nothing to do with your friends," Gabriel said. "The choice is for you and Baxter to decide," he added, patting Daro on the shoulder.

"Baxter?" Daro asked, turning toward the mage.

The men from Godhomme turned to regard him, understanding that he had a deeper purpose in this, which Daro had explained to them. It did not take Baxter long to make a decision.

"We follow these tracks," he stated flatly.

"Are you sure? To do so may be a waste of valuable time," Daro asked.

"Yes, I am sure. We lost the tracks of Cassandra and the others north of Godhomme, so it stands to reason that they are on the northern side, if they are in the woods at all. There are probably few to no clues at the site you lost the tracks, and as you said, time is of the essence. It is too coincidental that a large goblin party has set out to the north."

"Goblins are common here, my new friend," Gabriel reasoned. "This very well may have nothing to do with your friends."

"Understood. Either way, we will make the area safer by eliminating the goblin party, correct?"

A smile crept across Gabriel's face. "I like the way you think, Wizard! We chase the goblins, then," he said to his men.

There was a great cheer from the six men from Godhomme. They were more than willing to kill a few goblins, having dedicated their lives to just such a thing. But, as the cheering settled down, Gabriel had to deliver the bad news that not all of them would make the trip.

"Travis, you and Leonard take the horses back to Godhomme. Bring them back to this spot in two days, so we may return home with our goblin head trophies and hopefully with the missing party."

Gabriel's nonchalant words were followed by more cheering as the men dismounted, and Travis and Leonard began tethering the now riderless horses together for the trip home.

"So, you will have no use for your most wonderful carpet in these woods, Baxter," Gabriel explained.

Baxter nodded and began rolling the carpet up nice and tight so he could strap it to his back. Daro knelt to help and said, "Do not worry; we will find them."

Baxter stopped his rolling and looked into the ranger's eyes. The confidence he found there took some of the worries from his mind, and he smiled back at his new companion and completed his task with renewed vigor. Finally, he agreed they would find Cassandra and the others, and the gods help anyone who stood in their way.

The party was tired and discouraged as they entered the enchanted cottage for the third night of their journey. They had made little progress that day, with Cedric taking longer than usual to guess which was the correct way without a clear path to follow. They had even backtracked several times and felt like most of the day was spent going in circles. Besides that, they climbed higher altitudes, and the wind was blowing harder and colder than the previous two days. As the four friends stripped out of their heavy coats and boots and sat in front of the always-burning fire, Cedric sat at a small table, examining Cassandra's map.

"He is lost, and now, so are we," Cass whispered.

"No," Cassandra answered immediately, shaking her head, and looking over at the old priest. "His road is true, and his god will not let us become lost."

"You mean your father?" Cass asked sarcastically.

"Yes, exactly," Cassandra snapped back with more than a bit of anger in her voice.

"Ladies, we are in good hands, I am certain," Greyson interrupted while working the stiffness out of his bad shoulder.

Cass looked at him and smiled, her demeanor instantly softening. "Very well, lover, I will put my trust in the old man. We are in this together, and I support Cassandra's decision to follow him."

Greyson nodded as Cass got up and moved to set up her bedroll. Greyson glanced immediately at Binta, who looked more than a little angry. "What? You know my duties to Plath, my dear," Greyson said with a disarming smile.

"I know, but with her?" Binta hissed.

"Well, I would prefer this one join our bedroll tonight; that would bring us all great pleasure," he said, putting a hand on Cassandra's leg.

"No thanks," Cassandra said matter-of-factly and picked up his hand and moved it off her as if she were removing a piece of garbage.

"What is it, Cassandra?" Greyson asked, truly confused by the sudden change in her behavior.

"I am no longer interested," she answered, then got up and went to Cedric.

Greyson and Binta sat there for many moments, staring into the magical fire that danced in the hearth. Greyson tried to figure out what had happened with Cassandra. He had made no inappropriate moves with her since they had started their journey. Was it the fact he had slept with Cass? Was she jealous? Binta was very upset by it, which was strange behavior for her. Perhaps he didn't realize how much hate had built between Cass and the two friends. He decided then that he would not be involved with anyone but Binta for the rest of the trip. Once they were home, he would work on seducing Cassandra once more. Now was not the time; he had somehow pressed too hard.

Nearly an hour later, Cassandra still sat at the small table with Cedric as he pored over the small map piece. Occasionally, he would blurt out something, then turn the map in a different direction. She wasn't really listening, and her focus was on Greyson and Binta, who were now sound asleep. There was no mumbling or laughing coming from Greyson's bedroll this night, as had been the case the previous nights. Cassandra's anger flared at the thought of him charming her, and she would confront him about that soon. She wanted to wait until they returned from their quest, but now that he had hurt Binta, she was unsure how long she could go without confronting him. She silently vowed to take Binta away from him after they completed the quest. With Zolmex in hand, that wouldn't be much of a problem.

"Cassandra?" Cedric asked, snapping her out of her trance.

"Yes? What?"

"Tomorrow, I will have you at Leo's tomb."

"Are you sure?" she asked, suddenly very excited.

"Yes, I am very certain! However," he began, then turned to look at the three friends sound asleep on the floor, "you must not let these petty distractions ruin your chance at finding your most powerful birthright."

"They won't, I promise," she assured him.

"Come with me, my dear," he said, taking her by the hand and leading her to the couch. "I have waited forty years for tomorrow. It is my destiny to help you achieve this most important goal. I will not have these three interfere."

"I want Zolmex just as badly as you want me to have it, Cedric. Trust me; they will not get in my way."

He smiled and nodded. "I thought that was the case; I just wanted to hear it from you. Now, how about some chocolate?"

"Definitely," she said with a smile.

Her addiction to his hot chocolate had only grown during the trip, and she looked forward to their nightly talks after everyone else had turned in. He was slowly becoming the father she never had. She sipped on her chocolate and pondered what the next day would hold for her. She still had so many questions for the old priest.

"What will Zolmex do to make me so powerful, Cedric?" she blurted out.

He thought about it for a few moments and shrugged. "Let's just say you will be so powerful that you will no longer need your spells."

"In what way, though?"

"I'm not sure, dear, but the scepter is an artifact, do not doubt, and artifacts hold tremendous power. This one was designed especially for you; only your father truly knows its power. After you possess the item, we will discover its powers quickly, I assure you. But first, we will need to find somewhere to hide because I fear what comes next once you have it in hand. Therefore, returning to Pelesea is not an option."

The words struck her hard, and she understood she would probably never be allowed in Pelesea again. He had warned her they would not return, but something pulled her to do just that. Perhaps Pelesea did feel more like home than she cared to admit. After all, she had accepted the goddess, Gella, into her heart because of her stay there. She had also made friends with Baxter and Victoria and had found Binta. She put the thought out of her mind for the moment; she would deal with that later. She swallowed hard, her nerves starting to get the best of her. The next day held promises she could only imagine. She would become the most powerful person in the world, and she could not fathom that thought. The possibility of failure had her stomach churning with butterflies.

"Cedric?"

"Yes, my child?"

"What if we can't find the tomb?"

The old priest laughed at her question, then said, "Your father would never allow that. I can sense that tomorrow, something grand will happen. Tomorrow, your life will change forever!"

CHAPTER 8

AMBUSHED!

Kessi awoke to the smell of food. She was so hungry that it almost made her gag, yet she wanted nothing more than to eat her fill of whatever it was. She sat up slowly and remembered where she was, immediately seeing the cell's bars. The other cell inhabitants were huddled together in the far corner. The door to the cell was open, and two servants dressed in inadequate clothing and with their feet shackled carried the delicious-smelling food into the cell and placed it gently on the floor. Neither of the servants looked as if they had eaten for days. A giant of a man stood at the door with a whip in hand, watching them carry out their duties.

One of the servants placed a bowl of fresh fruit down, snuck two grapes in his mouth, and swallowed them fast. It made Kessi happy to see him get away with the little bit of food. He made eye contact with her then, and his eyes widened in terror, thinking she would tell the guard. She only met his gaze with a warm smile. Seemingly not knowing what to do next, he nodded slightly and turned to leave. His hunger made him greedy, though, and he took two more grapes before he moved. He did not stuff them in his mouth this time. Instead, he kept them in his hand, cuffing them to hide them from the giant guard. As he exited the cell, the guard slammed the door shut, then grabbed the servant by the wrist.

"Looks like someone has sticky fingers," the large man said with a grin.

He then twisted the more petite man's wrist until he fell on his knees and cried out in pain. The grapes fell from his hand and onto the floor. Two guards opened the far door and pulled the other slave out of the room. Then, with wide grins, they quickly shut the door to watch the thief's beating unfold.

"Now watch what happens when you steal food," one shouted.

The giant guard at Kessi's door unraveled his whip as the slave tried to crawl to the far door, where the two guards watched with glee.

"They are for my wife. But, please, she has not eaten today. I only want—" he began, but the giant guard kicked him in the ribs, and he fell flat on his back, moaning.

"You don't say?" the big man said, picking up the grapes and stuffing them into his mouth.

"No, please, master, I did not mean to do it!" the man pleaded.

The man with the whip only laughed and struck the man in the face with the weapon. Kessi could see lines of blood streaking his face before the man turned over on his stomach and covered his head with his hands. The guard continued to strike at the servant, cutting his back and hands and hitting the man on the ear, tearing most of it off. The slave tried to crawl away, but the guard grabbed him by the leg and pulled him back. The other two guards at the far door yelled with glee and cheered their fellow guardsman on while the other slave sat at their feet, holding his hands over his ears while rocking back and forth.

Kessi had seen enough, knowing all too well how those lashes felt. She vaguely recalled being whipped, or had it been her sister? She had not remembered it until that moment; the display bringing the memory back from the recesses of her mind. Although she felt very dizzy, she regained footing, nearly fell back down, and stumbled over to the bars. Once there, she held on tightly, needing the support to keep from falling in her weakened state.

She heard a voice whisper to her, "No, over here, do not speak out."

She turned to see Sabrina reaching for her, not daring to leave the corner of the cell where the other girls huddled together. She waved Kessi over, but the whip's snap and the poor man's screams had Kessi's attention. She could not bear witness to such brutality.

"Stop!" Kessi yelled as loudly as she could.

The man had curled up in a fetal position at that point. His shaking hands were bloody and still covering his head, one holding his torn ear and crying. The large guard with the whip slowly turned to her, and his smile somehow grew even more prominent. Then, he approached her, and still, Sabrina begged for her to come to the corner of the cell. She thought about it but decided she was so weak that she would collapse if she moved from the bars. So, she stayed where she was and used the poor man's sobs to fuel her resolve.

"What did you say to me, little cell rat?" the man hissed.

"I said stop," she whispered, trying not to sound scared.

"That's what I thought you said," he responded with a quick jerk of his hand.

The whip struck her right hand, cutting two of her fingers deeply. She yelped and fell back on her rump. The jolt made her teeth chatter, and she nearly fainted, still feeling frail. She could hear the man unlocking the cell, while the other girls huddled together, none of them daring to move. Some even started to cry, knowing what was about to come. Kessi lay down, holding her injured hand to her chest, blood quickly staining her gown.

"Now, you will feel my whip, child."

She looked up and saw that the man was above her, whip in hand, his smile larger than ever. She shut her eyes tight and waited for the biting whip to tear her skin. She knew how it would feel, and those memories flooded back to her. She braced for the strike, understanding the man would show her no mercy once he started, but the strike never came. Instead, the large man yelped in surprise, and she felt him move quickly away. She opened her eyes just in time to see him slam to the floor in the larger cell and slide almost to the far door, where the other two guards and slave watched in stunned silence.

A female now stood over her, a pretty elf with ashen skin. Kessi began to thank her, thinking she was one of the girls cowering in the corner who had suddenly become inspired to help. Then she noticed her eyes and realized she was incorrect in her assumption. They were a beautiful blue and held some powerful, supernatural strength and more than a bit of hate. Moreover, they were bloodshot and unblinking, unnatural. Then Kessi looked beyond the woman to the guard, scrambling in fear to exit the cell, pleading with his comrades to let him out. And as they struggled to unlock the door, she noticed the coffin with the lid set aside. She knew then, without a doubt, that the creature was undead.

The undead elf leaned over her and grabbed the wrist of her injured hand. Her touch was cold, and her grip was like stone. The creature pulled her wounded hand closer to her face, blood dripping from Kessi's fingers. The woman's nostrils flared, and her pupils dilated. She looked from Kessi's hand to her dress, now soaked with blood. She licked her lips and stared at the blood for many moments.

Kessi did not know what to do and was about to say something when a female voice called out from behind the creature, "Let her go, Emiline!"

A small, attractive woman made her way inside the larger cell and stepped over the beaten servant, who was now unconscious. Behind the woman was a large man carrying a wicked-looking spear. Both looked familiar to Kessi, but she couldn't place their names. More importantly, the name Emiline seemed to be a name from her past that she could not recall. She shook her head, trying to clear the cobwebs in her mind, but with no success.

The creature released her and backed away as the small woman made her way to Kessi. The man with the spear stayed outside the cells, along with the other guards.

"What happened here, my dear?" the woman asked the creature, stroking her cheek gently as she did so.

"He hurt one of the chosen," the creature hissed, pointing toward the large guard who backed away until the man with the spear grabbed him and pushed him back.

"And you protected her, did you not?"

"Yes, I did as you instructed."

"Excellent job, dear. I will reward you shortly."

The woman then turned to regard Kessi; the evil and hatred etched on her face left little doubt in her mind that this one was dangerous. She walked toward Kessi, who had propped herself up on her elbows. Once there, she knelt on one knee and took Kessi's hand.

"Haven't you caused enough trouble?" she said dryly.

"I—" Kessi began to respond.

"Shut up!" the woman yelled and backhanded her hard, making her fall to the ground and nearly lose consciousness.

Kessi rolled to her side and brought her uninjured hand up to her swelling cheek. The woman grabbed her roughly and turned her so she was lying on her back. She then straddled her and ripped open the top of her dress. Kessi tried to cover up, vaguely aware of her nakedness, but the woman swatted her hands aside and rubbed her chest, looking for a wound.

"You are quite the bleeder, aren't you? All of this blood from a cut on your fingers? I thought you were truly injured, child."

She grabbed Kessi by the hair and forcefully pulled her to a sitting position. Kessi tried to keep her dress shut and not expose herself to the guards, who all looked on eagerly.

The woman bent so her face was just inches away and said, "I don't know who you truly are, impostor, but I want you to know that I am on my way to find your sister and bring her here. I can promise you that I will find her, and she will watch you die before my blade finds her own throat. It will be quite spectacular. I just wanted to let you know and thank you for telling us her location."

Kessi just looked at her, trying to remember any of it. Who were these people, and why was she jailed? Nothing came to her then, and she could tell the woman wanted a response, but she had nothing to offer.

"Do you even know who you are, fool?"

Kessi just slowly shook her head. She honestly had no idea, and tears began to form in her eyes. The woman just smiled and released her, letting her fall to the floor, where she began to weep. The woman shut and locked the door, then said something else to the undead creature. Kessi had her eyes closed, but she heard the screams of the injured slave as the beast tore into him. She covered her ears and cried even harder. She just wanted the nightmare to be over.

Shortly after, Matilda and Cerus made their way up from the prisoner's cell block, followed by the three guards and the remaining slave. The guards were a bit shaken after the incident with Emiline. That was especially true for the guard with the whip who had been thrown aside by the volatile vampire. Nevertheless, the four wanted nothing more than to leave the dungeon area and put the vampire far behind them.

On the other hand, Matilda was relaxed and even wore a smile on her pretty face. The screams of the dying slave echoed through the cave behind them as Emiline feasted, unnerving them all, even Cerus. The only one that failed to acknowledge the dying man's screams was Matilda. She hummed a tune as she walked. Cerus looked at her inquisitively, not liking her casual attitude about the lost demon, much less on her upcoming journey to Pelesea.

"I don't like it," he said as they walked.

"What is that, my dear husband?"

"Your trip. I don't like it," Cerus repeated.

"I must go to Pelesea and collect the sacred offering before that filth Vasheba finds her."

"Not that trip."

Matilda stopped, followed by the other five. "You're jealous of Malikai, the wizard?"

"No. We don't need the old man," Cerus answered, wringing his hand on his spear.

Matilda smiled, gently pried his fingers from the magnificent weapon, and took it into her hand. The giant-sized weapon dwarfed her and gave her an almost childlike appearance.

"We do need him, my love," she said and began walking again, using the spear as a walking stick.

Malikai was an old acquaintance of Matilda's and the man she had lost her virginity to when she was far too young to know what sex was. She grew to love him at some point and still considered him one of the most excellent lovers she had ever taken. She would see him soon because he could get her to Pelesea in the blink of an eye. Since she already suspected Vasheba was roaming the city, she needed to get there quickly to find Cassandra before the demon could. Of course, Malikai would demand many sexual favors before helping her, but that was not necessarily bad, in Matilda's opinion.

Cerus quickly caught up to her and said, "He uses you and will ask for favors."

"We need his powerful magic to get to Pelesea quickly. I will not waste time sailing the ocean again. Besides, I will pay him whatever favors he wants," she said, stopping again and turning to him. "He is an excellent lover."

Cerus's face turned red, and he grit his teeth. Then, he turned to the guards, who immediately diverted their gaze, not daring to make eye contact with their dangerous leader, who could be volatile when angered. The slave held his head down already, knowing better than to look any of them in the eye.

"I will kill him, just like I did Kavince," he said to his wife with a growl.

"Nonsense, we need him. Besides, he is not nearly the lover you are." She leaned in and whispered in his ear, "Let us go to our chambers now, and you can show me things that Malikai could never offer."

Cerus nodded, and they quickened their pace out of the prison block. The portcullis, sealing off the block, was raised quickly by two more guards stationed outside. As the six exited the corridor and the guards lowered the portcullis back into place, Matilda turned to address the group, including the two guards manning it.

"I will have your word that the virgins will be well-maintained and stay intact. The five of you will answer for it if any harm comes to them while I am gone."

With that, she took up Cerus's spear and heaved it at the guard who had broken that most sacred rule just moments ago, the large man with the whip. Her throw was not very powerful as she struggled to balance the giant weapon, and the impact would typically not have been lethal to a ready opponent. However, considering the man had not expected the attack and that the spear's tip could easily cut through any material, the nasty weapon easily sank into his chest. His eyes widened, and his mouth silently moved up and down as if to ask her why. He gurgled something unintelligible and began to grab his whip once again curled tight on his belt. Instead, he slowly fell to the floor, dead. Matilda went over to him and pulled the weapon from his chest, handing it back to Cerus.

"Understood?" she asked the remaining men.

They all nodded and bowed, and one guard acknowledged, "You have our word, my lady; no harm will come to your precious virgins or pet vampire."

"Good. Come along, Cerus, I desperately need you before I leave on my journey," she ordered and walked away, leaving the men to themselves.

They stood there, looking at Cerus for a hint as to what they should do. He smiled and said, "Clean that up," pointing to the dead guard.

He then quickly started toward the chamber he shared with his wife. First, he would show her just how powerful and thorough a lover he was before she visited Malikai. Then he would kill the old wizard. It seemed like a reasonable plan to him as he made his way to his chambers, hastened by the articles of Matilda's clothing that he found dotting the corridor along the way.

Kratoo couldn't believe his good fortune when he found tracks on the second day climbing the mountainous region where he thought the human cemetery was located. Kratoo was brilliant for a goblin, and he understood that they could be someone else's tracks, but as he studied them, he understood them to be the same as those he had tracked earlier. The footprints were lightweight, showing that none wore the region's goblin hunters' metal shirts. Also, most of the tracks were small for humans, making him believe they were primarily females, just like his missing party. Finally, and most importantly, the tracks were very fresh.

"What you find, Kratoo?" Gramous asked from behind.

"The missing humans!" Kratoo announced confidently.

Gramous came over beside the goblin and studied the prints. Finally, after a few moments of poking around the area, the ogre agreed. "Puny humans, with no metal sticks?" he asked to be sure.

Kratoo smiled and nodded, and Gramous returned the smile, showing off a set of brown and green teeth. "Bring the nets. We is close," the ogre leader ordered.

Four teams of three goblins each ran up to stand beside their leader, each carrying a net large enough to entrap a human. Gramous smiled and nodded to Kratoo to lead the way. The proud goblin scout did just that, knowing that their prey was not far ahead.

It was early afternoon when Cassandra and the others stopped to rest. With their morale diminishing due to the hard climbing over rugged terrain and the icy wind that beat them non-stop, they were a miserable group indeed. The fact that Cass had hatefully teased Binta the day before was fresh on Cassandra's mind and didn't help her foul mood. Cedric decided not to call forth the magic of the cottage, not wanting to tax the magical device too much and knowing they would need it more at nightfall. Cassandra was disappointed that they had not found the cemetery yet, and she watched Cedric survey the area as Greyson built a small fire to warm their extremities.

"It is time to pass the boots, Cassandra," Cass said through clenched teeth.

Cassandra and Cedric were wearing the magical boots and had been all day. But, of course, that was Cassandra's intention all along since this was the day she would find her birthright, and she needed to be prepared.

She shook her head and replied, "No, Cass, I must keep them on.

Today is the day we will find Zolmex, and I must prepare for any challenges."

If looks could kill, Cass's indeed would have, but Cassandra was insistent. Her heart went to Binta, though, knowing her friend was cold. She considered giving her the boots at that moment but thought twice, knowing that would cause a confrontation with Cass.

The four ate silently, and the three huddled around the small fire, trying to defrost their hands and feet. Greyson even cast a spell of warmth, giving them a slight reprieve from the elements, even if only for a short time. Cassandra sat away from them, not needing the heat, and ate in silence. She watched Cedric look around as he chewed on some deer jerky, and it appeared to her that he had no idea where he was. Cassandra sighed and put away her lunch. She wasn't hungry, and her patience was wearing thin. The exhausted young woman did not want to travel another day in these extreme conditions. She got up and went to the old priest, hoping he had some good news.

Kratoo smelled the smoke long before he had a visual of the group. Once confirmed these were the same weaklings he had followed earlier, he circled back to tell Gramous. The ogre leader was pleased and positioned his party to optimize a sneak attack. He brought forth his shamans to prepare their magics and dispersed his net troops to various spots surrounding the clearing. Kratoo knew that they would soon have five new slaves, most of them female, which would fetch a high price from the other tribes. It would all be because of him, and Gramous would reward him. With a smile, he took his place as the other goblins moved into position.

"This looks very familiar, child. I am certain I was in this spot during my vision with Kane. That was many years ago, though, and much has changed. The snow also hides the terrain, making this process all the harder," Cedric explained to Cassandra.

The mountainside loomed all the more significant right in front of them as they stood in a snow-filled clearing. There were no signs of a cemetery, and Cassandra did not like the idea of climbing steep slopes.

She examined that treacherous terrain when Cedric said, "Move back with your friends, Cassandra."

"What is wrong?"

"Nothing is wrong, but I feel we are standing on the very ground for which we have been seeking. So, stand back with your friends, and I will clear this snow."

Cassandra made her way back to the fire and told the others that they had possibly arrived at their destination. All of them rose and watched the old priest, but Binta and Cass did not move away from the fire, or the warm radius Greyson had magically created around himself. Instead, they watched as Cedric began casting a spell. Suddenly, a small ball of fire shot from his fingertip and made its way to the clearing. Then it exploded into a giant fireball, engulfing most of the area.

"How did he do that?" Greyson asked in amazement. "That is arcane magic, not priestly magic."

Cassandra only smiled, remembering what Cedric had told her about Kane blessing his followers with arcane magic; then, she ran up to the clearing as Cedric surveyed his work. She stood beside him and looked out over the hissing ground; with most of the snow and ice melted in the blast, a small cemetery became visible. The stones were ancient, and some had toppled over, but it was a cemetery.

"Leo is buried somewhere in that?" Cassandra asked skeptically, as the other three friends stood beside her and Cedric with stunned expressions.

"I believe so. Now, all we have to do is find the old wizard's tomb, and once there, we will find your birthright," Cedric answered rather anxiously.

The group of five began searching the clearing, looking over the tombstones, hoping they would find Leo's resting spot, their spirits suddenly lifted.

Gramous and the goblin band had witnessed the powerful magic of Cedric's fireball, so the ogre whispered to his two shamans, "Focus magics on that one. Kill him, and we take the others as slaves. He too dangerous."

The shamans nodded and eagerly prepared their spells.

As the goblins prepared for an attack and closed in on the group, Cassandra and the others roamed the small cemetery. It contained no more than thirty or forty small grave markers, most unremarkable and without identifying marks. Cassandra was rubbing snow from a grave marker when an arm grabbed her gently and pulled her up to a standing position. It was Greyson, and he had a serious look on his face.

"Cassandra, we should talk," he said.

"Now is not the time, Greyson."

"But as we complete our quest, I want us to celebrate once we return home. I was counting on the three of us to become more acquainted."

"No," she interrupted.

"Will you not hear me out?"

"You've spoken quite enough, Greyson Kavince," she replied, raising her voice slightly.

Binta, trying to read a worn tombstone, heard her friend and rose from her work. She made her way to the couple, understanding the severe tone of Cassandra's voice, and she knew at once that her friend was upset.

"What is wrong?" Greyson asked, grabbing her hand gently. "I mean, the day we left the temple, you were very receiving of my touch, but now you seem angry with me. What has changed?"

She took her hand back from him just as Binta walked up to them.

"Is everything all right?" Binta asked.

"No, Binta, I'm afraid not," Cassandra replied.

"I have found something!" Cedric yelled from behind Cassandra.

He had made his way to the most northern part of the cemetery, near the mountainside's steep slope, and there he knelt, shoveling snow away from a tombstone. Cass was near him and bent down to assist with his work. Cassandra moved to leave, but Greyson grabbed her arm and held her tight.

"No, Cassandra, tell me what is wrong. Let us both know because this affects the three of us," Greyson said, nodding to Binta.

"Very well. Tell me, Greyson, did you charm me before we left Pelesea?" Cassandra spat.

She saw that the accusation caught him and Binta off guard. He released Cassandra's arm and took a step back.

Binta gasped and asked, "Greyson, tell me you didn't do that."

He looked back and forth between the two women, caught in his own game.

"Well?" Cassandra asked, tapping her foot in the snow, her arms folded across her chest.

"Yes," he admitted softly. "But not to hurt you—"

Binta covered her mouth with her hand and said, "Greyson, how could you?"

Cassandra appreciated Binta's reaction and knew it to be sincere. She had discovered that a few nights earlier, as the two had shared their private conversation in the small cottage. Even though Cassandra could feel her face turning red with anger, she felt relieved by Binta's reaction. It further proved Binta had nothing to do with Greyson's treachery. Unable to control her anger any longer, Cassandra summoned all her strength and slapped Greyson. Binta stepped back, her eyes widening, and before Greyson could recover, Cassandra struck him hard again.

She was about to hit him a third time, but Greyson caught her arm and said, "Enough."

"Cassandra?" Cedric asked in surprise, rising from his work, Cass standing next to him.

With the party split and arguing amongst themselves, Gramous decided the time to attack had come. The ogre leader signaled to his shamans, who both began to cast their spells. Then he signaled to the net bearers, who rushed into the clearing. Finally, he grabbed his giant spiked club and led the rest of the group into the cemetery.

"Cass, f… f… flee," Cedric stuttered between slow-moving lips as a wave of magic washed over him.

"What?" she asked, but he was unresponsive then and not moving, as if he were petrified.

She stared at him for a moment, then realized they were under attack as she heard the whooping sounds coming from around them. She looked past Cedric's still form to the many creatures charging in from the trees. A net flew over her from behind, and she was pulled down hard by its operators. She fell to her knees first, then the blunt end of a spear cracked the back of her head. Everything went black, and she fell face-first to the ground.

"What the—?" Greyson began as the goblins came at them from every direction.

He drew his mace, as he was the only one carrying an actual weapon, just as a net fell over Binta. She gasped in surprise and quickly became off balance by three small, green-skinned creatures tugging on the net. A fourth creature raised the blunt end of his spear to hit her, but Greyson cracked him across the back with his mace before he could.

Greyson's hit knocked the wind out of the little goblin, and he fell away, rolling on the ground, trying to catch his breath. But, as he fell, six more took his place, spears leveled at Greyson, advancing on the young priest. Greyson began to back away intentionally, trying to get the creatures to follow him and leave Binta and Cassandra alone. Soon, there were too many filthy little things for that idea to work.

Binta struggled to sit up, but the three goblins handling the net would not let that happen. One of them released his end and picked up his spear, turning it so the blunt end could subdue his prey. It all happened so quickly but seemed to be occurring slowly for Cassandra. She could see the group of creatures go after Greyson from the corner of her eye, but her main focus was on Binta. What were these green-skinned, smelly beasts? What would they do to them if captured? It wasn't going to be good, and she wasn't about to find out. Rage boiled within her; she would not let her quest end this way.

She pointed her finger at the creature rearing back to hit Binta and let loose two green balls of energy that flew from her hand. The two small spheres flew at the beast and struck it in the chest before he could strike. The dumb thing stood there for a few moments before realizing it was dead and finally fell over. Cassandra had never killed anything before, and the shock of that act had her staring in disbelief at her hand like it was a strange new growth on her body. She felt the force of that spell when she cast it; it was much stronger than the same one she had used months earlier against Ronnis. Still, as the little creature fell dead, her heart ached at the fact she had killed.

"Cassandra, behind you!" Binta called from under the thick net.

Cassandra felt a presence behind her while Binta was warning her. She turned just in time to see another net flying over her, and she cursed herself for showing pity toward the vile little beasts. Cassandra managed to step back enough not to be entangled, but it clipped her shoulder, knocking her off balance. She was amazed at how heavy the rope net was and realized then that the little creatures had to be strong to toss such a thing. The three net throwers converged on her as she stumbled backward, eventually falling over a rock. Cassandra landed hard on her back and hit her head on the frozen ground. Cedric's fireball had melted most of the snow in the cemetery, but the ground was still very much frozen. The world spun for a moment, and when she finally reoriented herself, two creatures stood over her, spears raised to bash her.

Cedric tried to register what was happening. He was victim to a relatively simple spell and was upset with himself for not resisting such elemental magic. The old priest knew that Kane was with them, and Cedric did not foresee such an end to their adventure, not with his god watching them. He had not ventured out from under the temple in many decades, and his skills were a little rusty, but he should have known better than to let this happen. Cedric tried to look around the best he could, but his muscles tensed, and they would not comply. He was utterly helpless and could not protect Cassandra. How had he let this happen?

He saw a group of creatures taking an unconscious Cass out of some netting. One of the vermin, which he quickly determined to be goblins, examined her decorative staff, turning it over and over in his hands before shrugging his shoulders and heaving it into the woods. The others began to bind her hands and feet with rope, and he realized that the goblins planned on taking them alive. That was good; given enough time to break the spell, he would unleash his powerful magic on the pathetic creatures.

Another wave of magical energy rolled over him, increasing the effect of the paralysis. He cursed his bad luck because he was beginning to defeat the effects of the first spell. Then he saw the source of the magic; two shamans standing at the tree line on the far side of the cemetery, waving their staffs and casting their spells in his direction. The old priest could beat this if he stayed smart; he just wished he could check on Cassandra. So far, he had not heard his traveling companions cry out in pain, so he took that as a good sign, though he could not turn his head to confirm.

Kratoo was so very proud. His guidance had led the tribe to a glorious catch, and he would sit with the chieftains during the celebratory feast when they returned home. They secured their first catch as Gimpy, Netty, and Gorp tied Cass's hands and feet together. A female was invaluable to them, so his glory would be all the more remarkable.

He then looked over at the female's companion. He had almost forgotten about that one, but the squawking from the shamans reminded him. The odd-looking human stood there, unable to move or cast his black magic. As the other three goblins ran off to secure more prey, Kratoo drew his sword, an old, rusty scimitar he had found on a dead human pirate at the elf lake years ago. It had many chips, and the hilt was loose, but it was a famous weapon amongst his tribe, and he planned on making it more prominent. He walked toward the paralyzed human with a sneer on his face.

He reared back with all his strength and rammed the scimitar home right into the human's gut. Nothing happened; there was no killing strike as his weapon bounced harmlessly aside, a temporary blue shield of energy visible around the human.

Kratoo growled and asked, "Dark magic?"

He waited for the human to answer, but he never did. Then he remembered that he couldn't, so he swung a cutting blow across the human's gut. But, again, the flash of some blue magic defeated his attack. He stood there scratching his head for a moment. Then he heard the unmistakably loud strides of Gramous from behind him.

Kratoo moved to the side and said, "Human has dark magics!"

"Move out of way! His magics won't stop this!" Gramous said, now nearly running, his giant spiked club reared back, ready for the killing blow.

Kratoo wasn't sure what to do, so he plugged his fingers into his ears in case humans exploded if you hit them hard enough.

The annoying little goblin was the least of Cedric's worries because when he saw the giant ogre approaching, he saw his doom. His mind raced, and his heart sank; how could this end their quest? He had spent his entire adult life living under the temple in Pelesea, only to bring the child of Kane out here in the wilderness to be ambushed by goblins, of all things? He had failed Kane and was helpless to save Cassandra. As the ogre reared back to swing, he only wished that he could close his eyes.

Greyson had six little creatures approaching him, and he could see more spilling out of the woods. They swarmed around Binta and Cassandra, and he saw Cassandra slip and fall, which meant she and

Binta were in deep trouble. He had to do something, but the creatures pressed him fully, surrounding him, their spears leveled his way. One spoke in a strange language that he could not comprehend but could only assume was an order to surrender. Then a wave of anger washed over him as the vision of Darian hanging from the tree in Tara, his guts spilling onto the ground, assaulted him. He rediscovered his courage.

To outsmart the creature, he played along with the order to surrender, patting the air with one hand, and wearing a look of defeat on his face. Then he slowly knelt on the ground and gently placed his mace at his feet. The creature barked more orders, and in response, he held up one finger and began slowly patting his pockets, pretending to look for something as he stood back up. All six little beasts stood there watching, unsure what to make of his actions. He then feigned surprise, pretending that he had found something in his right front pocket.

He slowly reached into it, and the creatures growled and tightened their grips on their spears. He slowly produced his fist from the pocket and offered it to the nearest one. It stood there puzzled as Greyson began to un-ball his fist. He silently prayed to Plath and called upon his priestly power to produce light. As he did so, he flicked his last finger open and summoned the light into the creature's eyes. It let out a squeal as it was suddenly blinded. It heaved its spear at him in response but missed badly. Greyson quickly stepped aside, and the spear hit the creature behind him in the throat.

It started hopping around, screaming in that strange language, which was a bit gurgled from the wound. One of the creatures beside the blinded one smacked it in the head for mortally wounding one of their own. That had the blinded creature drawing a wicked-looking knife and stabbing his newest assailant in the chest, thinking it to be Greyson. The other three monsters lost track of Greyson as they tried to calm their blinded friend, who was swinging away with his knife in random directions, all the while screaming in its abrasive dialect.

Greyson took the opportunity to pick up his mace and crack one of the little beasts over the head. A sickening sound followed as his mace broke through bone, and the creature fell away, unmoving. The other two finally turned toward him and ignored their blinded companion, who wandered into the woods, still swinging and cursing. Greyson liked his odds better at that point; two against one made him feel like he could win the battle.

He wanted to keep the confusion in place, so he was inspired to throw his hands up as high as possible and let out a yell of intimidation. He saw their eyes widen, lowering their spears in fear, their mouths hanging open. Finally, one of them said something to the other, who nodded. They were afraid, his tactic of intimidation effective.

"Well, that's more like it," Greyson said with a smile, then started walking toward them, his mace ready to finish the job.

Something flashed past him, barely missing him, and hit one of the creatures with a thud. It took him a moment to realize that it was an arrow, which was now quivering, stuck in the creature's chest. The other creature turned to run, but a second arrow followed, cutting it down before it took a step.

Greyson turned to see a small group of warriors cutting into the crowd of creatures, their swords quickly hacking them to pieces. He also discovered two men with giant-sized bows, letting fly their dangerous arrows into the suddenly confused mass of creatures. Then he spotted a familiar face, one of the wizards from the school of magic, an older fellow he had visited not too long ago. He couldn't remember his name, but he was busy unrolling some carpet. With renewed confidence, Greyson rushed to aid his friends.

Cassandra put her arm out in front of her, trying to block the coming attacks. She heard Binta scream the final phrases of a spell and listened to the familiar sizzle of a magical dart issue from her finger and slam into one of her assailants. She looked over her arm to see that creature fall away, and the remaining one jerk twice, then stand there with its mouth open. The spear slowly slid from its hands and fell next to Cassandra, then the creature fell on top of it, two arrows sticking out of its back. Cassandra looked at the dead monster, trying to register the appearance of the arrows.

She vaguely heard Binta say, "Cassandra, men have come; they are fighting these creatures. Help is here!"

She wasn't listening, now looking past the dead creature beside her to stare at an old grave marker. It was similar to all the others, except the base had a lion's face sculpted in it, the same sculpting that adorned the key her father had left her!

Cass was awake when the bone-crushing hit from Gramous's club penetrated Cedric's sphere of protection, then his chest, sticking him with those awful spikes and sending him flying through the air to crash into a nearby tree. He fell to the ground hard on his back, still unable to move, with a giant spike protruding from his chest. She pretended to remain unconscious, as there was only one of the creatures in the immediate area, along with the massive beast that had just attacked Cedric. She didn't want any part of that one and remained quiet until it ran off toward a new commotion at the other end of the clearing. That left the one little creature who immediately sheathed his sword and ran off into the woods.

With no remaining creatures in the immediate area, she sat up, nearly falling over from the pain that shot through her head when she did. She brought a hand up to rub the back of her wounded head, and realized then that her hands were bound. Blood was on her fingertips when she returned it. She remembered something hitting her from behind but couldn't remember what. Either way, the wound seemed minor. Cass looked at her hands and realized that a primitive rope bound them together. Since goblins are not so good at making knots, she was out of it in short order and quickly untied her feet afterward. Cass stood and staggered a bit, her head throbbing with every step. Finally, she blocked out the pain and made her way to Cedric's still form.

Cassandra knelt by the tombstone and tried to read the worn name on the smooth stone. She could not. Only a few characters remained, and not in a language Cassandra understood. She lay beside the marker to better look at the lion's face. Snow partially covered it, so she swept the remaining ice and snow from it, and her heart nearly beat out of her chest. One could only see it at this level while lying prone on the ground; the mouth of the lion made a keyhole.

"Are you two hurt?" Greyson asked as he made his way to Binta and Cassandra.

"No, I don't think so," Binta replied.

"Keep an eye out for Cedric; I need him," Cassandra answered, focusing on the tombstone and not on her friends.

Greyson looked up to see Cass reach Cedric, who seemed gravely injured. Binta saw it too, and they shared a knowing look. The fight was now on the south side of the cemetery, focused on the new group of warriors. The lumbering giant didn't even slow down as it ran right past them to join the fray, several arrows already protruding from its chest.

"I think Cedric is hurt," Greyson whispered.

"What? Then go to him, heal him, quickly!" Cassandra barked as she sat up and removed the necklace with the key from around her neck.

"Right," he answered and rushed off.

"Binta, keep a watch out for those creatures; this is important," Cassandra demanded, then lay flat.

"I have no more spells, Cassandra!" Binta yelled over the fighting.

"Just keep guard," Cassandra reiterated, inserting the key into the lion's mouth. The fit was perfect.

Cass knelt beside Cedric, who was gasping and struggling to breathe. A spike stuck from his chest but did not look too deep. Blood pooled from the corner of his mouth, and one of his eyes was primarily red with blood. He looked at her but did not speak and did not move. He raised a shaking hand toward the spike, but Cass batted it away.

"That looks like it hurts. Let me help you," she said grimly.

He lay his hand back down and nodded slightly. Cass could tell he was in tremendous pain, and she knew that Greyson could help him recover or at least make him comfortable during the brief wait for death to take him. But she had other plans.

"You nearly got us all killed, you crazy old man," she whispered as she took both hands and drove the spike deep into his chest, puncturing his remaining functioning lung.

His eyes widened, and blood spurted from his gargling mouth. Cass tried to avoid the mess as her hands went straight to the pocket that contained the jeweled necklace attuned to Cassandra. She stuffed it into her pocket, saying, "You won't need this anymore."

She then searched the dying man for the magical cottage. "Now, where do you keep it? Ah, here it is," she exclaimed.

He tried to stop her with a trembling hand but had little life left in him, and soon it was hers.

She turned to see Greyson running toward her, waved him on in a hurry, then turned back to Cedric one last time and said, "Don't worry about Cassandra; I'll take real good care of her for you."

His eyes widened even more before he let out a final, long exhale. His pupils dilated, and what little life that remained in him vanished. She stood and took a step back to let Greyson administer his healing, which Cass knew would be too late to save the crazy old priest.

Cassandra felt the magical force run through her body when she turned the key. Her muscles all tensed up in unison, and she rolled over on her back, unable to release the key. Instead, she stared straight up at the tiny bit of sky visible through the canopy of trees, caught in a trance.

"Cassandra!" Binta screamed and knelt beside her.

Cassandra's eyes were unblinking, and her arms and legs twitched slightly. Binta shook her shoulder gently, not knowing what was transpiring. She reached for her arm and tried to pull it away from the key, but she might as well have been trying to lift a boulder; it was not going to budge. Finally, she stood and looked up at Greyson, kneeling over Cedric with Cass watching them. She wasn't sure what to do, so she called Cassandra's name several times but got no response. Binta tried to figure out a solution, but before formulating anything, she heard footsteps behind her. She turned just in time to see two little creatures running straight for her.

Cassandra could hear Binta speaking to her, but it sounded as if it were very far away. She could not bring herself even to respond. The scene before her had her full attention, and Cassandra cared little for what was truly happening around her. She had a vision, not of the future or the past, but of the current moment. The image contained a different part of the cemetery, not far from where Cassandra lay. In the vision, she faced the steep grade of the mountain as it rose above the little clearing at the cemetery's north end.

It was as if she were standing there staring at the mountain, but she knew she was not and was lying many feet away from that spot. In the vision, and out of the corner of her left eye, she could see Cedric's still form, with Cass standing at his feet and Greyson kneeling over him. She could not change the view or even turn her head to see what was around her, so she studied the vision for a few moments, trying to let it sink in. Nothing seemed special about it at all. Her muscles finally relaxed, and the image slowly dissipated. She saw the blue sky and Binta standing nearby with her back toward her. Cassandra saw the charging creatures and knew Binta was in trouble.

Gramous charged right into the fray, giving the goblins courage once more, and the intensity of the fighting increased. Gabriel and Adam were busy picking off goblins with their bows as the vermin advanced. At the same time, the other two knights of Godhomme fought valiantly against the little creatures, their plate mail armor deflecting any minor hits that the goblins could score.

Daro squared off against the ogre, with several arrows already protruding from its chest. It swung a mighty swipe of his spiked club at him, and Daro jumped out of the way at the last moment. He then scored two quick minor stabs on the creature's forearm as he ran behind it. Unfortunately, the wounds only seemed to make the ogre mad, and it took its club in two hands for a powerful downward chop. The ranger barely dodged the strike, and the club cratered the ground next to him. He was about to strike with his two swords when a wave of energy rolled over him. He nearly froze in place from the magical attack, but managed to jump to the side at the last moment as another overhead chop struck the ground next to him.

"Baxter, there must be shamans. Find them, quick!" he yelled to the wizard, getting his magical carpet airborne.

"Gladly," he acknowledged, then shot a bolt of powerful lightning from a wand he was wielding, striking the ogre in the chest, and knocking it down to one knee. Then he flew off to find the shamans.

He started for the far tree line, where he expected them to be, but something else caught his attention before he had gone very far.

Binta had given up on stirring Cassandra from her trance and was set on protecting her friend from the attacks of those vile little creatures. She had used her one spell already and had nothing else memorized. She looked down and picked up a spear next to Cassandra that the dead goblin had dropped. She wielded it tightly, not realizing that she had it pointing in the wrong direction, with the sharp tip facing herself. She closed her eyes as they bore down upon her.

She heard the familiar sound of magical energy bolts and opened her eyes to see the two creatures lying at her feet, smoke wafting up from blackened holes in their backs. It made no sense at first as she looked down at Cassandra and was relieved to see her aware and in a sitting position. But she knew those strikes had not come from her. A familiar voice from behind her had her turning back around. There, Baxter's carpet hovered above the newly dead goblins.

"Cassandra, are you hurt?" Baxter asked, lowering the carpet, and jumping off quickly.

"No, I am fine," she said as he helped her to her feet.

"I am fine, too, Instructor Baxter," Binta said with a puzzled look.

Baxter was at a loss for words for a moment, nodded nervously at her, and said, "Miss Mulay, it is good to see you safe. I am thrilled that we have found you in time," he said, turning his attention back to Cassandra with an awkward smile.

"All of you," he continued after a few moments of silence, waving a hand at Binta, his face red.

He could tell that Binta suspected something, and he thought back to the rumors that spread through the school that Baxter and Cassandra had slept together. Her stare scrutinized his actions, and he became nervous. Was that a hint of jealousy in Binta's gaze?

The two knights from Godhomme showed few wounds, and the goblin bodies were stacking up all around them, especially with Gabriel and Adam firing their deadly bows into the crowd of creatures. But then the sun concentrated in the immediate area, and their armor and swords began to heat and eventually smoke. Goblins jumped back, becoming uncomfortable with the temperature change. The knights were slower and could not escape the area as the shamans kept their spells focused on them, moving with the knights. Unfortunately, they both knew what that meant and were helpless against that terrible spell.

"Split up," one knight said, and they began to do just that.

The little goblins, although not smart, knew what to do to keep the spell in effect. So, they came on then, herding the knights back together by the sheer number of them. Soon they were back-to-back once more.

"What now?" Siv asked, the temperature making the remaining snow and ice on the ground hiss in protest.

"We cannot see the shamans, and we cannot escape the spell. So, we fight," Josel responded, his armor already becoming unbearable and burning his skin.

"And die?" Siv asked.

Josel only nodded a solemn response. But battles like this were what they lived for; fighting and dying to kill the nasty goblins was their sole purpose. They understood that death was upon them. With a yell, they each charged into the goblin fray, killing many of them and ignoring the scorching metal that encased them.

Daro had stabbed the ogre with both his blades in the throat after Baxter's lightning bolt had dazed it. He watched as it slowly fell backward with a gurgling sound, dead before it even hit the ground. He turned just in time to see the two knights drop their swords, their plate mail turning bright red. Their screams soon followed as they were being cooked alive in their armor. He turned to find Baxter but could not locate him in the sky. His gaze finally caught him on the ground, conversing with several members of the party they had been tracking.

"Baxter, the shamans!" he yelled, then charged into the remaining goblins overwhelming the two knights.

Baxter heard Daro's plea and immediately returned to his carpet and had it hovering again. "I will be back; find a place to hide. Stay safe!" he ordered Cassandra and Binta.

Then he was gone, making haste toward the tree line. Shortly after that, lightning bolts ricocheted off the trees, splintering wood and melting snow and ice. Cassandra did not stay to witness the destruction. Instead, she took Binta's hand and said, "Come on!"

"Where are we going?" Binta yelled over the many lightning retorts.

"To Cedric, he is hurt."

The two ran to the fallen priest just as Greyson stood and shook his head. Cassandra ran up to the old hermit and screamed his name, kneeling beside him and taking his hand in hers. She looked up at Greyson in desperation, and he only shook his head solemnly.

"Cedric, no, you cannot leave me!" she yelled at the fallen man.

She hoped there would be some sign of life, but she knew it was too late. She bowed and put his cold hand on her cheek, closing her eyes. She then said a silent prayer to Gella. Greyson also prayed to Plath as Cass and Binta watched the sad scene. The commotion at the other end of the cemetery seemed so far away. The four of them stood in the clearing, mourning the passing of a companion that none truly knew, and understanding the adventure was failing.

"Your death will not be in vain," Cassandra said. "I promise you; I will find Zolmex. I will finish what you started."

Then she walked back toward the burial ground's grave markers at the north end.

"Where are you going?" Greyson yelled after her.

"To find Zolmex! I need the three of you to keep guard. Watch for those little creatures and make sure they do not disturb me. We are close," she answered.

She tried to orient herself so her view was the same as in the vision she had just received. She kept Cedric's body in her left peripheral while facing the mountain, trying not to cry over the loss. She had to stay strong and concentrate. Cassandra took several steps back until she thought she had just the right point of view that she remembered from the strange vision.

The other three looked on, and Binta still held the spear tightly. None of the creatures paid them any mind, and Greyson noticed that the wizard was now unleashing his deadly lightning on the goblins. The swarm began to disburse as their numbers dwindled.

"What is she doing?" Greyson asked Binta, then reached down, took the spear from her grasp, turned it around so the tip faced outward, and gave it back.

She shrugged and said, "She is finding Zolmex."

"I think she has lost her mind," Cass chimed in. "Now, where is my staff? Did those creatures take it?"

"Was it magical?" Greyson asked.

"No, valuable," Cass responded.

"Then forget it. Here is a spear you may use as a weapon. Help us stand guard; we need to make sure Cassandra is not interfered with," Binta said, handing Cass the spear and picking up another one for herself.

The three walked closer to Cassandra, who seemed to have her feet stuck in place, turning her head all around, looking for something. Luckily, the goblins were no longer focused on them, thanks to the new arrivals, and unbeknownst to Cassandra, Binta, and Greyson, the only real threat to any of them was the crude spear Cass held in her hand.

Cassandra saw no clues at all. She stood as close as she could remember to the spot in the vision but saw nothing. She planted her feet firmly and turned her head this way and that, looking for a clue. It took some time, but she eventually saw what Cedric had found a few moments before the goblin attack: another lion's head engraved at the base of the marker right next to her.

She quickly bent down and saw that someone had scraped the remaining snow from the base, revealing the lion's head. She thought Cedric had done that before the attack, and she was ecstatic about her good fortune. She quickly lay down on her stomach and looked into its mouth. Cassandra found there precisely what she thought she would: another keyhole. She quickly stuck in the key and turned it.

She prepared herself for another vision and fully expected her body to tense up once more. Neither happened. She looked around and saw nothing, so she stood once more in the exact spot she had been before finding the second lion's head sculpture.

"What do you know?" Greyson asked.

Cassandra began looking all around, and her three companions looked more confused than ever. "I told you, she has become daft," Cass said with a smirk.

Binta and Greyson looked at Cass then as she easily leaned on the spear, not impressed with Cassandra's actions, and not prepared to defend her if the little creatures decided to attack. Instead, she just shrugged and continued to look on with amusement at Cassandra's strange antics. A few goblins had broken from the fight and were running right toward them.

Greyson and Binta noticed and yelled a warning to Cassandra, then advanced to put themselves between the creatures and her. Cass just stayed where she was and watched Cassandra with great interest. Had she gone mad, or was she on the verge of finding the artifact? Cass was there for one reason: to ensure Cassandra failed in her quest. She watched intently as Cassandra desperately looked around.

Cassandra's desperation to find the next clue clouded her thinking, especially when she heard Greyson warn the others of approaching creatures. She tried to stand still, close her eyes, and calm down. She positioned herself the same way she was in the vision; her head turned toward the upward slope of the mountain that rose before her. Cedric's unmoving form still lay in her left-side peripheral vision. She could no longer see Greyson and Binta, but knew they were behind her, ready to battle. Cass stood almost directly in her way, just staring at her. Cassandra wanted to scream at her to move, but before she could, she saw the next clue, a third lion sculpture just over Cass's shoulder, about twenty-five yards up the steep incline of the mountain. It glowed slightly through the snow; she would never have seen it if she hadn't been standing perfectly and focused on Cass.

Greyson had his mace ready, and Binta held her spear in the correct direction this time. Just before the two creatures got to them, they veered off and ran into the woods. The little creatures had no fight left in them, and the two friends and lovers breathed a sigh of relief and shared a quick smile. They returned to Cassandra and Cass to find Cassandra on her stomach, retrieving her key from the lion's mouth.

"This way!" Cassandra yelled excitedly and waved her arm toward the mountainside.

She started climbing the slope, and Binta and Greyson quickly followed. Cass sighed heavily, then reluctantly joined them. She was considering at that moment how nice it would be just to run the spear through the annoying Cassandra. She had gotten away with it easily enough with Cedric, and Cass decided then that if the opportunity presented itself when they were alone, she might murder Cassandra and end the madness. Yet, there was hope that Zolmex existed, and she would need to keep her alive until they found it.

The four adventurers climbed the steep grade, finding handholds on rocks or small trees. Cass and Binta had to toss down their spears, the climb requiring both hands to keep from falling. The rise was steep; one slip could have them sliding and falling back down quickly. The goblin weapons tumbled to the bottom of the grade, about twenty yards from where they clung to the mountainside.

Cassandra stopped there and started craning her neck again, searching the terrain around her for the third lion's head. It had glowed briefly when she first witnessed it; to her estimation, it was precisely where they all currently clung to the mountain. But it was nowhere in sight. She looked back down at the cemetery, trying to get a bearing on how close she was, then started digging away with one hand at various rocks buried in the snow.

"It is here somewhere. It has to be," Cassandra said.

"What are you looking for?" Greyson asked.

"Another lion's head sculpture, this one a little bigger than the other two."

"You mean like this?" Cass said, pointing to a sculpture right between her and Cassandra.

Cassandra quickly and carefully made her way over to where Cass clung to a large tree branch. Her eyes widened when she saw it, and she immediately looked for a keyhole in the mouth. There she found what she had hoped for, and a smile widened on her face.

"Great, Cass! This is it!" she said excitedly. "Everyone hang on; I do not know what this will do. But, Greyson, please watch below if any scattering creatures decide to brave an attack."

Greyson looked over his shoulder and saw that all the little creatures were now on the run and the larger one lay motionless on the ground. "I think you're good. Go for it," he said with a nod of his head.

Cassandra nodded and smiled, sticking the key into the lion's mouth. Before she could turn it, the sculpture pulled the key in completely.

"Hey!" she yelled out in surprise.

"What?" Greyson and Binta asked in unison.

"The lion ate my key."

"Maybe this was the wrong sculpture," Cass said, unenthused.

Cassandra looked at her in disbelief, not expecting to lose her key and not knowing what to do next. She looked down at Cedric's unmoving form, and her heart sank. Had she done something wrong? She had no idea what to do next.

That is when the mountain itself began to tremble and shake. The four adventurers held on tightly as the hillside above them slowly cracked open. Snow, rock, and other debris rained upon them, and they held on for dear life. The small avalanche covered them in snow, dirt, and twigs, but none suffered injuries more severe than a few scrapes. And right above them now loomed an entrance into the mountain.

"That's it!" Cassandra yelled, spitting out dirt and shaking it from her hair.

"That's what?" Greyson asked.

"Leo's tomb!" she yelled, looking down at him with a big grin.

"If that is the case, you better get in there," Cass said, pointing toward the newly revealed cave.

"Why?" Cassandra asked as she realized the cave was starting to close once more. "Oh, good idea," she reasoned.

She looked for the key but couldn't even see the lion's head, which was now buried under snow and other debris.

"Hurry, everyone, climb!" she yelled and started climbing toward the closing entrance as fast as possible.

It was only about five feet above them, but the loose debris and steep slope made the going slow and treacherous. If any of them fell, they would not have time to make it back up before the cave resealed itself. The mountain trembled again as the entrance slowly began to close, making it even more challenging to hold on.

As the group struggled to cling to the mountain, Cass considered pulling Cassandra down from the slope but decided against that action. If Zolmex truly existed, perhaps Cassandra would find it. Cass would be glad to let her do all the hard work; then she would claim the artifact as her own. Cass climbed up and into the opening, pulling Cassandra up the last little bit and helping the others as quickly as possible. Cassandra assisted as best she could, and soon all four were in the cave with little time to spare.

Cassandra was relieved that everyone was in, but soon understood the potential dangers of where they were. Unfortunately, Cedric was no longer there to guide them, and the four of them, although still together, had little combined knowledge of such things. She quickly knelt and peered out of the closing cave, looking for Baxter and noting him coming toward her at full speed. She waved and yelled his name, but the cave entrance closed well before he reached them. The trembling within the mountain continued momentarily, and as it finally quieted, they could hear it magically sealing them inside. The sound popped their eardrums and sucked the air out of space briefly. Then all was silent, and they were on their own.

Baxter was satisfied with his work against the group of goblins. After finishing off the shamans, it had been easy for him to fly over the mass of creatures and scorch them with his lightning bolts. They had soon scattered, but his heart sank when he saw that two of Gabriel's men lay motionless in the field, smoke wafting from their armor from the shamans' deadly spell as Gabriel and Adam looked over them sadly.

That is when he heard the rumbling. He had heard it moments earlier but thought it to be the repercussions of his lightning bolts. When it continued after he had stopped his attacks, he realized it was the mountain itself. He looked just in time to see Cassandra and the others climb into a slowly closing cave.

"Cassandra!" he yelled and willed the carpet to fly to the spot hastily.

He knew he was too late and saw Cassandra wave and yell something at him, but he was too far away to make out her words. He watched helplessly as the cave closed shut right before he got there. He hovered at the entrance just a few feet away, looking for a way to reopen it. He watched in amazement as the edges of the door seemed to expand and seal tight, then the mountain itself seemed to hide it away. He looked on as soil fell above the entrance and settled on the hidden door. Next, vines, trees, rocks, and grass seemed to sprout out of that soil. Finally, snow and ice formed on top of everything, sealing the cave and completely hiding it from the outside world. The mountainside looked utterly natural and undisturbed.

"Cassandra," he whispered and touched the newly formed snow.

CHAPTER 9

CASSANDRA AND CASS

Kringus sat in the captain's quarters with Captain Biggles, both men sipping on some robust ale that Biggles only partook of on special occasions. He considered having a king aboard his ship a worthy event. Kringus's men were below deck, most of them sleeping. The captain knew the elvish brothers Von and Lenore were awake and most likely watching over Kringus at that very moment. A smile creased his face at the thought of having such powerful and faithful friends.

Biggles brought his mug up in a toast. "To safe travels to Pelesea."

Kringus nodded and tapped the mug with his own. He then downed most of the drink in one giant gulp. The drink was more potent than Kringus expected, and even though he did not cough it up, the wise captain caught on quickly to his discomfort. He smiled at Kringus and similarly downed his mug.

"Another?" Biggles asked.

Kringus nodded and held his mug out for a refill. This one he sipped on as they spoke. The captain followed suit, and they relaxed into a comfortable conversation. Kringus was glad to be on the water and finally heading home from such a disastrous journey. He thought of his good friend, Arrin, and the others he was forced to leave behind. He stared into the small stove, lost in his thoughts.

"You are concerned over those bodies we carry in the ship's hull?" Biggles finally asked.

Kringus's eyes flared as he shifted his gaze to the wily captain. He took a large gulp of the liquid, then nodded his agreement. "Men lost their lives on this journey, Captain. Good men who were even better friends."

"Aye, I understand completely."

"Do you?" Kringus asked skeptically.

"Of course. You are a king, ruling over many people. Each death affects you and haunts you. They remind you of your failings and make you question your decisions. You often think of them daily; worst of all, they become your friends. When they die under your leadership, you take it personally. Yes, dear Kringus, I understand you better than you know."

Kringus nodded with every word. "How do you know this?" he asked.

"I am the ship's captain; people are under my care, same as you, only on a much smaller scale. I remember every man and woman who has lost their lives on this ship. I remember them all, whether their deaths were due to my decisions or not. We are not so different, dear king."

Biggles then refilled both mugs, and the men sat silently for quite some time. Kringus stared into the fire, sipping the potent ale, lost in his troubled thoughts. Biggles just leaned back in his captain's chair and thought of the good sailors and, as Kringus pointed out, the good friends he had lost over the years.

"Don't you worry, Your Highness, we will have you home within a dozen days or so, and you will start to feel better. A king needs his queen in times like this, and from what I hear, you have the fairest in the lands, if you do not mind me saying," Biggles said, catching himself, hoping he had not offended the mighty king.

Kringus smiled at that and even gave a small chuckle. The king's joy made Biggles relax, and he stood up and tossed a log into the stove. Kringus took a big sip of the ale as the captain poked the fire, setting the logs in a favorable position for burning. Kringus watched him, his thoughts suddenly on Penelope. He did feel better just thinking of her. Biggles was right; home would make him feel in control once more.

His gaze drifted past the captain and out the small, circular window on the door that gave a view of the ship's deck. There he could see Boz sitting cross-legged on the bow, hands resting on his knees, staring out to sea. Kringus imagined the young carofex probably had his eyes closed but could not tell since his back was facing him. Despite the frigid temperatures, Boz was shirtless during his meditation, the giant flame tattoo covering most of his back on full display. Since they had set sail six hours earlier, Boz had kept to himself, and Kringus noticed that the ship's crew kept a wide berth of the carofex. Their new ally was an extraordinary character indeed.

"What of him?" Kringus asked.

Biggles stopped poking around in the fire and looked at Kringus, then out the small window, when Kringus nodded in that direction. He walked over and took a peek outside, noting the carofex. Then, he turned back to Kringus with a smile, but stayed at the door as if suddenly on guard.

"Your friend? Well, he is special," Biggles said.

"Why does your crew shun him?"

Biggles chuckled and shook his head. "Do not confuse fear with respect, my king. They do not shun the carofex; they respect him."

"So, why not converse with him? Why not accept him as a traveler on the ship? You speak to me; does that mean you do not respect me because you speak with me? Should I be offended, good captain?"

Biggles laughed at that and patted the air with his hands. "Very well, your point is made, Kringus." The captain turned to the window and the meditating carofex. His laugh faded, and his smile slowly melted from his face. Kringus watched in amazement as the captain even put his hand on the hilt of his saber and swallowed hard.

"The truth is, My Lord," he said, never taking his eyes off Boz, "the carofex of Mecca-Loraine are believed to be, how should I say it? Unnatural."

"How so?" Kringus asked, suddenly very concerned.

Biggles turned his attention back to the king, but subconsciously kept his hand on the hilt of his sword. "It is believed they are in league with a great demon, one that gives them power over fire."

"Demon? Power over the fire, you say?" Kringus asked skeptically.

"Yes, the demon is all hearsay, and there is no proof of a beast in the great monastery. Their control over fire is not an exaggeration, and I've seen them use it to decimate anyone who stands in their way. They are deadly fighters, but they connect physically with the fire element, or if the demon story is true, possibly to hell itself.

"So, you ask why my men avoid your friend? It is because the unpredictability of his race could have our beloved ship sunk, and all of us with it, before we ever see land again."

Kringus stared at the man as he told his tale and knew that the old captain believed every word he said. He understood then that there was much more to their new ally than Kringus knew. The fear in the captain's voice made it abundantly clear that Boz was dangerous. That was all right with Kringus as long as he was on his side. In truth, he knew little of the man and even less of his abilities.

"Let's just say it will be a long two weeks at sea," Biggles said.

He then turned his attention to the small window and noticed that Boz had disappeared. His grip tightened on his sword hilt, and he swallowed harder. Then, under his breath, he muttered, "A very long two weeks."

The next day, Kringus, Von, and Lenore stood at the bow of *The Siren's Scourge*, the ship bobbing as it cut through the waves, making each of them hold tight to the railing. The sun was setting, and they were anxious to put another day at sea behind them. Captain Biggles joined them after briefly meeting with Agatha, his first mate.

"Good evening, Kringus and good elves," he greeted them.

"Captain," Kringus nodded.

"I have excellent news, my friends; it seems we are ahead of schedule due to the good weather we have experienced since setting off from Mecca-Loraine. Therefore, we could make port in ten days or fewer if the sea continues cooperating."

All three of them glanced over the bow to the choppy sea, then shared a confused look.

"Believe me, this is mild compared to what it could be this time of year," the captain explained, sensing their confusion.

"Very well, Captain. That is great news," Kringus said with a friendly smile.

"I thought you would be glad to know. I'm sure all of you are eager to be back home and off my bouncing ship," Biggles said with a great laugh.

"You are not wrong, good captain," Kringus said and joined in the captain's laughing.

Kringus noticed that Boz approached them, having just come to the top deck. Biggles followed his gaze and quickly picked up the quiet but dangerous carofex. All four remained silent, watching in anticipation until the carofex joined them.

"Captain," Boz said, then gave a slight bow.

"Good evening, Boz. I hope your travel aboard my ship has been to your liking."

"It is not to my *un*liking," the carofex replied.

Biggles shifted uncomfortably to his other foot and stood there for a few moments as the party stood in silence. Finally, he smiled and said, "Very well, I must go now and study the charts to make sure we avoid some of the reefs near our course. I bid you all a good night."

"Goodnight, Captain," Kringus said, and the elves each copied his sentiment as the captain returned to his quarters.

Boz watched the nervous man leave, and all three of the others noticed that Biggles turned to regard the carofex one last time before shutting the door. When he saw the carofex watching him, he smiled and nodded slightly. Kringus could only imagine that the captain had his hand on his saber as he locked the door behind him.

Boz turned to the friends without acknowledging anything unusual about the exchange. "Kringus, I have checked the bodies of your fallen comrades, and they are well preserved and remain at a cool temperature."

"Thank you, Boz. I appreciate your concern over our most precious cargo," Kringus replied, turning back to face the ocean, and leaning against the rail.

"We will take our leave as well, my king," Lenore said, Von beside him.

"Sleep well, my friends, just another few days, and we'll be home," Kringus encouraged them.

The elven brothers stopped and nodded to Boz, who returned the gesture. The elves were soon gone after that, leaving Boz and Kringus alone. The king could see the carofex from the corner of his eye, standing firm, with his arms crossed over his chest and facing the ocean.

"Ever notice how everyone seems to flee your presence, good carofex?" Kringus asked, not diverting his gaze from the strong sea.

"Of course, as well they should."

"What do you mean?"

"They know my skill set, so they know it is safe to keep their distance."

Kringus then turned to look at the carofex, who kept his gaze on the ocean. He could only chuckle and shake his head at the strange man. "So, you are not bothered by the fact that every other person on this ship is afraid of you?" he asked.

His words got the attention of the carofex, who turned to look at him. "You think they fear me?"

Remembering the captain's words from earlier, Kringus said, "You think they respect you and not fear you?"

"They are the same. If I have earned the ship hands' respect, they should be afraid of me," Boz explained, then turned his attention back to the sea.

Kringus smiled and turned his gaze back as well. Perhaps there was truth to the words; maybe he, too, should fear the carofex. Those thoughts ran through his head as the two stood there for many moments.

Kringus finally broke the silence, "They say the carofex of Mecca-Loraine worship a demon and can call on its powers at any time."

Kringus watched for the carofex's reaction out of the corner of his eye but saw no change in his demeanor. Instead, the man stood perfectly still and replied without hesitation, "They are incorrect."

"I see. But you hold some great power over the flames?" Kringus pried.

"Yes, the carofex of Mecca-Loraine practice meditations that allow us to understand the element of fire more than most."

"I find that hard to believe, dear carofex, as I have come face to face with the worst fire imaginable," Kringus said, unbuttoning his shirt to reveal his scarred neck and chest.

Boz turned and took note of the many scars, obviously caused by intense heat. He nodded his understanding as Kringus buttoned his shirt.

"From a demon?" the carofex asked.

"An ancient red dragon."

"And you survived?"

"One of us did," Kringus answered truthfully.

The two stared at each other for several moments; the only sound on the ship's deck was the wind and the waves crashing against the hull. Eventually, the two shared a great laugh, and at that point, Kringus felt like Boz truly belonged beside him. They bonded during that conversation, putting the king's mind at ease. He trusted the carofex fully from that point forward.

"Who was he?" Daro asked, standing behind Baxter as he kneeled over Cedric's lifeless form.

"I'm not sure," he answered, taking Cedric's holy symbol into his hand, and studying it. "Looks like a priest, but I do not recognize this holy symbol."

"He must be the one responsible for the party? Perhaps the leader?" Daro reasoned.

"That would be my guess," Baxter answered, then stood to take in the sight of the mountainous slope in front of him where the others had disappeared.

Daro turned to look at the mountain as well, studying it from afar, searching for clues as to where the others had gone. "So, it just swallowed them whole?" he asked, turning back to the wizard.

"No, it was a cave—at least for a few moments," Baxter corrected, shaking his head. "Powerful magic did this, my ranger companion. I've never seen anything like it, and I consider its power almost god-like."

"God-like?"

"Yes, not even Lady Victoria could reopen that cave," Baxter confirmed.

He had performed a minor magic detection spell once the cave had sealed him from the party. The power he detected there was more potent and concentrated than anything he had encountered over his years as a wizard and as an instructor.

"So, what now?" Daro asked.

Baxter just shook his head and lowered his gaze in defeat. "I do not know."

"The perimeter is safe," Gabriel interrupted them, walking over to the two companions, his expression solemn.

"We are sorry for your losses," Daro said with a nod, which Baxter imitated.

"Thank you. Siv and Josel were great friends, and I will share their story with you this night over dinner."

"You are staying tonight?" Baxter asked in surprise.

"Yes, Adam and I will stay because the filthy goblins may return. We will have to leave in the morning, though, and take the bodies of our friends back to Godhomme."

Adam approached at that time and said, "Well, what do we know about him?" pointing to Cedric.

"Absolutely nothing," Baxter said, glancing back at the mysterious man's body.

"I assume you want him buried?"

Baxter glanced at Daro, who shrugged. Adam rummaged in his pack and produced a small spade. "I'll get to digging while the ground is semi-thawed. If we wait much longer, the digging will be impossible."

They all agreed with that course of action, and each took turns digging the newest grave in the cemetery. Once Cedric was laid to rest, Adam and Gabriel took the plate armor from their fallen friends and spread it around the gravesite as a marker. Gabriel shared stories about Siv and Josel, past adventures, and of forging great friendships. Daro and Baxter learned that Siv was the father of two young boys, making the event more tragic. They kept a tight watch that night, each taking shifts to ensure that the goblins would not ambush them, but the nasty creatures never returned.

As Daro took over the watch for Baxter and added a log to the fire in the early morning hours, Baxter thought he heard a female scream from the mountain that had swallowed Cassandra and her friends. He sat up and looked in that direction, but when he noticed Daro not reacting, he brushed it off as a figment of his imagination.

"Oh, Cassandra, what are you doing in there? Hang tight; I will find you, I promise," he whispered as he lay back down and tried to sleep. It took many hours before he dozed off, that phantom scream keeping him awake most of the night.

All was dark, and all was quiet. The four adventurers could not see as the darkness engulfed them, and the only way they knew they were still together was from their heavy breathing after the treacherous climb.

"Don't move; I will produce some light for us," Greyson instructed.

Shortly after that, his holy symbol lit as brightly as a torch, Greyson having used his Plath-given power to summon the magical light. The four adventurers looked around and found themselves in a large room with smoothly polished stone walls. There appeared to be no visible doors in the room, roughly twenty square feet.

"Now what?" Cass asked with a bit of sarcasm.

Greyson ignored her and said, "Cassandra, let me see your holy symbol."

"What?"

"You are wearing a holy symbol, correct?"

"Yes, here," she said, handing it over.

He called upon his power to conjure light once more, and her holy symbol lit up with the same intensity as his own.

"There, now we have two sources of light that will last well after we leave this place," he said as Cassandra placed the symbol back around her neck.

"Well, there has to be a door somewhere in this room," Cassandra said, moving close to the wall where they had just entered, finding no trace of the opening that was there just a moment ago.

She ran her hand over the smooth surface, feeling for the door's outline, but found nothing. She put her ear to the stone and listened, hoping to hear Baxter on the other side. She heard nothing, but she did feel a slight vibration that seemed to be coursing through the stone.

"I hear something. The wall is—" Cassandra began before the sound of grating metal and stone echoed through the room.

Suddenly, a heavy set of metal bars slammed down from the ceiling, cutting the room in half and nearly crushing Binta and Cass, who both had to dive to the side awkwardly. The impact of the heavy bars reverberated loudly through the small room and made Cassandra brace herself against the wall to keep from falling.

Once the initial shock wore off, the party found themselves separated, with Greyson and Binta on one side of the bars and Cassandra and Cass on the other. Greyson helped Binta back to her feet, and all four approached the barrier. After examining it, Greyson determined that the bars were cut perfectly into the stone ceiling and now were anchored just as perfectly below the stone floor. The room was divided in half by the thick, polished bars of steel, each about four inches apart.

"How?" Binta asked.

"It is more magic than mechanical, I believe," Cassandra answered, understanding better than the other three precisely who was behind such a creation.

"I agree," Greyson said, running his hand up one of the bars and trying to see where it began in the ceiling, then following it to the floor, where it disappeared in a perfect hole that wasn't there before.

"This reminds me of the holy caves of Plath. However, since this is not Plath's creation, it seems much more dangerous. And now we are separated, which I assume is what the architect of the cave wants," he added.

"What now?" asked Binta.

They all looked to Cassandra for guidance, as she knew more details about the quest than anyone now that Cedric was gone. She looked around the small room and put two hands on the strong bars, tugging them, hoping they were not as sturdy as they appeared. But unfortunately, they were, and Cassandra began to panic, for she did not know enough of what was yet to come. All she knew was that her birthright was somewhere in the tomb of Leo, hopefully somewhere in the mountain. She had relied on Cedric to provide those kinds of answers, and now everyone else relied on her for them.

Before she could answer, a sound echoed from beyond the walls, something deeper in the cave. It was a clicking sound and the rattle of a chain at first, but soon it was followed by the grating of stone as two slabs began to rise at the far end of the room, revealing two doorways, one on each side of the dividing bars. After the clicking and grinding stopped, the four friends let the sudden events register in their minds. Not one of them made a move for many moments.

"Time to play," Cassandra whispered, and the others looked at her with more than a little fear on their faces. Cassandra summoned a weak smile, which did nothing to lighten the mood.

The food was delicious, and the water was pure. Kessi ate and drank her fill, then some. The other girls understood her need for food and gave her more than her just share. After she ate, she sat back on her straw bed and tried to understand what was happening to them.

"So, why give us this food if they plan to harm us?" she asked.

"There is some kind of sacrifice we will be a part of, as far as we can tell," Sabrina answered.

"Yeah, they are fattening us up, just to kill us!" a younger girl of about sixteen years of age named Sara blurted out.

All the girls looked at her then, and her face turned red with embarrassment. Kessi smiled at her innocence, but the humor was short-lived. She looked through the bars to the coffin that lay dormant in the larger cell. Servants had cleaned up the mess after Emiline had eaten her fill and crawled back into her coffin. The dead servant was pale, his eyes wide with fear as they had carried his body away. Kessi could still see the horrible image in her mind.

Her thoughts were interrupted by Sabrina, "Don't worry, Emiline is on our side. She is here to protect us from the guards."

"She seems unstable, at best," Kessi argued.

"She is quite insane," another girl named Kimmie said in a whisper, not wanting the vampire to hear her words.

Kessi shook her head, still not making sense of any of it. She could not remember how she arrived at her cell, much less about her life before her imprisonment. She was sure she had a sister involved but could not remember her name.

"It is all so frustrating. I vaguely remember the names Matilda and Cerus, as you call them, and it took me a bit to even recognize their faces. Still, I do not know what they did to me. Even Emiline sounds familiar, but I can't remember why or how."

"Perhaps they brainwashed you before putting you in here," Sara pipped in again.

"It is possible," Sabrina agreed with a nod.

"But why? I mean, they didn't do that to any of you," Kessi answered, looking at the other girls.

"Perhaps you know something they don't want you to remember," Sabrina reasoned.

Kessi rubbed her temples, trying to remember anything, but she simply could not. Finally, she looked at the younger girl and smiled. "Sara, your name also has a special meaning; I wish I could remember why."

The girl smiled at her and took Kessi's hand, squeezing it gently.

"Either way, you are one of us," Sabrina said.

"Yeah, welcome to your new home," Kimmie added sarcastically, with a dramatic wave of her hand.

That broke the dour mood, and they all shared a much-needed laugh. Sabrina quieted them down quickly, not wanting to awaken Emiline. Kessi felt a special kinship with the other girls in the cell and immediately liked them. Whatever terrible fate was in store for them, they would face it together. In the meantime, hopefully, her memory would return. Perhaps she knew something; hopefully, that knowledge would allow them to escape whatever Matilda and Cerus had in store.

"I have been through this before," Greyson said, standing next to the bars.

"You have been here before?" Cassandra asked doubtfully.

"No, the elder priests tested my faith back in Tara; all young acolytes are tested or *were* tested back home." He paused there for a moment, remembering his childhood and his friends, especially Darian. It took him a moment to continue. "There was a cave, blessed and enchanted by Plath. I went through the cave and survived the test. I was alone then, but now we have each other. We can survive this, just like I did those years ago."

"So, how did you survive?" Cassandra asked.

"I put my faith in Plath," he answered proudly.

"I don't think that will help here," Cassandra sighed.

"Of course it will. Always put your faith in the gods, Cassandra. You wear the holy symbol of Gella, so pray to her."

"It wouldn't hurt," Cass said with a shrug of her shoulders.

Cassandra nodded and took her symbol in her hand, partially covering the powerful light it was omitting from Greyson's spell. She glanced again at Cass and then turned back to the bars. Cassandra wished that Binta was on her side of the bars instead of Cass. She did not trust Cass and did not like the prospect of venturing deeper into the caves with her. She had little choice and could tell by the look on Binta's face that she was not too happy with Cassandra and Cass as traveling partners, either.

"So, we must be smart," Greyson continued. "What weapons do we have?"

The three girls shook their heads, and Binta held her hands helplessly beside her. Greyson looked around and drew his mace. "We have one weapon, which we cannot share. But it will assist Binta and me in surviving whatever tests we will come across," he said, trying to put a positive spin on the situation.

"What spells do you have available for the remainder of the day?" he asked, taking inventory of their resources.

"I have two," Cassandra answered.

"So do I," Cass was quick to reply.

"I have none; I used my only spell fighting the creatures in the cemetery," Binta answered and shared a knowing smile with Cassandra, who recalled Binta killing the creature before it could strike her.

"I have three left," Greyson added.

"We have a weapon and three spells, while you two have no weapons and four spells. So, it is an even split. Just be smart and use the spells sparingly. We will see you at the end of this," Greyson continued.

The four stood there, frozen for a few moments, as a calm silence overcame them. The open doors offered no sounds of danger and gave them a deafening silence as a clue to what was beyond.

"Binta, you promise me you'll make it through," Cassandra said, reaching her hand through the bars.

"I will," she said, coming up to take her hand and push up against the bars so that she and Cassandra were face to face and only inches apart. "You, too. Be careful," she whispered and glanced briefly at Cass.

Cassandra smiled and squeezed her hand; her eyes shifted to Greyson. "You protect her, Greyson. I know that is your intent, but I will never forgive you if anything happens to her."

Greyson only nodded and offered a slight smile, but she could see behind the façade. She knew by his expression that he was not very confident in the possibility of surviving. Whatever lay beyond the doors was enough to unsettle the one amongst them who had previous experience with this type of situation.

She turned her attention back to Binta, tears welling in her eyes. "I'm sorry I got you into this," she whispered.

"I wanted to come," Binta said, shaking her head. "I would do anything for you."

Cassandra smiled as the tears flowed down her cheeks. Binta meant so much to her, and she didn't realize her deep feelings until that moment. The possibility of never seeing her again was too much to bear.

"If you two lesbians have finished, I think we should get going," Cass said, interrupting Cassandra's thoughts.

The abrasive way Cass referred to them as lesbians offended Cassandra, and it took all her willpower to bite her tongue. She did not want to start bickering with the vile woman before they had even started through the caves. Instead, Cassandra released Binta's hand and stepped away from the bars to see Cass standing there with her hands on her hips and a sour expression. Cassandra could only shake her head in disbelief that she had allowed the troublesome woman to come. She would have a few choice words to share with Greyson once they retrieved Zolmex and left the caves far behind.

"Be careful, you two," she said to Greyson and Binta, wiping the tears away and swallowing her fears. "Well, let's get going, then," she said to Cass as she walked confidently past her and toward the doorway.

Cass shrugged her shoulders once more and waved to Greyson and Binta as she followed. Binta watched them approach the doorway. Cassandra turned to her, flashed a smile, and said, "I will see both of you soon. Stay safe," before disappearing through the portal.

Binta stared at the doorway for many moments after the two rivals exited the room. Then she jumped when Greyson put his hand on her shoulder.

"Are you ready?" he asked.

"No," she answered honestly.

Cassandra and Cass walked side by side down the small corridor, wide enough for two people to walk comfortably. The walls and the floor were made of the same polished stone as the first room but sloped slightly downward.

"It's almost as if someone knew there would be two of us walking these corridors," Cass said uneasily.

Cassandra looked at her and could see the fear in her eyes, something she had not witnessed before.

"We'll get through this, Cass, don't worry. If we work together, we'll make it."

Cass stopped and chuckled. "We'll get through this?" she repeated, putting her hands on her hips.

Cassandra stopped and turned to face her, the look of fear on Cass's face now gone, replaced by the arrogant look she usually wore. Her expression reminded Cassandra that she would not be the best traveling companion and could not be trusted. Cassandra would have to handle her carefully to avoid starting the feud again.

"Yes, Cass, we will be fine. We will work together to overcome anything that stands in our way."

"I thought you wanted to be here. I thought you were after some artifact birthright. Is this not everything you expected? Is this not everything you wanted?" Cass asked mockingly, holding out her arms wide for effect.

"To be honest, I didn't know what to expect. I relied on Cedric to provide the answers. Now he is gone," her voice was loud at first but trailed off to a whisper at the mention of Cedric, his loss still painful to her.

Cass snorted and started walking again, saying, "I think you know more than you are letting on," over her shoulder.

Cassandra's face turned bright red, and she clenched her fists at her sides. She was already losing her patience with Cass and wanted nothing more than to slap her. Finally, Cass stopped at the edge of the light given off by Cassandra's holy symbol. She turned and gave her a sour look, waiting for her light source to catch up. So many thoughts ran through Cassandra's mind then, and she recalled the fight in the schoolyard. Her breathing quickened, and her heart raced. She was up to the challenge if it happened again in these caves. She reached up and grabbed the magical pendant that Cass had gifted her. She had the advantage this time. Both women stood there for a few moments, measuring each other, before Cassandra finally started walking again.

They walked silently for the next hour as the passage continued to slope downward, and the temperature dropped even further. Cassandra knew Cass had to be cold because they eventually began to see their breath come out in puffs when they exhaled, the temperature dropping significantly. There were no cutting winds or snow, but a numbing cold enveloped them. Cassandra still wore the magical boots, so she felt comfortable, making it hard to hide the smile on her face.

Greyson and Binta traveled through a parallel tunnel to the one Cassandra and Cass walked. The floor was similarly made of polished stone and did slope downward, although not quite as steeply. The temperature dropped, but Greyson refused to use any of his remaining spells, understanding that they had to conserve them. Finally, after several hours of walking and noting nothing of interest, they began to hear the sound of running water. It was a murmur at first and seemed far away, but as they proceeded, it became louder until it eventually roared through the cave. The smell of natural water filled the cold air, making them both shiver.

"Stay close and keep alert," Greyson instructed.

Binta moved in closer to him, wanting to share his heat. Unfortunately, the cold was nearly unbearable then, and she kept looking behind her to ensure no one was following them. She almost expected one of those nasty creatures from the cemetery to be there.

But, more importantly, she thought of Cassandra. She did not trust Cass, and her behavior deteriorated as the trip progressed. She did not like Cassandra being alone with her, although none of them had a choice given the circumstances.

"Look, light," Greyson said suddenly, breaking her thoughts.

Up ahead, the tunnel spilled into what looked to be another room, and there they could see the light flickering from a fire within, making shadows dance on the tunnel wall. Although from their angle, they could not see the fire or, more importantly, who or what could be causing it.

"You ready?" he asked.

"No," she said flatly once again.

At the same time that Greyson and Binta were discovering the end of their tunnel, Cassandra and Cass were also beginning to hear the sound of falling water. It was distant at first, but as they continued to walk, the sound echoed through the tunnel. They eventually came to a similar opening, seeing firelight dancing wildly on the tunnel wall, identical to what Greyson and Binta had discovered.

"Torchlight?" Cassandra asked.

"Possibly, and a waterfall?" Cass asked.

"Possibly," Cassandra answered.

They nodded to each other, then proceeded toward the source, sure to stay side by side, not knowing what creatures lurked beyond the doorway. Cassandra thought back to when she first encountered Cedric's room and her anxiety then. Yet, that somehow dulled in comparison with this unknown. The danger seemed tangible and hung in the air all around them.

Once they reached the doorway and peered through, they found the tunnel opened onto a small ledge about ten feet squared. At the far end of the small ridge was a rope bridge that disappeared into the darkness. There was a stalagmite beside the bridge, protruding from the lip of the tiny ledge. There, two torches danced wildly in sconces on either side of it. There was a booming sound of water falling, so loud that the two women had to yell to hear each other. Mist rose from under the bridge, making the ledge slippery and the temperature almost unbearably cold.

"Where do you think that bridge leads?" Cass yelled in Cassandra's ear.

"That will tell us," Cassandra replied, pointing to the stalagmite.

Cass followed the direction of her finger and noticed a parchment lying on the top of the stalagmite. It was open, with the ends fitting perfectly into the corners of the smoothed-off formation. They walked gingerly toward the parchment, being extra careful on the wet and slightly icy stone ledge. Once there, they noticed writing on the scroll. So intrigued were they with the strange stalagmite and ancient writing found there, and due to the fact the waterfall drowned out the sound, they never heard the stone slab lowering behind them, sealing them off from escape. When it slammed shut, they both jumped with a start and turned to see that there was no way to retreat.

"I guess there's no turning back now," Cass yelled.

Cassandra could only nod her agreement.

Greyson and Binta found a similar scene once they exited their tunnel; a tiny ledge with a rope bridge and a stalagmite with an open parchment, flanked by two torches. Instead of a roaring waterfall under the bridge, they found an underground river rushing from right to left with a giant whirlpool about twenty feet beneath it. They both peered over the edge, Greyson's light shining on the swirling water. Like the other bridge, this one disappeared into the darkness, Greyson's light falling well short of illuminating the destination.

Both shared a concerned look, then made their way to the unusual stalagmite. There, they found the parchment written in an old language, but similar enough to their tongue to be able to read it:

"See the swirl and try to cross.

Touched by two and all be lost."

"What does it mean?" Binta asked.

Before Greyson could answer, a hideous laugh echoed throughout the small cavern. It sounded evil and dry, almost like the effort to laugh was strained. Greyson pulled out his mace as Binta took a step behind him. Suddenly, additional torches sprang to life at the far end of the bridge, about one hundred feet away, leading to another small ledge. At the end of the bridge stood a robed figure, its face and hands concealed by its old, black robe. It stood unmoving, and the hair stood on the back of their necks.

"Who is that?" Binta whispered in his ear.

Greyson shook his head slowly, unable to provide a possible guess. He took a quick inventory of his remaining powers in his head and knew that he and Binta could be in serious trouble. He began a silent prayer to Plath, but it was quickly interrupted by the sound of the doorway closing behind them. He and Binta both turned to see it shut, sealing off any retreat. Greyson promptly turned back toward the mysterious figure, assuming an attack was imminent. But it was gone, and an open doorway now appeared on the opposite wall where the mysterious, robbed figure stood just moments before.

"Where is it?" Binta asked nervously, looking around and expecting it to show up beside her at any moment.

"It is leading us deeper into the cave."

"Do we follow it, then?"

"We have no choice."

He turned his attention back to the parchment and re-read the instructions. As he did so, there was a rumbling sound within the mystical cave and the clicking of chains and pulleys. Soon after, both walls of the small ledge began slowly closing in, threatening to smash them if they did not move.

"Greyson, the walls!" Binta screamed. "We must cross the bridge," she continued, walking toward it.

Greyson stopped her with an outreached hand and said, "No, get on my back."

"What?"

"On my back, and be quick about it," he repeated, lowering himself to one knee so she could climb on.

She did what he asked, and he slowly stood. "Do not touch the bridge, for I fear it will collapse."

Binta did not respond; her attention focused solely on the approaching slabs of stone that promised a horrible death.

"Binta?"

"What?"

"Do not touch the bridge, or we will plunge into the water, understand?"

"Yes, just go!" she answered in a near panic as the walls inched closer.

"Can you swim?" he asked, placing one foot gingerly onto the bridge.

"Of course not."

"Great," he said sarcastically, then stepped fully onto it, expecting the worst.

When Cassandra and Cass walked up to the stalagmite, they found a message similar to the one Greyson and Binta had found. They read it together:

> *"Over the falls and down to die.*
> *More than one you should not try."*

"What is that gibberish?" Cass asked.

"It looks to be written in old dwarvish. I learned it in Instructor Le'More's class."

"Of course you did," Cass said with a roll of her eyes.

"Did you not have him for your history lessons?"

"Who cares? Just tell me what you think it means," Cass yelled over the thundering waterfall.

Suddenly, the ledge began to shake, and both girls held onto the stalagmite for support. They soon found the source of the vibrations as the walls on each side of the ledge began to close in on them, just as they had with Greyson and Binta.

Cass quickly moved to the bridge and stood on it, holding tightly to the rope sides. She began to cross and never heard Cassandra yelling at her because of the falls. The young woman took several steps onto the bridge before realizing the light source was not following her, and Cass could not see where the bridge was going. She turned to see Cassandra standing on the ever-shrinking ledge, yelling something.

"What?" she yelled.

"Run! Only one of us on the bridge at a time!" Cassandra screamed at the top of her lungs.

"What?" Cass screamed back, holding a hand up to her ear.

"Just go!" Cassandra yelled, waving franticly with both hands for Cass to continue across the bridge.

Cass hesitated because she could not see well, and the bridge was icy. She knew Cassandra needed her to cross, but what was at the end of the bridge? It was suicide to continue without a light source. She stopped after several more steps and turned back to Cassandra just in time to see her desperately jump onto the bridge, narrowly escaping the crushing walls as they sealed shut behind her.

Greyson's trek across the swaying bridge was challenging. He knew from the broken language of the parchment that Binta could not touch the bridge without something terrible happening. Keeping his balance on the unstable thing while trying to keep his head up in case the hooded phantom appeared again proved unbearable. By the time they reached the far ledge, his legs were trembling, and he was sweating profusely.

As soon as he got off the bridge, Binta hopped down and helped Greyson into a sitting position. She hugged him tightly, realizing it had been a chore to carry her across. He took out his waterskin, took a giant gulp, and then handed it to Binta, who politely shook her head.

"Well, that was easy," he joked with a smile.

His light of the situation made her laugh, but they heard the mysterious chuckle again, echoing all around the cavern. Finally, they both stood, and Greyson took up his mace.

"Who are you?" he asked, getting no response. The laughing stopped as quickly as it had started, but it reminded them that they were not alone in the strange cave.

"We passed your test," Greyson yelled out. "Show yourself; we've earned that much."

They both waited for the cloaked figure to appear on the small ledge. Neither knew that the mysterious person or creature was the owner of the creepy laugh, but they both assumed that was the case. Nothing happened, and the only noise was the swirling water behind them.

"Let's move on then," Greyson said, nodding toward the next doorway.

Binta nodded, so they moved side by side through the doorway, which took them deeper into the mountain. After several more hours of traveling through the new tunnel, which seemed to twist and turn every few feet, sometimes climbing upward and dropping back down, they finally reached a level area. It opened into a small chamber with three passageways leading deeper into the mountain.

"I've seen this before," Greyson exclaimed as they made their way into the area.

"During your test?" Binta asked.

Greyson only nodded, his eyes trained on the three passages. His thoughts drifted back to the caves of Plath and how he had taken the right tunnel then because that is what he thought Plath had demanded of him. Blindly, he would guess the right tunnel again but decided the matter called for prayer, and he would not make a rash decision this time. Binta had taken a seat on the stone floor and was winded. He surveyed the area, not liking that there were four entrances to this little nook, counting the one from which they had entered. He felt there was no danger behind them unless that cloaked figure appeared again. He decided it would be wise to set camp there and sleep a while; then he could spend plenty of time praying to Plath for answers and replenishing his spells.

"We camp here," he stated with a certain finality.

"Fine by me," Binta agreed with a nod.

They made their camp and ate some dried meat. Their food stores were beginning to run low, and they dared not create a fire. The cave was supernatural, and neither knew what exactly could be drawn by a fire. Greyson tried to sleep sitting up to remain vigilant. However, weariness overcame him soon after Binta drifted off, and he succumbed to sleep. Neither heard the soft chuckle fill the air.

As soon as Cassandra landed on the bridge, it gave out; the anchors connecting the bridge to the cavern wall closest to her vanished, leaving nothing to hold it together. She tried to grab it before it fell away, but she missed and found herself free-falling toward the icy waters. When she finally plunged into the water, it took her breath away, and she immediately knew something was amiss. The water numbed her limbs dangerously fast, and the iciness threatened to paralyze her entirely. The water was unnaturally cold, magically cold.

It took her a long time to swim back to the surface, her body not responding well to the numbing water. When she finally poked her head above the water, she found a strong current pulling her toward the roaring waterfall. The water seeped through her clothing, and her limbs began to ache. Cassandra knew she had to keep moving as much as possible to avoid paralysis, so she paddled toward an outcropping of rocks to avoid being swept over the falls and managed to climb partially atop them. Unfortunately, they, too, were icy, and she found it very difficult to hang onto them, especially with her arms quickly growing numb from the cold.

She looked around, trying to get her bearings and catch her breath for a moment. She looked to be about fifty feet away from the waterfall. If she let go of the rocks, nothing would keep her from going over them. The stones were her last chance at surviving. To the left of the falls, directly on the other side of the icy rocks, was a shallow cove surrounded by a sandy beach. The water was calm in that cove, and she knew she would be safe if she could reach it. That meant she would have to swim at least thirty feet while battling the greedy current. She did not think she had the strength, as she could no longer feel her legs. Even if she were not freezing, it would be a challenging swim. Her grip on the rocks was slipping, and she needed to do something soon. That is when she saw Cass walking toward her on the sandy beach, just at the edge of her light radius. She did not appear wet or injured, and Cassandra thought it might be an illusion at first. She did not question her good luck and yelled over the thundering falls for Cass to help her, waving her hand desperately at the only person who could save her.

When the bridge first gave out, Cass had been quick enough to grab the rope sides of it, one in each hand. The end of the bridge she could not see had remained attached, creating a makeshift ladder out of the bridge. The other end, where Cassandra stood, fell away, and she turned in time to see Cassandra splash into the water. Cass held on tight as the collapsed bridge she clung to swung blindly into the darkness that enveloped her. She closed her eyes, expecting to slam into a rock wall or similar obstacle. That impact never came, and she felt herself swing over the falls. The bridge caught on to something above her and brought her back again the other way. She swayed over the falls repeatedly, back and forth, like a pendulum.

Eventually, the momentum played out, and she hung above the water. As Cassandra resurfaced, her holy symbol provided partial light so Cass could see the falls right under her. She let her eyes adjust to her surroundings, but Cassandra's light source only allowed her to vaguely make out the water beneath her while the area above was still shrouded in darkness. Cass needed to reach the shore, spotting the same one Cassandra did, but she needed to get the bridge moving sideways to do so. She examined a magical ring on her finger, showing a dove's wing on a blue gem. She had taken it from her father's inventory a few weeks ago for such emergencies.

A plan began to take hold in her mind, and she knew she would have to find something solid above her to rappel herself toward that sandy shore. She began to climb, and a few feet into the darkness, she felt the bottom edge of a wall. She reached out and patted the smooth stone, which she could vaguely see. She looked back down and estimated she was only about thirty feet above the water, but some fifty feet from shore. She could see Cassandra swim toward some rocks, and the woman looked sluggish, perhaps hurt or in shock. Cass used the wall for leverage to jump toward the shore the best she could, and as soon as she released the bridge, she called upon the ring's power. The magic of the enchanted jewelry took effect, making her as light as a feather. She hoped her momentum would carry her past the wicked-looking water as she floated slowly toward the shore but descended simultaneously toward the icy water.

The ring made her nearly weightless, but it was impossible to move in any particular direction while under the effects of the ring. Luck was with her as she coasted softly toward the shallow cove and managed to land lightly on the sand, only getting one of her boots partially in the freezing water. She then turned off the power of the ring and kissed it for saving her life. She quickly realized she had a decision; did she want to save Cassandra or just let the fool drown? She wanted that light source that hung around Cassandra's neck and decided the idiot might be helpful enough for a bit longer. She started toward her and realized then that Cassandra seemed to be struggling to maintain her grip on the rocks.

"Cass, help! I cannot hold on much longer!" Cassandra spat through the water as her grip continued to loosen.

Cassandra watched Cass drop her pack, but now her vision was blocked by the rock she held onto for dear life as she slipped further into the water. She made one final lunge to prop herself further up on the icy stone so she could see Cass. She was surprised by the lack of strength remaining in her arms. Her legs were numb, and the water was quickly freezing her to death.

She saw Cass throw something her way that looked to be a rope. Unfortunately, it fell short of the rock, and Cass had to reel it back in. Cassandra knew she had to reach that rope and hoped her arms would work when the time came. She was quickly losing the strength in her appendages, the numbing water draining them.

Cass reeled the rope back in and realized that ice had formed on the small cord after its brief time in the water. She stared at it in amazement to see the ice form that quickly. She could only imagine how miserable Cassandra must be in that water, and she smiled despite herself.

"Must be cold, bitch," she whispered.

She tossed it again, and it skipped off the top of the rock as Cassandra reached for it with tired and frozen arms. She reeled it in again, and the cord had more ice stubbornly clinging to it. The weight made it heavier and easier to throw, and her next toss was nearly perfect.

After several attempts, Cassandra finally grabbed the rope, but holding onto it was an entirely different story. Her arms were weak, and she couldn't feel her hands. The rope was icy, and she immediately began to slide toward the end of it as soon as she released her death grip on the rocks. She twisted the cord around her numb hand the best she could, stopping her from being pulled entirely off the line by the strong current. Cass appeared to take her time reeling her into shore, but that couldn't be, unless Cass was actually trying to kill her. Finally, she put the thought out of her mind and concentrated on hanging onto the slick cord.

Cass seemed amused at Cassandra's struggles to hang onto the rope and offered little assistance. Once she was close enough, Cassandra let go of the rope and tried swimming to shore. Luckily, the water seemed to push her into the cove and out of the current. Her struggle was real as the shallow water still drained her of heat and energy. Cassandra worried she did not have the strength to make it to the sandy beach and might drown in the two feet of water at the shore's edge. But, again, Cass did not assist her and seemed to smile. Cassandra crawled the last few feet, splashing her way to the sand and collapsing there, unable to feel much of her extremities.

"Looks like you lost one of your magical boots," Cass observed as she wound her icy cord and threw it next to her pack.

Cassandra looked down to see her naked foot turning blue from the cold. She knew then that she had to get out of her clothes, or she would freeze to death. Cassandra managed to stand on shaking legs and remove her pack and coat, nearly falling over several times as she struggled with the simple task. Then she pulled off her shirt, which was starting to freeze stiff. She was soon naked from the waist up but cared little. She had to remove the cold, icy clothes and fast. She knew her life depended on it.

She half-fell, half-sat on the sand, and struggled to undo the laces on her remaining boot. It took her quite some time to remove it, her teeth chattering as she did. That left only her pants covered in a layer of thin ice. She struggled to her knees, her body shivering badly from the cold, and she unfastened her belt with trembling hands.

"What are you doing?" Cass asked, standing in front of her with her arms crossed over her chest.

"I-I'm so c-cold," Cassandra stuttered.

"Well, I'm not having sex with you down here, Cassandra, so you might as well leave your clothes on," Cass said with a smirk.

Cassandra looked down at her bare breasts and felt ashamed of her nakedness, but she did not care; the cold was too much to handle, and Cass would have to deal with it. She managed to undo her pants but couldn't get them off by herself, so she pleaded with Cass to help her. Cassandra was on her back, with her pants partially down her thighs, the fabric stiffening as the freezing water made it impossible to remove them. Finally, she could do no more; her arms and legs were no longer following her commands.

"P-please, C-C-Cass, help me," she pleaded desperately.

Cass rolled her eyes and went to Cassandra's feet, tugging on the frozen pants with little success. Her heart was not in the effort; that was obvious, and Cassandra could not help at all as her body began to shut down. All she could do was hug her arms to her chest and try to keep her chattering teeth from biting off her tongue. Finally, Cass removed the quickly freezing pants and threw them down. That left Cassandra in her underwear, which was very wet and cold, with a sheet of ice forming on them as well. She could deal with that if they could get a fire going where she could get warm. She struggled to sit, hugged her knees to her chest, and rubbed her legs with her hands.

"Cass, p-please make a f-fire," she pleaded.

"Are you cold?" Cass asked innocently, kneeling next to her.

Cassandra gave her a sour look, understanding that Cass was mocking her. Flashbacks of the beating she took in the schoolyard came flooding back to her. Cassandra remembered thinking then that Cass might not stop, as the woman had seemed to gain momentum and an edge of cruelty as the spectacle had proceeded. Unfortunately, Cassandra was in no spot to defend herself this time, and if the situation escalated like it had that day, she would be in considerable trouble.

"Let's j-just make a f-fire and think o-of a w-way out of h-here," Cassandra stammered through chattering teeth.

"Sure, I'll build you a fire," Cass said, standing back up.

"G-great, m-my pack has s-supplies," Cassandra said, pointing to her backpack that she had taken off at the water's edge.

Cass went and retrieved the pack, which was dripping with freezing water. "I hope the water did not ruin the supplies you brought," she called.

She walked back over to Cassandra, seeming to take her time, opening the pack, and rummaging through her belongings.

"P-please h-hurry," Cassandra pleaded once more. "T-the water… it's u-unnaturally c-cold."

Cass made her way to stand next to Cassandra, the dripping pack in one hand, her other hand on her hip. She just stood there with a smirk, seeming to enjoy Cassandra's misery as she slowly froze to death. Cassandra just stared at her, watching Cass go through a range of emotions, and Cassandra assumed none of them favored her. She knew this was a crucial moment and that there would be a fire in her future, or Cass would let her freeze to death. She was at Cass's mercy and unable to build a fire alone.

"You know, before I start a fire for you, it is appropriate that you lick my boot. Remember, just like you made me do?"

"C-Cass, this is n-not the time!"

"Oh, I think it is a perfect time!" Cass interrupted and bent so she was face to face with Cassandra.

"Do you see this place?" she continued, waving her hand around the cavern. "You have led us all to our doom! Well, you and that crazy Cedric. I think you owe me more than a boot-licking, but I'll take that for a start. I suggest you get started if you want that fire soon."

With that, she stood and stuck her right foot in front of Cassandra's face. Cassandra just gave her a hateful look and tried to think of a way around the situation, but there was nothing she could do but proceed with the humiliating task. After all, she had made Cass do the same thing before they had left, even if Greyson had been behind her actions. She silently vowed once again to pay Greyson back for orchestrating those events, but only if she survived the concentrated evil known as Cashmere Ruben.

"Well?" Cass asked.

Cassandra shook her head and moved to her knees. Her joints ached, and her arms and legs were still very numb. It was hard for her to position herself on her knees to perform the task, but she grimaced away the pain and tried to think of the fire that would hopefully be roaring soon. She leaned forward and hugged her arms, trying desperately to find some heat. Unfortunately, the act made her face rest on the boot. She tried licking the best she could, but Cassandra could barely feel her tongue and had no idea if she was licking the boot. She hated Cass more than ever at that moment.

"Good job; I knew you could do it," Cass taunted, moving her foot around so Cassandra could lick the entire surface.

Cassandra only hoped that Cass would eventually build that fire; she was simply at her mercy. She could feel the ice fragments in her hair rubbing against her face as she licked the boot clean. Once done, Cass switched her feet and presented her left foot.

"Good job, now this one," she demanded.

Cassandra tried to pick the dirt off her tongue, but she was too numb even to feel the grit if it was there. Finally, she spit out what she could, but with her body starting to shut down, the drool just fell on her chin, mixed with a trail of grime and grit.

She began eagerly licking the second one, trying to complete the task quickly so that she could get warm. She was seriously worried about her body going into shock or just shutting down altogether. She knew she was in serious trouble now, and the only person that could help her was Cass. She did not like her chances.

"Does your little girlfriend lick as well as you?" Cass teased.

"What?" Cassandra said, stopping and looking up at her tormentor.

"Just wondering. I might visit Binta if we ever get out of this place. I'm not gay, but she seems to be submissive to Greyson. I bet she would be submissive to me, too," Cass said teasingly.

Cassandra's eyes narrowed, "You l-l-leave h-her alone," she hissed.

Cass knelt and grabbed Cassandra by the hair, pieces of ice falling from it as she roughly pulled her head back and screamed in her face, "You are in no position to make threats, little girl!"

"I h-hate y-y-you!" Cassandra spat out the best she could between shivers.

"And I hate you; as a matter of fact, I've had quite enough of you," Cass shouted, rearing back, and hitting Cassandra squarely in the mouth.

Cassandra fell to her back and brought her hands up to her face. She did not feel the hit because her face was numb, but she could feel the warm blood leaking from her mouth. Cassandra curled up into a fetal position and began to moan softly, bringing a wicked smile to Cass's face. Darkness crossed her features, and Cassandra could tell that Cass was thinking of bad things to do to her. Unfortunately, there was no one there to witness her actions or help Cassandra.

All she could do was lay there in the sand and shiver and watch as Cass took Cassandra's pack and heaved it into the water. Cassandra heard the splash and summoned enough energy to prop herself on one elbow. She saw her pack floating toward the falls. Then she saw Cass pick up her pants and throw them in.

"N-no, Cass!" Cassandra tried to scream, but her vocal cords would not work correctly, and her scream came out as a whisper.

"You won't need this anymore," Cass said, tossing her shirt into the water next. Cassandra's possessions were now gone, except for the holy symbol and magical medallion, both frozen stiff with ice and hanging from her neck.

Cassandra turned over on her stomach and tried to crawl away. She didn't know where she was going; or how she would outmaneuver her nemesis, but she had to try. Her legs screamed in protest as the frozen joints stiffly moved her at a snail's pace. She tried to summon her legs to move quicker, but she barely felt them and, therefore, barely moved with each strained effort of her frozen muscles. Finally, she could see Cass walk past her and make her way to her pack, where she picked up the iced-over cord. Cassandra tried hard to keep moving, but she was nearly frozen stiff and now out of time. She had only crawled about ten feet before Cass caught up to her.

"Where do you think you are going?" she asked, grabbing Cassandra's hair hard and jerking her back so her head was facing the cave ceiling. "I'll take those," she continued, removing Cassandra's holy symbol and medallion, then releasing her, making her fall face-first into the sand. Cass shook the ice from them, then slipped the light-bearing symbol around her neck, followed by the medallion, which would protect her from any magical attacks Cassandra could conjure in her weakened state.

With a smile, she took a handful of Cassandra's icy locks, pulled her head back again, and then began wrapping the cord around her neck. Unfortunately, the ice clung to it, making Cassandra even more uncomfortable and colder. She reached up with her hand to try to dig at the cord, but Cass slapped it away and kept to her evil task. Finally, once it had made its way around her neck several times, she released Cassandra's hair. Cassandra collapsed face-first in the sand again.

Then Cass began to pull Cassandra by the cord as if leading a dog.

She tugged it hard, and once the rope started to choke her, Cassandra made a feeble attempt at crawling once more to avoid being strangled.

Cass smiled and shook her head. "You are pathetic, Cassandra Rho. How you made it this far in life is beyond me. But I assure you, I will get out of this nasty place, despite your efforts to doom us all. You will not be so lucky," she teased, leading Cassandra back to the water's edge.

Cassandra desperately brought herself to a kneeling position and began unraveling the cord. The lack of strength in her arms made the task nearly impossible, and she made little progress before Cass was on her. Finally, she grabbed Cassandra by the hair and pulled hard, making her fall forward into the sand. Cassandra looked up to see the deadly water just inches from her face. She could feel the unnatural coldness it emitted even without touching it. She knew she couldn't go back into the water and survive. She simply couldn't.

Cass pulled her up again to a kneeling position, using the cord and her hair for leverage, then she pulled hard, tearing more than a few hairs out of her head, and throwing Cassandra forward once more so that her face splashed into the water. Cassandra felt the rest of her life's energy quickly zapped out by the freezing water. She managed to prop herself up on her elbows, sliding her arms underneath her and barely lifting her head out of it. It took all of her strength, and Cass was there to defeat her efforts. As Cassandra steadied herself on shaking arms, Cass sat hard on her back, keeping her from moving.

She felt Cass take back up the cord again, wrapping it around her neck several more times. Cassandra could not prevent the action, as she had to use all her energy in her numbing arms to keep her face out of the water, which was just inches beneath her chin.

"C-C-Cass p-p-please—" she tried to say, but her tormentor was not listening.

"I hope you enjoy the water because it is time to be cleansed of all your faults before you die," Cass teased, yanking hard once more on Cassandra's hair with one hand and pulling the cord back with her other hand. Poor Cassandra could do nothing but try to put weight on her arms, which could not support her. Every time her arms gave out, the cord cut off her air, and Cass pulled more hair from her head. All she could see was the darkness of the ceiling, and even that vision began to fail as the cord dug tightly around her neck.

"So, before you die, I want to know: who is superior to you in every way?" Cass asked with a wicked smile.

When Cassandra didn't answer, Cass let go of the cord and Cassandra's hair at the same time, making her arms collapse and her face splash into the ice-cold water. Before Cassandra could muster the strength to pull her head out, Cass pushed it further under and held it there. Cassandra had no strength left, and the water greedily drained the minimal warmth left in her. She knew her doom, then, and she accepted that she would die. She felt the ice beginning to form on her cheeks and could feel it clump in her hair. Her lungs ached for air, but that air would never come unless Cass let her breathe. She could do nothing about it, and so she accepted her fate. Just before she sucked in the freezing water, Cass pulled on the cord and her hair simultaneously, taking her head out of the water.

Cassandra gasped for air, but she received little of what she needed, the cord also having a strangling effect at this angle. Cass was in her ear once more. "Tell me, pathetic Cassandra, who is superior to you in every way?"

"Y-y-you a-are," she managed to whisper.

"Good girl, glad you finally admitted the truth. Goodbye, Cassandra Rho. Enjoy dying in this tomb you so desperately sought out," Cass breathed in her ear.

She then took both hands and pushed Cassandra's head back under the water. Cassandra's life flashed before her: she saw herself as a little girl in the forest, young Kessi alongside, the birds saving them from the giant wolves. She saw Sera brushing her hair, a smile upon her pretty face. She saw Binta and her heart ached, knowing she would never be able to hold her friend in her arms again. And last, a vision of Cedric's dead body flashed in her mind. She had failed him and her father. She was sad about that, disappointed that her greed for power had brought her to this very moment. She reached over her shoulder in one final attempt to push Cass off of her, but there was little strength in her arm, and she could not hope to pull her off her back.

"Die, you stupid bitch. There is no need to struggle; just die!" Cass said with a laugh as Cassandra's weak grasp finally found hold of Cass's newly acquired medallion.

Cassandra felt the magical device and knew what it was. The one thing that protected Cass from her spells, even if she were strong enough to cast one. She held onto it, pulling with what little strength remained in her frozen arm.

Then something clicked in her mind that Cedric had told her about seeing the magical energy around her. She could cast spells without a spellbook, but even if she did, the brooch would quickly negate her magic from harming Cass. Her lungs ached, and she had no choice but to breathe icy water.

The water filled her lungs, freezing her from the inside. She could feel the water inside her, killing her quickly, but she also distinctively sensed the abundance of magic within it. She could also feel the magic contained in the medallion, all the pent-up energy of the magic it had absorbed over time. In that near-death moment, she could sense the magic all around her.

She realized then that she didn't have to see the magical energy; Cassandra could sense it. As she blacked out, she forced the magical essence from the water through her arms and into the medallion, using herself as a conduit. It began as a slight tingling sensation throughout her body, but soon it concentrated in her arm and eventually fully into the magical amulet. Finally, the device exploded as a surge of energy flowed through it!

Cass flew off Cassandra and onto her back, a black cloud of smoke wafting from her chest. Cassandra raised herself from the water on her arms that barely functioned, gasping for air, and spitting up water, trying to shake the darkness that beckoned her. It took her several moments to shake the fog from her mind to realize she wasn't dead. Somehow, she was alive. Water poured from her nose, and she coughed up the freezing liquid. It took her a long while to open her eyes, which were nearly frozen shut by the cold water. She saw at that moment Cass stagger to her feet not far from where she lay.

She had a hole in her shirt where the medallion had once hung around her neck, and blood and blackened flesh were evident. Shrapnel from the blast was scattered throughout her neck and under her chin, blood gushing from many wounds. She staggered toward Cassandra, her eyes wide in shock.

"How?" she asked as she approached.

Cassandra had no strength left in her, but she knew she would die there from the cold if she didn't try to move. She managed to get to her knees, her joints aching and burning as she did, and her limbs weak and shaky. Finally, with all the strength she could muster, she got to a standing position with wobbly legs.

Cass was holding her torn neck and trying to make her way to the water, ignoring Cassandra altogether, still reeling from the explosion's shock. Cassandra staggered behind her on stiff legs, struggling to keep her footing. She felt as if she were frozen solid, and she knew that wasn't far from the truth. Dizziness overcame her, and she nearly lost consciousness several times during the small trek it took to reach Cass.

Cass knelt and began gently splashing the cool water on her neck. She also splattered some on her wounded chest, letting the coldness soothe her injuries. She never noticed or even suspected Cassandra approaching from behind her. By the time Cass turned to her again, Cassandra was right behind her and managed to kick her leg out awkwardly, connecting solidly with Cass's mouth.

Cass's head jerked back violently, and she lost consciousness for a moment. She fell into the water with a splash, immediately returning to her senses. She sputtered and splashed in the strong current as it swept her toward the falls. The impact of the kick made Cassandra lose her balance, and she nearly fell behind Cass. She managed to dig into the sand, and only her legs fell in, but that was enough to burn them even further, and she struggled mightily to pull herself out of the water's grasp. She turned just in time to see Cass go over the falls, her arms flailing as she did. Immediately, the cave went dark as Cass took the enchanted light source with her.

Cassandra wanted to die right there, face down in the sand. She coughed up more water and lay there listening to the falls for a long time. Sleep was taking her, but she realized as she passed in and out of consciousness that if she fell asleep, she would surely die. Thoughts of Kessi, Sera, and Binta made her sit up and fight the sleep. It took her a while, but she managed to loosen the ice-covered cord around her neck, and it took her numb fingers a very long time to unwind it.

She tried to remember the location of Cass's pack in relation to where she sat in the sand. She remembered seeing it when she tried crawling away from Cass moments ago. She gathered the cord with all her strength and tossed it in that direction, trying to hit it. She could not hear the impact because of the roar of the falls, but she hoped she could feel the vibration in the rope if she hit it. She dared not move from where she was because she did not want to get lost in the darkness or crawl into the water. She was as good as dead if she didn't have a fire soon. She had to find Cass's pack.

After many tries of tossing the cord, she finally hit something. She followed the tiny rope, crawling the best she could, and to her relief, it led to the pack. She opened it and rummaged through it, finding a lamp, oil, a tinder box, and a spellbook.

It took her a very long time to summon the strength to make that tinder box work, to strike a flame that ignited the oil-covered spellbook and start the fire she so desperately desired. Luckily, with some dry wood near her, she soon coaxed a roaring fire to life. She crawled around the area and gathered as much wood as her freezing body would allow. She put some on the fire and left the rest beside her.

Once it started, the warmth from the fire was the best thing Cassandra had ever felt. She curled beside it, with the wood pile within easy reach. She was naked and alone but had never felt more comfortable in all her life. The fire burned for a long time, and she slept as it did. The fire warmed her back to life and rekindled her determination. She would not only survive the cave, but she would find Zolmex and never be bullied again by anyone.

Cass had not caught her breath from the freezing water before she went over the falls, so she could not scream. She was glad because she didn't want to give Cassandra the satisfaction of hearing her cry out in fear. The dazed young woman had just enough wits about her to activate her ring once more just as she went over the falls. Her descent slowed, but not nearly as much as she had hoped. Her wet clothing weighed her down, and she fell more rapidly than she should have.

She could see the approaching water at the end of the falls, and luck was with her, as the only rocks were far to her left. She did not want to touch that water again as its magically enhanced coldness left her body numb and shaking. Also, she struggled to breathe from the injury the exploding necklace had caused. It felt like one lung was not functioning correctly, possibly not at all.

She gasped for breath and prepared for the cold plunge into the dark and icy water. She looked around as far as her light source allowed and saw nothing but water at first. She knew the current would probably take her straight ahead, and there would be little she could do to control that. Finally, she could barely make out another sandy beach to her right just before she splashed again into the water.

She hit the water rather softly but harder than she wanted, and immediately the current pulled her away. It took her freezing fingers longer than it should have to turn off the ring's power; by then, the rushing water had dragged her far away from the beach she had glimpsed. She rode the current for a bit, then tried to swim to her right the best she could. She was losing feeling in her limbs and now knew what Cassandra had gone through. She had to escape the deadly water, so she swam with all her might. If there were no beach that way, or if she was disoriented and swimming in the wrong direction, she would surely die.

Luck was with her once more as she eventually found land and crawled on very shaky arms and legs until she was safely onshore. Her clothes began to freeze immediately, and she struggled to get them off. It took her a long time to remove them as they quickly stiffened, and she shared the misery Cassandra had endured just a few moments before. She eventually pulled off her iced-over pants with tremendous effort and lay on the ground, shivering. She had no supplies, having left her pack on the beach with Cassandra, and if she didn't find heat soon, she would die. She crawled over to her shirt and reached into the frozen pocket to retrieve the magical cottage. She barely registered the fact that the third medallion she wore underneath her shirt, the one attuned to Cassandra's life force, was frozen to the inside of her shirt, but appeared unharmed by the explosion.

She half-placed, half-dropped the cottage on the sand and gave the command word. It took several attempts through chattering teeth, but she finally managed to spit out the proper command to activate the device. Soon she was inside the extra-dimensional space where a small fire awaited her. She lay down in front of it and curled into a ball. It felt so good as she and her clothes thawed out in front of the beautiful fire. Cass realized as she dozed off that she was wheezing and struggling to breathe, and there was a sharp pain in her chest if she breathed too deeply. It took her a while, but she eventually found a semi-comfortable position, and exhaustion overtook her.

In the darkness, a creature watched Cass enter the magical cottage. The beast was magical, and the extra-dimensional device did not fool it. Cass would have to come out eventually, and it would watch her, learn about her, and then take her to its master. It had time to wait, all the time in the world.

CHAPTER 10

KANE'S PLAYGROUND

Baxter awoke the following day to a robust and frigid wind blowing through the cemetery. He had found little sleep the previous night, and his muscles ached from sleeping on the hard ground. The tired wizard stretched out the stiffness in his back and examined the mountain face where he had last seen Cassandra. Unfortunately, there was no way to enter that spot; he just hoped he could find another entrance.

"Gabriel and Adam are going home," Daro said, interrupting his thoughts.

He turned to regard his ranger companion and nodded, looking over Daro's shoulder to see the two brothers preparing a way to transport the bodies of their deceased friends. He looked around at all the dead goblins and the lifeless form of the ogre and knew they had been victorious in the battle, but the losses would weigh heavily on the shoulders of the brothers from Godhomme.

"And what will you do now, good wizard?" Daro continued, refocusing Baxter's attention.

"I will stay and complete our quest," he said with a shrug, turning back to look at the mountainside.

"How do you plan to do this?" Daro asked, his eyes scanning the mountain as well.

Baxter turned to him and said, "I will use the magic carpet to find another entrance, hopefully."

Daro nodded but was not confident in his evaluation. Baxter could read it on his face and asked, "You don't think that will work?"

"You will need someone on the ground to look since you may miss obvious clues from far above," Daro suggested.

"Perhaps I shall do both if that is what it takes to find them."

"I will stay and search at ground level while you look from up high," Daro reasoned.

"You do not have to stay, Daro. Unfortunately, there is little hope that I will find a way in," Baxter said.

Daro glanced back at Gabriel and Adam, sensing that they were nearly ready to depart, and said, "They do not need my assistance. I will stay and see this through with you."

Baxter smiled and nodded, patting his new friend on the shoulder. He then scanned the mountain for clues. How they would find a way in was beyond him, but he knew time was of the essence.

An hour later, they said goodbye to their friends from Godhomme and began their search. Baxter flew his carpet slowly from up high, and Daro started his search on the ground. Finally, they agreed to meet at the cemetery at dusk to share any discoveries they may obtain. Baxter hoped it would be productive, still haunted by the scream he had heard the night before, whether it had been real or just a dream. He had an awful feeling Cassandra was in trouble and needed him.

Binta awoke with a start, sat up, and quickly discovered Greyson was missing. His mace lay next to her and glowed with a bright light. She stood and picked up the mace, calling his name softly. Her voice echoed through the multiple tunnels, and she cringed when she heard it carry. She was immediately concerned when Greyson did not answer her call. She held the mace out in front of her, the light disbursing some shadows. She glanced in the tunnel from which they had come, expecting to see the mysterious hooded figure at any moment. Instead, her hands began to sweat, and her heart pounded in her chest. What if that creature had Greyson?

She tried to steady herself and even gathered her things. She had studied her spellbook before she had slept and, now armed with one spell, ventured forward. She felt so inadequate at that moment. She was not an adventurer; Binta was a first-year student of magic and a mediocre one. She felt more like a burden than an ally in Cassandra's cause.

She made her way to the tunnel on the far right. Before they slept, Greyson told her that was the one he thought they should take, but he would pray to confirm. Before she could step in that direction, a light began to fill the middle tunnel. Someone was approaching from within it. Binta backed up until her back was against the cave wall and waited. She tried to steady the mace in her shaking hand, but with little effect. If the hooded creature appeared, or something even worse, she knew she was doomed. She could not use the mace proficiently, and her one spell would do little more than provoke a powerful creature. Perhaps it had already killed Greyson, and she was next? She held her breath and waited.

To her relief, Greyson eventually emerged from the tunnel and smiled once he saw her. "You are awake," he greeted cheerily.

"Yes, but you frightened me! Why did you leave me?" she scolded as she moved up and hugged him tightly.

"Your heart is racing," he said, pulling her to arm's length.

"I thought you dead. I thought that person in the hood had come as we slept."

"No, nothing like that. I prayed about our decision and am confident that the right tunnel is correct," Greyson answered with a smile.

"Then why were you in the middle tunnel?" she asked curiously.

"To find what was in it and to ensure there is nothing within that will follow us. I have also ventured down the first tunnel."

"Why did you go without me and your mace?" she asked, his story not sounding compelling.

"You needed sleep, and I left the mace in the event you were attacked and needed to defend yourself. I only went a short way in each tunnel. We are safe, do not fear, and I am certain the right tunnel is our true path. Also, I found this for you," he said, presenting a sheathed dagger.

"Where did you find that?"

"Back there, in the first tunnel," he answered, nodding his head in that direction.

"This is weird, Greyson," she said as they exchanged weapons.

"Why is it weird? You needed a weapon, and a dagger is perfect for you."

She reluctantly took it and looked at the nondescript sheath. "This was just lying there?"

"Of course not; there were many weapons to choose from; I selected this one for you. Would you prefer something else?"

She looked down that dark tunnel and let his words sink in. She did not understand the strange events and knew they had an important decision to make. Perhaps Kane decided that first tunnel was simply a way to provide weapons for their upcoming challenges. Maybe she should not question their good fortune; after all, they were safe and armed better than the day before. And the strange, hooded creature had not made an appearance. Binta wasn't sure if she even believed they saw such a creature. Perhaps it was an illusion or a figment of their imagination? Greyson showed her how to strap the dagger to her belt. Once it was there, she felt much better.

"Shall we go?" he asked.

She reluctantly nodded, but something about the situation seemed unusual. She thought something seemed out of sorts as the two headed down the right tunnel side by side. She stayed close to Greyson, the uneasiness only affecting her as he hummed a song to Plath that she had heard him sing before. His casual demeanor made it seem like he hadn't a care in the world as if he were walking through a warm forest with a gentle wind blowing his priestly robes. That upset her more than anything because she was terrified.

Her thoughts turned to Cassandra as they traversed the tunnel. She wondered how she was doing with Cass as a travel partner. Binta could only assume it was miserable, but she had faith in her friend and knew Cass wouldn't do anything stupid. To do so would jeopardize her chance to survive the strange place. She let out a nervous chuckle that Greyson seemed not to hear.

They walked along the empty tunnel for many hours as it twisted further into the mountain. Greyson said little and did not seem as vigilant as the day before. Binta had relied on his minimal adventuring wisdom to keep them safe, but now he carried himself as if he had all the confidence in the world and with no fear. She watched him from the corner of her eye, knowing something was not right, but not knowing exactly what was wrong or how to fix it. Even walking beside him, she felt alone somehow. She wished the party was still whole; she needed Cassandra. But instead, she buried her feelings and followed Greyson as he bravely ventured into the unknown.

Eventually, they came to a small room with a table in the center of it. On that table sat two flasks, both adorned with labels. There were no doors in the tiny room, with several drainage holes in the floor at each corner. Greyson and Binta stood at the edge of the room, looking in.

Greyson turned to her and asked, "What do we do now?"

She looked at him curiously, wondering why he would ask her such a strange question after he had led them through the mysterious cave.

"Greyson, what has happened to you?" Binta finally asked, afraid to hear the response.

"Whatever do you mean?"

"What happened as we slept? You wandered away from me, and now you are acting strange."

"Binta, I know you are afraid, but we will survive. Nothing has happened to me; I feel fine, and I am fine. Do you believe me?" he asked, grabbing her gently by the arms and gazing reassuringly into her eyes.

At that moment, Binta saw the familiar gleam in his eyes. That gleam assured her that he was all right, just as he promised. She smiled and hugged him. "I am sorry I doubted you; I am tired and afraid."

He smiled, hugged her once more, and said, "Let's enter the room; this is our next test."

They entered the small room, and the door slowly closed behind them, a large slab of stone that would seal them off.

"Greyson, we should leave; this feels like a trap," Binta said nervously, tugging his arm to go back before the door cut off their retreat.

Instead, Greyson only smiled and stood firm. She pulled on him, but she might as well have been trying to move a tree. Suddenly his strange demeanor was back, and she stopped her tugging.

"Greyson?" she whispered, but he did not respond for a long while.

"It is meant to be, my love," was all he finally said.

She gave up and turned helplessly back to the doorway. The pair watched the closing door, and once it shut and the echoing finally subsided, there was an immediate gurgling sound echoing from the drainage holes.

"Greyson!" Binta shouted and pointed to the nearest one.

Water began to pour forth and fill the small room. Binta panicked and grabbed Greyson's arm. But, again, he did not seem to notice and continued to wear a peaceful expression.

Cassandra awoke to the dying embers of her fire. There was still plenty of heat there but very little light. She was still chilled from her ordeal in the water but not so near death as she had felt earlier. She did not know how long she had slept, but it was long enough to dry the icy water from her underwear. She knew it was time to move along; staying in that spot would only invite danger, assuming there were creatures in the caves.

Luckily, Cass still had several days' worth of food in her pack, so Cassandra ate a small portion of it and lit the small lantern. She had plenty of oil for it and several more days' worth of food, but she had few other supplies other than the rope. Also, being nearly naked, with no footwear, did not make her feel good about her chances of staying warm. She had no choice but to take the current circumstances and move on. Zolmex awaited her somewhere within the cave.

She quickly looked around the beach area and discovered two ways to proceed. She could go over the falls as Cass had done and most likely plummet to her death. She felt a little guilty about Cass finding that fate at her hands. But, if Cassandra had not defended herself, it would have been her lifeless body falling over those falls instead. So, she did what she had to do to remain alive. Cass was the instigator this time, not Cassandra. Deep down, she knew Cass was dead; there wasn't a way to survive a fall like that. Cassandra felt relieved but guilty at the thought of it.

Her other option, and the more feasible of the two, was to establish a hold on the broken bridge that dangled from the ledge above. She had to reach that bridge if she wanted to live, and she quickly looked around for a way to do just that. If she could grab it with something, she might be able to pull it over within reach and use it as a ladder to leave the dark beach and deadly water behind.

An idea gradually came to her, but she wasn't confident in the possibility of it working. She looked around and eventually found a stone that was not too heavy but would add some weight to the end of her rope, making it a potential grappling hook. She tied it to the rope's end the best she could, and after the makeshift grapple was ready, she made her way to the water's edge. The unnatural coldness immediately seeped through her bones, making her joints scream in protest. She looked into the dark water and knew she would not survive another dip. She lay her lantern on the shore, as close to the water as she dared to get it. The light's radius showed the damaged and dangling bridge about fifty feet from the beach. She would hopefully use the stone to catch the end and reel it to her.

And so, she began the long and painful process of tossing the stone, then reeling it back. She lost the first stone on the second throw and replaced it with a smaller one. Once she lost that one, she tied the third rock more completely so it would not slip out, then let it soak in the water for a few minutes. As expected, ice formed over the stone, holding it tight to the rope's end. It was heavier then, but she adjusted her throwing and soon had a few close shots at snaring the bridge. Finally, after several hours of trying, she felt exhausted. With tired arms and aching legs, she sat next to the lantern to catch her breath.

She took Cass's waterskin and filled it with the icy water, taking a giant sip, then refilling it. The water was unnaturally cold, and she could feel it burning her insides, but unfortunately, this was the only water source available to her. She thought of her battle with Cass and how close she had come to death with their latest altercation. Ironically, the water saved her in that battle and gave her unnatural strength. She had felt it course through her arm when she summoned the energy into the medallion and felt its magic now as she sipped it. She had used the deadly water as a weapon, milking its magical power and striking Cass. She stared blankly into the dark water, trying to understand how it had answered her call.

Only the hiss of some creature below the falls broke her from that vivid memory. She held her breath, her eyes wide, and she watched the edge of the falls, waiting for something horrible to poke its head above the drop and spot her. She was paralyzed with fear and could only sit and watch for a long while. She understood that her lantern could be drawing too much attention, luring creatures from the darkness, but there was no way she would put it out. The hissing sound came again, still from below the falls but much closer this time. She scrambled to her feet and began tossing the rock with renewed vigor. She had to get to that bridge.

Just a few hundred feet away from Cassandra's camp, Cass stirred. Her sleep had not been nearly as peaceful as Cassandra's, and her wound was severe. Her chest hurt inside and out, and dried blood caked the side of her mouth. She wiped it away but then coughed more of it, sharp pains shooting through her chest with the effort. After the coughing fit, she examined her burned chest and realized it would leave a nasty scar below her left breast. Cass was physically stunning in many ways and always had been. Her perfect body was now scarred, and she owed that to Cassandra Rho. Her injury was just one more reason to hate the foolish woman, and she vowed to pay her back if she survived this ordeal.

She gingerly put her clothes back on, but even that small chore left her catching her breath and spitting more blood. There was a mirror on the cottage wall, and she used it to gently pick out the various pieces of metal embedded in her neck and chin. Some were buried too profoundly and too painfully to try to pull out, but she removed most of them, which made her at least slightly more comfortable.

After that, she found the remaining chocolate that Cedric had left, which consisted of two bars. She had never tried the stuff, but she knew that little witch, Cassandra, loved it. Cass took a few small bites and also liked it. She put the remaining bars in her pocket and Cassandra's holy symbol around her neck. The young wizard only had two spells left, and thanks to Cassandra, she had no spellbook to prepare more. She had no way to carry water but decided to drink from the river before continuing her journey.

She reluctantly dismissed the cottage and put the token in her pocket, but at the ready in case she needed it. She then went to the riverbank and took several large sips, which burned her insides, yet cooled the wounds simultaneously. Next, she splashed some on her neck and a little on her chest, which provided great relief, and afterward, she was ready to proceed. But unfortunately, she knew of no way to climb the falls, which disappeared into the darkness above her. Tempting thoughts of finding a way to the top of them and finishing off Cassandra greatly appealed to her. But instead, she turned from the falls and headed deeper into the cave, walking along the river's edge.

She walked for a long time, following the river as it ran deeper into the mountain. She felt as if hundreds of tiny creatures were watching her and could feel their eyes all looking upon her as she walked by. Cass was thankful for her light source because she knew those unseen creatures would probably have already attacked her by now if she didn't have it. She knew the light served as a beacon, summoning the unknown inhabitants, but it was also probably too bright for their sensitive eyes.

It wasn't long before her chest began to hurt, and she wheezed with each breath. She toughed it out for several miserable hours but eventually had to stop for a break. She sat down on a rock near the water's edge and coughed up blood. The coughing caused excruciating pain, and she clutched her chest. She knew each cough damaged her lung a little more, and she suspected she had a piece of her medallion buried there. She needed a priest as soon as possible.

She cursed Cassandra under her breath and took out the topaz medallion that Cedric had carried. The jewel was attuned to the little witch from the conversation she had overheard between Cedric and Cassandra. According to Cedric, it could tell her exactly where Cassandra was or if she was still alive. She put her hand around the stone and closed her eyes. Then, she focused, using what little knowledge she had of the device to reach out and utilize its power. She concentrated on the stone's emanations, and sure enough, she could feel it trying to locate Cassandra; no, not trying, succeeding! It took her a few moments of deep concentration to fully understand the item and its directions. She eventually figured it out and understood that Cassandra was somewhere above her, perhaps slightly behind her, and very much alive. She smiled as she thought of her next meeting with the pathetic woman.

"Come to the spider, little fly; you will not escape my web next time," she whispered.

When she eventually opened her eyes, she found herself surrounded by three giant, hairy spiders, each the size of a miniature horse. They were hideous, and the light from her holy symbol reflected in their many eyes. The light bothered them but did not stop them as they worked together to close on her, to trap her. She realized with horror that she was the fly caught in a web!

Cassandra finally snagged the lowest remaining crossbeam of the crippled bridge. The stone held reasonably well when she tugged on it to test the hold. It seemed secure, but exhaustion set in, and she knelt as she pulled the bridge closer. It took every ounce of energy left in her tired arms to draw the broken bridge within ten feet of the sandy shore. Finally, there it stopped, stretched to its limit. She held the rope in shaking hands, her strength almost entirely exerted. She needed to rest before making her next move, but the hissing sound she had heard earlier coming from the bottom of the falls had her second-guessing that decision immediately.

She would have to dive into the water; the bridge was too far out of her reach. She stood and backed away from the bridge, keeping the rope taut. When she reached the length of the strong cord, she wrapped it around her waist several times and tied it the best she could. Hopefully, the rope would keep her from going over the falls and dying. But if her makeshift grapple failed, it would mean her demise. There were no other options, so Cassandra put on Cass's backpack, tightened it, and then attached the tiny lantern to it. She had not heard from the unseen creature below the falls for a long while. Cassandra wasn't waiting for it to appear; she was leaving this part of the cave behind. She climbed the rope as high as possible, then jumped and let the bridge pull her out over the water.

As she swung back to the bridge's original position, she climbed up the rope quickly, hoping to avoid most of the water. But, as she suspected, she could not avoid it altogether, and her legs splashed into the icy liquid. She let out a slight squeal, the familiar pain of the water seeping into her once more. She found herself sliding down the rope almost as quickly as she rose. She eventually pulled her legs out of the liquid death, but the ice had already formed, creating a thin shell on her numbing appendages. Cassandra knew that if she couldn't use her legs, she would not be able to climb the bridge.

With her dripping legs out of the water, she used them to help her climb the rope, which finally had her making progress on the challenging climb. Unfortunately, she didn't realize just how exhausting the rope climbing would be, and her arms and legs quickly became fatigued. She struggled the last ten feet before she reached the bridge. She barely grasped it with her hands before her legs gave out. She held on desperately, knowing that if she lost her grip, she would most likely die in the dangerous water.

She could not see well above her, but the crashing falls seemed as if they were right underneath. She knew the longer she hung there, the less of a chance she had of completing the climb, as the effort slowly drained the strength from her arms. After the bridge settled from its swaying, she untied the rope around her with numb fingers, unwrapped it, and let it fall. The makeshift rock grapple clung stubbornly to the bridge while the other end dropped into the water, and the falls greedily pulled it in. She hung there a few more moments before finding the strength to continue.

Cassandra climbed, one crossbeam of the bridge at a time, using only her hands at first as her nearly frozen legs dangled beneath. Eventually, she could also use her feet, which helped her tremendously, although she found little strength in her legs. Cassandra could not take her rope with her, but that did not matter. She had to get off the bridge; she did not want to feel that cold water again. The rope that had nearly killed her in the hands of Cass had just saved her life; it had served its purpose.

The room was filling rapidly with water, so Greyson and Binta quickly moved to the small table. There, they examined one of the flasks, which contained a label with *"Poison"* etched on it with a strange, reddish ink. The other one was labeled *"Vigor."* They also found the following words on the stone table:

> *"One of each must drink a flask without a frown.*
> *To not do so will have you drown."*

"What now?" Binta asked.

Almost as if it were a scripted response, Greyson answered immediately, "I have a plan."

He held his enchanted mace up high, which glowed with his power of light and brightened the small room's ceiling. Unfortunately, no exit was visible, but that did not deter him.

"I have a spell that will protect me from the poison so I will drink from that flask. You drink the other one, which should not harm you. Once we have each done this, I believe a new door will reveal itself to us."

Greyson reached for the poison, but Binta caught his arm. "No, do not drink it!"

He looked at her with that weird smile and responded, "Do not be afraid for me, for Plath protects me. Besides," he continued, glancing down at the rising water, "we haven't much choice."

Binta looked down at the knee-deep water and reluctantly nodded, releasing his arm. She took her flask up and drank down the refreshing liquid. She then stood still, waiting for something horrible to happen to her. She expected to fall ill, be stricken with a disease, or even worse. Instead, the potion rejuvenated her, made her feel strong, and cleared her thoughts. She watched Greyson quaff his down and waited for the result. He had just drunk poison, and they would need Plath to protect him.

"Are you all right?" she asked, looking into his eyes, searching for some sign of discomfort.

As she looked there, she realized that she had been silly to think his actions over the last few hours had been strange. He was protecting her like he always had; he would bear the risk of being poisoned to save them. But had he cast his spell first? If he did, she had not witnessed it. Before she could inquire, he smiled and pointed to the ceiling, which now revealed an opening in the center. He helped her stay afloat as the water continued to fill the room, so they rose as the water did. Soon they reached the exit in the ceiling. He helped push her through the opening first; then, she helped pull him up as the water rose and eventually spilled into the tunnel in which they found themselves. The overflowing water soon ran into a crack in the new tunnel and drained away.

"How do you feel?" she asked him, still looking for signs of poisoning.

"A little wet," he answered jokingly.

She gave him a big hug, and they rested just a bit before proceeding. Binta thought at that time how lucky she was to have such a person to call her lover. Her mind drifted, and as they sat there, clothes dripping and feeling miserable in the cold caves, Binta thought of Cass. She was an arrogant woman who was now alone with her best friend and true love. Cass had also slept with Greyson, flaunting that fact to Binta every chance she got. For some reason, that bothered her at that moment. It hadn't affected her when she first discovered the indiscretion, but her anger began to boil the longer she contemplated things.

As they started their trek down the new tunnel, Binta's wet clothes clung to her, and she shivered with every step. Her breath was visible, but she did not notice. She also overlooked that Greyson did not seem bothered by his wet clothes, nor did his breath show. She didn't stop to think about why those thoughts of Cass filled her head so suddenly, but soon she was worked up quite a bit and even mumbled curses under her breath as they walked.

They traveled that way for some time, and the longer they went, the less Binta noticed her surroundings. She barely noted that the tunnel had many twists and eventually began to slope upward. The tunnel branched off in many directions, but most of the tunnels were too small to fit through, and the few that were big enough Greyson seemed to ignore. Binta followed him faithfully, not questioning his disinterest in the side tunnels. Instead, her mind focused on Cass as she thought of how she could pay her back for sleeping with Greyson. Then, finally, she would have her revenge.

She did not notice Greyson's smile as he watched her demeanor change. Instead, she grit her teeth and cursed Cass under her breath almost constantly as they traversed the tunnel.

Greyson awoke with a start to find himself bound to a stone slab, all four limbs spread and tied to the four corners of it. He was in a small room with one doorway at his feet. A brazier to his left emitted enough light to bathe the entire room. He tried to remember how he had even gotten into this predicament. He recalled having a horrible dream about the hooded figure and witnessing the thing's gaunt face. The vision had been vivid and left him feeling terrified. Now, he awoke and was somewhere unfamiliar and bound tight.

"What kind of evil magic is this?" he whispered to himself, testing his binds to no avail.

He stopped soon after, understanding he could not break free and recalling something in his dream; the hooded figure had taken his holy symbol and mace.

He stared helplessly at the ceiling and whispered, "Binta," to himself, realizing his love was somewhere in the tunnels without him, and that creature had disposed of him, most likely to get to her. He had never felt so helpless.

Cass sat motionless for some time, taking in the scene around her. How could this be? She had just made a metaphor in her head using spiders, which somehow came to be when she opened her eyes. It was almost as if the cave was somehow reading her mind. She slowly stood on the large rock and glanced at the three giant, hairy monsters. They closed in on her as one, seeming to use a coordinated effort to cut off her escape.

She had little time to react and even less time to think about the situation, so she did the only thing she knew to do: cast a spell. Unfortunately, she only had one bolt of magical energy remaining, along with the sleep spell with which she had defeated Cassandra. She summoned the energy quickly, and two blue darts erupted from the fingers of her left hand and hurled toward the spider in front of her, the one that blocked her escape.

The darts hit the creature in the face, and it made an angry, hissing sound in response, folding its legs to its front and shaking its head. The missiles did minor damage, but it was enough to occupy its attention for a few moments while she jumped off the rock and moved past it. She ran hard but was winded immediately, the sharp pains returning to her chest. She grasped her wound tightly and grimaced away the pain, knowing the hideous spiders were closing fast. She did not dare look back but kept her attention on finding some hole to hide in or exit from the cave. The only option she could think of was the river; she didn't want to take it, knowing all too well how dangerous the water was.

She could sense the things gaining ground behind her then, and she was slowing down, the pain in her chest becoming unbearable. Finally, she considered diving into the water when she caught a glimpse of a giant stag, moments before it jumped out of the darkness, narrowly missing her. She screamed out in shock and fell face down on the soft sand. She closed her eyes tightly and waited for the newest creature to trample her. However, the killing blow never came; instead, she heard a commotion behind her.

She turned to see the giant stag, which had a solid white coat and a set of antlers that dwarfed anything she had ever seen before. The creature stood at nearly six feet at the shoulder. The beast was not intent on trampling her to death; it wasn't even trying to hurt her. Instead, it was protecting her! It lowered its antlers and skewered the closest spider that rushed right into them. The thing hissed and squealed, making a horrible sound as it thrashed around, impaled on those magnificent antlers. She did not question her good luck and managed to regain her feet and continue her run into the unknown darkness of the mountain.

She glanced back several times to see how her new ally was doing, and the stag seemed to have the situation under control, but she did not dare stop. She did not know how many more spiders were with her in the dark. She scanned the pitch black and considered jumping into the water again, just out of sheer desperation, the pain in her chest getting the best of her. Then she saw something that caught her eye: a stairway barely visible within a small doorway built into the wall to her right. The light from Cassandra's holy symbol revealed it just before she had passed it by. She glanced back to the fight somewhere in the darkness behind her but could see nothing. Then, finally, she heard the stag cry out in pain, alerting her that the battle was far from over. She quickly made her way toward the stairway, hoping it was a safe place to hide from the dangerous creatures of the open cavern.

She quickly climbed the stairs that swirled tightly in the mountain wall for a long while. She was relieved that the spiders were too large to follow her into this small space. The climb winded her quickly and aggravated her wounded chest, making it flare with pain. She did not know how much longer she could survive without healing, but at least she was traveling upward. Hopefully, that would mean she was closer to an exit.

The stairs finally gave way to a vast cavern that stretched out in front of her in every direction. The light from Cassandra's holy symbol provided light to the immediate area but could not begin illuminating the entire cavern. The ceiling was low, only six or seven feet in some places, and stalactites and stalagmites were abundant. Most of these formations had joined to form columns, giving the illusion of supporting beams for the small ceiling. Cass stood at the edge of the stairs, using the holy symbol to light up as much of the cavern as possible. It did not help, though; the strange place remained a mystery.

She took a few steps into the cavern and immediately felt uneasy. She sensed something was watching her as she made her way through the field of stalagmites. She wandered for quite some time, trying to maintain a directional course, but once she was deep in the cavern, every turn looked the same as the last. Soon she was hopelessly lost, and she desperately searched for an exit. Her chest burned now, and she developed a croupy cough. She needed to leave the caves and find a priest, or she would die. Again, she felt she was being followed, and she stopped to listen.

She heard the familiar hissing out of the darkness, similar to the sound made by those giant spiders she thought she had left behind. She froze in place and listed intently for several moments. Then, a scurrying sound behind her had her moving quickly, running as fast as she could through the strange terrain. She assumed she would eventually run into a dead end and be eaten alive by the nasty creatures. Her chest hurt, and she wanted to rest. A noise behind her made her turn back. Unfortunately, that glance behind her cost her footing, and she stumbled into a pit.

The freshly dug soil surprised her, since everything in this cavern seemed composed of stone. The smell of fresh-dug earth was abundant, and she slowly discovered the pit seemed just her size. She shook away the suddenness of her fall and turned her attention to the opening above her, expecting the giant spiders to follow her down into the earthy hole. If not them, then something else just as horrific would surely come to kill her. She lay that way, petrified, for a long time. When nothing came, she eventually found the courage to crawl out of the pit. As she did, she realized it was roughly six feet deep and shaped like a grave. Once out, she scrambled away, trying to register what it could be. It had the look and smell of a freshly dug grave, but she noticed there was no displaced dirt.

Then she spotted a grave marker made of stone at the head of that pit with the following engraving: *Cashmere Ruben*. Her eyes widened with fear, and she quickly backed away, never taking her eyes off the gravestone. She eventually backed into a stalagmite and nearly fell, but she could not take her eyes away from the scene in front of her. Next to the hole from which she had crawled were two more gravesites, one on either side of it. One was freshly dug, just like hers, and was also empty. The other grave was old and filled with dirt, as if something or someone had been buried there long ago. Each had a similar stone marker that she could not read from where she stood. She collected her wits and looked around to ensure no creatures were ready to pounce on her. When she discovered none, she stepped closer to the graves and read the markers. The freshly dug one read: *Cassandra Rho*, and the older one had a much more aged and worn engraving that read: *Aust Goodwright*.

She did not recognize that second name, but as she walked around the grave reserved for Cassandra, she was disappointed to find Cassandra was not there. A wild thought entered her head then. She thought of Cassandra tripping into the hole and lying there unconscious for her to find. Cass would have so enjoyed killing her and leaving her in the ready-made grave. As she peered over the edge and her light source lit the bottom of the pit, she saw something metallic reflecting the light. Cass knelt and looked closer, moving Cassandra's holy symbol over the lip of the hole to get a better look. Her heart raced as she discovered a partially sheathed knife, the blade seemingly made of gold. None of this made any sense to her; three graves, two freshly dug and one much older with an unknown corpse buried there. What did they represent?

She stared at the knife for a long time, mesmerized. What kind of magic dug the graves, and who would leave a dagger in one? She began to believe that Cassandra's father indeed was a god and that the caves may hold the artifact Cassandra so desperately desired. But why would her father leave a murder weapon against his daughter if that were the case? She didn't think about that for too long and gladly accepted the weapon. As Cassandra said when they first entered the mysterious caves, it was time to play.

She eventually climbed into Cassandra's grave and retrieved the small blade. When she grasped the hilt, she knew immediately that it was no ordinary weapon. The handle consisted of a finely sculpted lion's head, depicted in a roar. The golden blade extended from its maw and appeared to be made entirely of gold, coming to a fine point, and vaguely shaped like a tooth. She immediately felt a special connection with the beautiful weapon, almost as if she bonded with it just by holding it in her hands. She liked the idea of owning it and felt safer with it in her possession. She climbed out and spat on Cassandra's empty grave for good measure and then walked away, leaving the mysterious scene behind her.

Cassandra reached the top of the bridge after what seemed like an eternity. It eventually ended on another small ledge, similar to the one from which they had started. She climbed onto the smooth stone and lay down, exhausted, rubbing her legs to bring back the feeling. She listened to the roaring falls underneath her, and although they were still loud, they seemed to be far enough away that she was safe from any creature lingering there. A feeling of relief washed over her, knowing she had escaped that part of the cave.

Although she was happy to have survived the encounter, the fact that she had killed Cass did not sit well with her. She peered over the ledge into the darkness, knowing Cass's body was down there somewhere, that place now her tomb. A strange feeling washed over her, and she cried for a long while. She was exhausted and alone and could now truly be called a murderer. Her actions had been in self-defense, but the fact remained that she had killed someone. She eventually cried herself to sleep.

Sometime later, Cassandra awakened and slowly sat up to look around. The lantern still burned brightly, so she knew she had not dozed for long. The ledge on which she sat was small, similar to the first one she and Cass had started from, and there was a doorway awaiting her. There were no other options, so she picked herself up and started through the opening. Although Cassandra was freezing from being nearly naked, moving away from the unnaturally cold water seemed to help. She felt her strength returning as she made her way through the new tunnel.

She walked cautiously along the corridor, now wishing she had a companion. Cass was the worst person she could have traveled with, but now she felt alone and vulnerable. Mostly, she didn't know what to expect from the cave. Cassandra needed Cedric there to help guide her, to help her find Zolmex. Of course, she missed Binta terribly and longed to see her friend again. She hoped Binta and Greyson had better luck making their way through the mountain caves.

She traveled for a long time without incident, and the passageway seemed to continue straight into the mountain, turning very slightly every so often. Eventually, she reached an enormous chamber that took her breath away. She stood cautiously outside the doorway to the room, peering in, and saw that it contained many pots filled with gems lining stone shelves along the far wall. She estimated that several hundred large gem-filled containers called the magnificent room home. Some even spilled their valuable contents onto the shelving and floor, leaving sparkling gems all about. Near the shelving was a set of steps leading up to a small landing that she assumed contained a secret door, though none was currently visible. There was a stone statue of a prominent, broad humanoid figure on either side of those steps. She recognized these immediately as golems from her studies at the school. She took a deep breath and stepped into the room. As expected, the doorway behind her began to shut, and she could do nothing but watch it seal off her means of retreat.

After the door closed fully, sealing her in, she turned her attention to the beautiful containers. Cassandra walked around the room, examining the various pots of gems. The light from the lantern sparkled within the stones, dazzling her. She was amazed by their beauty, but she dared not touch anything. From her studies of golems, she understood that to do so would possibly activate the magical structures. Wizards built them to protect and defend treasures or used them as bodyguards. This place looked to Cassandra to be precisely the place one would support with golems. The gems were of various colors and hues and were stunning. Cassandra assumed they had to be worth an endless amount of gold. She did not notice for a long while, but finally saw a set of instructions chiseled into the smooth stone on the wall. She approached the carvings and held her lantern up to read them:

If you are the offspring of Kane, you must pay the golem the gem of your birth.

She digested the information and tried to make sense of the words. Then, after reading it several times again, she turned to focus on the golems. They stood at attention on either side of the stairway, silent but promising death if she made a wrong decision. She approached them, and to her estimation, they had to be at least eight feet tall. She looked them over for any clues to help decipher the instructions. They appeared made of stone and fashioned after human warriors, complete with chain mail. But they carried no weapons. She could only imagine their strength and how a solid blow from one would probably kill a person.

She looked them over, daring not to step past them upon the small flight of stairs for fear of activating them. She found no clues to help her until she realized one wore a stone ring. That ring was missing its gem. The answer became apparent: she needed to place a gem into the ring setting to pass the stone golems. She could only imagine what would happen if she chose poorly, and Cassandra knew she would not get a second chance. Now all she had to do was find the correct gem. She turned and looked hopelessly at the many pots that lined the shelves.

A long while later, Cassandra sat with her back against the wall, observing the various piles of gems, trying to determine the appropriate pot from which to pick. She had been in the sealed-off room for a long time, carefully considering her pick and knowing she had only one chance to get this right. Even though Cassandra was nearly naked, the young woman was sweating profusely as the temperature continued to climb in the stuffy room. She realized then that her breathing was becoming more labored, and the air supply slowly dissipated with the doorway sealed tightly. She would be forced into a decision very soon.

She stood slowly and took a sip from her waterskin, feeling the water refresh her; it was still unnaturally cold and helped cool her against the growing temperature. Then, she walked to the shelves and found the pots containing the purple gems. It took her a long while to summon the courage to touch one, but she could not examine them properly without disturbing them. The golems did not move when she lifted the first pot and sat it on the floor, to her relief. The other containers holding purple gems followed, and soon she had many scattered across the floor, examining them intently. Eventually, she discovered only five different purple gems, hundreds of each, but only five different hues. She lined them up, side by side on the floor, and studied them. She did not know much about birthstones, but she did remember Kessi discussing it with her at some point over the last few years, and she remembered hers being a darker purple. That eliminated three of them, leaving two from which to choose. She took the darker of the two, guessing that was the correct stone, and made her way toward the golems but lost her nerve once she stood before the giant constructs.

It seemed too simple to her; add the correct stone, and she would be free to go. She returned to the engraving on the wall and read it over and over, then examined the purple stone one last time. She took a deep breath and made her way to the golem with the empty ring setting. She stood in front of the thing, the giant creature towering over her small frame. She brought the stone up to the ring, which looked like it would be a perfect fit. She placed it in the setting and took a step back, hoping a new doorway would appear at the top of the stairs. It did not.

The golem came to life and swung at her incredibly fast for something so massive. She ducked at the last moment, losing her balance, and falling hard on her rump, which sent shockwaves of pain through her still-cold legs. The stone fist barely missed her head, and she crawled backward, away from the fast-approaching behemoth. She soon found herself lifted off the ground by the second golem as it grabbed her backpack and hoisted her in the air. It brought its other fist around to smash her to a pulp. She had little time to react and folded her arms in a way as to drop from the pack and back on the floor. The giant fist smashed the backpack, destroying it and all its contents, with water from the waterskin splashing the golem and the floor around it. Somehow the tiny lantern survived the impact, falling onto the soft remains of the pack, so there was still light in the room, or she surely would have been doomed.

She barely had time to register the events before the first golem was on her, trying to crush her with a giant foot. She rolled out of the way just in the nick of time and somehow found her feet, running away to the far wall as the foot smashed the floor, making the entire room shudder. She glanced around, trying to develop a plan. Unfortunately, no doorway appeared at the top of the stairs, and there was no obvious way out of the room. She had no way to battle these creatures; her spells were nowhere near powerful enough to help her. As she ran past the shelves of gems, she knocked over several pots in a desperate attempt to slow down her pursuers.

The golems made their way quickly across the room, smashing the gems that were scattered underneath their massive feet, crushing them to little pieces or sometimes entirely to dust, and not slowing at all. She ran back past them before they could coordinate their attacks, narrowly dodging two fists as she did. She went toward the stairs, cutting her feet on the broken gems. Blood poured from her right foot as a large chip of rock lodged into its sole, and she nearly fell from the slickness when she tried to change her direction at the last moment. She did not want to climb the stairs for the risk of being trapped there. Her situation was becoming more desperate by the second.

How could she escape this? Why had her birthstone not worked? The two golems turned in unison, but one stayed on the far wall while the other approached her. They were separating; they were smart enough to develop a plan to catch her! There was nowhere to run, so she desperately considered her options. Her eyes darted around, trying to find an answer to the golems. Sweat drenched her body, and her wet hair clung to her face, her breathing becoming more labored as panic set in.

Then she saw a gorgeous, blue-colored stone, sparkling far more than the others! It was lying in the center of the room and somehow whole. She had knocked over several pots of the blue and orange gems, and this one was amongst them. It caught her eye immediately, the reflecting light dancing wildly. The rock was nothing like the other blue gems surrounding it and had somehow remained intact. No, this one was special, triggering a deep memory. She had seen rock of this color only once before but on a much larger scale. She had viewed it many times in her recurring dream about Zolmex. She thought back to that all-so-vivid dream of the birthright sitting on the table, calling her to grasp it, and her father standing on the other side beckoning her to pick it up.

That was it; Zolmex was the answer! Her purple birthstone had nothing to do with it; the unique topaz laying in the middle of the floor would deactivate the golems. A swinging fist came at her fast, and she let out a yelp and moved to her right at the last possible moment. It hit the stone wall hard enough to send flecks of stone flying, one cutting her under her left eye, and the wall cracked in several places with the impact. She ran with all speed toward the blue gem. She intended to grab it and keep running, but the blood gushing from her foot made her slip and fall hard.

She grabbed the blue gem up in her left hand, but before she could regain her footing, a golem grabbed her by that hand and lifted her easily off the ground. Its grip was so tight that it felt like her bones would crack and break. She noted that the hand that held her also wore the ring with the incorrect stone. She reached around with her right hand and began prying off the purple stone. Before she could get it out of the setting, the second golem grabbed her right arm and pulled her back.

So now she was stretched out between the two creatures, one of her arms held by each, her feet dangling a good two feet from the floor. Pain shot through her arms as the vise-like grips tightened even further. She screamed and kicked her legs, trying to pry an arm loose, but there was little she could do. She was at their mercy. She looked at the blue gem, still in her left hand, but could not figure out how to switch the correct rock for the bad one. Her focus was short-lived, though, as each golem grabbed a leg with their other hand, pulling her to a spread-eagle position.

She knew this would not end well, and she refocused on the gem she held in her hand, the only possible hope for survival. She tucked the precious treasure into her palm using her pinky and ring fingers. She then stretched her middle and pointer fingers toward the ring setting, trying to pry the purple stone free.

That is when the golems began backing away, stretching her limbs in directions they should never go. She screamed in pain, but that did not phase the unthinking golems. Finally, tendons stretched, ligaments tore, and her right shoulder popped out of place. Her screams continued as the golems slowly pulled her in half. Tears poured down her face as the pain overwhelmed her.

She vaguely heard a gem drop to the floor and noticed that the purple stone she had loosened had worked its way out of the setting and had fallen. Unfortunately, this did not disable the golems, and they took another step apart, stretching her arms and legs. She quickly worked the blue gem from her palm and brought it into her fingers. She yelled defiantly, fighting off the pain the best she could, and reached the rock out to the setting. The sweat on her arm was the only thing that allowed her to move enough to accomplish the task. The skin on her left arm tore under that effort, nonetheless, and the pain wracking her body overcame her just as she somehow placed the blue gem perfectly in the setting.

Everything stopped. The golems ceased moving, and Cassandra hung there, stretched to her limit, head down and sobbing. The immense pain kept her conscious, but barely, and when the creatures finally dropped her to the ground, the pain from the impact was dull and insignificant compared to her wounds. She fell awkwardly, and the two golems marched back to the stairs and took their place as guards, becoming immobilized.

She was face down, among the various gems, her legs still spread out impossibly wide and her right shoulder dislodged and torn. She used what little strength she had left in her battered body to witness the golems standing silently, guarding the stairs. Then, to her relief, she heard the familiar sound of gears, pullies, and chains moving from within the far wall, and shortly after that, a stone slab moved to reveal a new doorway at the top of the stairs. She smiled weakly and lay her head back down on the bed of gems and knew no more as the pain and exhaustion took her from the conscious world.

Greyson and Binta came to an area in the cave that opened into a cavernous room with many stone slabs about eight feet long with leather straps at the corners. All ten slabs were located together in the center of the room, placed in a circular pattern, and it was apparent sacrificial rituals were performed there. Many rooms surrounded the larger room, with light flickering from one of them, making shadows dance on the floor and adding eeriness to the scene.

"What is this place?" Binta asked in amazement.

"It is a sacrificial altar for the god Kane, my love," Greyson answered without hesitation.

"What?" she asked, her eyes never leaving the slabs.

"A place where you may sacrifice your greatest enemies to the king of gods and rid yourself of vermin that plague your life."

She swallowed hard, and her hand instinctively went to the dagger that Greyson had given her. She had never carried a weapon before, but the blade felt good in her hand, and she drew it from its sheath before she even registered the action. She held it up to her face, Greyson's light source reflecting in the blade, and studied it. Thoughts of Cass suddenly filled her head, evil thoughts that felt so appropriate in this particular room.

"These rooms on the outside are for special sacrifices, where the one performing the sacrifice may have a private experience with their enemy. There is one room ready, a sacrifice awaiting its doom," he said, pointing to the room bathed in light.

Binta's eyes were wide and unblinking, and she slowly turned her head to view the room he referenced. Her breath came in short gasps, and her mind swirled with the possibilities. She knew that Kane had offered her a gift; she knew she would find Cass in that room, bound and helpless before her. She did not realize that the elixir she had consumed had done its work, distorting her reality and focusing her hate for Cass. Her mind was a lump of clay, now sculpted to believe Binta would find Cass in the room. No matter what she found there, her eyes would deceive her into believing it was Cass. She also did not understand that the person she traveled with was not Greyson.

"Go to it; find your most hated enemy. Then, do what you must do," the impostor whispered in her ear.

Her head slowly turned to him, her eyes still unblinking, and a lone tear ran down her face. She licked her lips in anticipation, slowly nodded, and turned toward the room but still would not take a step. The fake Greyson smiled as the turmoil played out on her face, fighting her desire to kill Cass yet hoping she would have that opportunity. He leaned in and whispered a final suggestion, "She is in there, the one I consider my greatest lover."

Binta's grasp on the dagger tightened, whitening her knuckles. Her face turned red with rage, and she clenched her teeth.

"I am falling in love with her and cannot wait to be intimate with her again. Perhaps I will go to her now," he added with a wicked smile.

He stepped toward the lighted room, but Binta grabbed his arm and held him back. She slowly shook her head when he looked at her with feigned surprise. Binta said nothing as she walked briskly toward the room, dagger in hand. The impostor laughed evilly, but Binta never heard it; her mind focused on only one thing.

The true Greyson could hear someone conversing outside his tiny room but couldn't make out the words. He waited anxiously, sensing that someone was coming, and was so relieved when Binta entered the room.

"Binta!" he exclaimed excitedly.

She did not say a word and only walked up to him quickly, silently surveying his predicament. Then, she was by his side, looking over him as a hungry person might look over a delicious feast before gorging themselves. She slowly brought the dagger up above her head with two hands as if to plunge it into his chest. He could see the traces of tears on her cheeks, and he knew she was fighting a spell controlling her actions.

"Binta!" he screamed, trying to break the strange trance she seemed to be under. She only smiled in response.

"Binta, it is me, Greyson!" he yelled in desperation.

She brought the dagger down fast, stabbing him deeply in his thigh. Her hand quickly covered his mouth tightly, stifling his scream. She flashed a wicked smile as his muffled scream lasted many moments.

She leaned into his ear and whispered in no uncertain terms, "I am going to kill you, whore. It is nothing more than you deserve, so shut your mouth and accept my wrath."

The pain in his leg was unbearable with the dagger buried deep in it, and it took all his effort to focus on her words. She spoke strangely and called him a whore, which made no sense. Did she not recognize him?

"I will now remove my hand to hear your screams of pain and desperation, a fitting punishment for one such as you," she promised through gritted teeth.

He had to find a way to break her trance before she killed him. The waves of unbearable pain made it difficult to focus, but he had to ignore it.

"I will start by cutting off your toes," she whispered in his ear, pulling the dagger from his thigh.

The pain nearly had him blacking out, but he knew to do so would mean certain death. So instead, he tried to focus on a spell or an effect he could cast while bound to the table. He had to try something for Binta's wicked smile and crazed eyes made it clear she meant what she said. He glanced at his throbbing leg and noticed blood gushing from the fresh wound. He felt nauseous and nearly blacked out.

Binta's words had him refocusing, "I will then cut off your fingers," she whispered.

"Binta, it is me!" he yelled in desperation.

She answered that outburst with a slash of her dagger toward his face. He turned enough, so it cut a deep groove in his cheek and did not take an eye. Then, before he could scream in pain, Binta tightly covered his mouth with her hand and whispered, "Shhh."

Tears and blood pooled in his ears, and he concentrated on remaining conscious. He could feel the blood soaking his pants and knew he was losing too much blood from the wound in his leg. He also understood that whatever spell she was under would be hard to break.

Before he could do anything, Binta said, "After that, I am going to take your feet, then your hands, and eventually your arms and legs, too. As you lie there on the brink of death, the last thing I will take will be your heart. I will remove it from your chest and present it to you as you perish. Think of it; we will have hours of fun."

She stepped away and giggled hysterically, and Greyson knew she was not kidding. He could only assume that the skeletal creature in the hooded robe had gotten to her and had poisoned her mind against him. He had to think of something quick because Binta was eager to start cutting. She moved down to his feet, placing the dagger between his legs on the table, then began unlacing his boot.

"You know, you should have left him alone. He is mine, and you shall never touch him again," Binta whispered hatefully.

"Binta, it is me, Greyson!" he screamed.

She said nothing but removed his boot and picked up the dagger once more. The look in her eye told him she was lost. She did not see him; instead, she saw someone she hated, and her words made it easy for him to understand just who. He began to speak again, trying to break the trance, but could only stammer when he saw her hold his foot tightly and rear back with the bloodied weapon. He wanted to scream and kick, but his leg hurt too much to move, and the binds restricted him, anyway.

It seemed like it happened in slow motion; Binta brought the dagger forward with tremendous force, her hate fueling her attack. It plunged through his naked left foot, and he saw the blade protruding from the top of his wounded foot, covered in blood. He witnessed that sickly view for just a moment before the pain set in, and he didn't even hear his screams as it took him in and out of consciousness in a continuous battle to remain awake. Binta's smile only grew at his discomfort.

He tried to hang on to consciousness, to tune out the pain, but it was no easy task. He grimaced and groaned and pulled on his binds, trying to deal with the tremendous pain that wracked his leg and foot. The wound in his thigh still gushed blood, and the cut on his face was more profound than he cared to admit, but the pain in his foot was the most intense. His left leg was now on fire from his foot to his waist, and if she began sawing off toes, he wasn't sure he could remain awake. He had to think of something quickly before she continued her carving.

He closed his eyes and prayed to Plath, asking for answers, and when he opened them, he felt Binta working on his right boot. He peeked at her and noted she had placed the dagger between his legs again, and he knew his only hope was to keep that weapon from her. As she worked with his right foot, he moved his injured left leg the best he could to cover up the dagger. Binta seemed to be in another world and did not notice the movement. He knew that would not save him from this predicament, so he closed his eyes and prayed for divine intervention from his god.

An idea came to him then in his panic and through his pain. He credited the thought ultimately to Plath and thanked him silently several times before summoning his power of light. Binta had just removed his boot, and before she could grab the dagger, he called light into her eyes to blind her and remove her sense of sight. She let out a little yelp and rubbed her eyes, trying to blink away the blindness suddenly there. Then, she swung her fists around and growled like a wild animal.

"Binta," he said calmly.

Her fit continued, and she nearly backed herself into the corner of the room. Greyson yelled her name loud enough that it startled her, and she jumped at the sound of his voice.

"Greyson?" she asked in response.

He sighed in relief, grateful that her lack of sight had somewhat broken the spell, but he had to be careful because he assumed her mental state was fragile. He would have to choose his words wisely to keep her from slipping back into that trance and continuing her attack.

"Yes, it is me, my love," he answered.

"I... I can no longer see," Binta said, backing into the wall.

She put her palms flat against it and looked around wide-eyed, trying to get her bearings and locate the direction of his voice.

"I know, my love; I can help you if you release my restraints."

"What?"

"I am bound to the slab," he answered hopefully, knowing this would be the turning point if he were to break the trance.

There was no answer at first, as Binta wrinkled her brow in confusion.

"No, Cass is on the table—"

"No, Binta, it is me. Do I sound like Cass?"

She slowly shook her head. "No, of course not."

"You cut me, Binta. I am injured."

"What? No, I cut—"

"You thought I was Cass, but you were under a spell from the hooded figure. Would you hurt Cass? Kill her?" Greyson interrupted, knowing he had to attack her moral fiber to break the spell entirely.

"No, of course not. I... " Binta began but trailed off.

Her eyes widened as the remnants of the elixir's power diminished. She covered her mouth with her hand and stood there for a moment.

"What have I done?" she whispered, tears forming in her blinded eyes.

She returned to the slab, feeling around with her hands until she found him. She touched his blood-soaked pants, retracting her hand in horror.

"Greyson, what have I done? You are hurt!" she said, using her hands to move up the slab and feel his face, again retracting her hand when she felt the wet blood there.

"I am injured, but I will be fine if you release me."

"Oh, Greyson, I cut you. I did not—"

"You did not know what you were doing. It is not your fault, my love," he interrupted her soothingly.

She bent low, feeling his lips with her hands, and kissed him. The tears were flowing freely now as she began to sob. She rubbed his hair gently, buried her head in the nape of his neck, and cried. He let her for a short while, but the pain was getting the best of him, especially his foot, and he began to feel faint. He had lost too much blood and needed to attend to his wounds soon.

"Binta?"

"I'm sorry, Greyson," she said, raising her head and stroking his face.

"I know."

"Will you forgive me?"

"Binta!" he screamed, breaking her out of her stupor. "I need you to focus. I am hurt but will survive."

She nodded and wiped her eyes. "Of course."

"First, let us pray to Plath, and he will remove your blindness."

She leaned back close to him, and they quietly prayed together. Greyson summoned his power to dispel the effect, removing her blindness. She blinked it away, and it took her several moments to see again. Once she laid eyes on him and no longer saw Cass in his place, she nearly burst into tears. He calmed her down with a reassuring smile.

"The dagger is under my left leg. Please cut me loose, and I will perform some healing on myself."

He moved his leg so she could see it, and she quickly picked it up. He held his breath, knowing she would start cutting him again if she were not entirely free of the spell. But what choice did he have? Giving her the weapon was the only natural choice he had. To his relief, she went to work, cutting him loose. Soon Binta had him free from his binds. He did not want to use all his healing powers since they were limited, and he knew he would need to save his healing for future ordeals. So, he healed his leg and foot with minor spells, which enabled him to stand and walk independently.

She hugged him tightly once he could stand and whispered in his ear, "I am so sorry, my love."

"There is nothing to be sorry about; you were not yourself. There is nothing for you to feel guilty over," Greyson said, taking her head in his hands and looking her in the eyes. "You need to forget this. The deception is just part of the cave, part of the test. I am alive, so you have passed that part of it, and now we move on to the next thing. Do you understand?"

She nodded and hugged him tightly. Afterward, she helped him walk back into the larger room to find his mace and holy symbol lying on the floor. The impostor had left them lying where she had last seen him. There was no sign of the fake Greyson or the hooded figure, and Greyson and Binta assumed they were the same person. A shiver ran down Binta's spine as she hugged him tightly. He knew she was frightened, but he also felt it would not be the last time they would deal with the sly creature.

Later, they searched the area, finding no sign of the mysterious villain, and all the side rooms were empty except one. That one room did not contain a sacrificial slab but a stairway leading up into the darkness instead. And so, they climbed, Greyson leaning heavily on Binta for support.

Cass had traveled through the stalagmite catacombs for many hours with no interruptions and no signs or sounds indicating that the giant spiders were still following her. As she walked, she examined the unusual knife she had found. Cass did not currently have a spell available to confirm her guess, but she believed the item to be magical and very powerful. She could sense the magical energy it gave off. A collector of magic, she very much enjoyed the tooth-shaped blade. She studied every inch of it, marveling at the fine craftsmanship of the lion's head hilt and the perfect golden edge. It would cut Cassandra efficiently and effectively; she had no doubt.

Her interest in her new weapon was why she did not notice the giant white stag until she was almost upon it. It emerged from behind a stalagmite; its head lowered so as not to scrape its antlers on the ceiling. She was a mere twenty feet away when she finally saw it. She froze in place and gently put her weapon away, then slowly moved her hands to her sides to show the magnificent creature that she was unarmed. It pawed the stone floor with its front hoof, then turned and began to walk through the stalagmite maze. It stopped after a few steps, then turned toward her, waiting for her to follow, so she did.

After the creature had saved her from the spiders, she had no reason not to trust it. It was there to protect her; she welcomed the ally. It seemed to sense that she was injured and slowed to a leisurely pace. The pain in her chest was constant now but not unbearable. She grew to trust the creature even more during their trek through the maze.

To her delight, the maze finally ended, as did her adventure in the mountain altogether, for the stag had led her to daylight, pure and wonderful daylight. The cave opened into a large field of flowers, and the sun shone brightly in the sky. She stepped out into the warmth and breathed in the fresh breeze. Her sensitive eyes could not handle the brightness, but she didn't care; she kept them shut and spun around in the field of fresh flowers, hands out wide, basking in the sun. Finally, she was free of the dreadful mountain; she had survived the ordeal.

Once her eyes adjusted to the brightness, she took in her surroundings. A field of flowers stretched around her, along with a river spilling out of the cave. She knelt next to it, cupped her hands, and took a small sip. The water was cool but not dangerously cold like it had been in the mountain. She splashed some on her wounded neck and chest, and it soothed her wounds.

Then the wonderful scent of freshly baked bread filled her nostrils. She realized that she had not eaten for a very long time, and the smell was intoxicating. She stood and looked around, trying to find the source, and she noticed the stag on the far side of the field of flowers, standing there, looking her way. When it saw that she noticed, it pawed the ground, just like it had done in the caves. It was waiting for her to follow it, and so she did. She quickly made her way across the field, and when she got close to the beast, it turned and started walking into the nearby woods. She followed it, and the scent of bread became stronger.

Her trip into the woods was short as the stag led her right to a small cottage nestled in a grove of giant oak trees. She knew that was the source of the wonderous smell as it now permeated the area. The stag drifted off and began munching on a small clover patch. The quaint house was her destination; it was where the magnificent animal intentionally led her. She made her way to the creature cautiously, and it made no move to flee. She stretched out her hand and stroked it on the neck. It looked at her, munching on its snack, but did not react. Instead, it simply went back to grazing.

"Thank you," she said with a genuine smile, for the beast had saved her life.

She made her way to the cottage to find that the door was open, and the smell of baked bread wafted from within. Her stomach growled, and she stuck her head inside and called out, "Hello?"

"Hello?" returned a friendly female voice within.

Cass took a step back and waited on the small porch. Soon a beautiful woman, somewhere in her third decade of life, appeared at the door, a giant smile on her face. She had attractive features, including a magnificent smile and long, golden hair that reached down her back. She was dressed in a simple blue dress and wore no shoes. It took Cass a moment to soak in the woman's beauty, and she just stood there staring at her.

"Hello, and welcome to my home," the woman began before recognizing Cass's wounds. Her expression turned to horror, and she rushed over to gently take Cass by the shoulders. "Oh, my, you are injured!"

"Oh, yes, I am, but it is not bad," Cass began, but the woman rushed her inside and toward a large and comfortable-looking chair.

The décor matched the terrific scents as the place appeared immaculate. Plush furnishings, soft rugs, and beautiful paintings adorned the place. Cass noticed fresh-cut flowers in a beautiful glass vase as she entered the sitting room.

"You stay here, and I will get a cool washcloth for your wounds," she said, then made her way into the kitchen to fetch a basin of water and a cloth.

"My name is Cass, and I appreciate your hospitality. I don't mean to be any trouble."

"Nonsense," the beautiful woman exclaimed as she returned and set the basin on a small table next to Cass. "You are a most welcome guest, for I receive few visitors here."

"I imagine that is the case, being this close to the caves," Cass said as the woman gently lifted her chin and began cleaning her wounds.

"Yes, that is true, I guess. Is that where you came from?"

"Yes, your beautiful stag saved me from them."

"Oh, yes, you mean Magist," the woman nodded. "He is a good friend and has saved many people from those horrible caves over the years."

After a few moments of gently cleaning her wounds, the woman exclaimed, "There you are," then sat back and offered a warm smile.

"Thank you; you are very kind," Cass said.

"Now come with me, and we'll get you some food. Are you hungry?"

"Yes!" Cass exclaimed a little more eagerly than she intended.

They both shared a laugh at that and made their way into the kitchen, where many wonderful smells assaulted Cass. First, she smelled the fresh bread, which was cooling on a windowsill. In addition, fruits, spices, and fresh stew blended in a most intoxicating aroma. Next, the beautiful woman offered Cass a chair at the table, which offered a view of Magist outside the window, still grazing peacefully.

Cass suddenly grew confused and asked, "When I entered the caves a few days ago, it was bitterly cold outside. Why is it so warm now? Where are the snow and icy wind?"

The woman laughed and said, "I am afraid that the magic of the caves has kept you there longer than you believe. But I assure you, it is very much summertime now."

That made her wonder if any others had already made it out of the caves. How long had she been in there? She panicked a bit at realizing time had moved differently than she had believed. Perhaps some had died in there; perhaps Cassandra had expired? She secretly did not want that; she planned to pay her back for her injuries. She would check the amulet when time permitted.

The woman served her some of the bread and some delicious stew. It was the best food she had ever eaten, and she had a second helping of each, which was totally out of her character. Being the daughter of a wealthy merchant of Pelesea, she had learned the appropriate etiquette in social situations as a child, but she was so hungry that she could not help but be a bit of a glutton. She ate her fill and, after her second helping, slid her chair away from the table, yawned, and stretched. Finally, she felt so full and comfortable that she closed her eyes for a bit.

When she awoke, her arms and legs were bound tight with a thick rope to the chair. All of her magical belongings sat on the table: her ring of floating, the golden knife, the cottage token, Cedric's amulet, and even Cassandra's holy symbol, which still glowed duly in the daylight spilling into the kitchen. The beautiful woman, who she realized had never given her name, sat at the table across her, her pretty face wearing a frown.

Cassandra awoke to find the lantern barely burning and the room mostly dark. She could see the two golems standing at the edge of the shadows, the low, dying light giving them an eerie appearance. The battered girl raised her head slowly, bits of broken gems clinging to her cheek. She tried to rise from the floor, but as soon as she tried to move her right arm, a bolt of unimaginable pain shot through her shoulder, making her scream and fall back down. More gem fragments cut her face, and she had to stay motionless for a few moments until the pain subsided.

Once the pain had passed, she tried it again, using only her left arm. But moving her legs proved to be especially difficult as well. Both legs had been stretched to their limit, and she slowly closed them together and sat up. Both hips screamed in pain, and her pulled groin muscles shot red-hot waves of agony through her thighs. She sat there for a long time, trying to fight the waves of nausea. She picked out the remaining gem shards from her chest and stomach, and when she finally worked up the courage, she used her left arm and her battered and stretched legs to get her into a standing position slowly. The pain nearly overwhelmed her, but after some work, she was standing. She was battered, bruised, and very wobbly on her feet, but she was somehow standing.

She limped over to the remains of her pack and somehow managed to retrieve the remaining oil for the lantern with her one good arm. After a good deal of work, she even refilled it. But unfortunately, nothing else in the pack was salvageable, so she limped up the stairs, taking one at a time, then stopped to take a deep breath before trying the next. It was a slow and methodical process, but she eventually made it to the top. Once there, she limped out of the room with only a tiny lantern and no other supplies.

The pain in her legs was unbearable and made walking very difficult, but that did not compare to the pain in her shoulder, which ached with every movement. Her right arm hung uselessly by her side as she made her way gingerly down the newest tunnel. She knew if more encounters were similar to the golems, she would not survive them. She could make no more mistakes. Not for the first time since beginning the adventure, she questioned the wisdom of being there. Without Cedric's help, she felt she was doomed.

She walked a very long time, with the tunnel slowly rising upward. She had to climb several sets of stone steps, which was slow and excruciating due to the condition of her legs. So, when she reached the next obstacle of her journey, she knew she was in trouble. At the top of a very long set of steps, she found herself in a large room with a burning brazier standing in each corner. The middle part of the floor was covered with squares about two feet in diameter, with a different letter in each square. A doorway continued into the mountain on the far side of the square pattern. Unfortunately, this time there were no instructions for the puzzle before her.

The pain overwhelmed her, which turned to frustration. Eventually, doubts about continuing filled her head. There was no one to help her solve the mystery of this puzzle, and she desperately needed the help. She had little energy left even to try. Her lantern finally burned out as she looked over the strange floor. Even though she could see because the braziers offered plenty of light, the lantern dying represented how she felt emotionally. She had nothing left, no energy, possessions, or hope. When it finally winked out, she dropped it to the floor, stood there, and cried for a long time.

Greyson had to lean more and more on Binta as they traveled, for the wound on his left foot had reopened and was bleeding profusely. He dared not use another healing spell, fearing they would need them again. Binta's pleading to do so fell on deaf ears as he would hear none of it. The tunnel became less polished and more natural, with pockets of soil popping up and the walls becoming rough and raw the more they traveled. Soon, all signs of the worked stone were gone, replaced with irregular borders, an uneven floor, and even a stalagmite or two every so often.

"The tunnel has changed; does this mean we are coming to the journey's end? Do you think this will rejoin with Cassandra and Cass?" Binta asked hopefully.

"We will see in time," Greyson answered, sitting on a rock, and removing his boot to tighten the bandage on his foot.

Viewing the blood-soaked cloth, Greyson understood the seriousness of his wounds. He didn't want Binta to know; after all, her guilt from causing such injuries weighed heavily on her shoulders. He silently vowed to destroy the hooded creature if they encountered it again. Of course, he was equally frightened and secretly hoped they would escape the caves without ever seeing it again. It was very powerful and beyond either of them.

Greyson worked his bindings the best he could, and they were soon on their way again. After a few hours of difficult traveling, the pungent odor of rotting flesh began to fill the tunnel. There was no source for it that they could see, but Greyson drew his mace, recognizing the possible stench of the undead.

"I wish you had kept the blade," he whispered.

"I could not. It may well have been the charming device used to trick me into cutting you," Binta answered, shaking her head.

Greyson smiled at her and took the lead, now limping alone. He would protect her as he readied his mace, expecting something to rush forth from the darkness. He recalled the encounter with his zombie back in the caves of Plath and how frightening that was. He did not want Binta to experience that kind of fear. Nothing ever came, but the smell grew stronger, making him believe an encounter was imminent. Nevertheless, he kept them moving since there were no other options.

"Follow me closely, and keep your eyes open," he instructed.

Binta did just that, but neither saw anything until a great deal of time had passed, at which point they both saw a flickering light further ahead. As they approached, the source became evident, and they could barely make out a brazier standing in a vast opening into which the tunnel spilled. And, besides the lone brazier, they could make out a pole about six or seven feet tall near it. A stone slab also rested nearby, only a bit smaller than the one in which Greyson had been tied. They looked at each other hesitantly.

"What could it be?" Binta whispered.

With a sigh, Greyson answered, "Just like everything else in this place, there is only one way to find out. Are you ready?"

"Of course not," she said.

"Do you still have a spell?" he asked her with a smile.

"Yes."

"Be ready with it, my love."

Greyson kissed her on her forehead and marched toward the strange scene. His limp was more profound now, but he tried to put the wound out of his mind. When they got closer, they noticed that the pole had shackles hanging down from the top, and the slab had writing chiseled across it. Visible just outside Greyson's light source was a wall behind the pole and slab, and they understood the area was not as vast as it had first appeared. Also, the stench of death was much more profound near the pole.

They shared a knowing look, understanding that another test was before them. Greyson smiled and nodded to Binta, who returned another weak smile. They proceeded toward the brazier, battered and bruised, ready to put the next test behind them.

"What have you done to me?" Cass asked, trying to shake the sleep from her mind.

The woman only smiled, but she didn't seem as beautiful as before; her face seemed drooping, and her skin and teeth were darker. Simply put, her attractiveness had significantly diminished. She rose from her chair and fetched a pot filled with foul-smelling liquid from the stove. The stench made Cass gag, and she tried not to be sick, but she fell gravely ill when she saw the flies gathered around the pot.

The woman laughed at her, but it wasn't a pleasant, dainty laugh as before; now, it was more of a cackle. "What is the matter, my dear? Don't you want some more?" she teased, spooning out some liquid onto Cass's plate.

She saw the maggots crawling in the meat and swimming in the foul concoction, and could no longer hold back the waves of nausea, so she bent over and vomited on the floor, which made the woman cackle all the louder.

"You liked it the first time; why not try a few more bites?" she teased.

It took a while for Cass's body to finish rejecting the foul food she had consumed, and when she finally rose her head, vomit dripping from her chin, she caught a glimpse outside, and it was pitch black now, all traces of the sun extinguished. She only saw two red eyes staring in at her from the window. She kept her gaze fixed on those horrific eyes, afraid to look away.

"Yes, Magist wants to play with you. He will love playing with your corpse once I am done with it," the woman further teased.

When she looked back at the woman, Cass was shocked to see that her golden hair was now black and greasy. She was changing right before Cass's eyes. Cass shook her head and tried to focus on her surroundings. She noted that the bright and cheery kitchen was a dark and scary place with things crawling in the shadows, and the only light came from the wood stove and Cassandra's holy symbol.

"Who are you?" Cass asked.

The woman slammed her open hands on the table, making the magical trinkets jump slightly. Cass noticed that the woman's hands had turned into claws, her fingers now much more prolonged and crooked, and her fingernails long and black.

"You are in no position to ask questions, fool!" she hissed.

One of her eyes fell onto the table and rolled away, leaving a dark socket with a tiny, red glowing light in its place. The woman smiled, and Cass watched in horror as her mouth widened and her teeth elongated until her mouth was full of razor-sharp fangs. She took her finger and poked out the other eye, revealing another one of the tiny, red lights.

"And now you see the folly of your time here. Your death is imminent," she teased as an extra-long tongue darted out from behind her prominent teeth and licked the air in front of Cass. "Now, I ask you what these items do and their activation words. Cooperate, and I will make your death much less painful," the creature said, motioning her hand to the trinkets on the table.

"*Call to me,*" a voice echoed in Cass's mind.

She wasn't sure if the words were actual or she imagined them, but the creature in front of her evidently had not heard anything as it took no notice of it. Cass strained her ears, trying to pick up the source of the communication. Then, after a few moments, she brushed it off as her imagination. The horror in front of her had her full attention.

A powerful slap from the creature had her turning over in her chair. The strength from that hit was equal to that of ten men, and Cass had difficulty staying conscious as she lay there sideways. It did not surprise her when she felt blood trickle across her nose and drip on the filthy floor. Cass guessed that perhaps one of those claw-like fingers had cut her cheek with the strike. The gash stung, and she could almost feel it becoming infected immediately.

"*Call to me,*" the words came again. They were real; Cass had heard them a second time.

Cass tried to detect the source and briefly considered it Magist the stag, but she dismissed that idea after seeing the creature's true self. She felt her chair being righted, and soon she was sitting again and facing the evil creature that had grown even more hideous in the last few seconds. Her mouth drooled a blackish substance similar to putrid swamp water, her hair had thinned, and the remaining strands seemed to glisten with oil. Her face even drooped as skin hung from her cheeks and her chin.

"Answer me, stubborn one, or I'll eat your fingers," the creature threatened.

Cass looked around, trying not to look the thing in the eyes. She did not doubt her doom, but someone or something was trying to communicate with her. Why, unless it was to save her? Who, or what, could it be? Her eyes darted back and forth in the grey kitchen, and the only thing there that seemed to glow brighter than the gloom itself was the gold knife.

"The knife," she whispered, realizing the magical item was trying to communicate with her.

The creature looked back at the knife and then smiled at Cass. "Yes, we will start with the golden knife. I know this does not belong to you, little thief. It was the key weapon of Leo, the grand wizard and member of the old New Order. So, tell me, rogue, where did you find it?"

Cass needed the name of the blade. She had traveled for several long hours, communing with it, but knew nothing of it or its powers. But it felt enough of a connection with her to reach out during her most desperate time, or perhaps it just didn't want to be in this creature's clutches. It didn't matter; it was her only way out of this.

"What is it called?" she blurted out.

The creature grabbed her by the throat and squeezed with enough strength to cut off her air. The beast nearly crushed her windpipe, put its mouth up to her ear, and whispered, "You do not ask the questions; you answer them. Shall I infect your already mortal wound?"

It then brought a long, crooked finger before Cass's eyes and waved it menacingly. Cass could almost sense the disease emanating from the black tip of the unnaturally long digit. Then the creature stuck it deep into Cass's chest wound, digging deeply, tearing her injured lung even further. Cass tried to scream as the burning pain wracked her body, but the creature's tight grip on her throat only allowed tears to stream down her face. She gurgled and spat blood as the creature worked its finger to and fro, ripping her open and the filth of her clawed finger infecting the wound immediately. Finally, after many moments of digging and Cass nearly losing consciousness, her tormentor removed her finger from the open wound.

Cass slumped over in her chair, her chest on fire and sweat dripping from her face. Her breaths came in long wheezing gasps as her lungs refused to work correctly. The filth the creature had deposited in her chest began to eat away at her, and she knew she was doomed. She made eye contact with the beast, which mocked her by licking the blood off its blackened finger. Cass had seen enough and knew she would die if she didn't do something.

"Tell me about the blade, then, and I will give you what you want," she dared to demand as she started a severe coughing fit, spitting up blood.

The creature stood there dumbfounded for a moment and was about to strike Cass once more when Cass blurted out, "I am dead; there is no escape. Just tell me its name so I will know it before I die."

Her desperate words stayed the vicious creature's hand, and it looked at Cass with confusion at those words.

So, Cass continued, "There is no motivation for me to give you what you want. So, instead, give me this little knowledge as I go to the grave, and I will give you what you desire. You will then be able to add my powerful magic items to your collection. Otherwise, they will be useless trinkets to you."

The creature stood there for a moment, not knowing what it should do next. Finally, the two just stared at each other, Cass sweating and panting hard, trying to grimace away the searing pain in her chest, the creature simply trying to process her unusual request.

Finally, it spoke, "The blade is called 'Tooth of Leo', dear girl. It is the weapon constructed by Leo himself, the wizard enchanting it with an invincible ward that will keep the blade intact for eternity."

"Come to me, Tooth of Leo," Cass called telepathically to the knife.

She could immediately feel the hilt in her right hand. She glanced at the table and noticed the knife was no longer there; it had answered her call! Without looking down, she started sawing the rope binding her right hand.

"And the blade, although pretty, can cut through any material, having been enchanted heavily by Leo. Moreover, the soft gold metal is tougher than any steel blade. Nevertheless, it is a beautiful knife, one I will wear to remind me of how nice you were to find it for me," the creature taunted.

"Now tell me what the cottage token does," she demanded.

"Come closer, for I cannot say it too loud for the risk of activating the item," Cass lied.

The creature smiled, slid closer, and cocked her ear to hear Cass whisper the magical word. The overwhelming odor of the beast had Cass nearly losing the remainder of her lunch. Instead of whispering in its ear, she brought her freed hand up in a desperate swing, holding Tooth tightly. The creature's eye sockets widened for a moment, but the red dots of light remained the same. It had no chance to react as Cass buried the beautiful blade in the side of the thing's head.

The creature started to scream out, but its mouth never finished opening, nor did her vocal cords form the sound before she stood perfectly still. Dark, black blood began to pour out of her wound, but the creature didn't move or make a sound; it stood perfectly still. All the while, dark blood poured into Cass's lap with a sickening splatter.

"It paralyzes?" Cass whispered in astonishment.

When the creature didn't respond, Cass released the knife and began untying the remainder of her binds. The task burned her chest, and she continued coughing, spitting pieces of darkened flesh from her lung. In a few moments, she was free, and she stood from the chair and backed away, wiping the black blood off of her the best she could. Cass held her wounded chest and felt it festering under her fingers. She looked down and saw that it was indeed infected. She coughed up some blood, and Cass thought she might die from the pain in her chest as the nasty infection took hold. After coughing, she looked at the paralyzed creature and saw its beady red eyes move. It was still alive, even with the wound. An idea came to her at that moment.

She rummaged around and found some oil near the stove. She took it to the creature, bent so they were face to face, and said, "And now I take my leave of your nasty home, along with my possessions," she added, placing the ring back on her finger, the holy symbol around her neck and the cottage and medallion in her pocket.

"I want to repay you for your hospitality. You've been so kind; it is the least I can do," Cass said with a mocking smile.

She splashed the oil all over the thing's face and partially open mouth. Once she saturated the creature's face, Cass took a burning log from the fire, waved it menacingly in front of her, and said, "Goodbye, ugly one."

The creature tried desperately to move, but no matter its strength, it was no match for the magical blade. Cass took her time to bring the log back, flung it hard into its face, and immediately set its head ablaze. The smell was awful, and Cass quickly left the kitchen while covering her mouth and nose to reduce the foul odor. When she reached the door, she turned to regard her work. The petrified creature whined pitifully as its head melted. Finally, Cass moved outside the evil cabin and shut the door tight.

Then she called her weapon, *"Come to me, Tooth of Leo."*

The weapon instantly appeared in her hand, and just as she suspected, it was cool to the touch, even though it had just been in flames. Suddenly, there was screaming inside as the creature was once again able to move. It thrashed around, trying to douse the fire, but ignited the cabin in the process. Cass heard a loud crash, and the pitiful screams continued as the thing burned to death, igniting anything it touched. Cass took great satisfaction in those screams as she walked away.

She looked around for Magist but did not see the creature. Glad of it, she walked briskly away from the burning cabin, the screams now silenced. She tried her best to ignore the pile of corpses gathered in the river at the edge of the water, around the same area she had drunk from earlier. She recalled how good the water had tasted, which had her dry heaving for a bit. The effort brought her to her knees as her chest burned from it. She was lucky to be alive and took great satisfaction in her escape. She held up the golden blade and witnessed the reflection of the burning cabin within it.

She returned to her feet and hurried away from the area, just in case that thing still lived. Cass also wanted to distance herself from Magist or any other minions that could close in on her. She looked over Tooth once more and marveled at the blade. She could not wait to wet it with Cassandra's blood.

"Where are you now, bitch?" she whispered, taking out Cedric's amulet.

To her delight, the amulet told her without a doubt that Cassandra was still alive and somewhere above her. She needed to find a way up to the next level of the cave, and there she would find her prey.

"I'm coming for you, Cassandra," she said with an evil smile, then picked up her pace, thoughts of revenge racing through her mind.

Cassandra stood at the edge of the mysterious floor, trying to make sense of any obvious pattern, but she could find none. She had no idea how long she had stood there, but it felt like an eternity. Her arm ached, and her legs barely supported her weight. She was miserable and nearing exhaustion. She would have to make a move soon; she was in too much pain to continue standing as she was.

She knew she could not use her right arm in its condition, but she had little choice. She sensed a significant amount of magic emanating from the strange floor, and whatever mystery it held would require her dislocated shoulder to be usable. She reached around with her good arm to try and push the shoulder back into place, but to little effect, and the unbearable pain brought her to her knees. Waves of agonizing pain shot through her groin muscles, and she felt her hips nearly pop out of place. She sat there for many moments, rocking gently, and waiting for the pain to subside.

She closed her eyes and took some deep, meditating breaths, willing away the pain the best she could. She silently prayed to Gella and greatly missed her holy symbol, feeling closer to the goddess when she wore it. She hadn't prayed for a long time, and it felt good to relax and put her troubles into the goddess's hands. Then, as she opened her mind and asked for help, the answer became apparent. She opened her eyes slowly and glanced at the closest brazier, the answer to that prayer.

Shortly after, Cassandra was sweating profusely and shut her eyes tight, saying yet another prayer to Gella. She had maneuvered her right arm so that it was perpendicular to her body with her right hand tightly grasping the brazier, which was anchored securely to the stone floor. The pain was excruciating, and she whispered her prayers aloud now as the intensity grew more unbearable with each passing second. Again, she closed her eyes tight, spitting her words between clenched teeth in short gasps. As the moment neared, her words became louder and louder, echoing through the cavern. Finally, she could no longer stand the waiting, knowing she was about to feel the worst pain of her life. It took all of her willpower and determination to do what she did next.

She pulled hard on the brazier with all her might and leaned to her left, pulling her dislocated shoulder back into place. The pain was unbearable, and her blood-curdling scream echoed deep into the caves. Once her shoulder snapped back into its socket, the pain subsided, but she found herself writhing on the floor by then. The pain was worse than she expected, but as she relaxed and held her arm close to her chest, she said a prayer of thanks to Gella. Her arm felt better immediately after it popped back into place, but the pain of doing so had her entirely spent. She lay there a long while, holding her injured arm and praying to her goddess. Eventually, she found sleep.

> *"Sacrifice your greatest love*
> *to leave this place of death for life above."*

Greyson and Binta read the words on the stone slab together, then took a moment to register them.

"So, one of us needs to be sacrificed to proceed?" Binta asked in astonishment.

"Evidently, that has been the hooded creature's plan all along."

Greyson noticed Binta wince at recalling her actions which nearly killed him while under the creature's trance. He squeezed her hand, and she gave him a weak smile. He knew she was still carrying the weight of that guilt, which he did not want her to do.

"Listen, this place is evil and vile. We should not have come here, and I will get you home safely," Greyson reassured her.

"I just hope Cassandra makes it," she replied weakly.

"And, what of Cass?"

"Yes, of course. I hope we all get out of here. I did not mean to exclude Cass, I—"

"You love Cassandra, I know. It is easy to forget Cass, but I know you wish for her well-being, too," he responded.

Binta nodded with another forced smile, and he knew her guilt was getting the best of her. He needed to get her out of this place, but this test could prove fatal for one of them.

His thoughts were interrupted by the sudden intensity of the nauseating stench. The smell of rotting flesh had been present in the caves for some time, but it suddenly became overwhelming, making them both sick. Binta covered her mouth but still gagged from the odor, and Greyson soon followed suit. He presented his glowing mace, walked to the wall, and followed it, soon discovering they were in a rather large room, and the wall corned and cut to his left. He followed it for a bit, moving past Binta and the pole until they were nearly out of sight. Then he discovered bars extending from the wall, the ends of the bars disappearing in the ceiling and floor, creating a cell before him.

Eventually, he found the source of the awful smell, and the sight initially startled him, making him break into a cold sweat. Behind the bars was a cell full of zombies in various states of decay. His mace did not emanate enough light to see the full size of the room, but he could see at least two dozen unthinking creatures. They stood at perfect attention, waiting for something, it seemed; waiting for the bars to retract, he reasoned. They did not respond to him or his light.

He returned to Binta and said, "Many undead are watching, awaiting our next move, I'm afraid."

She blanched and asked, "Many?"

"A room full of the things are caged and awaiting release," he informed her with a frown, nodding toward the darkness. "The only thing now is to figure out exactly what this test is all about and how the zombies play into it."

Greyson went to the slab of stone to re-read the instructions there. Binta looked into the darkness where Greyson had just emerged and shivered. Whether it was from her still slightly wet clothing or fear, he could not tell. He figured it was probably a little of both. Either way, Greyson knew this test, like the others, would not be easy. He studied the slab and the instructions there, hoping he could find a solution to this newest puzzle.

After a long while, he studied the shackles on the pole and could not find a way to lock or unlock them. Each consisted of a solid metal ring and looked to fit a human's wrists, but there was no way to open them. The contraption perplexed him, and he let out an audible sigh.

"They must magically seal," Binta suggested.

He somberly nodded his agreement, "Most likely."

"So, what do we do?"

"We sacrifice the one we most love. One lives, one dies."

"Just like the hooded figure wanted from the beginning," Binta whispered, remembering the murderous trance it had bestowed upon her.

Greyson suddenly took Binta in his arms and kissed her lips gently. She leaned back, looked him in the eyes, and saw nothing but love.

He smiled knowingly and said, "I love you, Binta. Remember me and remember Plath. Live a long and happy life."

He turned to grab the shackles, but Binta caught his arm. "Wait, what are you doing?"

"I am sacrificing myself so that you may live, my love."

"No, there must be a different way!" Binta said, tears welling in her eyes.

Greyson sighed again and smiled, feeling her pain but having no other solution. The caretaker of the caves, the hooded one, wanted this, and he truly knew no other way. He would gladly sacrifice himself to save her if that was Plath's will. She would be an excellent priest one day, and although he planned to convert her, perhaps Plath would take her under his wing. A tear formed in his eye as he thought of the life now lost to him with this unfortunate circumstance.

It took some convincing and lots of tears, but Binta finally relented. He gave her his mace and what little supplies he had left, including two healing potions and a little food. Then the two lovers shared a long, emotional hug with Binta sobbing in his neck. He shed a few tears of his own, and finally, she pulled away just a bit to see his face. Her eyes were red, and her cheeks streaked from crying, but she was still beautiful to him. He would genuinely miss her.

"Thank you," she whispered, which elicited more tears.

"Go now, live a full life. Call upon Plath in your times of trouble, and he will listen. And do not doubt that every time you pray to him, I will hear your voice as well."

That revelation made her start crying again, but she nodded reluctantly. He kissed her on the forehead, then pushed her away gently.

"Be prepared; a doorway should open once I close the shackles. Leave as soon as it does; I do not want you to witness my demise. I guess it will appear on the opposite wall from the zombies," he said, nodding to the far side of the cavern.

Binta nodded back and held the mace high to light her way as she took a few steps in that direction. She turned around and saw Greyson standing at the pole about forty feet from where she stood. She could still see his face as his holy symbol glowed defiantly in the darkness.

He smiled and waved, and she returned the wave, wiping her tears away.

"Goodbye, my love," she said softly, then turned to the wall to watch for the signs of a doorway opening.

Greyson didn't know how to apply the shackles, but as Binta walked away, the solution presented itself as they opened on their own. He knew it was a magical device then but did not delay putting his hands in them. He stood with his back to the post, facing the zombies, and raised his hands over his head and worked them into the opened shackles, and they closed on their own, perfectly fitting his wrists. He tested their strength, but they held tight. Soon he heard the tell-tale rumbling of the gears that would open the door for Binta and simultaneously lower the bars for the zombies.

He turned back one last time to see Binta standing at the wall, watching as a nearby door slowly opened. He nodded, which she reciprocated, but she struggled to remain strong. Finally, he heard the undead approaching, and she must have seen them because she put a hand over her mouth and exited the room through the new doorway. She was crying as she did, and it broke his heart. He had never felt more alone than when she walked through that doorway.

Cass found herself wheezing and eventually coughing up more blood. She leaned one hand on the cave wall and spat out blood and pus. She grabbed her chest with her other hand as more pus oozed from the infected wound.

"Witch," she whispered, referring to the creature she had left to burn a few hours ago, understanding now that the foul creature had mortally infected her wound, just as it had promised.

She had to get out of the caves, or she would surely die. After her coughing fit, she picked up the sound of falling water ahead. It was not nearly loud enough to be another waterfall, but perhaps it was a way out. She staggered forward, hoping she would find an exit.

To her delight, she soon found the source of the water. The river seemed to disappear under the cavern wall. But the second water source flowed down from the rocky wall before her and trickled into the river. She looked into the darkness above her, searching for the start of the water flow, but could not see that far into the pitch black. So, she activated her ring, reduced her weight considerably, and prepared to climb. She examined the rocks on the wall, and although they were wet and slippery, they offered plenty of handholds for her to climb. She kissed the ring in appreciation and began to climb slowly.

She had made it about ten feet up without much trouble, primarily due to her reduced weight, when just by luck, she heard an approaching creature over the trickling water. She turned to see Magist charging at her from the dark. The thing was not white and beautiful as when she had first laid eyes on it; it was not the majestic creature that had led her to the despicable witch. Instead, the beast had those evil red eyes she had seen back at the cabin, and most of its skin was missing, revealing bones and rotting muscles underneath. The beautiful white coat was now pitch black. It charged at her, head down, antlers angled to skewer her.

She hustled up the cavern wall as quickly as possible and lifted her legs just high enough to avoid the strike from the enraged creature. Several chunks of stone hit her feet and ankles, motivating her to climb faster. Magist pawed the stone wall and snorted, wrath playing out just a few feet below her. She turned her attention to the wall and climbed, ignoring the echoes of the bellowing beast.

She had climbed several hundred feet before Magist grew quiet but did not realize how high she had climbed. Her arms did not ache as they usually would, but she felt her weight returning to normal. She had to find a way off the wall; hopefully, the water source would be large enough for her to do so. But unfortunately, her ring was taxed, and soon its power would fade entirely. She glanced down, saw nothing but darkness beneath her, and climbed faster.

She found a solid hold and maneuvered enough to reactivate the ring. As she expected, the power did not return, and she felt her weight normalize, making her hold tentative on the slippery rocks. Panic set in as she realized the ring required recharging before it would work again. She would have to climb the slippery wall on her own now. She tried not to glance down, for falling would mean certain death.

Cass nearly fell several times as she climbed steadily but shakily up the cliff face. She badly needed to cough but dared not for fear of plummeting to her death if she started one of her coughing fits. Then, to her relief, she spotted an opening, a tunnel large enough to fit a human about ten feet above her. She refocused her efforts and eagerly moved toward it, wanting to be off the cliff face, which she had scaled for nearly an hour. She dared not guess how high up she was, but she knew a slip would result in her doom.

She made the opening shortly after and hauled herself up with exhausted arms. A stream of water about a foot deep gently poured over the lip and trickled down the enormous rock wall and into the river far below. Once she was safely off the cliff face, she collapsed in the small stream of cool water and let loose a coughing fit that had her spitting up pus and blood once more. Her chest felt like it was ripping in half with each cough.

She lay there for a long while, and once she found the energy to gain her feet, she took the amulet in her hand and asked, "Where are you, Cassandra?"

To her delight, she was near, very near. The revelation lifted her spirits, and she started again with renewed vigor.

When Cassandra awoke sometime later, she found the braziers burning low, and she realized she would need to make a decision concerning the mysterious floor soon. She struggled to a sitting position, her hips aching severely with the effort. Her groin muscles were also on fire. They had been stretched badly by the golems, and she needed healing before her legs would ever function normally again.

She gingerly tested her sore right arm, moving it in a circular motion. There was little pain, but it felt very shaky, as if she pushed too hard; it might pop right back out of the joint once more. She wasn't sure she could face that pain again. Cassandra knew she could not use it as usual, but she would be fine as long as she didn't move it suddenly. She didn't like her chances, given her ordeal thus far through the mountain, but she got to her feet after great effort and faced the grid of letters on the floor once more. Cassandra studied it for a long while and could see no pattern. With the braziers burning low, she felt pressured to make a quick decision to avoid being stranded in the dark. Finally, she spotted a letter "C" on one of the first tiles, corresponding to her name, and decided it was as good a place as any to start. After a quick prayer to Gella, she stepped on it.

She hoped that if she started matching the first letter of her name, she would find a solution to the puzzle. Unfortunately, it was apparent right away that she had chosen incorrectly. The tile was as thin as paper and collapsed with the first bit of pressure. She nearly pitched forward, which would have meant her doom. First, the entire tile with the letter "C" on it crumbled to pieces; then, all tiles within the floor grid that had the same letter similarly crumbled and fell. She managed to step back before stepping fully on the tile, so she did not fall.

None of the falling debris made a sound, which told her that the fall was a long way down. The weakened light source gave little indication of what was beneath the fragile floor; all she could see below was pitch black. The quick reaction of pulling her leg back had shot pain through her hip and leg, and she cursed under her breath. She grimaced it away, though, and determinedly crawled to each tile first in line and pressed on each one enough to determine if they were solid. Unfortunately, none were, as they all crumbled and fell, which made each other similarly marked tile fall. When done, at least a third of the tiles were gone, having turned to dust.

"What do you want from me?" she screamed, her voice echoing above and below the tiled floor. "Am I here only for your pleasure? Do you not want me to find my birthright? Do you not want me to summon the demon filth known as Marnelphion? Are these not your plans? If so, my dear father, why do you make me jump through these hoops?"

With her anger playing out and her echoing words finally silencing, she examined the floor again. Unfortunately, she did not have long as the light had grown dimer since she had awoken from her sleep. She found no patterns that made any sense to her, and she nearly screamed out in frustration once more, growing tired of the game. If the braziers burned out entirely, she would have no hope of crossing the trapped floor.

She closed her eyes and took a deep breath, trying to calm her nerves. Since childhood, she had the uncanny ability to "see" magical energies when she had focused enough to do it. She remembered when she first met Baxter and had stolen his cantrip. She recalled the time in class when she had seen the fire energy of the magical ring, and she had also seen through the illusion of Cedric's messy room. She had felt the power of the water rush through her before she had lashed it out at Cass. She opened her eyes and examined the tiles for magical energy.

As she focused, she could see that the tiles radiated powerful magic, almost god-like. However, the energies gave her no indication of which tiles were the correct ones to walk on. She assumed that some were solid, and if she could figure out the pattern, she could walk across. She relaxed her mind and let the vision fade. The low light made the tiles very difficult to see, so she had to decide soon.

She stomped her foot in frustration, which she regretted immediately as waves of agonizing pain shot through her leg. She crumpled to the ground, clutching her wounded hip. She screamed out in pain and anger and noticed the small, unlit lantern within reach. It was her last possession, besides her underwear, which now showed holes in several locations. She picked up the dead lantern and threw it with her one good arm toward the tiles, tired of the game, tired of the pain, and tired of simply being in the magical cavern. To her surprise, it hit something solid, bounced, crashed through a neighboring tile, and fell. But it hit something substantial first.

She gradually regained her footing and peered through the dim lighting to locate which tile had survived the impact. It looked like one in the third row, marked with an *X*.

"*X*? What?" she began before the obvious answer came.

"Zolmex!" she exclaimed excitedly.

It had never occurred to her that whatever the answer to the code was, it could be backward from her direction. It had to be Zolmex; she was sure now. Unfortunately, it was too dark for her to see all the tiles from her vantage point, so she would have to finally take that leap of faith and hope to pick out the remaining letters. The tile marked *X* was about four feet away from the ledge, which generally would not be a difficult jump. But with her injured legs, she was very concerned about the attempt. Time was up; the braziers nearly burned out. She took a few steps back, then ran the best she could and jumped.

Her battered legs prevented her full range of motion, and the effort had her grimacing in pain. To her relief, she landed safely on the tile, which did not collapse. She quickly found the *E* tile, only two feet away. No other tiles were even near that one, so she would fall to her death if she was incorrect in her guess. It seemed to hover in the darkness, beckoning her to try the jump. She did not have time to pray since time was of the essence; she jumped. To her relief, she landed easily, and the tile held.

There was a new problem now, though. The *M* tile was six feet away, and she wasn't sure if it was an *M*. The light was minimal here in the middle of the tiles, but she saw no other options that resembled an *M*. She backed up on her current tile the best she could and got a short running jump. She made it to the *M*, and it did hold, but her legs buckled when she landed, and she pitched forward, leaving the top half of her body hanging over the chasm below her, and she nearly toppled over.

It was a precarious perch, and she nearly fell several times before finally pulling herself back to the safety of the tile. The glimpse she had beneath her was terrific as she saw no supporting column for the tile she was on; an invisible force was holding the suitable tiles. She wanted across the pit as soon as possible. She struggled to her feet again, and her poor legs barely supported her. There were three more tiles to go, and she could see little of the markings on them.

Nevertheless, she wasted no time jumping to the next tile, hoping she was correct with her guess. To her relief, she was.

She had little trouble with the remaining tiles, and made the last leap, exhausted and in a lot of pain. She fell to her knees and caught her breath for a bit. Her hips were on fire, and her legs were unsteady at best. She turned to regard the tiles and the smoldering braziers that gave little light now. She knew of no options for light at this point and cared little; she just hoped she wouldn't have to use her taxed legs anymore. She made her way out of the room and into the next tunnel, and soon the darkness enveloped her.

Greyson watched Binta leave, and he smiled, feeling she would be fine. He did not feel fear, and he suddenly did not feel alone, Plath dousing that feeling once Binta was gone. Although the stench of death was all around him, he did not panic. His god was with him. He tried to pull his hands from his shackles, but only for a moment; there was simply no escape. So, he did the only thing he could. He turned to meet the undead, who were now visible at the edge of the light. There were dozens of them, and more were coming. They saw him and made their way to him as quickly as possible, stumbling and growling along the way. They were in various degrees of decay, a perversion of death.

Plath was with him, more so than he had ever felt before. He assumed the feeling was strong because Plath was ready to take him to the afterlife, and he was more than willing to go. Greyson began a song to Plath, and his holy symbol began to glow even brighter in response. He could see how many of the undead there were now, and he took comfort in the fact that they would kill him quickly, and Plath would spare him the agony of a slow death. He thought of Darian then, and his adoptive family in Tara. Greyson would see them all soon, and that lifted his spirits. And, at that moment, he was not afraid to die. His song became louder, and it echoed throughout the chamber.

"Come on then, filth. Plath rebukes your existence. Come and feel his wrath!" he screamed out at them.

Come on, they did, smelling the kill.

Greyson's smile widened as they approached, especially when he heard the familiar rumbling behind him of the doorway sealing again. They would not be able to follow Binta.

"My god, the greatest god of them all, the bringer of light and destroyer of undead, rid the world of these atrocities! Use my soul to devour the evil! Take me under your wing, my god, for I am your servant in life and death," he screamed out over the moaning of the undead creatures.

As he spoke, he could feel the power swell in his symbol as it grew brighter and brighter. He felt a familiar surge of power run through his body, similar to when he called upon Plath for his spellcasting. The power overwhelmed his senses as he felt the spirit of Plath pulsing within him.

He used that power to lash out at the undead as they neared. His symbol grew so bright that its light bathed the entire cavern in the most brilliant, holiest light he could have imagined. The power surged through him, and the light became so bright that he was temporarily blinded. Many of the closest undead creatures had been utterly destroyed when it subsided, turned to dust in the holy light.

Greyson's arms and fingers tingled from the effort, and he slowly brought them down in front of him, turning them over and examining them in amazement. It took a moment to register the events and realize that his hands were no longer in the shackles. He looked to the bonds above him to find his holy symbol now shackled in place of his hands. He instinctively felt around his neck to find the emblem gone.

"Sacrifice the one you love the most," he whispered in awe.

Plath was allowing him to live, was filling the sacrifice so Greyson could survive! He noted then that plenty of zombies remained, and they continued to close. Greyson suddenly looked back at the stone door from which Binta had exited, which was half-closed. He moved as fast as possible to the closing portal, pain shooting up his left leg and foot. Blood sloshed in his boot, making it very difficult to move quickly. When he finally reached the door, the opening was only a few feet wide, and he squeezed through at the last moment. The door closed behind him, leaving him in total darkness but very much alive.

He stumbled along for a bit, unable to see much, feeling the polished walls as he moved. Eventually, Greyson found the light from his mace up ahead, dimly at first, but he quickened his pace and finally caught up to Binta. She was looking his way, holding the mace defensively in her hand, ready to defend herself, when he limped out of the darkness—the look on her pretty face when she saw him warmed his heart.

"Greyson!" she yelled excitedly and ran into his arms.

They hugged for a very long time, both crying tears of joy.

Cassandra made her way through the dark passageway for quite some time, feeling the walls with her hands, similar to how Greyson had done for a brief time. She was alone in the pitch black, battered and bruised, with no weapons or supplies. Despair and panic began to set in; Cassandra needed to see the light of day again, see her friends again, and kiss Binta. She could not take much more of the cave without having a breakdown.

She eventually saw a light source ahead, and she hastily made her way toward it, hoping against hope that it was not another test. As she neared, she felt a slight breeze blowing from that direction, and it rekindled hope that she had finally found an exit. She quickened her pace the best she could with her wounded legs.

When she finally rounded a bend in the tunnel and saw the source of the light, her heart sank a bit. It was not an exit to the outside world but an entrance to yet another cave. She made her way to the end of the tunnel and peered in. The cavern was so large that she could not see the ceiling or walls. A small ledge on the far wall, nearly fifty yards away, contained another brazier, fully lit, which was the only light source in the cavern. The small ledge had a set of stone stairs leading to the floor, and there appeared to be a ravine at the base of those stairs. She glanced to her left and right before entering the giant room. Once she did, she could see many other tunnels spilling into it on either side.

She felt very vulnerable as she entered the magnificent cavern and felt that at any moment, some snarling creature would jump out of one of the other tunnels and make quick work of her. She would not be able to defend herself if it did. Nevertheless, she reasoned that she needed to reach the ledge with the brazier for her next test, so she limped toward the ravine. To her relief, no creature attacked her, and no test presented itself for her to solve. Once she reached the lip of the ravine, she could see that it once housed a river but was now dry. She stood on the edge of the gently sloping bank peering down to the dry riverbed about fifteen feet below her.

The riverbed seemed to start at the steps of the small ledge and make a loop to the middle of the cavern where she stood, then turned back to the same wall where it disappeared through another tunnel. She took in the strange view and puzzled over it for many moments, trying to understand what this place once was. She could still feel a slight breeze, which seemed to come from the tunnel the dry riverbed fed into. A hooded figure was standing on the ledge when she looked up again.

It had not been there a moment earlier and seemed to have just appeared from nowhere. It extended a skeletal hand in Cassandra's direction and reached out to her telepathically, *"Your time here has ended."*

"Who are you?" she asked aloud, her voice wavering with a bit of fear.

"I am the caves' keeper and your executioner, trespasser."

Her heart raced, sensing that the creature was far beyond her capabilities. She stood in defiant silence, trying to be strong and find a way to avoid a confrontation with the mysterious creature. She did not have to see the arcane energy to understand it was there; the air was thick with it.

"I am the daughter of Kane. I have come for Zolmex, my birthright."

The creature slowly lowered his hand and telepathically reached out to her once more, *"If you are truly the offspring of Kane, then he surely must be disappointed. You stand before me without weapons, supplies, or even clothing to cover your filthy skin. You are a pathetic wretch, coming to my home demanding an artifact as powerful as Zolmex."*

She could not argue with his words, and her eyes began to fill with tears as the truth of them stung her profoundly. And, it had just confirmed the existence of Zolmex! The thing was right, though; she did not deserve the artifact. Her friends were lost to her, possibly dead, and it was all for nothing. She had failed and realized then and there that her life, in general, had been a failure.

"I feel your despair. Excellent! You are a failure, and now the two of you must decide which will live and which will die."

The puzzling comment made no sense to her, and after a few moments, she responded weakly, "There is only me; there are no others—"

Her words cut off as all the muscles in her body tensed up, and she could no longer freely move. The blade had plunged deeply into her back, and although the pain was excruciating, she could not move or even scream.

"Little Cassandra Rho, tramping through the forest, being far too loud and bringing the wolves upon us," Cass whispered in her ear, reciting the old nursery rhyme that Cassandra had heard many times from mocking children at the orphanage.

Cass had stabbed her in the back, and she knew immediately that the wound would be mortal. The worst part was that she couldn't even fall or react to the vicious attack; something paralyzed her. So, Cassandra just stood there, eyes wide, releasing tears to stream down her face, the pain overwhelming her. She felt her body shutting down and growing cold. She could not move but wanted nothing more than to fall and sleep.

"Excellent, you have made your decision. You have sacrificed your friend and must live with your guilt for the rest of your days. Leave this place," the skeletal figure said telepathically to both women.

A door slowly opened on the left side of the cavern, and arctic winter wind and natural daylight spilled into the cave for the first time in centuries.

"Gladly," Cass whispered in Cassandra's ear and began her walk toward her freedom, leaving Tooth buried in Cassandra's back.

She had to pause for a severe coughing fit that had her nearly on her knees, but when it had subsided, she looked back at Cassandra and called for Tooth. The knife appeared immediately in her hand, and Cassandra fell into the ravine, released from the blade's paralyzing effect. Then, with a smile, Cass shielded her eyes from the bright daylight and made her way to freedom.

CHAPTER 11

LEO'S TOMB?

The entire crew of *The Siren's Scourge* lined the ship's rail with Kringus, Boz, Von, and Lenore, flanked by captain Biggles and first mate Agatha. The boat slowly passed within five hundred yards of the ruined docks of Novafontera. The cursed city spewed forth the poisonous gas and, from this distance, looked enveloped in a green fire. The crew was deadly silent, and the only sound was the lapping of the water against the hull.

"The sight never ceases to amaze even the most seasoned sailors," Captain Biggles whispered to Kringus.

The king nodded and kept his eyes locked on the poisoned city. The echo of Daro's words from a few months earlier rang in his ears: *"Something is awake in the cursed city."* He could almost sense the truth in that statement as they passed. Something evil seemed to lurk within the dead walls of the place. He knew that he and the New Order would soon make Novafontera a priority, and a chill ran down his spine at the thought of it.

"About two more days, Your Highness," Biggles said, interrupting the unpleasant thoughts.

"What?" Kringus asked, shaking his head.

"We will have you home in about two more days," Biggles reiterated, then nodded and walked away with Agatha, ordering his men to get back to their stations and move along at full speed.

The crew quietly dispersed, and soon the ship picked up speed, sailing quickly toward Pelesea. Kringus and his allies watched the cursed city until it was out of sight. Home sounded good to the king; he longed to see his queen.

Greyson and Binta had just emerged from one of the many tunnels, similar to Cassandra and Cass before them. By this time, Greyson had become desperate enough to consume one of his healing potions for his wounded leg, leaving only one. Binta had emerged just in time to see Cassandra fall into the ravine, her joy at seeing her best friend replaced with sheer horror as Cassandra seemed to pitch forward. It appeared to Binta that her friend was either unconscious or even dead.

"Cassandra!" she screamed and ran to the lip of the ravine.

Greyson followed her as quickly as he could, but soon fell behind. He had not seen Cassandra's fall, but from Binta's reaction, he knew something was wrong. As they exited the tunnel, he felt the cool temperature filling the cavern and the blinding light penetrating the darkness from what appeared to be an exit. Then he saw Cass walking toward the opening, holding her chest.

"Cass?" he yelled.

She turned in surprise and quickly tucked away what appeared to be something golden and metallic that reflected the sunlight. She seemed injured but was alive, and Greyson was relieved to see her.

"Come this way, Greyson," she called, pointing toward the exit.

"Greyson, the creature!" Binta screamed at the same time.

Greyson turned back and saw the hooded figure walking down the steps of a small ledge on the opposite side of the ravine.

"Cassandra's down there," Binta yelled, pointing into the ravine.

Once again, the grating of stone had him turning toward Cass, where the exit was beginning to seal.

"Hurry, Greyson!" Cass yelled, waving him on franticly. "The door is sealing!"

Greyson turned to catch a glimpse of Binta making her way down the hill toward Cassandra. He turned again to Cass one last time, standing outside, waving him on, in the middle of a coughing fit. The door was about to shut, and if he intended to join her, he would have to be quick to reach it before it sealed. He would not leave Binta or Cassandra behind, so he turned his back to the door and ran after Binta.

Cass couldn't stop her coughing fit and spit up quite a bit of blood onto the white snow. She heard the door shut and looked up to see no sign of it on the mountain. The mountainside looked ordinary and undisturbed, and Greyson had not made it through. He had not come with her as she'd hoped. She needed healing quickly, so she staggered away in the freezing temperatures, hoping to find help.

She considered summoning the cottage to sit by the fire and sleep. She was afraid doing so would mean she would curl up next to the fire, and the infection would worsen and take her life. Instead, she continued her trek, concentrating on putting one foot in front of the other. She had no idea where she was, but Cass knew enough to follow the slope down the mountain, hoping she would find help soon.

Daro had been close enough to the opening mountainside that he had heard the rumbling of stone. He was quick to investigate the sound, and when he got to the spot, he soon picked up Cass's trail, starting with a pool of blood. It didn't take him long to find her lying unconscious in the snow. When he gently turned her over, she was in bad shape, too bad to move in her condition. He did not recognize her but assumed she must be from the party they were trying to find.

The ranger quickly set up a camp and built a fire so Baxter could locate him. He gave the girl extra blankets and brewed a home remedy from roots, dried berries, and several rare herbs he carried in a pouch. The brew was hot and bitter; but the ranger hoped it would temporarily stave off the infection in her chest, which was one of the worst he had seen. He gently cradled her head and forced her to take a few sips. Even in her unconscious state, she tried to reject the foul liquid by turning her head. Finally, he forced it down, and soon she was sleeping soundly.

Sure enough, Baxter did not take long to spot the smoke from his flying carpet. He circled the area first to see who had built it and saw Daro attending to an injured person. Baxter knew that if he could see the fire, so could their enemies, but he understood the fire was necessary and that Daro had built it so Baxter could find him.

Baxter landed the carpet quickly and ran toward Daro, who was bundling his patient tightly in the blankets. Daro tried to intercept him and began to speak, but Baxter walked briskly around him, moving to the injured person. He pushed the blanket away to see her face, hoping it was Cassandra.

"Cass Ruben," he whispered.

"You sound disappointed," Daro said from behind him.

Baxter shook his head and stood. "No, not at all. I am thankful we found at least one of them. My objective is Cassandra, but I am glad we found Cass alive. So where are the other three?" he asked the ranger.

Daro shrugged and shook his head. "I only saw tracks of one person, and they came from the mountain, which gave no clue of ever having a doorway."

"And she hasn't spoken, I assume?"

"No, she is very sick, Baxter. You must use your carpet to get her to Godhomme quickly."

Baxter nodded his agreement but looked at the mountainside, and Daro knew he was scanning it for any signs of caves or other doorways. Daro clapped him on the shoulder, startling the wizard. Baxter turned to see Daro smiling at him.

"Do not worry, my friend; I will continue my search and build a fire each day so you may find me. We will find the others if the mountain releases them. For now, though, this one is very sick," Daro said, nodding at Cass's still form.

Baxter nodded and said, "Of course, I will make haste to Godhomme and return after I am certain they have adequate healing for her."

"Adam and Gabriel will have the means to heal her," Daro assured him.

"What is wrong with her?"

"An infection, one of the worst I've ever seen. The wound is deep in the girl's chest, and the infection is aggressive. She also has many smaller wounds on her neck and chin. I'm not a priest, but she may have a collapsed lung. She badly needs healing, my friend."

Soon after, Baxter had her on his carpet, making haste for Godhomme. Daro could tell that his new friend was worried about Cassandra and knew that if one of the adventurers was as injured as Cass, the others could be as well. And if attacked by something within the mountain, they may not even be alive.

Greyson crested the ridge in time to see Binta reach Cassandra, who lay face down in what appeared to be a dry riverbed. He winced when the stone door closed behind him, knowing his path to freedom had become sealed off. Nevertheless, Plath had helped him thus far, so he again put his faith in his god, knowing he would be in good hands. His heart skipped a beat when he saw the hooded creature rushing toward the two women.

"Binta!" he screamed, trying to draw her attention, then pulled his mace and ran down the ravine with all haste.

"Cassandra, what has happened to you?" Binta asked, kneeling beside her friend, nearing tears. "Oh, no," she whispered when she saw the pooling blood and the vicious wound on her friend's back.

Cassandra was still conscious and lifted a finger toward Binta, her lips moving as if she were trying to speak. Binta knelt even further and put her ear up to her mouth to hear her dying friend's words.

"I'm sorry, Cassandra, I cannot hear you," Binta said, fearing her friend was leaving the world.

Before Cassandra could speak, Binta was grabbed from behind by the hooded figure, who quickly lifted her by the throat. He turned her so she could look into his eyes, and she saw the creature's true face for the first time. Her eyes widened in fear as she looked at the hideous skull. The beast appeared as nothing more than an animated skeleton. Both eye sockets contained pure black orbs, swirling with smoke that spilled out of the sockets and dissipated in the air, giving the illusion that the thing's eyes were burning with black fire. She saw her true doom in those horrible, mysterious eyes, the most horrific images of her demise. She could do nothing but tremble in his grasp.

Greyson was only a few feet away when the creature grabbed Binta and lifted her off the ground. He saw the terror splayed across her face as she stared at the thing. He summoned the power of Plath and focused a light spell on the thing's eyes, but suddenly everything went dark. At first, he thought the brazier had snuffed out, but gradually realized that his attack had turned against him. He had inadvertently blinded himself!

Binta didn't notice Greyson's approach or hear him yell out in surprise at his sudden loss of sight. Instead, she became lost in the visions of fear and despair she saw in the thing's dark eyes. The creature briefly regarded Greyson, understanding that he was a minor threat.

"Fool!" it hissed at Greyson telepathically.

It then tossed Binta down like a rag doll, and she curled up in a fetal position, cowering in fear. Next, the creature turned its full attention to Greyson, who swung his mace wildly and felt the air in front of him with his free hand. Then, after one of his wild swings, the beast backhanded Greyson across the face, sending him flying to land hard on his back.

"Now meet your doom!" the creature threatened.

It pulled back the hood of his cloak, revealing its dark eyes, the magical smoke emanating freely from them. It cackled and raised a bony finger his way. Greyson could not see the small ball of fire that darted out from the end of that skeletal digit, as he was still coming to terms with his blindness. Once the small ball of fire reached him, it exploded powerfully, consuming him in its incinerating heat.

"Greyson, no!" Binta screamed out, witnessing the explosion, the sight temporarily bringing her out of her trance.

If the creature could have smiled, it would have, with Binta's misery and despair feeding it, exciting it. Instead, it made its way toward Cassandra, and as it passed Binta, she curled up in fear, unable to bear the negative thoughts the creature had imparted to her. It paid her no heed as it walked straight to Cassandra, who struggled to reach Greyson's discarded mace.

Cassandra struggled to remain conscious, but the numbing pain was getting the best of her. She knew the wound was lethal, and Cass was the reason for her demise. Cassandra had resigned to the fact that Cass had somehow cheated death and returned to best her. She was happy that she had not murdered Cass as she first thought, but the conniving woman was relentless, and in the end, it would cost Cassandra her life. But now, all she wanted to do was go to sleep, let the darkness take her, and sleep. However, she could not just lie there and witness her friends' slaughter as she died. She had to do something, so she reached with her one good arm to retrieve Greyson's mace, which had landed within her grasp.

Just before her stretching fingers reached it, a skeletal foot stepped on her forearm, the unnatural weight of the creature making her cry out. It bent low and grabbed her by the hair, dragging her away from the weapon, leaving a trail of blood as it did. The pain in her back nearly made her black out and had her screaming in agony. Her battered body was tired, and the wound in her back continued to pour blood and was made excruciating by any movement.

"You are doomed, child of Kane. Your blood is dark, which means the wound is mortal. How does it feel to know that your friend betrayed you? She sacrificed your worthless life so that she could live. You understand now that you meant nothing to her and that I will make your last few hours of life most miserable."

He flipped her over as if she were a rag doll, eliciting a painful scream. She didn't have the energy to writhe in pain, or she would have. So instead, she tensed up and waited for the agony to subside.

Then it was in her mind again, *"I have destroyed your friends, just like your friend has destroyed you. So now, a gift for your last few hours of life, the birthright you deserve."*

He produced a small metal flask from the folds of his robe and quickly picked out a giant maggot from it. He dangled it in front of Cassandra's face teasingly and said, *"This, my dear, is a borer maggot. A creature I am sure you are unfamiliar with because it is ancient like me. Allow me to enlighten you: most larvae feed on decaying flesh; this one enjoys the living flesh. I will place it in your wound, and it will eat you from the inside out.*

"I hear the pain is unbearable, so you will suffer immensely for the last few hours of your life. But, as you do, I want you to think about the one who did this to you. She will live a long, happy life without a second thought about your death. You are a pathetic wretch, and your father will seek appropriate punishment for you in the afterlife."

A magic dart hit the creature's hand, and he dropped the maggot beside Cassandra. She craned to see Binta standing again, her finger pointing toward the beast.

"Leave her alone!" she said, but Cassandra could see her trembling with fear.

The creature turned on her, and Cassandra saw Binta's eyes widen as she took a step back. Cassandra tried to grab the creature's foot as it left, but she couldn't hold back the thing. Her arm fell limply beside her, and Cassandra immediately felt a sharp pain near her elbow. She had little energy left, but she managed to lift her arm to find the maggot digging into her skin. She pulled it out, squished it between her thumb and forefinger, then turned to regard Binta, who was now being held off the ground by her throat once more, her feet kicking the air.

Greyson felt the heat of the fireball and knew he was in trouble. The explosion caught him solidly, and he felt the oxygen being consumed for a moment by the hungry flames. His blindness caught him so off guard that he hadn't realized what was happening but understood that a powerful spell consumed him. The flames licked at him and should have easily incinerated him. He quickly realized that his magical ring of fire protection had resisted the blast, leaving him unscathed. He called to Plath once more to dispel his blindness, and when it dissipated, he saw the beast holding Binta in the air by the throat. He rose to his feet, a little dizzy from the hit he had just absorbed, and ran to help his love, rage forming deep within him.

"Now, I'll let you witness the devastating effect of the borer maggot before you get your own," the creature taunted Cassandra, slamming Binta to the ground and knocking the air out of her.

It pained Cassandra to see her friend hurt so. Binta lay next to her now, the creature straddling her as it produced another of the larvae. Cassandra weakly reached out and took her friend's hand, squeezing it to let her know she was there and sorry. A tear trickled down her cheek as she watched the thing pry open Binta's mouth with solid, boney fingers and drop the maggot inside. Binta gagged and kicked, trying to spit it out, but the thing held her mouth shut until she swallowed it. Only then did Cassandra notice Greyson fast approaching.

Greyson picked up a rock as a weapon as he ran toward the creature. It was standing over Binta, who was squirming with both hands over her throat, choking and gagging. The thing had done something to her, and he could sense its pleasure at her discomfort. He saw red, and when he reached the thing, he used all his strength to bring the rock around and crack it in the face. He did not expect it to do much damage, but he wanted to draw its attention from Binta before it killed her. As he swung, he felt the power of his god running through his arm, and his aim was true.

The stone hit the face of the monster directly in its left eye socket, eliciting a loud crack, and time seemed to stand still for just a moment as it froze in surprise. Greyson managed to swing the rock again, hitting it again in the left eye, which collapsed the socket, and the magical smoke billowed out for just an instant before the side of the thing's face exploded. The force of the explosion disintegrated the rock, which saved Greyson's hand from being turned to dust. Unfortunately, he lost most of the skin on his palm from the force of the blast. He screamed and held his wounded hand to his chest as he lost his balance and fell. Cassandra's limp form rolled several feet away, moved by the power of the explosion, like some strange human tumbleweed. Binta was underneath the creature and felt no effects from the explosion, and she was still unaware of her surroundings as she writhed on the ground, coughing and gurgling.

Greyson hit the riverbank hard and nearly lost consciousness. His right arm tingled with a million pinpricks, and the palm of his hand throbbed. He tried to shake the cobwebs and noticed the monster staggering toward him. Then, in the distance, he was vaguely aware of a crashing sound, and the ground beneath him seemed to come alive as it lurched to and fro, throwing him around like a rag doll.

When the ground finally settled and he regained his feet, he realized that the entire cavern was rumbling, that the crashing sound he had heard was large pieces of the cavern roof falling and crashing to the floor. He looked around in amazement, realizing that he had severely wounded the hooded creature and that, in turn, had weakened the magic of the cavern.

"Look what you have done, fool!" the thing hissed at him telepathically.

It was in front of him now, and the hood was lowered, exposing his skull. A large piece was missing around the left eye socket, and scorch marks were visible all around that scar. The strange, magical smoke emanating from the eye was no longer visible. The thing seemed as unstable as the rest of the cavern. With a clawed hand, it took an awkward swipe at him, and Greyson quickly ducked out of the way. A large rock from the ceiling narrowly missed him as he moved. It took him a minute to catch his bearings and understand the roof would crush them if they remained there. He looked over to Cassandra and

Binta, both lying perfectly still in the chaos, and understood he needed to reach them quickly. If not, they would surely be crushed by the falling debris. Before he could react to that thought, the creature moved in for another attack.

It had regained its balance a bit and was much faster this time, which caught Greyson entirely off guard. It grabbed him around the neck and easily lifted him off the ground. Greyson brought his hands up to loosen the grip, but it was vise-like and would not budge.

"You take one of my eyes, so I shall take one of yours," it hissed in his mind, and its clawed hand came up to stab at his left eye.

Greyson could not hope to free himself from the creature's grip, and the ceiling continued to crumble, although that seemed to subside a bit as the monster found its bearings again. Large chunks of the roof still crashed all around them, and one narrowly missed Binta, showering her with debris. She didn't seem to notice as she was now in a fetal position, holding her stomach tight.

He didn't know what the thing had done to her, but he needed to get to her fast. If one of those rocks fell on her or Cassandra, they would surely die. He could not see Cassandra from his position, but she was lying perfectly still the last time he had glimpsed her. For all he knew, she was already dead. He thought about summoning his power of light once more to blind the creature again, but he remembered what had transpired the last time and thought better of it. Also, as his depleted powers dictated, he needed to save his spells for healing his friends.

He felt the sharp tip of the finger dig into the corner of his eye, and he reflexively jerked his head to the side before it could gouge out his eyeball. Instead, he took a deep cut to his cheek and realized how razor-sharp those claws were. He reached desperately for his holy symbol, feeling the power of Plath well within him, but quickly remembered it was gone, having sacrificed it to save himself.

"I rebuke you, foul beast!" he choked out as he struggled to breathe.

He brought his hands up to scratch at the face of the creature and hook that dead eye socket and hopefully cause more damage. Instead, he caught the right eye socket with his fingers and pulled with all his strength. As he did, the magical smoke pouring from that eye caressed his fingers, making them numb. The creature was ready to dig at Greyson's eye once more when its right eye socket cracked. The new wound surely hurt the beast as the magical smoke spilled from the fresh wound. It shrieked and released Greyson immediately, who fell to the ground. The creature stumbled around, holding both skeletal hands over its wounded face. The ground began to tremble again, and the walls started to crack and sway once more.

Greyson wasted no time finding his footing and ran to his mace, which now lay next to Cassandra. He noticed the ground she lay upon was saturated with so much blood. She lay on her back as the blood continued to pool around her. He could not help her, not now, not with the creature so close to being defeated. He admired her nearly naked form for just a moment, and he briefly wondered how she had lost her clothing, which sparked some lustful thoughts. Those would have to wait, as well.

He glanced at Binta, who was at least moving and moaning slightly, still clutching her midriff. Greyson looked back at the creature, still stumbling around, and his anger and hatred for the thing came to the surface, his face contorting into a mask of pure rage. He charged at the monster, both hands on his mace. The ground rolled, and he nearly lost footing as it cracked slightly beneath him. That did not deter him; nothing would stop him from destroying the hooded creature.

He swung the mace, and the creature noticed the attack at the last moment, bringing forth a hand to shield its face. Greyson struck with all the strength he could muster, and the hit shattered more than a few of the creature's fingers as it pulled its hand away from its scarred and battered face. Greyson could only imagine the surprised look it might have worn if it had skin and muscles to change its facial expression.

"Goodbye, filth!" he screamed and slammed the mace right into the thing's face as hard as possible.

The hit knocked out a few teeth and cracked the skull even more. Then, finally, it fell back and tried to crawl away on its elbows. It did not try to communicate with him at that moment, but Greyson could sense the pain, anguish, and even the fear it now felt. Greyson struck again and again, the power of Plath coursing through the mace with each strike.

Finally, the last blow was a direct hit on the remaining eye, which exploded, just like the left eye socket had done previously. The thing's entire face seemed to vaporize, and Greyson felt himself flying again, engulfed in a ball of fire. He did not feel the flames as they lapped at him; the ring preventing the damage once more. When he finally regained his footing, he saw that luck had been with them. The radius of the blast seemed to stretch out a good bit from the creature but was just short of enveloping Cassandra and Binta.

He had difficulty standing now as the ground lurched and split open in many directions. He regarded the hooded figure only to see the earth split apart and snatch the body. That crack enlarged and split the cavern floor from the riverbed to the ledge where the creature had first appeared. The ceiling dropped in several parts of the cavern as the cave-in began in earnest. When the floor split, he had to dive to the side, and by the time he had regained his footing, the crack in the foundation was about ten feet wide and still widening. He was on the same side of the fissure as Binta but was now completely cut off from Cassandra.

He ran to his love and pulled her away from the edge of the widening split. Binta moaned and kicked, so he called upon Plath again and sent waves of healing energy through her body. She stopped kicking and moaning but remained unconscious. The far wall cracked and nearly had the entire roof caving in. It split in a way that opened the door that Cass had used to escape. Sunlight crept in, and all he could see between himself and that door was dust, dirt, and flying rocks as pieces of the roof continued to fall.

He looked over at Cassandra and saw that the split in the ground had grown to about fifteen feet wide and continued to expand. Soon it would devour her. The young priest felt helpless, knowing that if he left now, he might be able to get Binta to the exit, but there was no way he would save Cassandra. He noticed through the dust and haze of falling debris that her eyes were slightly open, and she was smiling at him. She pointed to the door, indicating that he should leave.

"Cassandra!" he yelled, but he did not know why he even tried.

She was doomed; Greyson knew, and he was sure she did as well. But he could still save Binta, which is what he set out to do. He took out the last flask of healing potion and called on his celestial power to summon light once more, making the flask glow brightly. He then tossed it to Cassandra. His aim was not perfect, but he got it close to her.

"Drink it; it will heal you!" he cried over the constant rumbling.

She smiled and waved weakly, then pointed to the door once more. Greyson turned and picked up Binta, carrying her as gently as he could, and made haste toward the exit, using the rays of sunlight as a guide through the thick dust. His leg and foot throbbed, and the old injury from Cerus's spear made his shoulder spasm, making it difficult to bear her weight. The ceiling fell all around them, and he prayed loudly to Plath as he made his way, hoping his god would keep them from being crushed by falling rocks before they reached the door.

Cassandra watched Greyson pick up Binta and move toward the exit. He struggled to carry her up the riverbank, but she knew he wouldn't leave her. He was Cassandra's hero at that moment. They would escape, she knew, and she loved him for saving her friend. She lay there and felt very cold, but strangely at peace with her surroundings. Large rocks crashed and bounced all around her. She waited for one to crush her, but she felt she would pass into the afterlife before that even happened. She no longer felt pain, not even the knife wound in her back.

A giant ceiling piece landed next to her and showered her with rocks and dirt. It was such a large piece that it cut off the sunlight trickling in. She turned her head and squinted the dirt out of her eyes, but she could no longer locate Greyson and Binta, the giant rock now blocking her view. She smiled, knowing the falling rocks slowly created a tomb around her. She relaxed and let herself succumb to the sleep that beckoned her.

Before embracing that most beautiful notion, she noticed that although the rubble had blocked her view of the daylight, it was still very bright around her. She took that as a sign that an angel would take her to the afterlife. She had heard tales of such happenings during her short stay at the temple in Pelesea, so she understood she was probably experiencing that phenomenon now. But the light did not brighten nor fade as she lay there. She expected one or the other. Instead, a rock the size of her head landed beside her, showering her face with small pebbles. She instinctively turned to her side to avoid the spraying rocks. She felt the pain in her back then, a very sharp pain that reminded her she was not dead yet.

Once on her side, she saw the source of the continuous light: the vial Greyson had tossed her. It lay next to her, and even though dust covered it, it had avoided the crushing rocks. She reached for it with her bad arm, grimacing with the effort.

Greyson struggled mightily to climb the riverbank with Binta slumped in his arms. A large chunk of the ceiling fell behind them as he crested the top of it, cutting off his view of Cassandra. For all he knew, the large stone had just crushed her. He stood there for a moment, dumbfounded, until Binta softly moaned, which had him moving again. She was not a heavy person, and her tiny frame would have customarily been easy for him to carry; however, he couldn't hold her for long with his wounded foot and his bad shoulder.

He used the dim light as a guide and continued his prayer to Plath as dust, dirt, and rocks flew all around them. He had to squint his eyes to keep soil from filling them, making the light even harder to follow in the chaos. Then, suddenly, a large stone landed near him and rolled across his injured foot. He screamed and fell, dropping Binta as gently as he could. She cried out once but did not regain consciousness. He estimated they were less than one hundred feet away from the exit, and there was simply no way he could put any pressure on that foot.

He stubbornly tried to regain his footing but was suddenly pushed back to the ground as dirt, rocks, and silt poured on him from the collapsing ceiling, burying his legs and lower torso. Now there was simply no way for him to save Binta. He could not dig out of the mound of dirt, and even if he could, he doubted he could make the trek to the door, with or without her. Yet, he would not give up on her when they were this close to freedom. Inspired by Plath, he began to sing loudly over the rumble of the cave-in, defying the rocks that promised to crush the life out of them. He worked frantically to free himself so that he could save Binta.

Daro heard the rumbling shortly after Baxter had left to fly Cass to Godhomme. He had climbed back up the mountainside where Cass's trail of blood had begun, and sure enough, there was an opening in the side of the mountain. Dust and small rocks flew from it, and it was evident to the ranger that a cave-in was in progress. He got as close as he could without getting pelted by the rocks and tried to peer inside.

He knew that if anyone from the party was in there, they could not survive. He inched closer and took a small rock to the arm for his efforts. He shook off the pain and kept going, thinking of the young adventurers for whom he searched. He called out to see if he could get a response, but the entire mountain seemed to be rumbling at that point, and he knew that no one would be able to hear him. Daro turned to leave the area to avoid being crushed by the cave-in or swept away by an avalanche, but as he did, he heard a song echoing from within. It sounded like a prayer to a god but was faint and unintelligible. It was not his imagination; someone inside was still alive.

He quickly lit a torch and ran into the chaos of falling debris. He could see nothing, and as soon as he entered, a rock hit his forearm, making him drop the torch, burying it in the falling silt. It was pitch black, with dust and debris assaulting his senses, so he let the song guide him and did not rely on his eyes. The source of the song was close, but he knew he had little time left before the inevitable cave-in buried them. He walked on unsteady legs as the ground continued to roil, and he only hoped falling debris would not crush him.

Cassandra drank the liquid and spat up most of the first gulp. It was almost as if she had forgotten how to swallow, and it frightened her to feel her body shutting down, preparing for death. Nevertheless, she had to concentrate on getting the refreshing liquid down, and she chugged the whole thing once her dying body cooperated. She immediately felt the effects of the powerful potion as the knife wound on her back closed quickly, and the throbbing in her arm and legs subsided substantially. She propped herself up on her elbows, basking in the relief. She felt so much better that she began to laugh out loud. Rocks and debris fell all around her, and some smaller rocks hit her arms and legs.

She made her feet quickly and held the glowing vial tightly. The cracked earth and the fallen debris made it impossible for her to reach the exit Greyson was trying to find. The light from her vial cascaded on the large ceiling piece that had landed beside her. She realized then just how close she had come to being flattened by it. She turned the other way, trying to get her bearings on the far wall opposite from which she had entered. It seemed to her that there had been a tunnel that the dry riverbed ran through. She needed to find it fast to protect herself from the hail of stones.

An awful noise behind her turned her back just in time to see the large chunk of ceiling that had almost crushed her disappear as the ground swallowed it up! The earth shook and buckled and knocked her down. A small rock hit her knee simultaneously, tearing her skin and making it bleed. She held her injured knee and grimaced away the pain, knowing the injury wasn't bad. She knew her chances of being crushed out in the open; the next rock might do more than tear the skin from her knee. The ground continued to tremble and split open, which had her up and running as quickly as possible for the far wall, hoping there was a tunnel. Just a few feet behind her, the floor began caving in, swallowing everything with it and followed her, quickly gaining.

Greyson continued to sing and dig his way out of the mounting silt that continued to pour on him. A ridiculous notion passed through his head that he felt like an ant trapped in an hourglass. The more he worked, the further behind he was getting. He would soon be buried alive. He looked back at the doorway that was so close, mocking them and the promised freedom. Binta lay motionless just a few feet away. He would try to wake her so she could escape alone.

Before he could even fathom doing such an impossible task, a figure blocked the sunlight. He could not determine who or what stood before him due to the thick dust and debris filling the air. At first, he thought it to be an angel, recalling the caves of Plath and the angel he had met there. What else could it be but an angel sent from Plath? But whatever it was, it extended a helping hand, and he did not hesitate to grab it. His rescuer was strong and pulled Greyson free from his fast-forming tomb.

As Greyson regained his feet, and before he could give thanks to the stranger, the man spoke. "Can you walk?"

"Yes, but she cannot," he screamed over the dying cave, pointing to Binta's prone form.

The man reached down and gently lifted her in his arms, then yelled to Greyson, "Follow me and be quick!"

Greyson did just that as they somehow dodged the falling debris and made their way outside the collapsing cave. Once out, the man carried Binta safely to the side and laid her gently in the snow. Greyson followed, coughing up dirt and dust as he made his way clear of the chaos. He had no idea who the stranger was, but he was no angel; he understood.

"I am Daro, sent from Pelesea to find you and your friends. Is anyone else in there?"

Greyson coughed, nodded, and wanted to tell him about Cassandra and that the ceiling had cut them off from her.

"How many, and where?" the ranger pressed.

Greyson just shook his head and squeaked out, "Too late."

Just then, there was a booming sound of rocks dropping from within the mountain, and the whole thing seemed to tremble as if it would fall flat and be no more. Both men turned to see a large cloud of dust and dirt fly from the partially open door. The mountain shook violently and rumbled for a long while as both watched helplessly. Finally, many large rocks filled the small opening they had just used, sealing off the door.

"It's too late," Greyson repeated, still catching his breath.

Cassandra ran as fast as her injured legs would let her. They had significantly healed with the potion Greyson had given her, but even at full strength, she doubted she could outrun the collapsing floor. She felt it giving away just at her heels and knew her time was up. Then she spotted the tunnel with the dry riverbed ahead of her and dashed toward it. She eventually made it without being crushed, and it protected her from the falling debris, but to her horror, the collapsing floor followed her in. She ran faster somehow, her worn legs beginning to scream in pain. Then, just as the collapsing floor threatened to pull her down, side passages appeared in the tunnel, one on either side of her. She ran on, trying hard to reach one before the floor swallowed her.

The ground gave way just as she reached the intersection, and she dove inside the left opening, dropping her glowing vial into it as she slammed hard against that tunnel's wall. Her shoulder screamed in protest as the waves of pain made her slide slowly to the ground, the cool stone wall the only thing keeping her from falling. It didn't take long for the entrance to seal behind her with rocks and debris. The walls shook, and the ground trembled beneath her, but the new tunnel held; even after the trembling stopped, there was no sign of the new tunnel collapsing. It took a very long time for the dust to settle and even longer for the rumbling to cease. All the while, Cassandra sat there, exhausted and injured, but happy to still be alive.

Soon, the only sound was her labored breathing. She sat with her back against the smooth stone, her hair matted to her face, holding her bad shoulder, and waiting for the dust to settle. She realized then, for the first time, that she was sitting on a flight of steps leading steeply down into the darkness. The vial lay just a few steps down, covered in dirt and dust, but still shining brightly through the layers of filth. She smiled weakly, glad for Greyson at that moment. She was all alone, but he had given her some strength back and had provided her with light. She would have already been dead without his help; he had truly saved her. She closed her eyes and said a prayer to Gella, not only for the strength to continue, but also to ask that Greyson and Binta make it to freedom. She smiled at the thought of them making it out and finding their way back to Pelesea. The idea truly made her happy.

Cass lay peacefully in a fluffy bed in Godhomme, the priests attending to her. Baxter stood by impatiently, fearing Cassandra was in trouble, but would not leave without an update from the priests. Of course, if he had to take Cass to Pelesea, he would, but that would take a great deal of time, something Cassandra probably did not have. Adam entered the room then and patted Baxter on the back. Baxter nodded at him, and his new friend returned the nod with a smile.

"So, what do you think, Salena?" Adam asked one of the priests.

The young priestess came over and spoke quietly to them, "She is very sick. The infection is unlike anything we have ever seen. We have made her comfortable and have slowed the infection, but we do not have the means to cure it."

"She will need the priests of Pelesea?" Adam asked.

"Yes, or the elves of Nessor," she added.

"Pelesea is closer," Adam reasoned.

"Yes, but elven magic is needed to save her," the priestess reasoned.

Baxter and Adam shared a knowing look that indicated they understood the seriousness of the girl's health. Salena bowed and returned to her work.

Once they were alone, Baxter spoke. "She needs to return to Pelesea. Her father would want that."

"Of course. We can always send for the elves if they are truly needed," Adam agreed.

Baxter looked back at the girl, the priests working diligently to fight the infection. The situation looked bleak to him, but he was no healer. "I am needed back at the mountain as quickly as possible. There are three more missing people."

"I understand, but I must insist you stay the night here. Then, if Cass is stable in the morning, you may return to your mountain; if not, you will need to take her to Pelesea."

The idea of sleep took Baxter off guard; how could he rest? He had no time for this kind of delay. Adam saw the unrest in his eyes and gently grabbed him by the shoulder.

"Please, my new friend, rest. Daro is scouting the mountain, and your missing adventurers are in good hands. You need the rest, and this one is critically ill," he reminded Baxter, nodding toward Cass's still form. "Would you have her perish for the sake of saving others? She has a chance to live; we should help see that through."

Baxter knew the man's words were valid, but he also knew his heart belonged to Cassandra. He could not let her die in that mountain. The wizard would sacrifice himself to save her, so why would Baxter not sacrifice Cass? He shook his head at the absurdity of it and eventually agreed with Adam to stay the night. He took a refreshing bath, studied his spellbook, had a great meal, and slept in a bed made for a king. But all the while, his thoughts dwelled on Cassandra and her well-being. Rest eluded him that night.

"So, what is wrong with her?" Daro asked after they had made Binta as comfortable as possible.

"I'm not sure. There was a creature; it did something to her," Greyson tried to explain.

"She has no visible wound; did she suffer an attack that would have injured her internally?" Daro asked as he gently examined her for injuries. He had some knowledge of rudimentary medicine, but not enough to determine what was wrong with her.

"Again, I am unsure. All I know is that my healing does not affect Binta's condition," Greyson answered, kneeling beside her with a grimace, the pain shooting up his left leg and making his foot throb.

Greyson stood then, helplessly unable to answer any of his questions, and as he stood, he noticed for the first time the trail of blood in the snow, and he limped to it. "Cass?" he asked, turning to regard Daro.

The ranger nodded and made his way to join him. "She is also very sick, but with an open and infected wound."

"Where is she?"

"Baxter took her to Godhomme."

"Godhomme?" Greyson asked curiously.

"Yes, a stronghold within a day's journey from here. Hopefully, she has found healing as we speak."

"Can we get Binta there?"

"Very soon, for her sake and your own," Daro said, pointing to the blood oozing from Greyson's boot.

"Thank you for saving us."

"Of course, that is why I came."

Greyson just looked at his foot and the amount of blood he was losing and wondered if he could consider either saved.

"What in the hell happened in there?" Daro asked, breaking him from his contemplation.

Greyson turned to regard the mountain, which still rumbled occasionally, but with less and less frequency.

"Nothing good, dear ranger. Nothing good."

"Why did you even go? What was the point?" Daro asked curiously.

Before Greyson could answer, Binta screamed out and threw her blankets aside. By the time they reached her, she was clawing at her stomach, digging her nails into her soft skin, and making it bleed. Greyson restrained her arms before she could seriously injure herself, and Daro felt around her abdomen, looking for signs of trauma or a severe injury. He still could find nothing.

Binta screamed and thrashed and nearly tore from Greyson's grasp. It took all he had to hold her back. The fit eventually passed after what seemed like an eternity, Greyson holding her in his arms. She looked up into his eyes, tears staining her face. She whispered something between cracked lips, then fell unconscious again. Greyson's face turned as white as the snow surrounding him, and he gave Daro a concerned look.

"What did she say?" the ranger asked.

"She said it is eating her from the inside."

"What?" Daro asked, rising to his feet once more.

"That's what she said," Greyson reiterated, holding her tightly and stroking her hair.

"We are leaving now," Daro said as he took out an ax and began chopping limbs from a nearby tree.

"Where are we going? Godhomme?" Greyson asked.

"Of course."

"What are you doing?" Greyson asked as the ranger chopped the limbs to specific lengths.

Daro stopped for just a moment and looked up at the young priest. "Constructing a gurney to carry her. Do you think you can walk?"

"If it means saving Binta, I'll walk until my foot falls off and keep going, even after that."

Daro smiled and returned to his work, but the way he did told Greyson that he was probably hurting more than he realized. He wondered how long it would take for Binta or himself to succumb to the wounds they suffered. He looked at his aching leg and bloody boot, then to Binta's still form, and dropped that line of thinking before it went too far.

Cassandra stood and tested her legs. Her hips still had a dull ache, but nothing she couldn't handle. The battered girl reached around and felt the knife wound on her back. It had reopened when she dove into the side tunnel, but she thought it was no longer life-threatening. The potion had fully healed the internal damage from the attack. She thought briefly of Cass and how the wretched girl had tried to murder her twice. How had she survived the waterfall? It didn't matter; she didn't matter; all that mattered now was finding a way out of the mysterious caves.

She took a few steps down the stone stairs to retrieve her glowing vial. When she stepped on a specific polished stone, she felt it give just a little. She immediately heard the familiar sound of gears turning and chains pulling. She expected a door to open somewhere, but to her surprise, the steps folded perfectly into the floor, leaving a smooth, slick stone surface in their place. The vial began to roll down the steep slope, quickly picking up momentum on the smooth floor. She tried to keep her footing, but there were no handholds, and the slope was too great. She fell on her back, and soon she slid down the tunnel behind the vial.

She grabbed at the walls and floor, trying to grasp anything to slow her descent. She quickly learned that there was no hope of that, and it was as if the steps never even existed. Although the vial got a head start on her, she quickly caught up to it and tried to grab it once more. She was sliding faster and faster, and her mind began to race. Would the tunnel end have a wall of spikes, a cauldron of fire, or some other trap that would end in a painful death? She was moving too fast to grab the vial, and it bounced over her, and quickly she had little light as she moved faster away from the glowing beacon.

Soon she was sliding so fast that there would be no way to avoid any deadly traps. She stopped struggling so that she could prepare for whatever was in store for her at the end of the tunnel, the vial and its light falling behind. By the time she reached the end, the vial was bouncing far back, and she was shrouded in darkness. She never saw the end, and it took her breath away when she reached it. There was no wall of spikes or fiery trap, just nothingness as the tunnel spat her out into a chasm. It took her mind a few moments to register what was happening and when it caught up, she elicited a scream and waved her arms futilely, like a flightless bird.

Although the vial followed her descent, it was just a spec of light as she free-fell, and she could barely make it out high above her, giving the appearance of a tiny lightning bug. She could not see the cavern floor that would inevitably end her life, and she couldn't see any walls to the place. She was falling, falling into darkness of unimaginable depths. She eventually stopped struggling and just focused on the shrinking firefly. She relaxed her body and waited for the imminent splat that would signal the end of her ill-advised quest. She fell so fast that her hair whipped against her face, stinging her as it did. She didn't care, she just focused on the vial, which seemed so far away now, and her thoughts were on her friends and family.

She prayed to Gella that Greyson and Binta had escaped the collapsing cavern. She also prayed for her mother and sister, and it broke her heart to know she would never see them again. The hooded creature was right: she did not deserve Zolmex, and her father had to be disappointed in her. She would die down there alone, and for all she knew, her father would animate her again to be the new guardian of the place. She hoped not; that was not the ending she desired. She shook the thought from her head, closed her eyes, and waited for death.

She hit something then, but not the hard ground she had anticipated. Whatever it was, it was soft yet firm and cushioned her fall. Unfortunately, it gave with the impact, and she continued to fall for many feet, although her incredible velocity diminished significantly by the unexpected cushion. Eventually, it stopped, then just as quickly threw her back up the way she had come before pulling her back down. A sticky substance covered the giant cushion and wouldn't let her go, so on it went for many cycles, her bouncing up and down until her momentum slowly played out and she stabilized on the soft material.

She tried to sit up, but her arms stuck out to her sides, and she realized the sticky material held her tight. She tried to move her legs, but the effort shot sharp pains through her thighs as they were held fast as well. She was stuck to it and helplessly so. Only when the shining vial fell beside her many moments later, starting another wave of motion on the soft bed, did she realize her plight. To her horror, the vial showed a vast spider's web stretching in all directions! She could not see the ends of it, the pit was so enormous, and the web stretched out into the darkness. She knew it had to attach somewhere to hold her weight, especially with the force she must have hit it with from her fall.

"I do not want to see what made this web," she whispered.

On cue, she felt the web tremor slightly as if something else had touched it, something she assumed would not stick to the webbing like herself. What could she do? She had to move, had to free herself. The trembling increased, and it felt like many things were touching it now. She could only assume they were spiders, and she was dinner. She was caught just like a fly.

Then she saw one rushing from her right. She was correct; it was a spider, but much more significant than she could have ever imagined, about the size of a miniature horse. It was swift on the web and ran straight for her, its multi-eyed face so hideous she had to look away. She closed her eyes and tried to think of a way out, but she only panicked with the giant spider that close. Suddenly, falling to her death seemed a much more desirable way to die, and she cursed the presence of the web.

The thing was on her, and she could see the fangs as the creature closed, venom dripping from them. She desperately pointed her finger at it, unable to manipulate it much, but just enough to cast her spell. She summoned as much energy as possible for a magical attack. Two green darts came forth and sizzled through the air, slamming into the spider's many eyes. It shrieked and rolled along with the web, right past her and over the side. She watched it fall, realizing then that the web had broken at her feet, leaving an opening to the chasm below. The thing was gone and had hopefully fallen to its death.

She exhaled a huge sigh of relief and closed her eyes. Then, she turned to the vial and said, "That was a close one, huh?"

Her humor was short-lived, though, as she realized the web was still trembling. It slowly bounced up and down, carrying her like an ocean tide. She looked at the vial and closed her eyes; she had seen Greyson perform the light-summoning spell many times during the adventure. She needed that light; she needed to see what was coming. Unfortunately, she had very little energy left to produce effective spells and needed to use it wisely. She had no choice but to try to amplify the light spell. She couldn't create the light, but perhaps she could make it more intense.

She closed her eyes and focused. She could feel the energy, the magic that held the place together. It was part of her father and, therefore, part of her. She saw the familiar arcane symbols in her head and tried to piece them together into something she could use quickly. She funneled the energy to the vial and focused on making it brighter and much more brilliant.

She felt the warmth first and opened her eyes to find that the vial was now a blinding light in the cavern and lit up three times the radius it had before. It felt as if she were outside on a bright summer's day. And the warmth it omitted was intoxicating. She could also see where the webbing stretched out to both sides of the cavern, which she estimated to be about one hundred yards wide. She was immediately sorry that her vision had grown because now she could see what was coming for her. On both sides of the cavern were tunnels similar to the one from which she had fallen. Unfortunately, those tunnels housed more giant spiders. Dozens poured from these tunnels and ran across the web to reach her. Both sides of the web were full of them. She could not stop them all, especially with her spell powers waning.

The intense light at least slowed them as they shielded their sensitive eyes from it with their giant, hairy legs. She had to think quickly; what could she possibly do? She closed her eyes and tried to focus on the energy once more. She had enough power to summon one more spell, but she had nothing in her repertoire to deal with this many enemies. A thought occurred to her as the brutes slowly began to advance on her once more, somewhat recovering from the blinding light. She vaguely remembered the day Baxter had rescued her from Oldorburg. Her mind had been foggy that day due to the poison she had ingested, but had he eaten a spider? Yes, he had, Cassandra remembered suddenly. She craned her neck to look to her left and right. The web would not let her move much, but she could see that her doom was close. She returned to her inner thoughts and recalled Baxter climbing the side of the temple after he had eaten the spider. It was a spell, of course, and one she had never studied.

She was heavily drugged then, but she tried to recall the energies he had swirled together to create the spell of wall-climbing that day. She closed her eyes and remembered that foggy event; she had to, and so she did. She summoned the energies for the spell and wove them perfectly together to create a replica of the magic. She felt the energy wash over her and sat up, the webbing no longer restraining her. But it was too late; the spiders were only twenty feet away on each side of her. There was no escape!

She thought about grabbing the vial but reconsidered when she saw the smoke wafting from it. The intense light was also producing heat and, therefore, beginning to burn the web. It would fall through soon. She stood on the web and stuck her arms out to hold her balance against the waves that the spiders were producing. She looked around for an answer and eventually spotted a possible exit below the web. There was a tiny tunnel on the far wall, perhaps large enough to fit someone her size, which would be too small for the spiders, she hoped.

As the spiders closed in on Cassandra, she understood that was her only hope to escape, so over the edge she went, not jumping to her death but instead, using the hole at her feet to crawl along the underside of the web, making her way desperately to the small tunnel she had spotted. She ignored the fact that she crawled underneath the mass of arachnids; she was on one side of the web, and they were on the other. They swatted at her with their coarse, hairy legs, some cutting her in a few places; some bit at her, but none could score a solid hit. Finally, she was too quick for them and continued her run, hanging upside down on all fours. She tried not to think of what was above or below her.

She glanced behind her to see the vial burn a hole through the web and fall. She also saw many spiders crawling behind her, underneath the web, and they were much faster than she. She turned back to the small tunnel and marked its location well, as the light quickly diminished and was soon gone as the vial fell from sight. She nearly reached the small opening before the light disappeared. But soon, she was in total darkness, feeling around the wall with her hands and promptly locating the entrance before she lost her bearings.

She quickly squeezed into the opening and was so focused on fleeing the spiders that she did not consider what she was getting into so hastily. There was nothing to grab hold of, so she took a small spill into a room, and as she did, a brazier flared to life right next to her. Another one on the far side of the room lit up moments later. She glanced at her surroundings as she sat there for a moment. Besides the braziers, the room contained a stone stairway leading up into the darkness, a pile of what looked to be torches lying on the floor next to the first brazier, and, more importantly, a casket sitting alone in the middle of the small room.

"Leo!" she gasped.

Before she could do anything else, a horrible pain shot through her calf. She looked down to see that one of the spider legs had reached in and cleanly stabbed right through her muscle. She screamed in agony, and the creature pulled her back toward the opening. She could see the thing's eyes reflecting in the flames of the brazier, and she knew she couldn't let herself be pulled out of this room, for that would mean certain death.

The spider was strong, and it quickly had her legs out before she could grab the lip of the opening and hang on. She pulled with all her strength but found little power in her wounded shoulder. Then she felt a sickening pain in her foot, and she could only imagine it had just bitten her. Her fear was soon confirmed as she felt the venom pumping into her system. It immediately numbed her leg, and she could feel it coursing through her body.

In addition to the vicious wound, webbing started to fill the small opening. Her spell that allowed her to resist its sticky hold began to fail. She could still move freely about the stuff, but as it grabbed her, the source of the webbing was also pulling her. There was no way she could hold long against the strength of the spiders. She could not see her attackers and could no longer feel her right leg. She knew she had to break the hold, or she was doomed.

She took her left foot and kicked straight out with all her might, scoring a direct hit to the creature's face. It hissed in pain and fell away, releasing the grip on her leg. The pain should have been overwhelming, but she hardly felt it, whether from the adrenaline or the poison; she wasn't sure. She pulled herself back into the room and fell limply to the floor. Her right leg gushed blood, but she felt none of it, as that leg was now completely numb from the poison and even had a greenish hue. Suddenly, she felt very sick to her stomach. She knew it was probably the poison and hoped it wasn't strong enough to kill her.

The webbing continued to pull her, and more spidery legs reached in to grab at her. She avoided them by lying flat and not giving them a clear target. Still, they scratched at her and opened several nasty wounds on her abdomen and upper legs. Finally, she untangled herself from the filaments and crawled away from the opening, staying as low to the ground as possible. Soon she was out of reach of the nasty spiders, and she watched as they continued spinning their webs in the opening, sealing it off.

She meant to get up and check on the casket. Was she in the great

Leo's tomb, the most powerful wizard known to exist? More importantly, was Zolmex in that casket? Exhaustion overtook her as the thoughts swirled in her mind. She was vaguely aware of the poison pumping through her veins as she lay on the floor near the steps and welcomed sleep. The casket would have to wait.

The journey to Godhomme was slow and dangerous. Getting Binta off the mountain slopes was trickier than either Greyson or Daro had thought. Greyson even took a spill, which reopened the wound on his left thigh. He put it out of his mind and focused on saving Binta. Daro didn't argue with him, hoping to make Godhomme before dawn. Neither was certain Binta would live much longer, so they kept up their travels through the night the best they could. Greyson was sorely injured, and the light from Daro's lantern made them stand out in the wilderness, ripe for a goblin ambush. Luck was with them, and they reached Godhomme just as the sun was cresting the eastern horizon. Men atop the wall saw them a good way off and opened the gate, sending out a contingent to greet them. It was a good thing, too, because as soon as Greyson knew they had arrived, he collapsed several hundred yards from the gate. Daro eased the gurney holding Binta to the ground and checked on him.

"You did great, kid. Now hang in there; help is on the way," he whispered.

The men from Godhomme helped Daro carry the two wounded adventurers into their stronghold, where the priests quickly attended to them. They were given a bed next to Cass, and the priests provided medical attention to all three. They worked hard to save Greyson's foot and to find a cure for Binta, who was very sick at that point. Daro stood by and watched the priests' work, just as Baxter had done the day before.

He never heard Baxter sneak up beside him, and he jumped when the wizard asked bluntly, "And what of Cassandra?"

The ranger turned to regard him, and the look on his face spoke volumes. Baxter's heart sank as Daro lowered his gaze to the floor and slowly shook his head.

"Where is she?" Baxter asked, his voice breaking.

"She fell in the mountain, caught in a cave-in."

"You do not have her body?" Baxter asked, holding onto false hope.

"Baxter, believe me, she is gone."

"You might be correct, but I am not giving up on her until I have proof," Baxter argued and started away.

"Where are you going, Wizard? I need you to help me get these three to Pelesea; they are all very sick."

Baxter stopped and turned back, his gaze shifting from the ranger to the three young adventurers fighting for their lives. He knew he couldn't give up on them just for the small hope he could find Cassandra. His heart sank as he knew what he must do.

Before he could answer his friend, Gabriel said, "We already have a wagon ready to take them to Pelesea, led by my finest team. They will make short work of getting them home."

Surprised by the kind gesture, both Daro and Baxter shared a puzzled glance.

"When can you leave, my old friend?" Daro asked.

"The team is ready; I'm just waiting on the priests to stabilize the two new patients. But I assure you, we will have them all there before the next dawn."

That seemed to satisfy the ranger, and he nodded to Baxter, who understood that he would feel no guilt for leaving and that they were in good hands. But as if on cue, a young priestess walked up to Gabriel with a concerned look and said, pointing to Binta, "Sir, you should know that our medicine cannot heal the girl, and she needs to be taken to Pelesea immediately."

"What is wrong with her?" Baxter asked, walking toward Binta's bed.

"We are not sure, but we feel there is an infection from within. For reasons unknown, our healing does not affect the wound," the priestess explained, as all of them gathered around her bedside.

Baxter knelt and gently lifted her shirt to expose her midsection, which was red and warm. He felt her gently, and she moaned even with his very light touch.

He looked up at the priestess and said, "She does not need priestly healing; she needs arcane magic. Lady Victoria will be able to help her."

Baxter then addressed Daro, "I am taking her to Pelesea on my carpet. I can only take one other person with me, so the other two can ride in Gabriel's wagon. Once she is healed, I will make haste back to the mountain, hoping to find Cassandra."

Daro smiled at him and replied, "Sounds like a good plan, my friend. However, my adventure ends here. Do you understand?"

Baxter returned the smile and nodded. "Yes, of course, and I will see you back at Pelesea once I have found Cassandra."

Baxter hurried off to pack his things and retrieve his carpet. He knew Binta was in serious trouble and needed to reach Victoria quickly, but his thoughts remained on Cassandra. Daro had warned him that she was dead, but he didn't believe it; he couldn't believe it.

Soon, he had Binta on his carpet, wrapped in a thick blanket to keep her warm and heavily sedated, so she would not squirm off the magic carpet during a thrashing fit. Luckily, she remained silent the entire trip, although her moans were audible and more frequent than Baxter would have liked. They made the trek to Pelesea in just a few hours and didn't even stop to land at the gate, but instead flew past the guards and straight for Lady Victoria's tower.

The guards must have recognized him because he heard no shouts of alarm and no sign of pursuit. He landed at the base of the tower and quickly dismounted. Baxter ignored the stares of students who witnessed his arrival and focused instead on getting to Victoria. He made his way to the tower door, of which he and only a handful of instructors knew the location and offered the password. The invisible door showed itself, and he was back on the carpet in no time, slowly floating through the doorway.

Once inside, the door sealed back, the golems activated, but he silenced them with the appropriate password and floated up the staircase and onto the main floor. To his delight, he quickly found

Victoria sitting in one of her conference rooms. To his dismay, Mr. Ruben, Cass's pushy father, was with her. His red face displayed a not-so-happy look. They both regarded him as he landed the carpet in the large hallway.

"Baxter, you have returned!" Victoria greeted him happily.

Her cheerfulness dissipated when she noticed a body wrapped in a blanket. She quickly rose to her feet and made her way to him, Mr. Ruben right on her heels.

"Binta," Victoria said, recognizing the girl right away. "What is wrong with her?" she asked Baxter.

Before he could answer, Franklin Ruben cut him off, "Where is my daughter, Wizard?"

Baxter ignored the man and spoke to Victoria. "Something has cursed her, I believe. The healing powers of the priests did not help her. If anyone could help, it would be you, Victoria."

Victoria nodded, making her way quickly down the hall of eternal doors.

"Remove the blanket and keep her still; I will return shortly," she called over her shoulder.

Baxter complied and knelt to unwrap the heavy blanket gently. Franklin knelt with him and whispered, "Is she going to make it?"

"I honestly don't know, Mr. Ruben," Baxter said as he continued his work.

"Where's my daughter?" Franklin asked once more, this time his voice sterner as he stood.

Baxter stood as well and tossed the blanket to the floor.

"She is on her way and will arrive at the north gate sometime before daybreak," Baxter assured the man.

The large man seemed slightly relieved at that information but still worried as he pointed toward Binta and asked, "Is she like this one?"

"No," Baxter confirmed, looking at Binta's tormented face, sweat streaking it in many places. "But she is wounded, and her wounds are infected. She should be fine but is in desperate need of healing."

"So, you brought this girl instead of my daughter?"

Baxter turned to regard the man and understood he was simply a protective father, but he was in no mood to listen to him argue that his daughter was the essential victim when Cassandra might be injured and need of help, or worse, dead.

When he saw Victoria return, he bit his tongue and said, "Binta is sicker than your daughter, and I only had room for one person on the carpet."

Victoria had a scroll and quickly knelt beside Binta and unrolled it.

"If anything happens to my Cass, and it's because you did not prioritize her—"

"We will all share in your grief!" Baxter interrupted.

The two men stood face to face, and many moments passed between them while Victoria read the scroll. Eventually, Franklin Ruben nodded and took a step back.

"I appreciate your efforts, Wizard, but understand, Cass is my everything."

"I understand your plight, Mr. Ruben, but you must understand that men have died to rescue these young people. Do not let their deaths be in vain."

"Of course. I will watch for Cass at the north gate. Good day, Wizard. Good day, Lady Victoria," he called behind him as she was finalizing the spell.

She glanced up at Baxter and gave him a nod, indicating he should call off the golems and open a door for the man to exit. Baxter made his way to the top of the stairs, where he could do just that. Mr. Ruben seemed not to notice the golems or the door opening at the last second. The distraught man took his leave, and Baxter ensured the door was secure behind him. Afterward, he quickly made his way back to Victoria. There, Baxter found her helping Binta stand slowly. He rushed up to them to assist, but Binta waved him off.

"I am fine, Instructor Baxter," she said warmly. "How did I get here?" she asked, looking around curiously. "Am I in the tower?" she added, her eyes wide.

"I will take her to the temple. She still requires healing, but I have defeated the curse from within," Victoria confirmed.

"And I—" Baxter began.

"Are leaving once more to find her," Victoria finished for him.

He nodded and activated the rug, which rose from the floor and floated beside him at knee height.

"She is still out there," he confirmed.

"Cassandra?" Binta asked.

"I will find her and return soon," he said, directing his answer to both of them.

"Cassandra!" Binta screamed, grabbing his arm tight. "Instructor, Baxter, she is hurt. That thing had her!" she added, recalling the creature they battled.

"What thing?" Baxter asked, suddenly intrigued.

"I don't know, a skeletal creature. It got in my mind; I almost killed Greyson because of that thing. Where is he? Where is Greyson?" she asked, the sudden rush of memories flooding back to her, sending her into a panic.

"Come, Miss Mulay, we need to get you to the temple," Victoria instructed, helping her toward the stairs.

Binta continued to speak gibberish that neither understood: something about zombies, skeletons, and magical rooms. Baxter watched them go and suddenly felt very ill. If Cassandra was alive, she was probably in serious trouble. Binta's words repeatedly rang in his head, *"She is hurt!"*

Soon he was flying out of Pelesea and toward the mountain, pushing the magical rug to its limits. But nothing would stop him from finding her. He had taken the opportunity to memorize some spells the night before at Godhomme. He was determined to find Cassandra, and the gods have mercy on anyone who tried to stop him.

Cassandra awoke with a start, bolting upright to a sitting position. Her hair matted her face and sweat covered her near-naked body. She knew the poison had something to do with her condition as her foot throbbed where the spider had bitten her. She had been having a nightmare, a very vivid nightmare, but could not remember the details. Though, she knew without a doubt that it had been about her father. She had that same uneasy feeling she usually had after her dreams back at the orphanage. She sat there for a moment, trying to remember the details, but she could not, and once she remembered she was in a tomb, she soon forgot about it.

They had been looking for Leo's coffin, beginning at the small graveyard when they were together and alive. She was the only one to reach their goal, assuming it was Leo's tomb. She sat there a moment longer, contemplating how long exactly she had been in the cave. How many days ago had those little creatures killed Cedric? She honestly didn't know; there was no day or night in the cave, only darkness.

She stood slowly, and her leg was still numb and tingling from the poison, but more noticeably, the wound in her calf where the spider's leg had impaled was excruciating and looked like it had bled quite a bit while she had slept. As she stood, dizziness overcame her, and she suddenly felt very ill. She realized then that she had not eaten for a very long time.

"Time to take Zolmex and leave this god-forsaken place," she whispered.

She made her way gingerly to the casket. It was a simple wooden box, with no extravagant markings of any kind, except for a lion's head carving on the side that matched the key her father had given her. It was old, rotted, and very plain; not precisely the casket she imagined Leo, the greatest wizard the world had ever known, would have been buried in. The lion's head carving verified that this was his tomb. It had to be, or all of this was for naught.

"Dear Leo, time to hand over Zolmex; it is rightfully mine. I appreciate you holding onto it for me all the years, but now I need it," she said as she slowly lifted the top.

It took some effort, but once opened, she saw a skeletal figure inside, dressed in a colorful wizard's robe decorated with many arcane runes. The robe stood the test of time and looked in perfect condition. The corpse's beard was long and white, similar to the drawings she had seen of Leo back at the school. There was a scroll rolled up with a wax seal sitting atop the corpse's chest, his skeletal hands resting on it, but she could see nothing else in the coffin due to the lack of light. She regarded the pile of torches, limped over to them, and lit one using the brazier.

When she made her way back to the coffin, she held the torch up high and moved it around so it would light all the dark corners and crevasses of the unremarkable box. There was nothing else there, just a corpse in a fancy robe with an old scroll across his chest.

She wasn't sure if this was Leo, but if it was, there was no Zolmex to be found as Cedric had promised. If it wasn't Leo, where was he, and who was this? Many thoughts ran through her mind as she just stared at the corpse. She felt so cheated after everything she had accomplished. Her eyes filled with tears, but she would not let herself cry; her crying days were behind her.

Her gaze slowly made its way to the old scroll. What was that? A clue? A map? Whatever it was, she didn't have the energy to keep playing the games her father seemed so intent on playing. All she wanted now was to go home, wherever home was. She reached into the casket and grasped the old, brittle paper. Her touch had pieces flaking off, so she tossed the torch onto the floor and used both hands, one to move the skeletal hands and one to pull the scroll free gently.

"Gross," she cried out, dropping the skeletal hand and wiping her hand on the side of her ragged underwear, removing any evidence she had touched the skeleton.

Once she had the scroll freed from the corpse's grasp, she took the torch, placed it in the brazier, and then sat on the steps to read it. The paper was old and very brittle, and the wax seal barely held the parchment together. The seal had a "Z" melted into it, which lifted her spirits.

"Zolmex," she exclaimed, then regarded the lion's head carving on the casket's side again.

"Tell me your secrets, Leo," she said aloud, her voice echoing up the stairwell.

She waited a few anxious moments, hoping her excitement had not stirred anything in the dark above her. When nothing showed itself, she removed the seal, which crumbled at her feet when she touched it.

Then she quickly unrolled the parchment, her heart racing in her chest. The scroll was not Zolmex, and Cassandra was tired of the games, so she needed the parchment to tell her exactly what she needed—where was Zolmex, and how could she reach it quickly? Maybe it would give her a clue on how to find the strange room in her dreams. She took a deep breath and unrolled the old paper.

She stood and held the parchment up to the brazier to ensure she could read it correctly. Unfortunately, the scroll was quite simple, and she confusedly whispered, "It cannot be. So, what does this mean?"

There, written in a simple, old language, were the words: Notel X.

She studied it for many moments, mouthing the words silently. What did it mean? What was she supposed to do now? She stamped her foot, sending waves of pain through her hip, and threw the scroll into the brazier, which hungrily ate it. Soon, there was nothing left of it. Someone wrote those simple words centuries ago, and until now, the scroll had lain dormant, waiting for someone to find it. Now it was gone, and Cassandra was not amused. It was time to leave.

"What does it mean?" she screamed at the casket. "I am leaving. I do not want your stupid artifact, Father!" she screamed, imagining he was immensely enjoying her discomfort and frustration. She grabbed a new torch with a growl, lit it, and began to climb the stairs, which spiraled steeply upward. She didn't even close the casket lid as she left the small tomb.

She climbed the stairs for many hours. She briefly considered that they might be trapped like the last ones and fold away to have her fall again. She dismissed the thought, not caring if that happened because she was too frustrated at having come this far for nothing. Why had they come? Why had she followed Cedric so quickly? Perhaps he was just a simple madman. She second-guessed all of it and hoped she could escape the horrible cave. None of this made any sense to her anymore.

"Notel X," she whispered to herself in disgust.

What did that mean? She didn't care; she just wanted out of the caves. She stopped and rested for a bit, not realizing how long she had been climbing, and needing water desperately. She had been lost in thought and had ignored her body until that moment. She was thirsty, hungry, and tired, and her calf screamed in pain at the spider wound, which looked like it was already infected. She climbed for what seemed like an eternity, her body drenched in sweat with the effort.

To make matters worse, her torch was slowly dying, allowing the darkness to creep in again. Why had she not taken an extra torch or two? She scolded herself for being stupid and careless, but it was too late to turn back. She sat down to rest her leg and put her head in her hands. She wondered how far the stairs went and what test or trap waited for her at the end. She sat there a few moments, tired, injured, and emotionally spent, when she suddenly realized she was cold, colder than usual. She could feel the goosebumps on her skin, her sweat-covered body reacting to cooler temperatures. It was much colder here than in the rest of the cave, the only exception being the magically enchanted water.

"An exit!" she exclaimed, standing up once more and vigorously climbing the stairs.

It had to be an exit. Had she climbed out of the mountain's depths and was nearing civilization once more? She had to hold on to that hope to keep her sanity. So, her heart leaped in her chest when she saw daylight up ahead. The light spilled out onto the steps, and the temperature was even colder now as she began to shiver uncomfortably. She didn't care; being cold had never felt so wonderful.

She tossed the torch down and ran as fast as her tired and injured legs would carry her up the steps. As she came around the curve of the steps, she saw a doorway above her and to her right, with natural daylight shining in. It wasn't bright, and she couldn't see where the doorway led from her current position, but it was not torchlight. She could also vaguely hear the howl of the wind. She ran on until she reached the doorway. Her heart sank as she saw an old metal door made of crisscrossing bars blocking the way.

"No," she whispered, and ran up to the old door.

There was no other way to go, either through this door or back to the tomb. There had been no other side passages on her trek up the steps.

"No!" she screamed as she grabbed onto the rusted bars.

The door reminded her of one in a jail cell and was in disrepair and hanging precariously on its hinges. Still, it remained partially shut and blocked the way. She looked beyond the door and found the source of daylight. There had been a bridge at one time spanning a great chasm, which she assumed was the same one that contained the massive spider web far below. The bridge had suffered enormous damage from some long-ago event, and now only a twenty-foot section remained. It reached out past the old door toward the far side of the chasm. About thirty feet above the bridge was the cave ceiling, which contained a small grate to the outside. Daylight poured in through that grate.

"An exit," she whispered to herself.

The heavy, rusted door was the only thing separating her from the bridge and possibly freedom. She pulled on the door, and it gave just a little. The movement of the old door gave her some hope that she could open it. She pushed hard on it, and it moved just a little more, and she saw that it carved a rut in the stone floor. She did this several times, and it opened wider each time. She labored feverishly to work it open; it was the key to her freedom. She was so close to exiting the cave, and she began to panic a little more with each passing moment.

Her senses started to play tricks on her as well. She thought she heard the spiders coming from the other side at one point, their legs chittering on the stone wall. She could imagine the corpse coming up the stairs to retrieve the scroll, or perhaps the skeletal creature had returned with a bottle of maggots. By the time she had the door open enough to squeeze through, she was in a cold sweat once more, despite the cold temperature. The door now hung precariously from the bottom hinge, leaning toward the broken bridge. She squeezed through the opening and out onto the bridge.

As she stepped out, she felt the blisteringly cold wind. She was close enough to the outside world that the snow, the trees, and all of nature's smells seemed to overwhelm her. She closed her eyes and took it all in, her hands out to her sides, relieved and excited to be this close to freedom. She slowly opened her eyes and walked to the edge of the bridge. The sunlight was weak, and she could barely make out the other side of the chasm. Something had broken the bridge long ago, and what had caused such damage did not matter to her. Instead, she imagined the missing piece was lying at the bottom of the chasm, far below the spider web.

When it was intact, she assumed the bridge had just led back to the mysterious caves filled with tricks and traps, and she was not going that way. She was going up. She craned her neck to measure the distance to the grate. If she could reach it, perhaps it was rusted and breakable as the old door she had just slipped through. She then looked over the edge of the bridge, down into the darkness. She could not see very far, but she knew what lurked there. A cold chill suddenly ran down her spine, and panic nearly overwhelmed her again. If those hideous spiders knew she was up there, they would come for her; she felt confident. There was nowhere to hide if they came for her now that the broken door no longer functioned. She glanced up at the grate in the ceiling again and pondered her next actions.

Suddenly, a loud booming sound shook the bridge, causing her to jump and scream. She turned to see that the door had fallen and lay flat on the bridge. It took her a moment to catch her breath, her heart beating out of her chest, but when she finally regained her composure, she realized that the loud boom of the falling door was still echoing far below her, traveling the length of the chasm. Her scream traveled closely behind.

"The spiders," she whispered, her eyes suddenly widening.

She dared to look over the edge of the broken bridge once more. Of course, she could not see anything through the thick blanket of darkness, but she could imagine those monsters pouring out of their holes and climbing the walls to investigate the source of the noise. She froze with fear at the thought of it. It took her many moments to tear her gaze away and approach the cavern wall. Finally, she recalled the wall walking spell Baxter had cast and copied it again, confident in its required arcane pattern. When she reached the wall, she walked up it on all fours, her hands and feet sticking to it as a spider's might. When she reached the ceiling, she walked across it the same way, hardly deterred. When she came to the grate, she pulled hard on it, testing its strength. To her dismay, it was solid. She pushed and pulled on it several more times, to no avail. It was shut and was not going to open easily. She tested the rock ceiling around the grate, trying to find a weakness, but there was none.

"No," she cried and stuck her hand through the grate, hoping someone could see her.

No one came, so she dared to shout, "Help me! Somebody, help!"

She glanced down into the darkness and saw the destroyed bridge beneath her. She wondered if the spiders were on their way, as her shouting had created new echoes to lure them out. She turned, screamed for help, and jerked hard on the grate, becoming desperate.

"I can't die this close to freedom," she whispered, on the verge of tears.

She heard something from far below, a clicking sound. She stopped and listened intently for a few moments and eventually heard it again. The spiders were coming! She screamed louder for help, pulled, and jerked on the solid grate. She was trapped. As the panic set in, she struggled more desperately. Eventually, she gave up, breathing hard. She could not open it, and no one was on the other side to help her.

She thought of that day all those years ago when she was a small child, the evening she and Kessi had ventured out with their mom into the neighboring woods. She had not felt that scared since then, but the feeling returned to her in a rush. That odd connection she had felt with the birds that day came with it. She could feel them in the woods all those years ago, and she felt them again. The ravens were there, and she needed them.

She took a deep breath and closed her eyes, calming herself. She remembered feeling very calm as a child, and she needed to do that to call the ravens once again. She remembered that evening like yesterday and how she had ignored her fears and focused on the birds instead. The way she had called to them when she was five had been an instinct, something she knew how to do. Now, she was older and understood better how to reach out to them, although she had never replicated that great of a summoning again. She felt her call go out to the surrounding woods for many miles, reaching many birds.

She felt them respond to her call to fly to the grate. They were coming!

She could feel more and more of them as she concentrated. They answered her call, and great flocks came to the grate and understood what she needed. As they swarmed around it, they began pecking at the snow and dirt at the edges. She moved to the side as debris rained down through the grate. They were digging her out! They were following her commands and digging her out. She did not relent in her concentration and instead spurred them on at a greater pace.

"Hurry, my friends," she whispered, looking into the thick darkness beneath her.

She could not see the spiders, but she could sense them. The hairs stood on her neck as she thought about the nest of creatures below her. She ignored her fears and called out to more ravens. Soon they were swarming the area, all fiercely digging to free her, but would they be fast enough?

Baxter stood at the cave entrance, the one Daro had told him about where Cass, Binta, and Greyson had all escaped the mountain. He had found the trail of blood quickly enough, and it led right to the spot, or what had once been the entry. Now, there only remained a pile of rubble blocking the way. It had been a full cave-in, just like Daro had told him. If Cassandra was caught in that, she was truly gone.

He put his hand on the mountain and lowered his head. "Cassandra, if you are still alive, I will find you. I will not give up on you," he promised.

He sighed and made his way back to his trusted carpet. He would make several trips around the mountain, fly low, and look for other possible entrances. His instincts told him it would be futile, and Daro had said it in not so many words. Nevertheless, he had to stay positive and do everything he could for Cassandra. The slim chance she was stuck inside the mountain or lay injured somewhere on the surface got him onto the carpet and up in the air quickly.

He made his way along slowly at first, seeking some sign that he could gain access to the mysterious mountain cave. He was desperate and time was not on his side. The longer he searched, the more he realized that it was a nearly impossible task. There was no visible way into the mountain; even if he found a way in, would he ever find Cassandra? If he did, was there a chance she would still be alive? Those thoughts tormented him, and he felt utterly defeated in his search until he spotted the swarm of birds. There were hundreds of them, and as they passed overhead, they temporarily blotted out the sun.

"Ravens?" he breathed.

Of course, he could not tell what kind of birds they were, but he knew they would lead him to Cassandra if they were indeed ravens. He quickly followed the swarm and watched them land near the top of the mountain to add to the hundreds already gathered there. More and more of them came in flocks and landed in the same place, working in a frenzy once they reached the ground. He could not determine what they were doing, but they all fought to gain one spot on the mountain. He hovered the carpet as close to them as he could, and only then did he see the grate. It looked like the ravens were trying to dig around the edges, and yes, they were ravens.

He lowered the carpet to within a few feet above the grate and peered into the darkness. He saw nothing there, but he knew Cassandra had to be there.

"Cassandra?" he called out.

"Baxter!" her voice returned, and her hand stuck out between the bars.

He lay prone on the carpet and grabbed her hand, which was cold.

"Baxter, you came for me!" she sobbed.

"I am here. Are you hurt?"

"Yes, but not bad."

"Good, I will have you out of there shortly," he said, releasing her hand and grabbing the bars of the grate. He pulled with all of his strength, but they would not budge.

"Baxter?"

"Yes, what is it?" he answered, still preoccupied with testing the bars.

"They are coming for me. I don't have much time."

A chill ran down his spine as she spoke the words. They were said with such finality as if she had resigned to the fact she would die down there. He examined the edges of the grate, and the ravens had quickly dug up the sides, but the bars just continued into the rock and dirt as if the grate had no end. He knew there would not be enough time for them to dig her out this way if something was coming for her.

"How much time do we have?" he asked, grabbing his spellbook and looking for something that might help.

"I don't know. Not long, I fear," the frightened girl answered between sniffles.

He felt so helpless at that moment. He was close to rescuing his love but couldn't complete the task. He could not live with himself if he let her die like that. An idea slowly came together for him then. He closed the book and lay back on the carpet to look into the darkness. He could barely see the outline of her face, which seemed very close to the bars.

"Call off the birds; I have an idea."

"What?" she yelled, her voice showing more than a hint of fear.

"Call them off; there is no way to dig around this thing. It runs deep along the mountain."

"But we must, I—"

"Trust me, Cassandra, I have a plan."

A few moments passed before the birds finally stopped their pecking and flew into the neighboring trees. After they had settled above him and away from the hole, he could see her face better as more light filtered into the cave. She looked breathtaking to him. Her face was filthy from dirt and dust, and her hair was sweaty and matted, but she was stunning.

Everything seemed quieter now that the birds had stopped their digging. Baxter could make her focus better this way. It was her only hope; she would have to do something he had never seen done before, except for one other time back in Oldorburg.

"Cassandra, do you remember when we first met, and you stole my cantrip from me?"

"Yes, why?"

"I need you to do that again, but with a different spell."

"What? Why? I need something that will move these bars, Baxter."

"I know, but I need you—" he began before his thoughts were interrupted by a chitinous echo below her. "What is that?" he asked.

"The spiders," she said, silently crying once more.

"Spiders?"

"Yes, hundreds of them, all huge. Get me out of here, Baxter."

"Focus on me, not the spiders, and you will be out of there, standing beside me soon enough."

"Hurry!" she screamed, nearing panic as the sound grew closer and closer.

"I will cast a spell, and you will take it from me, just like the cantrip."

"What? I can't!"

"Cassandra, you can, and you must. You can do things I've never seen anyone do, things that Lady Victoria cannot even do. And the best part is that you've only just begun learning about your powers. I believe you can do this, and I need you to believe it, too."

He watched her beautiful face, tears leaving trails down her dirty cheeks. She was frightened and unfocused, and that meant she would fail. He had to get her to focus.

"Cassandra, do you want to see your sister and mother again?"

Just as he had hoped, that got her attention, and she looked at him dumbfounded, almost like she didn't understand what he was asking her. Finally, it slowly sank in as she realized she would never see her family again if she didn't calm down and focus. She took a deep breath and closed her eyes.

"If you do, then do this for them. Do this and be free of that wretched place once and for all."

She nodded her understanding, so he stood on the carpet and began to cast his spell. Cassandra closed her eyes and fell within herself, and he could see her face transform and the distressed look melt away. Soon she was breathing calmly, almost peacefully, and he knew she was focused on the spell. He could hear many creatures below her but could not see them. All he knew was she had precious little time to do this, which would be impossible for anyone else.

Nevertheless, he believed she could do it; perhaps she was beginning to think it, too. He couldn't be sure, but it seemed like she was a beacon for the magical energies in the cave, that perhaps she was summoning them, sorting them, and bending them to her will. He felt confident in that fact because, as Baxter began casting his spell, he felt her pulling it away before he could finish it. So, he had to double his concentration to complete it.

He finished his spell, and an extra-dimensional door appeared a few feet below Cassandra, hanging in midair. He turned and pointed behind him, and a similar door appeared on the mountainside. The spell usually only worked for the caster to transport himself a short distance away. No other person could use the door; it didn't work that way. He was hoping that Cassandra could do just that.

"Cassandra?" he yelled into the darkness.

"Yes," came her calm reply from within.

Her tone and calm demeanor surprised him more than a little, especially since he could hear the crawling spiders around her now.

"The spell is complete; a door hangs below you. It is my door, but I need you to steal it and use it as your own. Do you understand?"

"Yes," she replied again, still with her eyes closed.

"Do it, now, Cassandra!" he yelled to her, panic growing as the spiders closed in.

He knew they were close, probably within striking distance, but she didn't seem too concerned with them. She was doing what he had asked; she was focusing. However, he didn't want her to become so focused that she forgot her surroundings. If she didn't or couldn't steal the spell, she would die, so she needed time to prepare. He looked on helplessly and could vaguely hear himself yelling for her to jump through the door. She was unresponsive and seemed almost to be asleep.

Then she opened her eyes and looked into his. They were

unnaturally blue, and they almost seemed to glow in the dark. It startled him, and he nearly lost his balance on the carpet. But then she released her grip and fell toward the magical door.

Baxter held his breath as he watched her fall. To his relief, she seemed to disappear through the magical door and did not simply fall through it. He turned anxiously to view the other side of the door behind him. To his delight, she first fell through the door, initially horizontal to the ground, then crashed to the ice and snow, where she slid a few feet and then lay motionless. Spider legs jabbed through the grate and slashed at his carpet just a moment later, and webbing began to shoot forth. He could see many spider eyes in the darkness now and understood what kind of death Cassandra had just avoided. He spurred the carpet away from the hole and landed beside her prone form.

He was surprised to see her nearly naked, with only her underwear to hide her most private parts, and not much of that material remained. It was transparent and torn in many places, leaving little to the imagination. He gently turned her over and took in her nakedness for a moment. He was so in love with her that he could not resist admiring her young body.

"See something you like?" she asked weakly, opening her eyes just a bit and smiling.

"Oh, yes, sorry," he stammered, looking away.

Before he could apologize, she sat up and hugged him tightly. Her actions caught him off guard at first, but he hugged her back.

"Thank you for coming for me, Baxter."

"Of course. I was not going to leave you here to die."

They shared a moment then, looking into each other's eyes. Then, he slowly moved toward her. He wanted nothing more than to take her in his arms and make love to her. His heart raced at the thought, and he moved closer; he would kiss her as no one had ever kissed her!

"Baxter?"

"Yes?" he asked with a gulp, ready to devour her if she was so inclined.

"I'm cold."

"Uh… Yes, of course," he said, the trance now broken.

He stood and retrieved a blanket from his pack. He then helped Cassandra up and wrapped her tightly in it.

"You ready to go home?" he asked her, waving toward the carpet, trying to move past the awkward exchange they had just shared.

She smiled and nodded, holding the blanket tight and stepping on the magical carpet.

"You know, we really should stop meeting like this," he said, half-jokingly and more than a little flirty.

"What do you mean?" she asked as she sat in front, and he took a spot behind her.

Once he settled, he pulled her tightly against him, and she just seemed to melt into his arms, not resisting a bit.

"Well, you being mostly naked, needing rescuing, then me swooping you up on a magic carpet."

She turned to regard him, her beautiful face making his heart race. She held that look for a moment, then kissed his cheek.

"Just take me home," she said with a smile.

He returned the smile and said, "Gladly."

Soon after, they were making haste toward Pelesea. Cassandra snuggled against him and quickly found sleep, just like the first time he had saved her. He loved her so much and wanted to tell her so. Baxter resolved then that once things were back to normal, he was going to. He daydreamed of the life they might have together, and that ride to Pelesea was one of the happiest moments of his life.

CHAPTER 12

HOMECOMING

It was midmorning when *The Siren's Scourge* made port at Pelesea. Unknown to the dockmaster, the ship made its way to the nearest dock and dropped anchor. The scruffy dockmaster came storming out of his tiny office and approached the lawless boat, whose captain and the first mate now appeared on the bow rails.

"Good morning, Dockmaster," Captain Biggles greeted the flustered man.

"It was a good morning until you broke nearly every rule concerning ship docking etiquette!" the dockmaster shouted back angrily.

The captain turned an unconcerned glance toward Agatha, who only wore a smile. Then, with all confidence, he answered the angry man, "I do apologize, but we were in a huge hurry, you know, precious cargo and all."

"And do tell me, what precious cargo you might be carrying that will allow you to ignore porting etiquette?"

Biggles smiled and moved out of the way so that Kringus could take his place at the rail. "Good morning to you, Dockmaster Harold!" the king said cheerily.

"My king! I... I—" Harold began before Kringus cut him off with a raised hand.

"You were doing your job and doing it well, I might say. I want you to forgive this ship's blatant disregard for our docking rules. Make a note of this ship, *The Siren's Scourge*, for it, as well as Captain Biggles and first mate Agatha, are free to dock here as they please from this day forward."

"Yes, my king, as you wish," Harold said with a bow.

"Now, send word to the queen that I have returned; I am most eager to see her beautiful face again!"

"Yes, Your Highness," Harold answered with a bow and summoned one of his younger dock hands to deliver the message. Soon, the young man was running with all speed toward the castle.

Kringus watched him go and noticed that a few city folks were beginning to gather near the docks. Word of his arrival would spread fast, he knew, and the excited reaction of his people made him happy. There was a murmur among them, and he saw a few point excitedly in his direction. He was glad to be home, and the people were just as happy to have him back. He still had a heavy heart from the disastrous trip they had just returned from, so the happiness didn't last long.

He looked back at the dockmaster and said, "Dear Harold, please summon six of your best deckhands; we have cargo to unload."

"Yes, my lord, I'll have them momentarily."

Harold hurried off to find the best men for the job, and it didn't take long as most of them were now gathered in one spot, talking excitedly about the king's return, and neglecting their work. Harold didn't seem to mind that part and started pulling men aside to help with the most delicate task. Kringus made a mental note of his actions. He would see the man rewarded for being such a loyal subject. He turned to Biggles, took off a ring he wore on his right hand, and placed it in the captain's hand.

"What is this, my king?" Biggles asked, holding the ring to the morning sun to examine it.

The item glistened in the warm light, and the craftsmanship was flawless and appeared very valuable. Looking over his shoulder, Agatha gasped and covered her mouth. He rolled the platinum ring with his fingers, examining its craftsmanship. It did not have a gem in its setting, but instead contained a raised "K" where the rock should have been.

"A signet ring?" he whispered.

"Yes, for you and all of your crew. Take this anywhere in my fair city, and you will find lodging, food, supplies, or anything else you need. This ring is my seal and will allow you to purchase what you need at no cost.

"My king," Biggles exclaimed while Agatha continued to hold her hand over her mouth, her eyes widening after hearing Kringus's words. "I cannot possibly—" Biggles continued, but Kringus quickly cut him off.

"You are an ally of my city. You brought us home when we most desperately needed it. Take this ring for as long as you are here and return it to the castle before you set sail. At that time, I will have the gold waiting for you that I promised to pay you for your services. So, take the ring and use it. I insist," Kringus explained, grabbing Biggles by the shoulders, and offering a sincere smile.

"Thank you, my king," Biggles said humbly, lowering his head.

"Call me Kringus," the king said and gave him a friendly pat on the shoulders.

He then turned to find the two elven brothers at his side. Von cracked a rare smile and said, "It is good to be home," and then nodded toward the gathering crowd.

Kringus looked back at the mass of people, all waving and yelling excitedly about the return of their king. Then, Kringus approached the rails and waved to them, eliciting a tremendous cheer. He continued waving for some time, giving the people what they wanted and basking in the fact that he was finally home.

He turned back to Von and Lenore and said, "No, it is great to be home! I will see you two at the castle. You proved your worth to me once again, my friends."

They smiled and nodded, but all three shared the same thought; they had lost men, which might already include Arrin. They shared a moment, their hearts heavy with grief from their loss. Then, with a slight nod from Von, the elves took their leave, turning toward the unloading plank. The dockhands climbed aboard using that plank to retrieve the bodies as the elves exited the ship.

Kringus watched the elves undock and watched the dockhands

disappear below deck at the same time. They were home, and it had been a lousy journey; they had possibly freed Oldorburg from the evil it held over the townspeople, but it was hardly a victory. And for what? To find the mother and sister of one girl? He ran his hand through his hair and puffed out a long exhale. The journey had been a failure, but he was home now. It was over. He turned to leave the ship, but he caught sight of Boz standing silently at the rail.

Kringus made his way to the carofex and asked, "Well, what do you think of my city?"

Without looking away from the gathering crowd, he replied, "It is everything I imagined. Of course, my brothers and sisters at the monastery would be most pleased to share the sight before me."

Kringus smiled and patted the man on the back. "Thank you for helping us back in Oldorburg. We might all be dead right now if it wasn't for you."

"No," Boz said, turning toward the king. "You would not be dead, but perhaps more of your friends would be. I did little to change the outcome."

"No, you did a lot, Boz," the king insisted. "I want you to stay on the castle grounds while you are here; I will make accommodations."

"A tremendous offer, but one I must humbly decline," Boz said politely.

"Why?" Kringus asked, his thick brows bunching up in confusion.

"I am more at ease living amongst your city folks. I will find a nice place within the city to settle for the night."

"Very well, but if you change your mind, come to the castle gate, and I will leave word for them to allow you entrance."

"That is very generous but unnecessary," the stubborn carofex insisted.

Then Boz did something that Kringus had never seen him do in the few weeks they had known each other: he smiled. It was such a strange look that the king was suspicious of it.

"What?" Kringus eventually asked.

"Your queen has arrived," he answered, even though his back was facing her and her entourage.

Kringus looked over the carofex's shoulder and saw a second mass of people cheering and walking toward the docks, the queen in the midst of them. Small children danced around her, and the city folks threw flowers in front of her as she walked. It was the most beautiful sight Kringus had seen in a very long time. His gaze became a stare, a trance induced by love.

Boz finally turned to regard the spectacle and was moved by the vision of the queen. She wore no crown and a simple but lovely green dress. Her long, red hair bounced on her shoulders as she strode confidently and excitedly toward the docks. He also made note that she had no guards around her. The royal couple of the grand city didn't act pretentious at all. He felt comfortable here and felt a kinship with Kringus and the lovely queen, whom he hoped to meet later. Nevertheless, he was honestly sad that his time in Pelesea would be brief.

"Enjoy your stay, my friend," Kringus said, patting the carofex on the back.

Boz watched him quickly leave the ship, then heard the crowd cheer as he made his way along the docks and onto the cobblestone street. There, the king quickened his pace toward the queen, and she, in turn, rushed to him. The crowds moved so the two lovers could find each other easily. The queen ran the last twenty feet and jumped into Kringus's arms as if they had not seen each other for years. There was a great cheer from the city folk as they pelted the royal couple with flowers.

Kringus spun her around a few times before gently putting her down, and the two shared a kiss to more cheers. Boz watched it all curiously and noted how he felt at that moment. It would be a great memory to share with his family at the monastery. The thought of his home snapped him out of his trance, and he quickly left the ship. Moments later, as he made his way across the massive docks, he glanced at the happy couple to see them smiling from ear to ear and sharing their greetings. He wished he could have stayed and joined the celebration a bit longer, but there was work to do. He slipped into the throng of people and disappeared.

Binta heard the cheers first and sat up in bed. The morning light peeked in the room from around the heavy drapes blocking off the balcony's entrance. She eased the covers off and slipped out of bed, trying not to wake Greyson. The priests had healed him and told him his leg would heal eventually, but he would use a crutch to walk for the next few days. The priests had restricted the amount of walking he was allowed to do, and they ordered him to stay in the temple until they deemed him healthy enough to leave.

So, the road to recovery had begun for him, while Binta showed only minor wounds from her first, and hopefully last, adventure. She made her way to the drapes, and as she neared, she could make out muffled noises on the other side, as if a large crowd had gathered outside. She slid behind the drapes and blinked away the brightness of the mid-morning sun. She opened the doors and quickly stepped through, trying to shut them again before the noise awakened Greyson.

It took her a moment to realize what was happening as a large mass of people gathered at the docks, only about one hundred yards away from the temple balcony where she currently stood. The crowd focused on a particular ship, and she could hear people shouting about the king. She could only imagine that Kringus had returned, and it made her sad thinking of it, knowing that Cassandra had longed for this very moment and was not alive to witness her family's return.

Her suspicions were confirmed moments later when another large crowd passed in front of the temple. She caught a glimpse of the queen among that crowd and, shortly after, a glimpse of Kringus as he made his way toward Penelope. The group blocked her view, but she knew the two had embraced as the crowd let out another cheer. She looked down at the railing of the balcony. She missed Cassandra and knew that her friend and first love was gone. From what Greyson told her, she had little hope Cassandra had survived.

"A copper piece for your thoughts?" came the familiar voice behind her.

She turned to see Greyson walk out onto the balcony, using his crutch to keep the weight off his wounded leg.

"You should be in bed," she scolded him, coming over to help him to the railing.

"The bed was suddenly cold without you. Besides, who can sleep with all of this racket, anyway?" the young priest said with a smile.

"The king has returned," she said flatly.

"Oh?" was all he could muster as he squinted to make out the royal couple amongst the crowd.

They both watched the reaction of the gathered city folk and understood that the couple was together again. The city was now complete with the return of the king. The crowd grew more prominent and joyful by the minute, but neither Binta nor Greyson shared the joy because their thoughts lingered on Cassandra.

"Do you think Kringus brought her family here?" Binta asked.

They shared a moment of silence, looking into each other's eyes. The pain on Binta's face spoke volumes as the return of Cassandra's family was important, but it was a minor event without Cassandra to witness it.

"I hope so," was all that Greyson eventually said.

He hugged her tight, and she wrapped an arm around him. She sniffed and wiped a tear away. Binta wondered what Cassandra's sister was like, and she hoped she would get a chance to meet her. She would share the sweet stories of her time with Cassandra, albeit a time that was too short. Would Kessi resemble Cassandra? Would she act like her, kiss like her? It was too much for Binta as she finally broke down and sobbed into Greyson's gown. He rubbed her back and let her get it out. She couldn't see, but he shed a few tears of his own that bitter-sweet morning.

Franklin Ruben watched the scene unfold at the docks from the third-floor bay window in Cass's room. He opened the window so he could hear the cheers for himself. Since it was unseasonably warm that morning, he felt confident the cold would not make his little girl uncomfortable. He turned to regard her in the oversized bed, surrounded by many pillows and with the finest down comforters that money could buy.

She seemed so small and fragile, tucked into the large bed, surrounded by all those comforts. But, regardless of the amenities Franklin had given her, he felt helpless because she was still very ill. She was unconscious and still battling the infection. So, he had hired a priestess from the temple to care for Cass. The young woman sat beside her, wiping her forehead with a damp cloth. His eyes welled with tears as he took in the sight. He had lost his wife when Cass was young, and he couldn't bear the thought of losing his daughter, too.

He cleared his throat and rubbed his eyes, turning back to the window so the priestess would not see him cry. He watched the king and queen embrace, and he smiled. It was short-lived, as he thought of his daughter not being able to witness the scene beneath him. He would avenge her death if anything happened to her; every person involved in that ill-advised expedition would suffer his wrath. Especially the Rho girl; she had already caused enough trouble for Cass at the school and now may be responsible for her death. She had better hope Cass pulled through because Franklin strongly believed in an eye for an eye. From the rumors, the troublemaker remained lost in the wilderness, and he smiled at the thought of her dead body lying in the woods, being picked clean by vultures.

"It is nothing more than you deserve," he whispered.

At about the same time the royal couple reunited amongst the many cheering city folks, Baxter gained sight of the northern city gate. Cassandra curled up against him, and he sniffed her hair. As filthy as the young woman was, she still smelled lovely to him. She had slept the entire way, and he was honored to think she trusted him enough to fall asleep in his arms. He had obsessed over her near-naked form being so close to him during their journey home. He conjured many images of the future the two might share, everything from passionate sex to marriage and even children. So, with great reluctance, he gently shook her awake, not wanting the magical carpet ride to end.

"Cassandra, wake up; we are home," he whispered in her ear.

She stirred slowly, and it took him several times to get her fully awake. They flew over the gate, and both noticed the large gathering of people near the docks. It was so large that the people blocked the entrance to the temple, which is where Baxter had intended to take her. Instead, he circled back to the gate and the four remaining guards. None of them paid the flying carpet much notice, having seen the magical device fly over the gate several times in the last few days. Baxter lowered the carpet to hover just a few feet off the ground.

"Gentlemen, what is the commotion at the docks?" Baxter asked them.

One guard turned to him to answer, "The king has returned. A ship brought him in just a few moments ago, and the queen has made her way to the docks to greet him. It is a most glorious morning, dear wizard!"

"Baxter, my family!" Cassandra whispered and tried to sit up, grimacing when she moved her injured legs.

Her cover fell slightly when she moved, revealing a naked shoulder that garnered the guards' attention, drawing their gaze from the docks.

"Easy, Cassandra, you need a priest, remember?" he said, putting an arm around her.

"Is everything all right?" one of the guards asked, suddenly understanding that Cassandra was not dressed appropriately and looked in feeble health.

She nodded to the guard, then pulled the blanket tight around her. She looked Baxter in the eye and made one request. "Take me to the docks. Please, Baxter."

Baxter nodded, then bade the guards good morning, lifting the carpet back into the air. He flew it slowly so as not to startle the many vigilant guards around the area. Cassandra craned her neck anxiously, looking for any sign of her mother and sister. Instead, they saw the king and queen locked in an embrace, talking closely as people cheered for them.

Baxter willed the carpet lower and toward the royal couple with a wave to Kringus, who wore a giant smile. It slowly disappeared as the carpet landed a few feet away. Baxter had a bad feeling when he witnessed the change in Kringus's expression, but Cassandra didn't seem even to notice as she hopped down from the carpet before he could lower it fully. She landed awkwardly after the small jump and grimaced away the pain in her leg.

"Cassandra," Baxter yelled after her as he landed the carpet, but she ignored him and limped toward the king.

Kringus stood there and turned as white as a ghost as she approached him. Penelope was beside him, and the concerned look she gave her husband told Baxter everything he needed to know. But, again, this exchange seemed lost on Cassandra, who continued her slow and painful walk. Baxter had landed the carpet about twenty yards away from the king, but it seemed to take a very long time to make that walk in her condition. She used the blanket Baxter had given her to cover herself, which hung around her shoulders. Her hair was dirty and matted to her filth-streaked face. She suffered grievous injuries as dried blood caked her calf and back. She was a sight to behold, which made the event even more tragic, Baxter thought, understanding by Kringus's expression that this would not end well.

Her eyes never left Kringus as she made her way slowly toward him, and the crowd, which was jovial just moments before, began to calm as a hush gradually spread through their midst. Soon, the only sound was the lapping of the water at the docks as all watched the wounded girl approach the king and queen.

When she was finally before them, she ignored all etiquette by not bowing and not addressing them with their proper titles. Instead, she looked into Kringus's eyes and asked, "My family, where are they?"

Kringus held her stern gaze with his own, then eventually shifted it to the docks and nodded slightly. Cassandra turned slowly in that direction and looked past Baxter, who had made his way to stand beside her. There she saw the unthinkable as six bodies wrapped tightly in cloth were gently carried off a large ship.

Her eyes widened, and she put a hand over her mouth, tears spilling down her cheeks. She would have fallen to the ground if Baxter had not been there to catch her. He looked at Kringus as Cassandra cried into his chest, her body limp. His eyes were wide, studying the king, hoping to pry some good news from him silently. Instead, Kringus slowly shook his head. Penelope came over and helped Baxter comfort the girl. Tears formed in the king's eyes as well. He did not have to deliver bad news often and was not used to failing at any mission. It was indeed a sad moment for them all.

"Greyson, it is Baxter!" Binta yelled when she first saw the magic carpet.

"What?" he asked before he followed her pointing finger toward the sky.

"Is that—?" he began before Binta interrupted him.

"Cassandra!" she yelled, nearly knocking the young priest over as she shook him hard by the gown with excitement.

She cupped her hands and yelled out to her friend, but she was too far away from the temple to hear her, especially over the cheering crowd. They watched as Baxter lowered the carpet and Cassandra jumped off.

"She looks terrible," Greyson whispered.

"Yes, but she is alive! We must go to her," Binta exclaimed, and headed for the patio door.

Greyson grabbed her arm and held her tight, shaking his head.

"What are you doing? We must get to her; she's hurt," Binta argued, trying to pry from his grip.

"No, Binta, we should stay here and see what transpires. You'll never reach her from the ground, not with that crowd."

She understood his point as she looked over his shoulder to see Cassandra limping toward the king. She could not make it there with the gathering of people and could probably see more from the balcony, anyway. So, she changed her mind, seeing Greyson's reasoning, and returned to the railing. But she was restless, wanting nothing more than to feel Cassandra again in her arms. So, she fell silent as the crowd did. Something in the air felt wrong, and she could almost sense the bad news coming.

Franklin Ruben saw the carpet fly by his house, so close that he quickly identified the Rho girl bundled in a thick blanket. He was none too pleased to see her brought home. With the description he had received of the girl after the incident with Cass and his conversation with Baxter about the one remaining lost adventurer, he knew it must be her. A disgust crossed his face as the angry father watched the carpet land near the king. He looked back at Cass, who moaned softly as the priestess patted her forehead with the wet cloth. Franklin saw red as he looked back to see the Rho girl approaching the king. She was not bedridden and in danger of dying like his little girl was. He could fix that.

"Leave us," he instructed the young priestess.

"But Mr. Ruben, your daughter—"

"Leave us; I will summon you again shortly. I will take care of Cass for a while. Wait downstairs until I call you," he interrupted.

"As you wish," the young woman said, offering him the cloth as she stood.

"And close the door behind you, please," he ordered, standing there, watching the confused priestess leave.

Once the door shut, he tossed the cloth on the bed and went to a secret compartment he had built into the wall. Once he opened it, he took out the loaded crossbow hidden within and returned to the window.

The crowd had grown mysteriously quiet, and he could hear the Rho girl sobbing. A smile creased his lips at the sound. It was good that she should suffer, and although the queen was currently in his way, if he got a clean shot at the girl and knew he could kill her, he would take it. He wasn't a warrior by any means, but he was proficient with a crossbow. Franklin waited for his opportunity, his knuckles whitening on the weapon as he opened the window fully and held the weapon at his side.

The bodies were gently laid on the cobblestone street by the dockhands, and the crowd began to murmur a bit as they recognized the precious cargo. Cassandra nearly swooned when she saw the bodies laid out before her. There were six, and Baxter had a horrible feeling that two were her mother and sister. If that were true, he knew Cassandra would not be able to handle such awful news right after everything else she had endured.

Nearly overcome with emotion, she turned to Kringus and asked, "My family?"

Kringus nodded and said, "We believe one to be your mother."

"Which one?"

She started crying again, and Baxter helped her walk to the bodies. Kringus made his way there and inspected the feet.

He pointed to one in particular and said, "This is the one we feel is Sera; we marked her wrappings with chalk so we could tell her from the others."

"I want to see her. I won't believe it unless I see her," Cassandra said between sobs.

"Are you sure, my dear? It might be unsettling," Penelope said soothingly.

Cassandra nodded and looked on as Kringus motioned to two of the dock hands to unwrap Sera. They bent low and began to gently and respectfully unwrap the face so Cassandra could see her. When they finally stood and moved away, Cassandra limped to the body and cried hysterically. It was her mother, and even in death, she was beautiful. Her face was a little discolored and bloated, but her mother was unmistakably lying dead on the street, her worst fear finally realized.

Cassandra knelt with Baxter's help as Penelope moved to stand beside Kringus and shared a concerned look with the king. Cassandra stroked her mother's face as her tears rained down on her dead body.

"I am sorry, Cassandra," Baxter whispered.

"And what of my sister?" she asked between sobs, not bothering to even look back at the king as she addressed him.

"We could not find her," he answered, swallowing hard as he did, feeling the guilt of his failure.

"Where is she?" she asked, more loudly, still not looking at the king.

The queen and Baxter looked at Kringus and measured his reaction to the hysterical girl. He did not seem to notice, so lost was he in his despair. Baxter saw several guards nearby act to her tone, and he hugged her tight, trying to comfort her.

"We do not know. Your sister escaped the evil town before we arrived. The leaders there seemed to think she had come to Pelesea, but I cannot confirm."

Cassandra listened while lovingly stroking her mother's hair. Her crying died down to an occasionally broken sigh as she tried to gain control of her emotions. After all the battered woman had been through, Baxter knew this was enough to send her over the edge. How many times had terrible things happened in her life? Both of her mothers were now lost to her, and her sister was missing. Kringus had waited too long, just like Cassandra had feared. She had told Baxter several times that was the case, but he refused to believe it. So now he took part of the blame upon his shoulders.

"I love you, Mother," Cassandra whispered, then kissed Sera on the forehead.

Tears poured down her cheeks. She held Sera for a few more moments, her eyes still closed and holding her tight. When she opened them, the sadness was replaced with a rage uncontested. Baxter saw it and knew the next few moments could hold dire consequences, yet he was powerless to stop it. Everything seemed to progress in slow motion.

"Oh no, Greyson," Binta whispered as she watched her friend kneel to inspect one of the bodies.

The crowd was hushed, and the scene, which had been so joyful moments before, grew very sad.

"Is it her sister?" she asked, unable to see clearly.

"I cannot tell. But, dear Plath, have mercy on her because I feel it is either her sister or her mother."

Binta hugged him tight, and he reciprocated, both overcome with emotion.

Suddenly, Cassandra threw Baxter's arm off her and stood to face the king. Baxter was taken aback by the action, and it took him a moment to realize what had happened. He quickly stood with her, ready to support her if she needed it, but she pushed him away without breaking eye contact with Kringus.

"You failed," she said between gritted teeth.

Those words, dripping with venom, finally got the king's attention, and he said, "What did you just say?"

"You failed, Your Highness!" she screamed, taking another step toward him.

Gasps erupted from the crowd, and four guards rushed up to the girl, hands on the hilts of their swords, but Kringus stayed them with an upraised hand.

"You are correct, child; I have failed you and them," he answered somberly, pointing to the other five bodies.

"I don't care about them," she hissed.

"Those are my friends," he clarified angrily. "They died trying to help find your family."

"Then they failed, too."

"Careful, ungrateful brat, I am in no mood to humor your wicked tongue," he said, warning her that she was crossing the line.

Penelope put a hand on his arm, and he glanced at her. Baxter knew that Penelope was Kringus's rock; she supported him during such awful times. That simple look on her face reminded the king he should be lenient and show compassion for Cassandra. Kringus half-smiled, and she returned it. He patted her hand and turned back to Cassandra, only to have a raven land on his shoulder. The bird's appearance startled all of them in the area except Cassandra, who continued her preaching.

"You come here, and people shower you with gifts and cheers! You walk amongst them as if you are some hero!" She screamed so loud that even Greyson and Binta could make out the words. They shared a concerned look as the spectacle continued to unfold.

"Cassandra, come with me," Baxter said, trying to take her hand, but she pulled away and never even acknowledged him.

Several ravens landed in the area, and the city folk began to nervously back away from the scene. Before Baxter could do anything to defuse the situation, twenty ravens perched in the immediate area, and more were coming. The crowd began to panic, and the guards grew nervous. Von and Lenore made their way to stand beside their king, along with Franklin and Jimmon, the two cavaliers who had made the trip. A raven landed on Lenore's shoulder, and he reached up with a finger, and the bird perched upon it. He brought it to his face curiously and looked at Von for answers. His brother shrugged.

Franklin Ruben raised his crossbow and quickly gained Cassandra in his sights. She was standing before the king, with only that fool wizard close to her. He could not hear what was said, but the brat was screaming something at Kringus. A smirk crept across his face; if he killed her, avenging his daughter, the city folk would probably hail him as a hero of the city. He would be known as the person who saved the king from her forked tongue.

"Goodbye, brat," he whispered.

Just as he pulled the trigger, something hit his crossbow, causing his bolt to badly miss the mark, flying over the group, and plopping into the water without anyone noticing. He looked down and saw a bird on the window's ledge, dazed and trying to find its bearings.

"What the—?" he began, puzzled at the strange sight.

He was about to squish the bird when another one landed on the crossbow and started pecking at the mechanism.

He yelped and dropped the weapon onto the flower bed below the window ledge. The dazed bird seemed to return to life then and join its friend, pecking at the weapon. Franklin drew the windows closed, but before completing the task, at least ten birds were biting and destroying his crossbow.

"Ravens?" he asked, perplexed, as he watched the scene unfold from the safety of the closed window.

"You are not fit to be king! You are pathetic!" Cassandra screamed, her fists balled up at her sides so tight that her knuckles turned white.

Kringus just watched intently as hundreds of birds began to fill the area, landing on the ground, in nearby trees, on tops of buildings, and several on Kringus himself. The king didn't flinch as he patiently let her anger play out. Finally, Baxter could sense the panic that began to spread through the gathered crowd, and he knew that Kringus would have to stop Cassandra's outburst and feared it would require force.

"Cassandra, please, stop this," Baxter pleaded, but his request fell on deaf ears.

Cassandra's rage boiled within her. Seeing her mother lying dead on the docks while people cheered for their king, the one who had let it transpire, was more than she could take. She didn't hear Baxter's plea, and barely even noticed he was there. Her focus was on Kringus, and Kringus only.

"You have failed me, Your Highness, and to be honest, I am getting a little tired of people letting me down," she threatened calmly, making the hairs on Baxter's neck stand.

She stood quiet then and relaxed her fists, closing her eyes as if in meditation. She stretched her arms out to her sides, and many birds flew from the trees and landed on them, covering both. She opened her eyes, and a smile found its way to her face. Not a pleasant smile, but one that promised revenge.

"How about it, Penelope? Are you proud of your husband's failings?" she teased.

Jimmon and Franklin moved to unsheathe their great swords, but Kringus's booming voice stopped them.

"Enough!" he screamed, and his voice echoed through the city streets, which remained deathly quiet, even with the large gathering of people. Surprisingly, not one bird moved or flew away at the sudden outburst.

"I've had it with your threatening words, ignorant girl! We risked our lives to save your family, and some of my friends died trying! Now, we come home ragged and saddened by our failure, and this is the thanks we get. Look at your feet; there lay the bodies of four of my friends!"

"Will you join them?" she answered with a smile.

Both cavaliers drew their swords, and the elven brothers followed suit, but Kringus held up a hand, stopping them from engaging.

"And so now you threaten my life? You have just committed treason in the most unforgiving way. What will you do, have your birds pluck out my eyes, then peck us all to death? Do you think that will save you; do you honestly think they will keep all of us at bay before we run you through with our swords?" Kringus threatened but made no move toward his weapon.

Cassandra just stood there smiling, her resolve unfazed by his words.

With a calm but clear voice, Kringus continued, "And if any of these god-forsaken birds cause me, my friends, my guards, or my people to lose even one drop of blood, I will cut you in half where you stand, and ship the remains of your body back to Oldorburg where you belong."

The threat was real, and Baxter knew Kringus meant what he said. Anyone who knew Kringus understood that he was good at his word, especially when someone openly threatened his crown.

Still, Cassandra continued to smile, and the birds became restless. They hopped around on her arms, becoming more agitated by the moment. She and Kringus stared into each other's eyes. Penelope, the elves, the cavaliers, Binta and Greyson, and everyone else who witnessed the scene would swear that time had stopped, and no one knew what would happen next. But everyone sensed that the ending was going to be tragic. There would be no winner this day, not under these circumstances.

Suddenly, Baxter was between Cassandra and the king, disrupting their field of vision. He wore a nervous but calm smile. Cassandra frowned at first, not happy with the distraction, but he did something she did not expect.

"Cassandra Rho," he said. "I love you."

The tension from her eyes melted away, and her body relaxed as he spoke the words, words she had heard so seldomly in her short lifetime.

"What?" she whispered.

He placed his hands gently on the sides of her head and pulled her face toward him. She did not resist as he kissed her gently on the lips. She gasped and looked into his smiling face, realizing his words were sincere. The birds slowly began to fly away, and he kissed her again, this time more passionately. The ravens flew from her arms as she kissed him back, the couple embracing as the birds flew around them for many moments.

There were some gasps from the stunned crowd as they watched all the birds take flight as one and leave the city altogether. There were also whispers of recognition from some, understanding this was the girl of legend who could control ravens. But the birds flew away without spilling one drop of blood, just as Kringus had demanded.

Cassandra and Baxter heard none of it as they shared that most beautiful and sincere kiss. When they finally broke it, several guardsmen were next to them, waiting to take her into custody. Baxter only smiled at her and never broke eye contact. He stepped back so the guards could do their job, and she let them. They took her, one on each side of her, holding her arms gently, and she gave no resistance at all.

"And now, girl, you shall be jailed until I determine your fate exactly," Kringus ordered.

"Fine," she whispered meekly, but kept her eyes on Baxter.

The guards marched her off toward the city jail. The crowd parted for them to make their way, and they whispered as she passed, none fully understanding what had just happened.

A large hand landed on Baxter's shoulder, and he turned to see Kringus. "You did well, Wizard; thank you for diffusing the situation."

Then the king and queen began to walk toward the castle, arm in arm.

"My king," Baxter yelled before they had gone very far.

Kringus and Penelope both turned to regard him, as did the two cavaliers and the elven brothers, and he could feel his face growing red with embarrassment. Then, after he composed himself, he said, "I do love her. Please be lenient on her; she meant no harm."

Kringus stared at him for a moment, looking at him as if he were crazy. Eventually, he gave a slight nod and turned to leave. Baxter looked back to find Cassandra, but the crowd had closed behind her, and she was out of sight. He had just taken a significant step into uncharted territory. Even though the circumstances were terrible and recent events had been stressful, his heart was whole for the first time since meeting Cassandra Rho.

Epilogue

Four days later, as soft snow fell on the city of Pelesea, the New Order met in the large banquet hall in the castle. All members were in attendance, save for Arrin, who was still, to their knowledge, recovering at Farmer's Stop near Oldorburg. Kringus and Penelope sat at the head of the table, followed by an empty chair for Arrin, Von, and Alleah on the king's side of the table; and Victoria, Lenore, and Daro on the queen's side. They were sharing breakfast since a meeting of the New Order would not be the same without some of the castle's finest food, a luxury Kringus insisted on for his friends.

They had gathered at Penelope's urging after what Alleah and Daro had discovered about Tara and Novafontera. First, the king and queen had taken a few days to reacquaint themselves and relax after Kringus's eventful trip to Oldorburg. Now the New Order was ready at last to discuss business.

"So, we are together again at long last. Welcome, my dear friends," Kringus began.

They all shared a few pleasantries, but the mood was somber in light of the theatrics that had occurred at the docks a few days earlier. They had also just buried their dead friends the previous day. None of them felt like taking care of New Order business, but they had made a pact to do so, so they put away their personal feelings and began the critical meeting.

After a few moments of small talk, Penelope began the discussion by saying, "Tell us, Daro, what you know of Novafontera."

The talking slowly died off, and all eyes turned to the ranger. Daro opened his mouth, and a large piece of ham on his fork dangled before it. He stopped his hand in mid-air and glanced around at his friends, who waited for his response. Then he slowly put the ham back on his plate and wiped his mouth.

"Very well. In simplest terms, Novafontera has come to life," he explained.

"In what way?" Kringus asked curiously, taking a large gulp of his wine.

"Undead have invaded my woods."

"Undead, as in zombies and skeletons?" Kringus pushed.

"Worse—vampires."

All eyes then turned to Kringus, who sat back in his chair. Then, after a few moments of silence, he spoke again, "Are you sure they came from Novafontera?"

"Yes, I fought a few in the woods the day after you left for Oldorburg."

Kringus winced slightly at the thought of him collecting Arrin and heading to the forsaken city.

"A female, I assume a lesser vampire, mentioned Novafontera and her master, Lord Heinsvick," the ranger continued.

"Does that name ring a bell with anyone?" Penelope asked.

"Yes," came the simple reply from Victoria.

All eyes turned to regard her. Her complexion had paled at the mention of the name.

"He was a warlock in his former life, but the stories say that he carried over his powers to his state of undeath," she continued.

"How do you know of him?" Daro asked.

She turned to him to answer, but before the words left her mouth, Penelope chimed in, "He existed at the time of the original New Order."

Victoria turned a surprised look toward the queen and nodded. "That is correct."

Kringus gave his wife a puzzled look, but she shrugged and said, "I did some research after Daro first came to me with the news a few months ago."

"So, you think this creature has been living in Novafontera for the last six centuries?" Kringus asked Daro.

"Perhaps," he replied with a shrug. "As I've said before, it is as if something has awakened the city, and now it stirs."

Kringus sat back and absorbed the information, taking another healthy gulp of his wine, then refilling it. "Alleah, is your group still going to Tara to investigate events there?"

"Yes, we leave in two weeks, a bit delayed because we are waiting for Greyson Kavince to heal," the beautiful priestess answered.

The mention of Greyson had them all recalling the events that had unfolded with Cassandra, but no one mentioned it. Penelope had warned them that Kringus had still not determined a suitable punishment for the girl, and it was still a sore subject for him. Everyone wisely let the moment pass without mentioning Cassandra's name.

"Daro, I am sure you wish to return to your home?" Kringus asked bluntly.

"Of course, though, I will miss this incredible food," the ranger agreed, which brought some chuckles and even smiles to the faces of the ordinarily inanimate elves.

"Then you shall return, continuing to monitor Novafontera for the winter months. Then, as spring arrives and the snow begins to thaw, you will watch for a caravan of Pelesea knights and priests. They will be coming from the south, returning from Farmer's Stop with our friends in tow. You will return with them and give us your report."

"Of course," Daro said with a slight bow, then picked up his fork and devoured his delicious ham.

"A caravan?" Penelope asked her husband.

He smiled and said, "Biggles is leaving in a few days, and he has offered to take our men to Mecca-Lorraine, where they can easily march to Farmer's Stop for the winter. I must get healers to Arrin and the others and sending them with Biggles is the fastest way I know."

"Perhaps you should not keep secrets from your wife," Penelope said, not being privy to that information before the meeting.

Kringus just winked and took another sip of wine.

She smiled but playfully added, "I will have to take this up with you in our next sparring session."

"I'd like to see that," Daro said around a full mouth.

The comment elicited laughter from all of them, and their spirits seemed to lift a little. They shared a hearty breakfast afterward, the meeting unofficially coming to a close. But, as with most New Order meetings, the gathering quickly turned into its simplest form, a meal shared by the best of friends.

Afterward, as they began to disburse, Kringus pulled Alleah aside and asked, "You will be back by spring?"

"It is my hope, my king," she answered honestly.

"How many warriors do you have?"

"Forty, plus Kavince."

"Do you need more? I mean, are you expecting a battle?"

She shook her head, golden locks bouncing in the morning sun that shone through the giant windows. "No, our mission is to discover the source of the vicious attack on Tara and for us to determine if Gorl was behind it truly."

"And if you meet an army of Gorl?"

"Then, there will be a fight," she answered honestly, and the fire in her eyes told him in no uncertain terms that she meant it.

"Very well. May Sinnis be with you."

She bowed and left as the others trickled out. Once they were all gone, Kringus stood sipping his wine, facing the door his friends had just departed through, deep in thought.

His wife slipped her arms around him and whispered in his ear, "Ready for that sparring session?"

The king smiled, gulped down his remaining drink, and took his wife by the hand, eager to teach her a lesson on the sparring field, though secretly, he had a feeling he had upset her, and she would better him this day. Nevertheless, knowing exactly how those sparring matches always ended was a winning scenario for him.

Across the ocean, on the other side of the world, Kessi sat in her cell eating a similarly delicious breakfast as the New Order had just shared. She had made friends with all her cellmates, their number growing to more than a score now. Her best friend was Sabrina, the cell's first occupant and implied group leader. The two sat and finished their eggs and fruit and sipped on the cool, refreshing water supplied in jugs.

They had stacked all of the plates at their cell door and moved to the back of the cell. Once the guards on the other side of Emiline's cell saw this, they sent in the slave to fetch the plates and empty jugs. Kessi watched him collect the plates and felt guilty, knowing that the starved slaves were allowed no food and were forced to collect their dishes. Kessi blankly watched him gather the containers, and guilt overcame her as it always did.

As she watched him quickly collect the plates and jugs, she quietly asked Sabrina, sitting next to her, "Why do they feed us so well?"

"It is easy to see. As I've told you, they are fattening us up for a sacrifice."

"A sacrifice to what?" she asked, genuinely curious. "I mean, these slaves don't get fed and even occasionally are fed to Emiline. Why are we so different?"

Before Sabrina could answer, Kimmie butted in, "We are virgins, all of us."

Kessi looked around at the solemn faces, each girl unspoiled by sex and pure by most standards. They all seemed to fit that description, Kessi realized as she made eye contact with each one.

"So, as the old stories go, they will sacrifice the virgins to appease the gods," Kimmie said.

"Yes, but I'm not sure I want to know what kind of god these people are trying to appease," Sabrina answered.

Kessi sighed and leaned back against the wall. Something didn't make sense; something she couldn't remember. She still didn't know who she was, not even her name, and she felt that her sister had something to do with this. She just hoped her sister was on her way to save them.

Her incoherent thoughts drifted as her eyes settled on the coffin in the next cell. Something about the vampire's name sounded familiar to her, and she tried every day, with Sabrina's help, to remember her past. Still, she had not given up hope that she would eventually remember something important; she had to. Something was there, deep in her memories, the key to their survival, and it was just out of reach for her confused mind to grasp.

The cellmates made a pact to keep their eyes open and look for a chance to escape. But Kessi knew that it was more realistic that they pray for someone to rescue them. And so, they also prayed to a goddess named Gella, whom Sabrina worshipped.

As the slave left with their dishes and the guard locked the door to the vampire's cell, the girls moved freely about the enclosure, breaking into groups, and chatting away. Kessi loved them all, but she knew their fate was doomed, and she could not and would not accept that.

She sighed heavily and closed her eyes, saying another prayer. This one was not to the goddess but to her sister, whom she firmly believed was out there somewhere. "Dear sister, whoever you are and wherever you might be, please save us from this awful place."

At the same time, Kessi tried to make sense of the jumbled thoughts in her fragile mind; Matilda found herself escorted into the grand wizard Malikai's stronghold. Two scantily dressed and beautiful young women escorted her.

The décor of the stronghold had not changed since her last trip to see the powerful wizard; the tapestries and paintings of nude women, most being used by several men, adorned every inch of the hallways and various rooms. The air smelled of incense and erotic oils, the scent promising sensual activity.

They led her to a large room, the one she knew to be Malikai's, and the large oaken doors opened before they arrived. She found Malikai standing at a bar, drink in hand. Matilda's two beautiful escorts stopped at the door as she continued inside. She walked up to the wizard, who had a drink prepared for her.

She took it from him with a flirty smile, and he directed her to an oversized, cushioned chair. The man was in his early sixties but had the body and the energy of a man much younger. He currently wore no shirt, and his long grey beard and hair spilled over his shoulders and chest. She admired his well-toned abs as she sipped her drink.

As she remembered it, suggestive art hung from the walls, and a large bed was the centerpiece of the room. Matilda knew from experience the bed was well used and a sleeping lover currently lounged there. As was Malikai's tradition, a bowl of fruit and chocolates rested on the bedside table. The bar took up most of the room, and she knew from experience that it stored some of the most excellent liquors in all the lands.

"It is as if you were expecting me," she purred.

"As I was," he acknowledged. "I would be a poor wizard indeed if I was not."

"And you know why I have come?"

"That eludes me. Please enlighten me," Malikai said with a smile.

He took her now empty glass to refill it and, on his way back to the bar, lifted his left hand toward the bed and whispered a command word. The blankets adorning it flew away as if a strong wind had blown them. The naked woman, who looked young enough to be Malikai's granddaughter, stirred and sat up.

"Get out," the old wizard said forcefully.

The girl quickly collected her clothes, made brief eye contact with Matilda, and hurried out of the room. The doors shut behind her, and Malikai offered Matilda another drink. He stood in front of her, his crotch at eye level.

He quickly downed his second drink in one gulp and said, "Now, let's determine why I find such an excellent lover in my quarters."

"I—" she began before he put a finger to her lips.

"Shhh, you know the arrangement; I expect prepayment."

He fell over her, and she gladly accepted the advance, embracing him passionately. Her business could wait.

Cassandra awakened as a soothing feeling washed over her, easing the pain in her legs and arms. She opened her eyes to find Maina in her cell with her. She smiled and sat up on her small cot with the priestess's help.

"You just healed me?" she asked, grimacing away the pain as she rose.

"Yes, but evidently not enough," Maina answered with a concerned look.

"I'm just stiff, that is all," she answered, rolling her right arm, testing the pain in her shoulder. "I feel good. Thank you for coming and for the healing."

"Of course, Cassandra. We are all worried about you in the temple of Gella and have been praying for you."

Cassandra gave her a sincere smile and asked, "How long have I been here now?"

"Four days," Maina said with a sigh, then stood straight. "I fear the king will enact his punishment soon."

When Maina stood, Cassandra noticed two guards in the cell with them.

"Why are they here?"

Maina turned to regard the two men and said, "They come with me every time I come to see you."

"You have been here more than once?"

"Yes, I come to heal you every day, but this is the first time I've seen you awake."

"I've been sleeping for four days?"

"You've been injured, seriously injured, Cassandra. You needed the rest."

She thought about the injuries she had faced in the caves, especially with the golems, and a chill ran down her spine. She glanced at her injured calf and saw it wrapped with clean bandages. She didn't feel bad, besides the stiffness from sleeping. Her eyes suddenly widened as she remembered the last time she had seen Binta, injured, with Greyson trying to carry her to freedom.

She stood with some assistance from Maina and asked, "Binta? Is she alive?"

"Yes, she is at the temple and in perfect health. Greyson, too," Maina answered happily.

Cassandra felt such joy at hearing the good news that she hugged the priestess tightly. "That is the best news I've heard in a while!" she said excitedly. Then, after a bit of a pause, she reluctantly broke the hug and asked, "What of Cass Ruben?"

"She is very ill and bedridden. We feel she may survive but is still in critical condition."

"I wish I could visit her," Cassandra said, with the most pleasant image of covering the girl's face with a pillow running through her head.

One of the guards interrupted her thoughts: "I'm sorry, but time is up."

Maina nodded and said, "Give me just a moment to say goodbye."

The guards looked at each other, and one just shrugged, so the other nodded his agreement.

"We do not know the king's intent. He is very secretive about your punishment. You may never see the light of day again," Maina whispered so the guards couldn't hear.

"I will, don't worry. The king is in the wrong, and he will see that in time," Cassandra said, keeping her voice to a whisper.

"His anger with you is great, and I do not share your optimism. Pray to Gella; she will see you through this," Maina said.

For the first time, Cassandra noticed then that she wore the acolyte clothing she had donned when she lived at the temple, making her feel a little closer to the goddess. She looked up at Maina with a smile and said, "Thank you."

"Of course, we couldn't exactly leave you in the attire you wore when you returned from your adventure."

Maina turned to leave, and the guards opened the door for her. Before she could leave, though, Cassandra blurted out, "Tell Binta I miss her and that I am fine."

She wanted to say more and let her friend know she loved her but didn't want that message relayed by anyone else. Instead, she would tell her the next time she saw her. Maina stopped, and the guards waited with the priestess standing in the doorway of the opened cell.

"I shall. And what of Baxter?"

The memories of the kiss came flooding back to Cassandra then. She had felt at peace during that kiss when she desperately needed it. It had been her first kiss with a man, and she had liked it. But Baxter did not hold her heart; that belonged to Binta.

"He sends his love," Maina said, breaking her thoughts.

Cassandra could only nod. Maina waited a few moments for her to say something, but she was at a loss for words. So, the priestess just smiled and left with the guards. They locked the cell behind them and walked down a small hall lined with similar empty cells. At the end of that hall was a metal door they unlocked and went through. Cassandra watched them go, and once the metal door slammed shut and she heard the key locking it, she sat down on the cot.

She looked around the small cell and noticed one tiny window at the top of one of the ten-foot-tall walls. It had a fogged pane of glass with bars lining the inside of it. She couldn't see through it, but it was enough to let in some light. Besides that, there was no light source in the cell or the hall.

She lay down and stared at the window, and a million thoughts ran through her mind. Her mother was dead; her sister might be alive and in the city; she wanted to murder Cass; Baxter loved her; she loved Binta; the king might execute her for her actions. She had never felt more alone.

"I vow to find you, Kessi. I'll get out of here, and I will find you. I will grow more powerful so that no one can hurt us ever again."

She made that pact for herself and her sister and was determined to become the most powerful wizard in all the lands. She thought of Zolmex then. Why had her father sent her through those stupid caves if Zolmex didn't exist? Perhaps it did, but it just wasn't located there, or maybe it was there, and she had missed it. In her dreams, she always found it in a desert mountain range. That was a far cry from the dark, cold caves she had just endured.

She sighed and put her arms behind her head, grimacing once more as her right shoulder screamed in pain at the movement. She adjusted her arm slightly and eventually, the pain subsided. She thought of her adventure and how it had almost killed all of them. And for what, to appease her father? Or maybe to sate some crazy old priest? She didn't have the answers. All she had was one clue, which still made no sense to her. The simple words "Notel X" were all she had received for her efforts, for her near-death experience. The meaning of those words eluded her, but she couldn't help to feel that they were just the next clue in the greater scheme of things.

Vasheba crouched over her prey, an old priest she had snatched from Pelesea. Black, sticky blood still leaked from the spear's wound in her abdomen. The demoness had gone to Pelesea, not to murder Matilda's great sacrifice like she had threatened, but to capture and torture the girl. Her plan was to eventually trade her for Matilda's husband who would pay dearly for injuring her. She would not only have Cerus but take possession of that nasty spear as well. Matilda would have no choice but to agree to the exchange.

She had not been able to locate the girl in the large city. Though her disguise—that of an old peddler, complete with long, white hair and hands knotted by arthritis—had been perfect, she was uncomfortable walking the streets. The goodness that she felt welling all around her, not only from the people, but from the buildings and even the ground of Pelesea repulsed her.

When she found no sign of the sacrificial lamb, she quickly made her way to one of the temples. She had not been able to enter the horrible place, but she had waited outside until a priest had exited. Vasheba asked the man in clerical vestments to pray with her.

To begin his prayer, he reached out a soft hand and touched her. That was all she needed to teleport him there, to the catacombs beneath Novafontera.

The deadly gasses that filled the city did not affect the subterranean area, so she could easily take humans there for torture or dismemberment. It would be the home of Cassandra Rho sooner rather than later. The priest lay atop a large stone table, with Vasheba's chain wrapped around him tightly, digging deeply into his skin. The man was unable to move and had already wet his nice robes at the sight of the horrific beast standing above him. Vasheba growled with glee at the urine stain.

"And now you will tell me what I want to know," she imparted telepathically, then reached out with a long, crooked finger to touch his forehead. The priest stared at her, his eyes as wide as saucers and his lower lip quivering in fear.

She knew that of all the citizens of Pelesea, the clergy knew of most happenings so if anyone could identify the exact location of Cassandra Rho, this man could. She easily tore through his thoughts, ripping away things of disinterest to her; rituals concerning his goddess, Anastia, and personal agendas and appointments. Trivial, mortal rituals and nothing more could be found in his weak mind. Her probing found that the man knew a Cassandra, but she was a lover from his twenties, many decades ago, clearly the wrong Cassandra.

She hissed her displeasure with him and ripped the heart-shaped silver pendant from his neck. It was his holy symbol, that of the insignificant goddess he worshipped. The man had wasted her precious time but wasn't completely without his uses.

"Please! I do not want to die," he said, then began to sob.

She smiled, a toothy, frightening sight that mortals found only in their darkest dreams. She did not respond to his pleas or his cries of desperation. Instead, she took the heart symbol that he had worshipped probably most, if not all of his pathetic life, and pressed it hard against his neck. His crying stopped and his eyes bulged at the immediate lack of oxygen. She kept the pressure so he couldn't breathe and giggled at his desperate thrashing, which made the barbs of her chains dig deeper.

She would have loved to play with the fool for a long while, but she would save that for Cassandra. She swiped the silver amulet across his neck, cutting his throat with one proficient stroke. Blood squirted with each pump of his dying heart, and he mumbled incoherently for a bit. She enjoyed the reaction, as she always did when a mortal was dying, but she needed his essence so couldn't enjoy the moment to its fullest. Instead, she took the heart-shaped symbol and cut open his abdomen. He half-screamed, half-gurgled as she did.

Once his guts were spilled, she tossed the bloodied amulet across the room where it bounced around and finally settled in the corner. She then stuck her fingers into the warm innards and pulled at his waning life force. His eyes grew even wider as he passed from the world of the living, and he was still. Vasheba continued to tug at his life force, absorbing every ounce she could. The nasty wounds caused by Cerus's lethal spear closed and healed as the man's body shriveled to a husk.

Vasheba withdrew her fingers out of the now-powdered insides of the man and smiled. She had failed to obtain Cassandra Rho, but she would find her in time, and Matilda would pay dearly for her. Vasheba would also make sure Marnelphion knew she had been the one to secure the great sacrifice.

Her wounds were now healed, and she felt better than she had in some time. The mortal world was to her liking and the new queen of Novafontera basked in the knowledge that the real fun was just beginning. When Marnelphion arrived, she would be set free upon the world to cause as much chaos as she desired. The hour grew near, Marnelphion stirred, and hope for humankind diminished.

About the Author

A fan of fantasy and science fiction from a young age, Phillip Martin dreamed about writing stories. He's used that desire to run roleplaying games and even develop them. His roleplaying stories have created countless adventures and worlds for the benefit of his closest friends. Finally, some of his vivid imaginings have been immortalized in print for others to enjoy. Phillip lives in Christiansburg, Virginia, and can be found at www.cassandra-rho.com.